BY CHRIS LOPARCO

COVER AND ILLUSTRATIONS BY CHRIS LOPARCO

In His Name

Chris LoParco

www.astorytoldbook.com

Quotations in this book were taken from the New International Version (NIV) of the Bible

ISBN-13: 978-1542345033

ISBN-10: 1542345030

Cover Design, Illustrations, and Page Layout by Chris LoParco

Characters created by LoParco, Olivera, Santarsiero

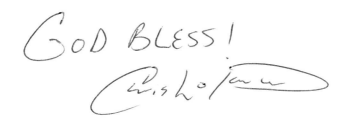

GOD BLESS!

Thanks be to the True and Ever Loving God,
without whom none of this would be possible.

And to all of those saints out there who have believed in and
continually help in this great journey
– Thank you.

*Jesus looked at them and said, "With man this is impossible, but with
God all things are possible." Matthew 19:26*

*But these are written that you may believe that Jesus is the
Messiah, the Son of God, and that by believing you may have life in
His name. John 20:31*

PROLOGUE
DEATH SPEAKS

Look up at the stars, each star in the night sky and beyond, all the billions you can see and those you cannot. God placed the stars with His own hands on the fourth day. Before that, the Darkness had dwelled on the face of the deep. But the Spirit of God hovered over the waters and God said, "Let there be light." His light pushed back the Darkness and the mortal world was made. But He placed the stars in the sky to keep it at bay. Each star represents an angel of the Lord. Their light holds back the Darkness, keeping it from the mortal plane of existence, keeping it in its own dimension, a dimension known to many as the Abyss. This Darkness is beyond the blackness of space. For in the dark matter that holds the Universe together is the hand of God. But in the true Darkness, the essence of all evil, God does not dwell, for that Darkness does not comprehend the Light and no light is inside of it, and in the Light is no Darkness.

Not all of the stars still shine. Those that have died out are the fallen angels; these are that third of all angels who fell from grace when they followed Satan in his scheme to take God's throne and others who fell afterward. God had many of these, with their leader, thrown into Hell, where they still plot and scheme until the last days. Some were cast into the Darkness itself. These are the stars that became black holes. There are seven of them who rule inside the Abyss. They call themselves the Angels of Darkness and hold themselves superior to the rest of their fallen brethren, including Lucifer himself.

So what exactly is the Darkness? It is pure, unadulterated evil personified in the form of a spirit. It has no physical form but is made up of a dark energy. The Darkness hungers for life, and it absorbs souls into itself, feeding on their energy, their life-force, draining them until these souls are almost lifeless. This is why it is said that the Darkness destroys worlds. Not that a

4

planet is completely obliterated from existence, but rather that all of the life force is drained from its people. But it does not stop there. The Darkness will also drain the energy from animals and plants, and even from the core of the planet, leaving it completely dead in every way. Only God can destroy. Only God can create from nothing, and only He can turn that very creation back into nothingness.

The planets, the stars, the galaxies, they all speak to the glory of the One who made them. But there is no glory for me. All I have known is the death of all things — the end of life. I yearn to see the light and hope for life. But my spirit only knows death, for that is who I am. I sit and wait for another to be reborn. A hope, a shining light in a world of desolation. I look for a new day. The end will come, but what I wait for is *after* the end. I, Death, wait for a new beginning.

CHAPTER I
THE THIRD DAY

The cold winter air filled the night sky. They had laid Nathan to rest earlier that day, and the small group of friends-turned-family had taken up residence in Esmeralda's parents' house. With Radix vanquished, Esmeralda slept soundly in her parents' bed, while Kimberly did the same in Esmeralda's old room. Lyles could not sleep, though. He was still concerned about the twins, knowing in his heart that some sinister plot was being strung together to snatch them away. Guarding them as best he could, the young man sat in a rocking chair next to their crib, sword in hand, ready to defeat anyone who tried to harm the children. Over the crib hung the St. Michael medal that Lyles had once worn. No one would dare try to take these defenseless babes as long as the mighty Archangel was their protector. But even with the protection of the winged saint, Lyles still did not want to take his eyes off of them. The night grew later and darker, and Lyles' eyes became heavy. He could not stay awake forever. He was still human. But that did not stop him from trying. As his eyes closed, he was awakened by the appearance of his good friend, Puck.

"Not mean to wake you, friend," the Djinni spoke.

"I wasn't sleeping — just resting my eyes," Lyles responded.

"Need you no more to stay awake. Here am I now. You sleep. Djinn need not sleep."

"I don't know. I'm afraid something'll happen."

"But if grow too weary you do, how then will you defend anyone? Rest you need. Trust Puck."

Lyles figured that his friend was right, and before he knew it, the young hero was fast asleep. Just as the serene state of dreaming was about to happily grace Lyles' tired body, he was awakened yet again — this time by a loud crash in the backyard. He got up immediately and went out back to have a look, while Puck stayed behind to watch the twins. The sly Djinni decided to cloak himself in invisibility, so he could catch any prowlers unobserved. There was nothing in the yard from what Lyles could see, but he could feel that something evil was definitely present, for the ring on his finger told him so.

The Ring of Solomon was a great weapon in the hands of good or evil. It had many wonderful powers. One of these included the ability to detect the presence of evil. Lyles' friend Nathan had used that very same ring to battle the evil Radix. The ring had given Nathan increased strength, stamina, and durability in his fight. But even the Ring of Solomon had limits. When Nathan realized that trusting in God was his greatest weapon, then he truly began to reach victory over his foe. Unfortunately for Nathan, victory came at the high price of losing his own life — a modern-day martyr. Lyles knew the ring had strengths, but he also knew that it was not perfect, and that he too must learn to lean on God in order to receive true strength.

Inside the nursery, something materialized before the twins' crib. It was one of Puck's former brothers, a nasty and vile Djinni. The demon looked much like Puck himself, just more sinister. Its sideways eyes, jagged tusks, and sharp claws were ready to attack its prey. Just then, Puck appeared behind the demon and dug his claws into its back. The Djinni squealed in pain, which not only alerted Lyles in the yard, but also woke up the women who were asleep inside the house. Kimberly and Esmeralda ran into the nursery. Lyles soon followed with his sword drawn to help Puck battle the adversary that was trying to harm the babies. At that moment, matters grew worse. Out of smokeless fire, a dozen more Djinn appeared in the room. The fight with Radix might have been over, but danger still lingered. It would not be so easy to protect the children when all the forces of evil in the Universe were ready to grab them at any moment. The battle was on, and even Kimberly and Esmeralda picked up lampstands and started to swing at the desert demons. The fight was taken out into the hallway, leaving the babies alone in the nursery. The distraction had worked perfectly. The stage was now set for yet another unwanted visitor to enter. But this monster was far worse than any Djinni. Satan's own bride, Lilith, had come, and she was ready to claim her prize. She was not here to play any games, appearing in her true demonic form. Her mouth was wide open, exposing her fangs. She reached out her hands to scoop up the children. Victory was hers, or so she thought. A blazing light blinded the succubus, causing her to back off. There before

Lilith stood Michael, the Archangel, with his fiery blade pointed straight at her skull.

"Leave this place now, wench," the righteous angel commanded. "Or I will be forced to place you into the second death."

"Always with the drama, Mike," Lilith responded. "Stay out of my affairs. You have no business here."

"That medal above that crib puts those babes under my protection. I will let no harm come to them."

"But who will protect you?" The wretched succubus let out an ear-piercing cry and pounced onto the Archangel.

Michael pulled back from Lilith, trying to get loose from her sharp talons. Her nails dug into his armor, and she sank her teeth into his neck. With lightning-fast reflexes, the Prince of Hosts threw her from him, causing the bride of Satan to fly out through the window. With wings spread and sword drawn, Michael flew after his prey. The warrior angel and the wretched demon fought in the cold winter night. Lilith proved to be quite the match, as she soared around her foe and sank her teeth into him again, trying to drain his life force. But Michael was fast as well, and knocked her off of himself with his fiery blade. Flashes of light could be seen in the dark sky as the two otherworldly beings battled. War had been unleashed in and around the Salvatore household, and all the while, the twins were left unprotected.

Esmeralda's heart stopped for a moment. She felt danger in her very soul. Her children were alone, and they needed her. Out of desperation, the young mother threw a lampstand at the nasty Djinni in front of her, and ran back to the bedroom. Kimberly ran after her to help. Each woman grabbed one of the babies. Kimberly had Bianca and Esmeralda had Gideon. They had to get out of the house and get to somewhere safe. If they could make it to the car, then they could drive to the Sisters of Saving Grace. Maybe the nuns who had helped to bring these children into the world could help to keep them alive. Esmeralda and Kimberly bolted out of the room, down the stairs, and rushed toward the front door. It wouldn't open, even though it was unlocked.

Kimberly ran to the back door, and Esmeralda decided to follow. But at that very moment, a bright light stopped Esmeralda.

An angel shone before her, much like the angel who had saved her after her horrifying moment with Radix. But there was something different about this angel's light. It did not comfort her; it brought no peace.

"I am the angel of the Lord," commanded the luminescent being in front of Esmeralda. "Give me the child and I will carry him to safety."

Esmeralda could not speak. She wanted to trust the angel and give her son to him for protection, but something was wrong.

"You must hurry, my child, for it is not safe for the boy here. Only I can save him."

The angel seemed to lose his patience as he repeatedly asked for the child; each time his voice growing sharper and angrier. Esmeralda knew that something was not right. The Spirit was guiding her heart, and would not let her give up the child. But the angel would not be opposed so easily, especially not by some mere mortal. He reached out and grabbed her, and a sharp stabbing pain shot through her body, sapping her of her strength and will. With ease, the being before Esmeralda took Gideon and began to transform. Esmeralda lay on the ground unable to move as she witnessed the angel become a demon, and not just any demon. It was Satan himself.

"You are a fool to think that you could deny me, girl!"

Fire shot from the beast's mouth as he spoke. "This child is rightfully mine, for it was by my power that it was conceived. Now the prophecies can be fulfilled, and Hell will come to Earth with power and might."

Esmeralda passed out from the pain and fear, and Satan disappeared with a maniacal laugh. His voice echoed throughout the house and beyond.

Kimberly ran to Esmeralda who was unconscious on the floor and barely breathing. She screamed for help, and Puck appeared before her with Lyles running down from the hall upstairs. The Djinn they were battling had retreated. Kimberly tried her best to resuscitate Esmeralda with CPR, but it was not working. The touch of the Devil was toxic and the poison was fatal not only to the body but also to the spirit. The team of friends that stood around the fallen woman was unable to help in any way. But when hope seemed at its very bleakest, another light shone. This one was brighter than the last and warm with the love of God. A true angel stood before them now.

"I am Raphael, one of the seven who stand before the presence of the Lord," the angel spoke with authority and compassion all at once. "Do not be afraid, for your friend will not lose her life today. The Lord still has much work for her to do here on Earth."

Lyles and the others backed up, and the angel drew closer to Esmeralda. He touched her gently over her heart and at once she began to glow, as did Bianca, who was still in the arms of Kimberly. All were amazed. Then, in the same manner that Raphael had appeared, he vanished in a radiant light. Instantly, Esmeralda opened her eyes and sat up, wondering what had just happened. Everyone was there with her, everyone except Gideon.

**

Lilith had escaped, and Michael soared through the planes of Heaven, seeking council with the Creator of all. But before he could reach his final destination, he stopped at the sound of his name. On the seventh plane of Heaven, Raphael stood waiting to speak with his brother.

"Michael, what are you doing?" Raphael asked.

"What do you mean, 'what am I doing?'" Michael replied. "I am going to speak with the Father, about what just happened, and ask His permission to go into Hell and rescue the child that Satan stole."

"We cannot allow you to do that," Raphael stated.

"We?"

"Yes, we," the sound of several voices sang in unison.

The Prince of Hosts looked around to see five more of his brothers standing alongside Raphael, glowing bright with the light of the Spirit. Together they were known as the seven who stand in the presence of the Lord, the very place they were standing now. This seventh plane of Heaven was heavily guarded on all sides by the four-faced cherubim — each had a face of a man, an ox, a lion, and an eagle. The next and last plane beyond here was the throne of God, which only Michael and the Seraphim could enter. Michael, the Archangel, was the leader of the Seven, also called the archangels by men. They included, Gabriel, Raphael,

Uriel, Phanuel, Azreal, and Metatron, all of whom were present at the moment. These were glorious angels, beautiful and strong, much like Michael, though his magnificence was slightly greater as was his rank. All but Azrael were clad in bright and shining armor. They glowed like the stars of the heavens. The Angel of Death, Azrael, kept his usual appearance, that of a man with long golden hair, pale blue eyes, and dressed in a long black robe. Michael looked at his brothers and wondered what their opposition was.

"You are being rash, a quality not fit for an angel, let alone one of your rank," Phanuel spoke. "You should know better than any of us that the Lord has a plan, and we need not worry."

"Need not worry? It is not about worrying, but about righting a wrong. That child was placed under my protection, and I allowed him to be taken by that foul beast. I cannot allow Satan to have this or any victory, especially at the sake of losing this child's soul."

"I wonder if you are as much concerned for the child's soul as you are about the fact that you failed," Azreal interjected.

"I'm tired of your attitude, Azreal!" Michael shouted. "I am certainly most concerned for this child's soul, and not just for his own sake but for the sake of all humanity. He is no ordinary boy, as we all know. If Satan were to corrupt him, it could prove to be fatal for all Creation. This can be the beginning of the end."

"And so what if it is?" Phanuel asked. "We know the final outcome. It has already been written. Or do you doubt that He will fulfill all that He has spoken into truth. The end is inevitable, but with it will come peace, and a new and better creation — a creation without Darkness and only Light."

"I know this, but my heart aches for all those who will be destroyed. I have feared this day since the beginning. Can none of you understand my pain?"

"He can," Metatron spoke, his voice booming throughout the Heavens. "He felt every ounce of it on the cross, and He still feels it now."

Michael stopped and knew that God had answered him, for Metatron rarely spoke and when he did it was for the Lord alone.

Without anything else to say, Michael was engulfed in light, and left his brothers.

***

Esmeralda was in a state of shock. She could not even shed one tear. Too much had happened too quickly in this young girl's life. First, her parents were murdered and she was raped, only to discover that she was bearing the seed of the evil monster who had violated her. Then, she lost her brother to that same vile creature, and now the Prince of Darkness had kidnapped her son. All she could do was stare out into space, not knowing why God was putting her through these trials. How could any of this be for a greater purpose? All of it just seemed tragic. Lyles put his arm around her and so did Kimberly. Puck stood back, not knowing what to do, and then the Djinni disappeared in a puff of smokeless fire. At that moment, for no good reason, Esmeralda burst out laughing. Lyles and Kimberly didn't know what to make of it. They expected her to either remain somber or start to cry, but laughter? This was odd indeed.

"Are you okay, Ezzie?" Lyles asked.

Esmeralda did her best to calm herself down so she could speak, but it seemed hopeless. Kimberly held Esmeralda close to her. Lyles backed away, thinking Kimberly was better able to handle this situation. And that is when the tears started, and they did not stop for quite some time. The young mother was broken. She took her daughter from Kimberly and brought the baby close to her heart. There was something soothing about the touch of the baby girl. It was as if she emitted peace from her very soul. Finally, Esmeralda was able to relax and remained still. Kimberly took Bianca back into her arms, and Lyles helped Esmeralda to her feet.

"We need to get out of here!" Lyles exclaimed.

"We need to go to that safe house with the sisters," Kimberly said.

"Yes, the Sisters of Saving Grace!" Lyles agreed. "Come on, Ezzie, let's go."

"No! I can't leave! We have to find him! We have to find Gideon!" The tears began again.

"I'm sorry, Ezzie, we can't get him back." Lyles tried to speak some reason. "We don't even know where he is."

"I need my son! I can't go without him. It's my fault. I was too weak to protect him. This isn't fair! God, why? God, why have you done this to me? Do you enjoy watching me suffer?"

Bianca glowed with an aura of white light. Her dark eyes seemed to grow lighter, and at once Esmeralda began to calm down again. Lyles and Kimberly were in awe, but this was not the strangest thing they had seen. They took this opportunity for Lyles to lead Esmeralda to the car while Kimberly carried the baby girl. As soon as she sat in the back seat, Esmeralda fell asleep for the entire ride. She was awakened by the sound of the car door opening and the voice of an old friend.

"Esmeralda, how are you?" Sr. Thomastina greeted her as she reached out to help Esmeralda from the back seat of the car.

"Sister, huh?" Esmeralda replied as she got out of the car. "Sorry, I didn't even realize that I had fallen asleep. My head feels fuzzy. I'm so happy you're here…"

Then, Esmeralda fainted.

Sr. Thomastina had caught her, and Sr. Catherine came over to help get her inside. Lyles and Kimberly followed them with Bianca still in Kimberly's arms. The baby smiled, unaware of the tragedy all around.

***

Death sat atop Nathan's grave. It had been about three days since he had passed and Death knew that something grand was about to take place that next morning. It was a strange night, filled with many odd visitors, but now Death sat alone, as he was much accustomed to do, watching and waiting. The morning sun began to rise in the east, painting the horizon with a multitude of beautiful colors. At that very moment, the ground shook and began to crack with the force of a great earthquake. Lightning struck the ground and split Nathan's tombstone in two. The ground began to open, and Death stood watching. Glowing in an aura of light, Nathan rose from his grave. He stood up. The light faded. Nathan did not know what had happened or where he was. He touched the suit jacket that he was wearing; it was his

14

father's once. But before Nathan could grasp the situation he was in, he heard a voice.

"I knew it!" Death cried out.

Confused, Nathan turned to the ghastly being before him and asked, "What did you know? And who are you?"

"I forgot, you can see me now. Now that you have transcended."

"Transcended?" Nathan questioned. "What?"

"Sorry, let me explain, I am…"

"He is Death," Gabriel interrupted, as he appeared from a beautiful, radiant light. "But there are much more important things to discuss. I will be taking Nathaniel with me."

"Hold up!" Nathan exclaimed. "I'm not going anywhere yet. I've had enough of this. First the whole Radix thing, the forty days in the desert, demons, zombies, God knows what else I went up against. Now the Grim Reaper, over here, and you show up, and already you want to take me somewhere. Well, I don't want to go. I want to see my sister and my friends."

"I am sorry to tell you, Nathan, but you can't do that. You died on that cross, and now you have been raised back to life. Your sister and friends already mourned you and laid you to rest just yesterday. You cannot go and see them; it would be unheard of."

"Died? Raised back to life?" Nathan grabbed his head and screamed to the heavens.

Gabriel placed his hand on Nathan's head and said, "Peace be with you, child of God," and with that peace was with Nathan. "We must go. Trust me. It is important that you learn about what has happened to you." He paused and turned. "Death, thank you for watching over him during the night. Please go and carry out your duties, for this chapter is closed and a new one begins."

With a wave of Gabriel's hand, the ground closed up from where Nathan had risen, and his tombstone mended itself back together. It was as if nothing had happened, just as the angel had wanted. In a flash of light, Gabriel and Nathan vanished. Seeing that there was nothing more to do, Death left as well, in a similar fashion.

***

In the Arabian Desert, beastly screams cried out from all around, filling the air with sin and hate. A word could be heard amid the screams, "Legion!" A man sat alone in the desert — poor with nowhere to go and no place to rest his head for the night. Ahmad had traveled far to see his family, but a gang of robbers had stolen his horse and all of his money. A group of demon-like birds circled over his head, as if waiting to eat his flesh once he lay down for the night. Their cries were horrendous, like devils in the sky, screeching for blood. And amid their cries, he heard that same word that traveled through the air, "Legion."

But Ahmad was exhausted and could stand no longer. No matter how hard he fought, he fell onto the sand. As he did, the flock of birds swooped down and seized him all at once. His eyes turned blood red and he cried out that very word that was being called out from all around, "Legion!"

Then all went black.

CHAPTER II
THE DAWN

The shadows that painted the office were paled by the dark soul of the man who sat amid them. The office was his throne room, which sat one floor below his penthouse apartment. A luxurious life for a man who, in his mind's eye, was more than just the ruler of all he could see, but all that lay beyond. No one was quite sure what work he did, not even those under his employ. All they knew was that he not only owned the business and the building that it was housed in but, as some suspected correctly, he owned the whole city as well. He had a clear view of Belvedere Castle in Central Park from where he sat. He had a clear view of many things, thanks to the altitude of his throne. Windows surrounded him on three sides, but from his den above he could see the whole city. The building was all glass and steel, very modern and slick. The man stood up and leaned forward on the glass of the floor-to-ceiling window before him, looking right down into the park, right at the stage of the castle, where not too long ago he had seen quite the spectacular display. This man was no fool about the truth. He had seen many things in his day, for his day had been very long, longer than time itself. A smile dragged across his face, but was broken by the sound of his phone ringing. He answered it.

"Yes, Ms. Winters, send him in," he said with a scowl.

Another man wearing a dark red suit with a black shirt and a white tie entered the office. He shut the door. It was difficult to see his face in the dark, but the two men knew each other well.

"Lucifer, what can I do for you?" the man said to his visitor in the red suit.

"Can't a friend just check in to see how you're doing, Sam?" Lucifer retorted.

"You're hardly a friend checking in on me," the man replied. He turned and leaned on the window again, looking out. "So what do you need?"

"You should know better than anyone that I need nothing. Actually, I came to give you a gift. Something I am sure you have been missing," the Devil said, and a large leather-bound book appeared in his hands.

Sam turned around to get a closer look. His eyes filled with greed. "*The Necronomicon!*" he exclaimed. "It's about time I reclaimed that book. I knew once your minion was defeated that it was only a matter of time before you came to your senses and returned it to me."

"Hmm, well, yes, I suppose you will put it to good use then. But my gift comes with a price. More like a favor." Satan paused and sat up. "You and I share the same desire to bring Darkness to this world. I know we have had our differences in the past, but I am hoping we can put those aside for a greater purpose. You know as well as I do that great things are afoot, but even you do not know the whole of it. The end is near, and it will begin with a child."

Sam looked into Lucifer's eyes, which were kindling with fire.

"I can't forgive you for what you did to me. It has been a long time, but the wounds haven't healed. Though, I might look past it for now if you are proposing what I think you are. This boy, I presume, is the son of Radix and that girl."

"You are very astute. Your eyes are almost as far reaching as mine. The boy you speak of has great power, but he is only an infant right now. I need you to raise him to be a man of strength and character. He will lead this world into a new age, an age of evil, an age of true and beautiful Darkness. Can you do this? Can you raise this boy, and usher in the truth that we have been waiting so long for. The other worlds have fallen. The seed of Adam only lies on Earth now. Let us bring this act to a close and let the next one begin. Imagine a world of endless possibilities, a world that both you and I have dreamed of. I may have been damned first, but you were damned also, both of us by the King that we served so dearly. He had no intention of sharing His power. I, on the other hand, would love nothing more than for all to possess the same great power that I do. What do you say?"

"Where is this boy?"

"Upstairs, waiting for you to care for him. This will be your chance to be the father you always wanted to be. To raise a son after your own heart — a son, who will be exalted as you once were. And together, we also will be exalted and glorified. This is the dawn. The beginning of the end."

"I accept. I will go see this child now, and he will be my son, for today I have begotten him," the man said with delight.

The Devil vanished from the room, and the man left his office to see his new son. The world was about to change once again. The shift toward Darkness had now begun anew.

***

"Oh, I'm so glad you're finally awake," Sr. Suzanne squealed.

Esmeralda looked confused at first and then could not help but smile back at the rosy-cheeked nun. Esmeralda was in the same bed that her brother had been in after he was wounded in a battle with Radix. It had not been long since she was last here, less than a week to be precise. Her twins were born in this very place on the last day of the year, and only two days later were they all released from the hospital so Esmeralda could bury her brother. Bianca slept in a crib next to Esmeralda's bed. The sound of her daughter breathing rejuvenated the young mother. Esmeralda sat up.

"How long have I been here?" she asked.

"It's been three days now," the sister answered. "You had suffered from tremendous shock. I'm very sorry for all you've been through."

She placed her hand on Esmeralda's face.

"Thank you, sister. Are Lyles and Kimberly here?"

"Yes, I'll go get them. Everyone will be so happy to hear that you are awake."

A few moments later, she came back in with Lyles, Kimberly, Sr. Catherine, and Sr. Thomastina. They had all been taking care of their dear friend while she was asleep, praying that God would wake her not only from her slumber but from the nightmares that continued to plague her life.

"Ezzie, how are you feeling, honey?" Kimberly asked in her ever-so-sweet voice.

"I've been better," she replied. "He's gone isn't he?"

"Yes," Lyles said, holding back tears. He needed to be strong for her, for all of them. Someone needed to be. But he was supposed to guard those children, and he let the Devil snatch

Gideon away. Lyles turned and looked at Bianca who was still asleep in the crib. She was so pure and innocent, it could only bring a smile to his face.

"Michael told me that he would do everything in his power to find Gideon and bring him home. He also assured me that you and Bianca will be well protected, and that you should stay here with the sisters. They will care for you both and pray with you every day for the Lord's protection. Remember, He will not forsake you or leave you. Nathan truly believed that, and so do I."

"I know, I believe that too, but that doesn't make it hurt any less. I lost my son. He was only two days old. It's too much for me!" Esmeralda said amid a flood of tears.

Lyles and Kimberly sat on either side of her and wrapped their arms tightly around her as she wept. Just then Bianca woke up. She opened her big beautiful eyes and let out a soft coo to let everyone know she was there. Esmeralda stopped crying and turned toward her daughter. Lyles picked up the precious babe and handed her to her mother, who held her tight to her bosom. All her pain seemed to slip away in the smile of this blessed child. This girl seemed weak to many people, but God knew her strength, because it was His own. He filled this child with the Spirit from the moment she was conceived, for a great destiny awaited her. She would be a child after His own heart, to turn nations back to Him and bring glory to His name.

Kimberly and Lyles stood up and held each other. The nuns left the room quietly, to leave this small family alone for a few moments, to finally have a moment of peace and happiness to share together. But that quiet moment would end suddenly as Sr. Catherine screamed from outside the room. Lyles ran out to see what was going on.

"A demon, a demon!" Sr. Catherine shouted and grabbed Lyles forcefully. "He's come for the girl!"

Lyles prepared himself for battle immediately. He grabbed his sword and slowly walked down the hallway, searching for the menacing beast that frightened the nun.

"Where are you? Show yourself!" Lyles screamed. "You can't have her! You hear me! I won't let you take her away!"

"Stop! Please no harm, I mean!" a familiar scratchy voice called from down the hall.

Lyles knew right away who was terrifying these poor sisters, and he looked on as his good friend Puck ran from a band of nuns, who were throwing holy water at him. Lyles began to laugh hysterically as he watched Puck scurry away.

"Sisters, stop!" Lyles exclaimed with laughter. "He's cool."

Puck disappeared and hid behind Lyles. The nuns stopped in front of Lyles, and slowly Puck began to reappear. They stared at the Djinni before them.

"This is Puck," Lyles continued. "And we all owe a lot to this little troublemaker. If it wasn't for him, Radix might have killed Nathan before the sun came up and we all know what that would have meant."

The sisters looked confused. But Lyles assured them that he would explain more to them later. Right now, he just wanted to greet his good friend, which he did with a big hug. He brought Puck in to see Esmeralda, Kimberly, and Bianca. They also were very happy to see the little Djinni.

Puck apologized for leaving them so suddenly after Gideon was taken. He explained that he felt the need to do something about what had happened. He had proceeded to the Gates of Hell and spoke to the gatekeeper about the travesty that took place, demanding that the child be returned. Lyles wondered how the Djinni had gained such courage. The Djinni said that since he took that blow for Nathan, he had felt different inside, empowered in a way. The group of friends wondered though, even with his newfound courage, why Puck went alone — why not bring Lyles or Ravenblade?

The Djinni could not bring his comrades with him because they could not go where he went. They were flesh; only the spirit can travel to such places. That is unless the flesh is empowered by the Holy Spirit like Christ was when He resurrected from the dead. Unfortunately, though, Puck was unable to get the child nor could he enter Hell to pursue the nemesis who took Gideon. The gatekeeper had cast Puck back to Earth. Upon his return, Puck came back to his friends to see how they were and to tell the tale of his quest and of his failure. The group gathered around their friend and they all held each other, praising God for each other, and praying for Him to bring back Esmeralda's lost son.

At that moment, Puck told them all some very sad news. He could not stay with them because his very presence would alert Iblis to his location and cause Bianca to be in grave danger. He felt as if it was he who led the Djinn and Lilith to the children the first time, when Gideon was taken. He told them that he would go back to the desert where he was created and stay with Ravenblade in hopes of devising a plan together to get back Gideon. With tearful eyes, they said goodbye to Puck, and at once he vanished in a puff of smokeless fire.

A few days had passed since their dear friend Puck had left them, and it was time for the group to part ways. Esmeralda and Bianca had been set up in a small cottage a little up the road from the retreat house where the sisters lived and worked. The cottage had not been used in years, and the nuns felt that Esmeralda and Bianca would need their own space. But the sisters would be close by to help them with anything and everything and, of course, Michael the valiant Archangel watched over the mother and daughter with his sword blazing with the fire of God. All seemed to be well.

Lyles and Kimberly said their goodbyes and packed up their car for the drive back to Manhattan. It was a quiet drive home with the only noise coming from the radio. Kimberly dropped Lyles off at his apartment. The two kissed each other goodbye, a kiss that lasted much longer than the two expected. With all the pain they were feeling, they sought comfort in each other's touch. Once inside his apartment. Lyles showered and changed to a T-shirt and pajama pants.

He sat on his bed and touched the ring on his finger, feeling its engraved designs. Could he ever be the hero that Nathan was, even with the ring he was wearing? Right now, all he could think about was his failure to save Gideon from Satan. Trying to clear his mind, Lyles casually picked up Reverend Reynolds' diary, which was on his nightstand. This book had revealed so much to the young man about the evil that he had seen for himself. But what other secrets did it hold? While reading some quick entries in the diary, he fell asleep.

***

The sun was shining in Central Park. It was a beautiful spring day, and everyone had come to have a picnic. Esmeralda held Bianca, while Lyles and Kimberly played with Gideon. Even Nathan, Ravenblade, and Puck were there, enjoying the time with their friends. Everything was perfect. But then the joy was broken. The Sun grew black and shined down dark rays to the Earth. The darkness was so thick you could not see anything. You could not even breathe. Lyles began to feel all life leaving his body. It felt empty and cold, as if he were evaporating from existence. Everyone and everything was gone, and only the Darkness remained. At that moment, Lyles woke up gasping for air. He could breathe again. He was indeed alive, and the world was still there.

He stuck his head out of the window and felt the cold winter air, sucking it in. It felt good to be alive. He closed the window and sat on his bed, thinking of the revelation he just had. It reminded him of the Darkness that Reverend Reynolds had written about in his diary. A presence that the good reverend had said was like the absence of God. This is how the Darkness that Lyles had just experienced felt. Empty, cold, and without love, exactly what he would relate to the absence of God. This thought frightened Lyles, and he picked up the diary to see if he could find out more about this Darkness.

***

In the Arabian Desert, Ravenblade sat alone atop a cliff. His eyes surveyed the land below. Tanks and jeeps filled with armed soldiers flooded the sand-covered terrain. It all seemed foolish to the immortal. He had observed this mortal race since they were first created by the Almighty. Nothing had changed since the dawn of time. The desire to control, to have absolute power, had led men since that day when the first man and woman chose to listen to the voice of the Devil, following his dark path. All of it was pointless, little more than a game. But the immortal also knew who the real players of this game were, and the evil that lived in their hearts. Yes, he knew much of evil, for it dwelt in his own heart as well. While surveying the action below, Ravenblade was interrupted by a visitor.

24

Without turning, he spoke, "And what brings you here, Death? I thought our business was done."

"I just came to give you some news about your friend, Nathan," Death answered.

"He has risen then," the immortal said with a half-smile.

"Risen?" Another familiar voice shouted.

Ravenblade put his hand on his head and sighed. He was not one for company and it seemed like visitors kept popping up to disturb him.

"Yes, Puck," Ravenblade spoke. "He has been raised from the dead. A fate bestowed upon only the greatest of heroes, those having true faith in their hearts."

"One of the many gifts that Christ gave to mankind when He first rose Himself," Death interjected. "This transcending of the body and spirit is a taste of things to come for all of creation when men and women are resurrected for the final judgment, a day I long for more than any. For after that day, my service will be complete and I will be free."

"Heard of such a thing, have I," Puck spoke softly. "But never met a mortal who had been raised, only stories. Djinn do not concern for such matters, as we will return to smoke at the end, just as we began. There is no eternity for such creatures as we."

"You are not the only one to never see these men and women," Death continued. "For they are not allowed to return to the mortal plane to tell their tales. They are lying in wait for the end, just as all others are, in Heaven and Hell and places in between."

"Well, the end sooner than later may be," Puck said.

"What do you mean?" Ravenblade asked, arching his right eyebrow.

"The child, Satan has, the boy. Much fear is inside me, for this. The legends I hear, the stories of the one to come. Great evil will be. Begun it has," the Djinni continued.

"I did not know of this," said Death. His eyes opened wide from under his hooded cloak. "This could be a great disaster — worse than Radix. Those children have great power and if that power is harnessed for evil that could definitely mean the end is upon us."

Ravenblade did not speak. He put his head down and pondered the fate of the world. His heart was changing more every day, but it still had darkness in it. He even wondered what side he would play on in the end. Would he fight along with his new friends, or fight against them as an enemy. Puck remained with the immortal, and Death quietly vanished. He could not stand by idly while the Earth was destroyed as the other planets had been in the past.

CHAPTER III
HEAVEN ABOVE

In a flash of pure light, Gabriel arrived at the Gates of Heaven with Nathan. The crystals sparkled with the light of the fire that surrounded them, and the two approached the entrance. The ceiling of the room captivated the young man. The dazzling display of stars and galaxies over his head left Nathan awestruck. Fiery portals surrounded him, and right there before his very eyes was the Gates of Heaven itself. The crystal structure engulfed in fire before him could take him to many levels and places that were housed in this infinite plane of existence. Nathan just stood back and with wonder took in all that he saw — until he was interrupted by a voice.

"Excuse me," a bearded gentleman said in a very polite tone.

Nathan looked at him and the two giant angels that stood on either side of him. They almost appeared to be pillars of fire shooting up to the sky.

"Kepha," Gabriel addressed the man. "I have brought Nathaniel Salvatore, as requested by the Lord."

"Gabriel, I know very well who this is. What kind of gatekeeper would I be if I did not know who our guests were?"

"Of course," Gabriel added.

"But I don't know who you are," Nathan said. "And I'm not sure where I am. Is this Heaven?"

"I see being resurrected from the dead did not equip you with any manners," the gatekeeper interjected. "I am Kepha, but you may better know me as Peter, the apostle of our Lord. Kepha was the Aramaic name that Christ gave to me, when he and I were together on Earth. And, yes, you are in Heaven. But it may not all be what you have imagined. You have a special calling young man, and your training will begin soon."

"Training? What? I can't even get a break once I'm dead? Does everyone in Heaven have to train? I thought Heaven was all rejoicing and singing with the angels as we relax on clouds and pray for people," Nathan said.

"Well, I am not at liberty to tell you more. That will be Michael's job once you meet with him. And if you cared to read your Scriptures, you would know Heaven is a lot more than what you have learned from television shows and movies. It is a grand place, and there are many levels in this infinite space. Now if you will just step into the crystal portal here, you can go to your destination," St. Peter continued, as he gestured at the Gates.

"I'm not going anywhere until someone tells me what is going on. You hear me. I am sick and tired of being pushed this way and that way and no one telling me a single thing. I'm staying put and that is final!" Nathan shouted.

"Nathaniel, please enter the portal," Gabriel said.

"No! Who's gonna make me!" Nathan said and folded his arms.

"Fine. Have it your way," Gabriel said and shoved Nathan into the crystal portal.

Before he could do anything, Nathan had vanished in a flash of light.

"I still wonder what the Lord sees in that one. He is very stubborn," Peter said to Gabriel.

"Hmm, reminds me of someone I know," Gabriel said and patted Peter on the back.

Just then, Death appeared.

"What brings you here, Death?" Peter asked.

"I came with a plea, and was hoping to catch Nathaniel before he was sent to Michael," Death spoke.

"Sorry, you're too late. But what plea would you have?" Gabriel wondered.

"Gideon was taken by Satan, and…" Death was cut off.

"Yes, we know. Michael already informed us," Gabriel said.

"Yes, and of course nothing goes past the eye of God. He knew this before it ever took place," Peter remarked.

"I still do not understand all of you, and how nothing ever concerns anyone. This can prove to be worse than Radix. Why is no one storming the Gates of Hell and demanding this child be returned?"

"You know we cannot interfere in such a matter. What is done is done," Gabriel stated.

"So when exactly are you allowed to interfere? Seems like Satan can just go and do as he pleases and no one lifts a finger to do anything? This makes no sense," Death questioned. "Does Nathaniel even know?"

"No, he does not and it is better it remains this way. He has much training to do and we should not cloud his mind with things that will distract him. Death, God knows all and has a great plan. We may not understand His plans but they are perfect, and will all work out for the best. Without His consent we angels have no power to do anything, for we are subject to His will."

"I find that hard to believe. If you were all so subject to His will, then none of you would ever have fallen, especially not Lucifer. Do as you wish and, as usual, I'll do as I need!" Death exclaimed and vanished from their sight.

***

Nathan awoke. It had all been a dream. He was alive and with his friends in Central Park, enjoying a picnic. His sister was there with his niece and nephew. Even Lyles, Kimberly, Puck, and the immortal Ravenblade came to celebrate. The day was beautiful, the sun shining brighter than ever before, and Nathan soaked up each and every ray with joy, for he was alive. But as always seemed to be the case for Nathan, the joyous day began to grow sour. The sun grew dark and painted its black rays across the sky. The Darkness was thick and impenetrable. Nathan could not see anyone or anything. He was all alone, being consumed by the Darkness around him. Hope had faded and left only despair. With his final gasping breath, Nathan woke up. It took a moment for Nathan to realize where he was, for the dream felt so real. He was dead in a way, yet alive in another. But can one who has died sleep? Can he dream? Somehow Nathan had dreamed. Maybe it was because he still had flesh. The young man wondered exactly what he had become and what it meant for his future.

Getting up from the ground, Nathan searched the land before him. It was a strange place. Nothing at all like what he had pictured Heaven to be, yet he felt a peace in his heart that he had never known. The land stretched out for miles and miles. It was as if he was in an endless field, filled with vibrant green grass, and bright blue sky. There was no sun above him, but a warm, calming light shone down from above and all around. It was just at this moment that Nathan noticed he was no longer wearing the clothes he had been buried in. Even when he had stood at the Gates talking to Peter and Gabriel his clothing had not changed, but now, after passing, through the Gates, he was garbed in a white robe, which was tied at the waist by a white sash. He wore golden sandals on his feet and he felt stronger than ever before. Curious to explore the world around him, Nathan began to walk. As he walked, he noticed that everything remained exactly the same. It seemed as if there was nothing to be seen but grass and blue sky. Nathan wondered where everyone else was. There were no souls to be seen, no angels, and no sign of anyone. It was very odd. He stopped and took in a deep breath. The air was sweet, and felt refreshing. It was strange indeed to still be breathing after being dead, but once again he remembered that he did have his flesh, making this a little more understandable.

Then, before him little sparks of light began to rise from the ground all around, across the whole plain. These lights rose up to the sky and began to gather together. They were forming an object. At first it looked like a cloud, but then it transformed into a face. The face was gentle and peaceful with wooly hair and a beard. It smiled at Nathan and opened its mouth. From its mouth shot a double-edged sword, magnificent in every way. It was forged with impeccable craftsmanship as if by the very hand of God. The hilt was fastened with a sizable pommel to counterbalance the large blade. The handle was wrapped in what seemed like the finest and silkiest of leathers and was dyed red. The metal that made up the hilt and the blade was pure white, refined in the Fire of the Spirit of God. On the blade were carved intricate designs, including the shape of an angel where it met the hilt. Above the angel was a large gem engraved to look like a fiery eye and the gem changed color from red to orange to yellow to green to blue and even to purple. The blade itself was long and sharp, and two more points protruded out at the base of the blade giving the weapon an imposing look to all who faced it. This wonderful blade shot forth and came straight for Nathan. This reminded him of a dream he once had, and like that very dream, he could not move. The sword pierced his heart, and began to glow. It vanished from before Nathan's eyes, but it felt like he had absorbed the sword into his soul. The face had also vanished, and to Nathan's surprise, he felt stronger and more confident than before. He also felt filled with the Spirit, and God's very Word seemed to be branded into his heart. Wisdom as he had never imagined flooded his head, yet he did not seem to be overwhelmed by it, but rather felt very calmed by this knowledge. Something inside told him to keep walking as if he were being led somewhere. Just then he saw it, over the hill before him — a garden, beautiful and lush with vegetation. But this garden was surrounded on all sides by a fiery wall. He ran ahead to get a better look. And as he got closer, Nathan could see that it was not a wall that surrounded the garden, but angels that glowed bright with fire. They were cherubim like those who guarded the throne of God on the seventh plane of Heaven. They watched the young man as he approached with each of their four faces, but otherwise they remained perfectly still.

From the sky came forth a sword of flame that turned in every direction. Nathan stopped and fell to his knees. His heart yearned for him to enter the garden but he knew that he could not get past the angels or the flaming sword. Nonetheless, he was drawn to carry forward and found himself standing before those great angels, and the sword of flame was pointed directly at his head. He stared straight at the blade, completely fearless. The power he had received from when the double-edged sword pierced his heart and filled him with God's Word, gave him a confidence that rivaled even the angels that stood before him. Instantly, the sword went up and the angels moved aside to allow the young man entrance into the garden before him.

The garden was filled with every type of plant and tree one could imagine, all together in one place. It was odd, yet beautiful at the same time. He walked deeper and deeper, through the foliage, smelling the wonderful scent of the flowers that surrounded him. Ripe and luscious fruit hung from branches and vines all around. Looking further on, Nathan could see a vast river that ran through the garden in the distance. He had definitely entered Paradise, and this indeed was a much more fitting view of Heaven for the young man. There was so much to explore. Time did not exist anymore for Nathan, and he had already lost track of when it was, or how long he had even been here. Honestly, he did not care. All he wanted to do was see more of this beautiful place that he had ventured into.

Peace consumed him with every breath he took. The smell of the fresh water streaming from the river beyond beckoned Nathan to approach its shores. He hiked and climbed until at last he reached the river's bank. Right away he sat down and took off his sandals so he could soak his feet in the cool water. The feeling was so invigorating, and it encouraged him to want to jump in for a swim. He took off his robe, and kept on only the undergarment, which was seamless. The water was cool at first but grew warmer as he stepped in. It was the perfect temperature. Nathan also noticed that the water was crystal clear, and it tasted fresher than any water he had ever drunk. He could stay here forever, alone in this paradise. No worries, no problems, no misery, only simple bliss. The calming silence was broken by a noise Nathan heard in the distance.

It sounded like the grunting of a bull, or some other large mammal, and it came from downriver. He was not alone. But what lived in this garden? Maybe it was filled with all the animals of the Earth just as it had all the vegetation. But where were these creatures. That noise was the first that he had heard other than the running of the stream. And apart from the fiery angels and the sword, there had seemed to be no other life on this plane of Heaven. With a shrug of his shoulders, Nathan kept on swimming. He was in Heaven, what danger could there be. If it was indeed some great beast, it must be friendly. Or so Nathan thought. Just then, he felt the water move under him, as if a large fish had passed by. He looked into the river to see what it may have been. Something large and fast swam under him again. Even in the crystal clear water, Nathan could not make out what it was. He swam as fast as he could to the shore, and as he did the grunting sound came closer and closer as well as the sound of charging hooves. Before he could reach the bank of the river, Nathan was thrown into the air and flipped around. He was about to crash right back into the water, when a giant set of jaws wielding razor-sharp teeth shot up and reached out for him. His time in Paradise seemed to have come to an end, and Nathan would quickly discover what angels and demons feared as the second death.

Before the jaws could close on Nathan, a tree crashed from the shore and smacked the creature on the head. Nathan plunged into the water, and surfaced, gasping for breath. He pulled himself onto the shore and crawled away from the river. Sitting up against a rock, he saw an amazing sight. The beast that Nathan heard charging from the distance had knocked down the tree. This great and powerful brute was unlike any animal Nathan had seen. It was huge, more than a hundred feet from its head to the tip of its tail. Its neck was strong and sturdy, and its four legs like powerful pillars of stone. A long thick tail much like that of a sauropod dinosaur shifted from side to side as it moved. The creature's head was almost like a rhinoceros, and in addition to the horns on its nose, it had two on the sides of its head like a steer. Nathan knew he was witnessing some lost beast from days of yore. It stood on the shore next to the stump of the tree it had knocked down, shaking its head and huffing through its nostrils. The monster in the water must have been killed by that tree, for now the water was calm and still again.

Nathan decided to get a closer look at this majestic animal that had saved his very life. He moved closer, trying not to rouse the beast, for God only knew that Nathan had no chance of taming it. Unfortunately, as hard as he tried to be quiet, Nathan broke a branch under his foot, and the beast was startled. It saw the man right away and charged with full force. Immediately, Nathan turned and ran. He tried to shake the beast, but it was no use. He had to think of a plan and fast. He could not climb a tree, as this brute would only knock it down as it had the one before. *The water*, he thought. The creature could not go into the water. Nathan made a fast track back to the river and dove right in. Since the beast had killed the sea monster that tried to eat Nathan, he would be safe in the water.

He looked on at the beast that stood on the shore, and he laughed, for he was still alive, in some sense of the word. But that joy would not last. The beast kicked up some dirt, gave a great snort, and charged into the water after Nathan. No, it could not swim, but it was large and could make it at least halfway into the water. Nathan swam for his life, hoping to reach deep-enough water where the beast could not follow. That is when matters grew worse, for out of the water shot that great sea monster that tried to feed on Nathan. Now both creatures were coming right for him. Nathan swam again for the shore, and the two monstrosities crashed into each other. This was his chance to escape, and he did.

As he got to the riverbank, he found his robe and sandals, grabbed them, and headed deep into the garden, far away from the river. Looking back, he could see the two great creatures battling each other at the edge of the river. The beast locked its horns around the sea dragon's neck, and the sea dragon snapped back with its powerful jaws. It seemed as if their struggle would go on for all eternity.

The original serenity of the garden returned as Nathan moved away from the river. He was at peace again, and the only sound he could hear was the rushing water in the distance. His undergarment had completely dried by now, and Nathan put back on his robe and sandals. He began to approach the central point of the garden, which was full of fruit trees, ripe and ready to eat. Even though he was technically dead, Nathan did have flesh, and he decided to eat some of the fruit. First, he picked some delicious berries, then something like a mango. The fruits were all exotic and only distant versions of what Nathan knew of on Earth. Each one he ate was sweeter than the last. As he made his way, he came to a clearing where only two trees stood alone. One had no fruit, and the other was filled with the most delicious-looking golden fruit that Nathan had ever seen. The sweet nectar of the fruit Nathan was already eating ran down his cheeks as he began to wonder about the even sweeter-looking fruit below. The golden fruits glowed like stars on the tree. It was magnificent.

"Take a taste," a voice whispered in his ear. "The juice is sweet, sweeter than any you have ever tasted," it continued in a seductive tone. "All for the taking. Just one bite alone will give you life everlasting. You will become like God, all-powerful, almighty. Then truly you will control your destiny and that of others, so that you will endure no more pain, but joy beyond belief."

The voice filled his head with an incontrollable desire to race down, pluck the fruit, and savor its sweet taste.

"Eat, eat, eat," repeated over and over in his head.

Nathan began to walk slowly, with every intention of grabbing the fruit from the tree and eating its sweet flesh.

The sword of flame came crashing down from the sky and sent itself flying straight for Nathan's heart, before he reached the tree. As if by mere instinct alone, Nathan rolled out of the way and braced himself. The sword came flying back to attack once again. Out of thin air, into his hand appeared the sword that had pierced his heart and filled him with God's Word. With the sword he was wielding, Nathan blocked the fiery blade. It was a standstill and Nathan pushed with all his might to conquer the blade that was trying to slay him. He had to get to the fruit. He needed to have a taste. But then, as the struggle got to its worst, Nathan focused his thoughts on the sword in his hand. The more he placed his thoughts on the sword, the less he thought of the fruit and his own desires. The Word, which was the sword, filled Nathan and he became strong. The temptation to eat left him, and with that the sword of flame rested and returned to the entrance of the garden.

Nathan fell to his knees, and tried to make sense of what had just transpired. He saw the fruit again, but no desire entered him. It still looked amazing and wonderful, but something inside him told him that it was not time for him to eat this fruit. Not knowing what else to do, Nathan sat down on the soft grass beneath the tree.

"Welcome, my child," a soft voice called to Nathan from behind.

He turned to see a beautiful man, glowing with the light of the sun, much like Gabriel, Enoch, and Elijah had when Nathan was with them on Mount Sinai. The man had wooly hair and a beard. His robe was so bright white that it made Nathan's almost seem dirty. Nathan could also see that the man had marks on each wrist and foot. Instantly, he knew who this was.

"Peace be with you," Christ spoke.

Nathan could not speak, for he was in absolute awe at who was in his presence. He remained seated, for he could not think to stand up, nor to even greet his Savior. Jesus seemed not to mind at all, and sat down next to him.

"The fruit looks good and ripe, though it is not time for it to be eaten," Christ said to Nathan. "That is the Tree of Life. Once you eat its fruit, you will truly live forever. That is to be reserved for the end of all things, when I make things new again. But for now, you have Me, and My Spirit who dwells in you. You saw that temptation was knocking at your door, and your own will could not fight against it. But only when you focused on the sword, which is My Word, did you find the strength to overcome your desires."

He looked at Nathan with a comforting smile and put his arm around him. "I love you, Nathan. I always have and always will. From the first day that I created you and even before that, I have loved you. You must know by now that you are special to me. Not because of your great battle against Radix, or anything else that you will do. But I love you because you are Mine, and I promise you will do even greater things than you've done before. Remember this always, and keep Me in your heart. My Spirit will abide with you forever. If you know this, then no enemy can conquer you. You heard that voice inside that begged you to taste the fruit. It was your desire, but it was also from the enemy. Satan has chosen to sift you like wheat. Do not think that because you are in Heaven now that you are perfect and have no temptation. The battle wages on, and will not be complete until I have said so. Your strength is Me. Remember that, and keep the sword with you always, for it will save your life, just as I have saved your life."

Nathan looked up at Christ with a smile. He felt safer in His arms than he had ever felt, at peace and without fear. Then as quickly as He had appeared, Christ faded away and His peace remained. The young man struggled to get up, for he wanted to just lie on the grass all day. It was so soft and comforting, but he had to continue on. He got up from the ground and saw something sparkling on a mountain in the distance. Squinting to get a better look, Nathan noticed that it was a golden temple of some sort.

The young man was not sure why he had not seen it nor the mountain sooner, for there it stood high over all the trees in the garden. When he next looked down, he saw a path on the ground before him. The path started from the point where Christ had been sitting. Something inside told Nathan to follow this path, so he did.

As he traveled down the path Nathan thought of his encounter with Christ and all that Christ said to him. Nathan was a little upset that he did not take that opportunity to ask all the millions of questions that he had. But for some reason, when Christ spoke, Nathan could not help but only listen. No words could form on his tongue, and Nathan wondered about his speechlessness as he moved along. The path led to what seemed to be a portal surrounded by crystals, much like the portal he was shoved into that brought him to this plane of Heaven. He stepped in and vanished.

As Nathan entered the next plane, all he could see was a vast whiteness. Everything from the ground to the sky above was pure white. He was uncertain at first how he could navigate, when he could not tell where the ground was. There was absolutely no dimension to this plane at all. Yet for some strange reason, Nathan was able to walk forward with no problem. He spun around to see if he could make anything out, but everything everywhere was white.

"You seem lost," a voice called out.

Nathan turned to see Michael shining forth before him. He remembered the angel from when he had saved Nathan and Lyles from Radix, outside of Divine Body Church. Next to Michael was another, who towered over him like a giant. He must have been nearly eight feet tall. His shoulders were broad and he was very muscular. The man was wearing the same white robe and golden sandals as Nathan, which led the young man to believe that this giant was like him in a way — dead but alive.

"Nathan, good to see you again, and this time in a much better manner," the Archangel said with a smile. He turned to introduce the man next to him, "This is Christopher. I am sure you have heard of his legend back on Earth."

Though he was glad to not be alone, Nathan could not muster up even one word to say. He just stared at the angel and the man who stood before him.

"Seems odd of you to be at a loss for words. From what my brother Gabriel tells me, you never stop talking," Michael jested.

"Honestly, since I have been here I have noticed that I have less and less to say," Nathan replied.

"It is the Spirit. It is transforming you. The more you allow it to dwell in you, the greater the transformation will be," Michael stated. "I just wish it would move faster in this one over here," he nudged Christopher in his side. "He seems to never shut up."

"I'm a big guy, so I have a lot to say," Christopher shot back in a booming voice.

"I just wish someone would explain to me exactly what is going on," Nathan inquired.

"We will, but first let's go someplace else," Michael said and the three of them disappeared.

All three reappeared in a grassy plain, much like the first place Nathan had entered. The sky was blue, and the air was sweet.

"I assume this will be easier for you to get accustomed to," Michael said to Nathan. "Heaven is unlike Earth. It is not a physical plane, but rather a spiritual one. All that you see is like an illusion in a way, for none of it really exists as you see it. Rather, it is just energy that takes the shape of these surroundings. Most of this is too complicated for you to understand right now. Over time, more and more will be revealed, as you are ready."

"Okay, that's enough. Let's get to the good stuff," Christopher butted in. "You must have noticed that you have your flesh. Not your typical spirit, right? I'm like you too, and so are many more. We are like Christ after He rose from the dead, and much like all the saints will be one day."

"Yeah, but why? Why make us like this, and why now?" Nathan questioned.

Michael readied to answer, but Christopher jumped in again, "So we can fight in the final battle, Armageddon. We are Christ's soldiers and we have been brought here to train for the last days. Now, you will join us in our training."

"So, once again, I'm enlisted to fight a war that I want no part of," Nathan spoke.

"I see you have not completely changed," Michael finally was able to speak uninterrupted. "Whether you enlist or not is beyond the point. The war will be waged regardless, and you will have to choose a side. It is not about you. It is about God and His perfect plan that He set in motion before time even existed. I just ask you to look into your heart. You know that you yearn to see evil conquered. You have a drive to battle the Darkness. All that you have endured, has it not shown you the truth."

"I know what it has shown me. That evil is real, and that so is pain. After I died, I was hoping for some peace," Nathan said.

"But the story is not over. It is still being told, and you are still a part of it," Michael continued. "And you have peace, the peace of Christ, the assurance that you have His salvation and love. But there will be hardships and pain until the end. And you will not find the peace that you seek until the war is over," Michael paused and looked at Nathan. "I thought you were a hero. I thought you, of all people, would want this more than anything."

"Sorry to tell you, but you're wrong. I don't want this. I want rest. I want to feel the way I did when Christ held me," Nathan said, grabbing his head.

"What?" Christopher asked. "When?"

"In the garden — he held me by the tree."

"The garden, you mean the Garden of Eden? You were there?" Michael asked.

"I guess. It was just after Gabriel shoved me into the portal. I appeared in a vast plain, much like this, and wandered until I found the garden, which was guarded on all sides by fiery angels with six wings and a sword of flames. But they allowed me to enter, and when I was there it was beautiful. Until I came across those two monsters that tried to eat me."

"Monsters?" Christopher jumped in again.

"The Behemoth and Leviathan," Michael stated.

"Probably, now that I think of it, it was them — the giant sea serpent, and that part bull part rhino, part dinosaur thing. It was crazy. I barely escaped, and…"

"How on Earth did you escape the Behemoth and the Leviathan? No one can," Michael added.

"Well, I was only able to get away because they began to fight each other and forgot about me. Then, when I got to the middle where those trees were, with all that tasty fruit, I saw in the clearing two trees. One empty and the other full of glowing fruit."

"The tree of knowledge of good and evil and the tree of life," Christopher interrupted.

"Can I finish my story?" Nathan shouted. The angel and the giant stopped and just listened. "That is when I met Christ. I was tempted to eat the fruit of the Tree of Life, and was attacked by the sword of flame. But I was saved by the sword that was given to me. He called it His Word. When I focused on it, I found the strength to fight the temptation."

"Sword? You mean the sword of the Spirit called the Word of God?" Michael was beside himself.

"It came to me when I first arrived. It shot down from a cloud that looked like the face of Jesus, and pierced my heart, filling me with His Word. When I saw Christ, He told me to keep it with me, and that it would save my life. When He held me, I felt at peace, safe. It was more than I could find words to explain. That is all I desire."

"And that you will have, for once He has you, He never lets you go. But the time for peace is not here yet. For even Christ Himself said, 'I have not come to bring peace but a sword, division. War must come first, then peace," Michael spoke from wisdom. "But I must say I am taken aback by all you have told me. What you saw has only been reserved for those who will be given peace at the end."

"Even I have never seen the Garden, let alone the Tree of Life," Christopher said. "Do you know what that means? You are truly special in His eyes. It will be an honor to train with you, Nathan," he stuck out his hand and it swallowed Nathan's as the two shook.

"Hey, I've heard about you, and honestly the honor is mine."

"So, you've heard my story. Most men don't believe in it any more. It is a bit fantastical, I must say, but all of it true."

"You really worked for the Devil?" Nathan asked.

"Yes, unfortunately. But now I'm on the right side. I was only concerned with power then. Now, I have true power, power in Christ."

"Okay, that's enough from the two of you," Michael spoke. "It is time for us to begin. There is much for you to see and learn, Nathan. Your training will not be easy, and it will feel like an eternity, for here there is no time."

Michael was correct. To Nathan, it did feel like an eternity. There was no day or night where they were, so there was absolutely no way the young man could tell how much time was elapsing. Training was nonstop, for there was no need for Nathan to rest, and it was nothing like he imagined it would be. At first, he was very resistant. As he told the Archangel, he sought only to be at peace in Heaven. But as time grew on and the training grew deeper, Nathan began to accept this new path and, then, to yearn for it. The training did not involve any form of combat. The war that Nathan was preparing to wage was of the spirit, and no physical training could help him to be ready for it. He did have flesh, but it was not like the flesh he had on Earth. He was a transcendent being now. God had glorified his flesh in a special way. He never grew tired, his muscles never lost their definition, he needed not to eat, nor anything that he needed to do when he was mortal. No work was needed, his body was perfect, even better than when he was a prizefighter back on Earth.

Many had been given this gift after Christ rose from the dead. Though not all were chosen to be soldiers, like Nathan, for the Armageddon. Some of these transcendent beings even lived before the time of Christ, but they transcended after His death and resurrection. No one could achieve this feat until Christ first did it Himself. But as the Word says in Matthew 27:52–53, "The tombs were opened, and many bodies of the saints who had fallen asleep were raised; and coming out of the tombs after His resurrection, they entered the holy city and appeared to many." Nathan needed to learn much about what he had become, and what he would do. The more time he spent training, which involved channeling the Holy Spirit and releasing his own will to the Will of God, the stronger Nathan became. But he still had a long way to go, and much to learn. But just as Nathan was now a soldier of the light, there were others who were soldiers of the Darkness. The Darkness, which Nathan battled, was more evil than he could have possibly imagined. This enemy was more ancient and evil than any known to those on Earth. But Michael, Christopher, and the others who trained with them would share a lot, and through this Nathan would know of things that many of us would not know until the end of time.

There would be a break from training from time to time, when stories were told to educate and enlighten those who were training in the way of the Light. Michael would cause the sky to be as at night with stars strung about. All the men and women who were training would sit around a fire. This ordeal was not necessary but set a certain ambience that those who were once mortal seemed to enjoy. It reminded them of times back home when they were alive, and it helped to fill them with hope.

Christopher had started off with his story. How he had been born of great stature and proclaimed to serve the strongest king. After serving kings on Earth, he discovered one not of the Earth, whose power brought fear to men. So Christopher joined Satan and played soldier to the Prince of Darkness. To think of what he did to serve that evil demon made Christopher hold his head down in shame, for now he had the truth. But one day, when he was on a mission with his master, Satan cringed at the sight of a Cross. This made Christopher curious, for he could not understand why the Devil, as powerful as he was, could be afraid of some wood. He began to lose faith in his master, and sought to find answers about this cross. Thanks to a hermit named Babylas, he discovered that the cross was a symbol of Christ. Christopher discovered that Christ was not only the most powerful King in the entire world, but also the only true King. Valiantly, Christopher left his former master, and was baptized into his new faith, which was when he was named Christopher — Christ-bearer.

He was not one for praying and fasting, so as part of his new life, Christopher agreed to take people across a raging stream. One day, a young boy came up to him, and asked him to carry him across the stream. Without hesitation, the giant man lifted the small boy onto his shoulders and began to head across. As he walked deeper and deeper into the stream, he realized that the boy grew heavier and heavier, until at last it was as if the weight of the entire world was on his shoulders. But with matchless strength, Christopher made it to the other side and placed the boy down. He inquired how the boy grew so heavy, and then the boy transformed into Christ. Jesus told Christopher to follow him, and serve him, and asked him to place his staff into the ground. When he did so, a miracle took place, for his staff turned into a palm tree. Many people witnessed this event and came to Christ that very day. Even though his days of combat were behind him, Satan was still enraged at losing such a powerful soldier like Christopher, and vowed his revenge. He enraged the king of Lycia, and had him test Christopher to go against his God and serve false gods. But Christopher refused, and after much torturing, he was beheaded. Like Nathan, he was brought back to life, to serve God and prepare for the final battle against the enemy.

Everyone listened intently at the story; each of them had one of their own. But they all loved how Christopher told tales, especially those of his life. Michael would go next, and his tale was about the Universe, and the Darkness that they fought against.

***

"In the beginning was the Light," Michael began, "and the Light was Life. The Father, the Son, and the Spirit — God the creator of all. First, He created the Heavens. It was a magnificent Universe within itself, a wonder to be seen. The first beings he created were the angels — the Seraphim, the Cherubim, the Thrones, the Dominions, the Virtues, the Powers, the Principalities, the Guardians, and the Messengers. The Father existed with all His creation in peace and harmony. God is Light and in Him there is no Darkness. But when He chose to create, He gave His creation a choice — first to His angels and then later, when He created the physical world, to man. Thus the Darkness was born, the absence of Light, love, and life — the absence of God. Heaven was filled with the Light of God and the light of His angels, while the realm outside of Heaven, a blank plane waiting for the physical world to be formed, was dark and void. This is where the Darkness, evil intent, grew and took form. Ideas and concepts in this creation became personified. Beings such as the angel with no name, who was the personification of order, Sin, and Death were born as these concepts came into place. Likewise, the Darkness was one of these beings, representing evil and the chaos that it dwelt in. And like these other beings it had a mind. The spirit of Darkness grew inside the void plane that it existed in. It yearned to expand passed its realm and to break through the Gates of Heaven and take the throne of the One who created all these things. But it could not, for God is all-powerful. This Darkness, no matter how it seemed, was a created being, and like all creation was subject to God.

In order to hold back the Darkness, the Father instructed a team of angels whose light was pure and bright to stand at the edge of reality — the space between Heaven and the uncreated world. One of these was a Cherub, who shone with a light greater than any angel. It was said that his light was almost as bright as the Son's, and he was called Heylel — Shining One, or more commonly known as Lucifer. He led the regime that held back the Darkness, and because of this he got too close, and succumbed to its evil. The Darkness twisted Lucifer's mind and made him desire the same evil the Darkness desired. Transformed by the evil, Lucifer led a revolution in Heaven with one-third of its angels fighting on his side, in hopes of claiming God's very throne. The war was vicious but at last God would win, and Lucifer, along with his cohorts, was caste into a new plane that the Almighty created called Hell. Then, in order to truly hold back the Darkness and stop it from corrupting the rest of His angels, God created the physical world. Let there be Light. Inside the realm of chaos was brought forth order, as it was in Heaven. The planets and stars were set in place. The light of the stars held back the Darkness and drove it to exist in its own dimension. God created man and placed him on Earth, which was the central focus of all spiritual energy that held this new Universe together. But we all know that is not where the story ends, for evil is still alive and well. And it would permeate the physical world. But one day, on the glorious day of the Lord, the Darkness along with all evil will be put to an end, and God will reign victorious."

As Michael concluded, the fire in the center of their circle shot up into the sky with a brilliant flash of intense light.

Those who sat around the circle shouted with great excitement, and begged Michael to tell more. They wanted to hear the tales of legends. How man fell, and how creation was spread across the galaxy, of the great wars on the mortal plane between the Watchers and those who followed the Darkness. But those tales would have to wait for another time. Story time was over, and training would begin again.

Nathan now understood the great evil that he was up against. The dream he had when he first arrived in Heaven, as well as the evil he saw in both Satan and Radix when he faced them on Earth. But he also knew that he could not fight this evil, only God could do so. All he needed to do was to have faith, and everything would fall into place.

***

Nathan was not the only one thinking of the Darkness. On Earth, his friends also were contemplating that great evil and what the fate of the world would be. Ravenblade along with Puck and Death conversed about how Gideon was taken and what they could do to get him back. None of them could enter Hell. There was no hope. In the distance, Ravenblade felt a great evil power for a moment, but then it faded. They all wondered what that feeling could be. A new enemy to fight, an old enemy returning — no one knew.

And in New York, Lyles sat up in his bed reading that very tale that Michael had told to Nathan, for at one time it was told to the good Reverend Reynolds. Lyles flipped through the diary, amazed at what he was learning about the true evil that he would have to face. How could he battle such an enemy? It seemed impossible, but somehow he knew that God would be with him, and with that thought, he fell asleep.

Not too far away, in his penthouse apartment, a dark man looked out over the city. Everything would be his, in this world and beyond, for the child he possessed had great power. He looked at the seemingly helpless baby, and put his hand softly on his head. This child would lead the world, not to life, but to destruction.

CHAPTER IV
TIME AFTER TIME

Four years had passed since Satan had taken Gideon from his mother. Esmeralda and Bianca, the joy of her mother's heart, still lived in the guesthouse down the road from the Sisters of Saving Grace. Bianca Marie was growing up fast. To her mother, she was the most beautiful little girl in the entire world. Her skin was milky white and she had her mother's nose and lips. But much to Esmeralda's chagrin, she had her father's eyes. They were big and dark, and reminded Esmeralda every day of the tragic event in which her daughter was conceived. Though Bianca did have Radix's eyes, they were not sinister as his were. Somehow there was purity in them, as if her soul was untainted in every way. Bianca's hair was black and long, mostly straight with just a touch of waves, much like her uncle Nathan's. And, of course, she had the sweetest and kindest of personalities, always polite and full of love. She made Esmeralda happy in every way, but even the happiness that Bianca brought to Esmeralda could not extinguish the pain of losing her son, Gideon.

Esmeralda wondered about Gideon all the time. Where was he? What did he look like now? Was his heart kind and loving like his sister's or was it corrupted with evil like the Devil, who stole him away? Nightmares plagued her as she slept. And her daughter watched her toss and turn at night, praying that her mother would find peace. Bianca was never told about her brother. Esmeralda did not want to cause her any grief. She was so young and innocent. It was better if she had not even known that he was born. But the girl somehow did know. In her heart, she could feel her twin, but she did not know why? Her mother would tell her not to worry, and that all children have strange feelings inside. That it was part of growing up. But Bianca knew there was more to it. She even swore that she could see his face. And she did not tell her mother, but she could also sense his heart — and it was dark, very dark.

Bianca was not frightened by thoughts of her brother, only concerned. She was very caring, and she loved all life. Esmeralda would take her on walks through the woods around the grounds. Bianca would stop at every creature she saw, even the ants and the squirrels, and look on them with wonder. All creation was marvelous in her eyes, and she always thanked God for what He made.

Prayer time was her favorite time, because Bianca could talk to her Father in Heaven. She had no Earthly father that she knew of and, of course, Esmeralda would not tell her the truth of her conception and birth. So the only father that Bianca knew of was God. She called him Daddy in Heaven, and would ask Him to bless the world as He blessed her and her mother. She was indeed a sweet girl, and held a special place in the hearts of those who knew her.

She was also quite a curious girl. Some of the sisters claimed to have seen her do some very amazing things when they were watching her for her mother. One of the nuns claimed to have seen Bianca touch a wounded bird that had fallen from its nest. Instantly, the bird got up and flew back to its tree. The nun said nothing to the child, and thought to herself that the bird had been okay, and not really hurt. But inside she knew that God was working through this child. Another sister was with Bianca one day after it had rained. The little girl was crouched in front of a puddle staring as if she saw something inside. The water of the puddle miraculously separated and the little girl lifted up a tiny bug and set it back on the ground. Her only reply to the nun when questioned about the incident was that the bug was going to drown, and she had to save him. Esmeralda marveled at all of the stories she heard about her special little girl. With all that she had seen and been a part of, this special child seemed normal to her mother. The angel had told her that her child would be special, but this only led her thoughts even more to Gideon and what special things he also might have done.

***

"Gideon, one day I will rule not only this world, but all the Universe, and you and your brother will sit at my right and at my left," Sam said as he watched the child sleeping from the doorway of his bedroom.

The boy's eyes were crystal blue, his hair fine and blond, and his skin was white as snow. Gideon had Darkness inside of him that he did not understand, for he was only a child. But his

49

foster father, Sam, knew exactly what it was, and planned to use it to bring destruction to all creation.

"And which will be at your right, and which your left," a seductive voice came from behind.

"Does it matter, Lilith, which side each sits as long as they both sit at my side?"

"Hmmm, you know you sound more like him every day," Lilith replied. "You men with your plots for power. I only want to live freely. And your first born of your own flesh and blood, should sit at your right side. I don't care what power this little brat has. He is not even yours."

"Of my flesh or not, he is mine. And only with him will I be able to accomplish my goal. Your husband and I might sound alike to you, but we are not the same. My desires are not as vain as his. He fought God because he wanted all of the power for himself. That is why his allegiance to the truth no longer stands. He wants to be God. I don't want to be God. I can't be. I know that. I just wish to rule as Lord with justice over all creation. Not to enslave mankind, but to allow them the freedom that has been stripped from them. I fight God because His justice is wrong, and twisted. Look at what he did to my regime and me. We were conned into failing and falling. He could have empowered us. We did not separate from Him during the rebellion; we held true to Him and fought for Him well for many millennia, on this world and on many others. Fighting back the Darkness."

"Like I said, you two are so much alike. Maybe that is why I fell for you both."

"Do you really love him, like you loved me, or like I love you?" Sam said, looking into Lilith's pale eyes.

"That is not a fair question, and you know it, Sam."

"Hmm, I guess not. Nothing *is* fair, though. The Darkness that I fought against turned out to be Light as I had never known, truth as I was never shown, and hope for what will be. Only the Darkness can bring true justice to this world. It only desires that we follow our hearts, and do what truly makes us happy."

"Like ruling the Universe," Lilith sassed.

"Make your fun," Sam said and paused. He looked at her again, and took her hand.

"I still love you. I always will. And I can never forgive him for taking you from me. You were not so cynical when I first laid eyes on you. You were innocent, young, and beautiful."

"Am I not still beautiful?" the succubus wondered.

"Of course, but you are far from innocent and I am too savvy to fall for your charms."

"My charms? I am not charming you like I do to men."

"Let's put the past to rest, and move forward to the future. I have the serum for you. Come with me."

Lilith followed Sam to a small office down the hall from Gideon's room. He did not turn on the light, but just walked straight in, and took a small wooden box from on top of the desk.

"Take this," he said and handed the box to Lilith, who was standing in the doorway.

"And you are sure this will work?" she asked.

"Of course it will."

"And what do I do afterward?"

"As we discussed. Once he comes to his senses, take him to Iblis. Keep him there, until we can find the skull of Miacah. The power that it holds should be able to transform the body he is in. That transformed body can house him long enough for me to finish recreating the one that he lost in the first place."

Lilith left with the box, and Sam walked to Gideon's room.

"Yes, my two sons will work together with me, and the world will burn with a purifying fire. Darkness will reign, and we will rule. All is going according to plan."

***

"Hello?" Kimberly answered the phone.

"Hey, Kim, it's Ezzie."

"Hey, how's it goin'?"

"Good, hon, just tough sometimes, you know. But good," Esmeralda sighed.

"Yeah, I know what you mean. One day at a time."

"Yeah, definitely. Are you and Lyles still coming up next month? Bianca is super-excited to see you both."

"Of course! It's been some time."

"Great! Wasn't sure if you would make it. I know you newlyweds have a lot going on right now," Esmeralda replied.

"Yeah, it's a little crazy, but exciting."

"Can't wait to see you and Lyles. We miss you guys so much. Have to get Bianca ready for bed, so I'm gonna go. Tell Lyles we said hi and send our love. Talk soon."

"I'll give you a call next week. Tell Bianca we love her and can't wait to see her. Bye," Kimberly hung up the phone.

In the last four years, a lot had changed for Kimberly and Lyles. They went from dating to being engaged to being married very quickly. The wedding was small but beautiful, just family and of course a couple of really close friends. They now lived in Kimberly's two-bedroom apartment in Manhattan. It was larger than Lyles' apartment had been, and, of course, more convenient for her to go to work at the law firm. Lyles had also started a new job about three years before, as a clerk in the New York Public Library. The pay was low, but between Kimberly's and his salary they got by. Things were not perfect, but what marriage really is. The most important thing was that they loved each other deeply.

"Hey, baby, was that Ezzie on the phone?" Lyles asked as he walked into the living room.

"Yeah, she was asking if we were still coming up next month," Kimberly replied.

"Of course! I hope you told her that."

"Yes, I did, and I told her how excited we are to see them again. It's been a while."

"Yeah, well a lot's gone on for all of us," he said and sat down next to Kimberly on the couch.

"So how's your paper coming along?" Kimberly asked.

"Almost done. Just need to figure out how to tie up the ending."

"I can help you if you want," she said and put her finger on his chest.

Lyles kissed his wife and said, "I bet you can."

Three years ago, Lyles had started to go to seminary to follow in the footsteps of Reverend Reynolds. Reading the diary of the late pastor had really changed Lyles' life. Sure the battle with Radix showed him the reality of the war between Light and Darkness, but the diary showed him how to be faithful to God, and how to cherish His Word. He began to dive into the Bible, reading it every day. The more he read, the more he learned. This desire led his heart to want to go into ministry, so naturally he enrolled in seminary into a Master of Divinity program. He was not sure if he would become a pastor one day, but at least he knew that he wanted to deeply study God's solemn Word more than anything. Kimberly was very supportive of his decision, and was happy to see her husband's desire to be closer to God. He was on his way to making an impact on lives for the Lord. Though he did not realize the true value of the education that he was receiving, nor how much it would help him someday soon.

***

"Still thinking about that boy, Death?" Ravenblade asked.

"Of course, how can I not. Four years may have passed on Earth since the boy was taken, but I know that Satan will use him for great evil. That boy is powerful and can shift the balance. He could even be the one that Daniel and John spoke of."

"If you ask me, the boy may be dead already. Satan was probably jealous of his power and killed the kid," the immortal replied.

"He is not dead, or I would know of it. That snake is far too cunning and crafty to let some petty jealousy come in the way of his dark plans. This child is the catalyst he has been waiting for — a true child of Darkness."

"So you know the child is evil."

"His heart is dark, that much I can feel. But where he is, I do not know."

"Sad is this news," Puck said, appearing from smokeless fire. "His sister so sweet, so innocent, so pure. Could not bear to tell such news to Ezzie. Break her heart, it would."

"Yes, better to not let the mortals know of what we know," Death said. "They never really understand things as we do."

"No one understands things as I do," Ravenblade said. "Maybe I should have let Radix kill those children before they were born. I'm not so sure the girl is any better than the boy. They are his offspring, and his evil was dark and deep."

"Like yours?" Death questioned. "Slaying the children is not the solution. And obviously God wants them alive. I just don't understand His plans sometimes."

"Who does?" Ravenblade said back.

"Some of us understand it better than others," a voice boomed from behind.

"Hmm, Azrael, what brings you here?" Ravenblade asked.

"As much as it pains me to visit you, Raven, I have come to discuss the child as well," Azrael replied.

"Why now?" Death questioned. "I have been pleading at the Gates for the last four years, and no one has even acknowledged me."

"Timing is everything, my friend," Azrael continued. "I also do not have any knowledge of where the child is. Somehow, his energy is being blocked from us. Only God has the power to know. And no one can go to Hell and ask the Devil for the child. You, Death, had already overstayed your welcome there last time. The little Djinni there also gave his best shot, and you, Raven, just simply cannot enter because of your flesh, immortal or not. I could, but God would damn me for such treason."

"So then why did you come?" wondered Ravenblade.

"There is someone who can go," the angel answered. "Nathaniel Salvatore."

"What? How?" Death asked.

"The young man has been training with Michael for some time now. In Heaven, time does not exist as it does here. God has chosen for us to respect and follow the timing of this mortal Universe, but a day can be as a thousand years, and even a minute as a millennium. Nathan has learned a lot from the Chief of the Angels, and he has the Word with him."

"The Word of God, the sword of the Spirit," Ravenblade said.

"Yes. It has made a home in his heart. He is a man, and therefore has forgiveness through Christ. If he were to go into Hell, God could and would forgive him of such an iniquity, unlike myself or the other angels."

"And how do you plan to do all of this?" Ravenblade inquired.

"There is a way. It will not be easy, but I think with his training, Nathaniel can do it," Azrael stated. "But I will need some help."

"Help with what?" questioned Ravenblade.

"A distraction," the angel answered. "I was hoping you three could run some interference for me and Raphael to sneak the young man away from Michael and Christopher."

"Raphael is in on this too?" chimed in Death.

"Yes, something needs to be done," Azrael explained.

"By putting your faith in a man?" Ravenblade asked.

"No, my faith is in God," the angel said.

"Then why go against His plan?" Death asked.

"How do you know this isn't a part of it?" Azrael pointed out.

***

Across the desert in a small village in Iraq, there were shouts of agony and fear. A man supposedly possessed by demons was swinging chains that were shackled around his wrists — swinging them wildly at the people around him. They had tried to kill him with bullets and explosives, but nothing worked. He healed from the bullet wounds and the explosions had no effect on him. Two men had managed to chain him to a rock, but he instantly broke out and killed them. This man was indeed filled with power and no one could stop him. Then as the people cowered, a woman appeared. She was dressed very provocatively in a short, red dress.

The men and women looked at her with disgust, as they were modest Shia Muslims and believed that women should cover their bodies and not flaunt them. The provocative woman walked up to the deranged man, who whipped his chains at her. She caught both of the chains in her hands and swung them around, wrapping the man up and luring him to her. In one smooth motion, she slipped her fingers into her bosom, pulled out a syringe, and jabbed it into the man's neck. He fell to the ground and began to foam at the mouth. All the people looked on, even more fearful, for this sinful woman was able to do what their strongest men could not. The possessed man convulsed on the ground and shattered the chains that were wrapped around him. He rolled to his knees, and gave a deep growl. Looking up, he let out a bellowing sound, and then grew quiet. As if completely transformed and cured, he stood up very straight, and dusted himself off. He turned to the woman. The crowd around them fled.

"Lilith, how did you do that?" the man asked.

"Consider it a gift," she replied.

"And how did you acquire such a gift?" he asked and cracked his neck.

"I have my ways."

"Yes, you do," he said, running his finger down her chest.

"I guess I should thank you then. I feel stronger, and in control, though still not strong enough."

"The serum is only temporary and will not restore your complete power. But it will finally give you control over your host body, so you no longer act like a crazed animal."

"Yes, my spirit is too strong for these mortal bodies, leaving me weakened and crazed as you called it. But now I feel like I can do so much more."

"And you will, in time. For now, I would like you to come with me."

"And why should I do that?"

"Because this is only the beginning. With my plan, you will be fully restored."

"Sounds interesting, but I really don't trust you."

"I wouldn't dream of you ever trusting me. But honestly, what do you have to lose. I have already given you but a taste of what is to come. Doesn't it only make you hunger for more?"

"I am hungry indeed, and not just for that," the man said and slapped Lilith on her backside.

"Don't get fresh with me, kid. I could be your mother for all you know," Lilith said with a smile. "So, what do you say, Legion, will you come with me."

"Like you said, what do I have to lose?"

A man ran out with an assault rifle, firing at the two villains. Legion and Lilith just looked on at the pathetic peasant who tried to kill them. The newly restored Legion walked solemnly up to the man holding the gun and ripped it from his hands. The villager fell to the ground and covered his face. With ease, Legion snapped the gun in half. Then, he looked down at the man on the ground and smiled. The skin of the body that Legion was possessing began to move and ripple. Clawed fingers and demonic faces began to push against the flesh from inside him. The poor man panicked in great fear, for he knew that his life would end today. Legion lifted the man by his throat into the air. Another arm with sharp talons grew from his wrist and reached down the man's gullet until it found his heart and crushed it.

"Let's go," Legion said, and he tossed the corpse to the ground. "I am Legion, for we are many," he solemnly said, as the two walked away.

***

"Death, what brings you here?" Peter asked his visitor. "Another request about the boy, I presume. I think it is time to let it be and let God work out His plan."

"Honestly, I am here to talk to Christopher. Maybe I *have* finally decided to let God work out His plan," Death responded.

"Christopher? Why would you need to talk to him?"

"He is training Nathaniel, correct?"

"Yes, he is," the gatekeeper replied.

"Then, I want to speak with him. A private matter that Nathaniel's friends on Earth would like me to relay to Christopher for him."

"Hmm, well, this sounds funny to me. You can just give me the message and I will relay it through one of the angels to him."

"No, they specifically said they wanted me to give the message to Christopher. I really do not ask too much of you, Peter, so how about you do me this little favor."

"Don't ask too much? You are here all the time asking things. Why can't God do this? Or why can't He do that? Maybe you should just do your job and only come here when you have souls to deliver."

"Why don't you do your job and give Christopher the message. Let him decide if he wants to talk to me or not!" Death insisted.

"Fine, I will have someone contact him and see if he comes to hear your message," Peter stated.

"Good, I will wait."

***

57

"Michael, thanks for coming," Ravenblade said to the Archangel, who had appeared before Puck and him.

"I find this rather peculiar that you requested my presence. So what is your need?" Michael replied.

"We wanted to talk to you about Nathan," Ravenblade responded.

"Yes, Master Nathan concerned we are for him," Puck added.

"What concern could you have? He is in Heaven," Michael said.

"I'm really not concerned, only this little guy here is. I just want to know how his training is going. There is going to be a big battle one day that will put to shame all the ones we have fought in the past. I want to make sure you are properly preparing him for the fight. You have been soft lately. Letting Lucifer get his hands on that boy and all…"

"You listen here," Michael cut Ravenblade off. "I will not take your criticism. If you think me to be soft, then best try me yourself."

"I would love to," the immortal said with a smirk. "But, honestly, it'd be a waste of time."

"You are incorrigible," the Archangel raised his voice. "The young man's training is going very well. But don't expect to get a full report. You might be playing nice these days, but I still don't trust you, Raven. I never have and never will. Your heart is still black, and with Radix gone from the Earth, I am certain you will return to your ways."

"You know nothing of me, Michael. I do not care to be good or evil. I only care to do as I please. But regardless of that, I never have nor will I ever serve the Darkness. So, unfortunately, that puts us on the same side of the playing field when the war breaks out. Therefore, I am choosing to play nicely. I want to win so I don't have time for petty garbage!" Ravenblade raised his voice in return.

Puck sat on the ground with his head in his hands, while he listened to the angel and the immortal argue back and forth.

***

"Death, you wanted to talk?" Christopher asked. He loomed over Death like a hulking juggernaut.

"Yes, about Nathaniel. But it would be better to do so in private," Death suggested.

"Why?"

"Just please do me this one favor."

"Fine, let's go talk then. Come with me."

Death followed Christopher through a portal. When they came out onto the other side, they were in a vast place with a cloudy sky full of thunder and lightning. The ground was rocky where they stood, and they were surrounded on all sides by the crashing waves of a great ocean.

"Where are we?"

"Does it matter?" Christopher answered. "It's all fake — the clouds, the lightning, the waves, all of it just for show. This is a good place to talk. The only one who will hear us is God Himself. But that would be the case no matter where we went. Of course, He knows it even before it is said."

"Yes, that I am already quite aware of."

"So what did you want to talk about?"

"About his nephew, Gideon. They are concerned that he is unaware that he was taken by the Devil. They really feel he should know about this matter. It might even give him the drive to train harder to one day rescue the boy from the hands of Satan."

"You know it's not that easy, Death. God has a plan. If it is His will for the boy to be saved, then the boy will be saved. But telling Nathan will only cloud his mind and take away from all we are trying to do, by training him in the Spirit."

"Yes, but shouldn't he know the truth?" Death returned.

Death kept on speaking about the matter in order to delay the hulking man for as long as possible.

***

In another part of Heaven, Nathan was meditating. He was training in the Spirit, learning how to focus the energy of God that filled him. This would help him in the war to come. For only with the Spirit of the Lord, would he be able resist the Darkness that he would face. Great power began to build up inside of Nathan as the young warrior focused deeper and deeper on becoming one with God's Spirit. And just when his focus was at its greatest peak, and the Light of the Lord shone out from him, he was stopped by an outside force followed by a voice.

"Nathaniel, please come with me," the voice called out, waking Nathan from his trance.

"Huh?" he said as if awakened from a dream.

"It's I, Raphael. I need you to come with me and quickly," the brilliant angel requested.

"What? Why?"

"Please just come, before it's too late."

In times before, Nathan would have argued with the angel and questioned why he had to go anywhere. But the more he grew in the Spirit, the more Nathan began to change. He was truly transforming into a warrior of the Light. He took Raphael's hand, and the two were transported to another plane of Heaven. Nathan stared at the vast volumes of texts all around him. The shelves went on for eternity.

"Where are we?" he asked.

"The Hall of Records," replied another.

"Who are you?" Nathan inquired of the other being who stood before him.

His hair was blond and long, tied back in a ponytail. He wore a black robe, which contrasted his glowing white skin. His pale blue eyes pierced Nathan's own.

"I am Azrael, the Angel of Death," the angel said. "I keep the records of all mortal life on Earth and beyond. Each of these texts contains vast information of the Universe, past, present, and future."

"Why am I here?" Nathan wondered.

"Azrael and I wanted to speak with you about something dire," Raphael answered.

"Please tell me," Nathan insisted.

"Very well," Azrael began. "Let's cut to the chase. Your nephew, Gideon, has been taken by Satan."

"No! When? How?" Nathan screamed. He was told that his sister gave birth to twins, but he had never had the chance to know or even see his niece or nephew.

Raphael put his hand on Nathan's shoulder, and radiated a light that soothed the pain in Nathan's spirit.

"Do not fear, for he can be brought back," Raphael said.

"Yes, you can help locate and return the young boy," Azrael continued. "He was taken four Earth years ago, just before you transcended from the dead. Satan came in and snatched the boy from your sister, almost fatally wounding her. If not for the aid of Raphael and God's healing touch, she would have died. No one knows where the boy is, for some kind of power is blocking us from this knowledge."

"No, no, no!" Nathan yelled out. "This is impossible! And why did you wait until now to tell me? God must know where he is. Why isn't He putting an end to this? Doesn't He care about an innocent child?"

"Of course He cares, for He cares for all things. But as you already know very well, it is not easy for even us angels to understand His ways," Azrael went on. "But you can help, by entering Hell and finding the child."

"Are you crazy?" Nathan exclaimed. "How on Earth can I enter Hell? With what power can I face Satan? I met him in the desert before. I can't beat him."

"You can with the power of God," Azrael professed. "You have been training in the art of the Spirit."

"And you have the Sword," Raphael added. "The sword of the Spirit, the Word of God is no ordinary blade. When wielded by a true warrior of the Light, no Darkness can stand against it."

"Yes, Christ told me to keep it with me. That it would save my life, when I met him in the Garden," Nathan stated.

"So you faced your Savior again, then, Nathaniel," said Raphael.

"What do you mean *again*. That was the first time, other than in a dream, that I actually met Jesus," Nathan responded.

"Not true. You met him in the desert. The night before I visited you there," Raphael spoke.

"You told me that I faced the Angel of the Lord, whom Jacob had wrestled."

"And whom did you think that was?" asked Raphael. "Did not Jacob wrestle with God? I called Him by the name that was used in olden times before His human incarnation, the Angel of the Lord. For if you know your Word, which I think you may, since it is in your heart, then you would know that the Angel of the Lord always proclaimed Himself as YHWH," the sound of God's Holy Name shook the Heavens.

"Yes, you had met Christ before, and wrestled with him to a standstill. But now you must stop wrestling with Christ and your destiny, and battle your true enemy. That snake is more cunning than all the rest, for by his hand all have fallen." Azrael commanded. "You will need the sword that is in your heart for this fight."

"But how will I get there, and how will I know what to do when I arrive?" Nathan questioned.

"There is only one way that you can get into Hell from here. You must return to the Garden. When the Behemoth and the Leviathan collide, the clash emits a great force of energy. If you use what you have learned from channeling the Spirit, you can enter this energy and be transported to any destination of your choosing. But you must focus on your target without breaking concentration," stated Azrael.

"And what exactly do I focus on?"

Azrael opened one of his books to an image of fire and brimstone.

"Focus on this."

"And how will I get back to the Garden?"

"That's easy," the Angel of Death gave a rare smile. "Just close your eyes."

***

Puck still sat watching the angel and the immortal argue back and forth. Ravenblade's plan was working without fail.

"Okay, that's enough!" Michael blared out. "You are lucky that I serve the Lord, or else I would slice you to pieces!"

"Hmm, well as fun as that would be. I think we can stop now," said Ravenblade.

Michael stopped and stared at the man he had been bickering with, confused at how it ended. "What? So is that all then?"

"Of course. We don't need you here anymore, so you can go now."

"I don't understand, was this all some big joke?" the Archangel asked.

"We needed you to stay down here for just long enough," the immortal added.

"Long enough for what?"

"For Nathan to make his break for it."

"Break for it?" Michael was confused.

"Yes, he should be on his way to Hell as we speak."

"No!" shouted the Prince of Hosts, and instantly he vanished in a flash of light.

***

"Death, I can't sit here and argue this matter forever." Christopher began to get restless.

"I just thought you would be more compassionate to it than Peter has been," the grim being insisted.

"Are you sure this is all you came here for? For some reason, I feel there is something else going on." The giant was cross and folded his arms.

"Well, maybe there is, but I can't say. We just needed you away from him for long enough."

"What?" Christopher shouted.

"I can't stall any longer," Death said.

"Tell me what is going on!" The giant was incensed at this point, but it was too late. Before he could say another word, Death had disappeared.

"We have to find Nathan," Michael shouted as he appeared behind the giant.

"Why?" Christopher asked.

"He is trying to go into Hell and get Gideon back."

"What? But he can't. He hasn't had enough training. He will be trapped there until the end of time," Christopher said.

"I know. But maybe we can get to him before he finds a way there."

"But how would he get to Hell from here anyway?" wondered the large man.

"The Garden!" they shouted in unison.

Nathan opened his eyes to see the lush Garden he had been to earlier, and right away he saw the temple glistening on the mountaintop in the distance. The feeling of peace he had experienced the first time that he was there came over him again. It was amazing. The sound of the rushing river water filled his ears. That is where he would find the beasts that he sought. Without hesitating, Nathan ran to the riverbank and looked around for the Leviathan and Behemoth. Those monstrous creatures almost destroyed him the last time he was there. If not for their eternal feud, Nathan never would have escaped. But this time, escape was not part of the plan. Instead, he would face them head on and somehow use the energy they would create in battle to teleport to Hell. This meant that he would not only need to get very close to these colossal creatures, but practically get in between them when they collided. How he would do this, he did not know, but Nathan was ready as ever to do the impossible, yet again. The river water was still. Nathan looked about, listening for the sounds of the beasts.

"Where are you!" the young man shouted at the top of his lungs in hope that they would hear him and come rushing at him.

Nothing happened. The water remained calm. There were no signs of life anywhere around him. Nathan took off his robe and sandals, as he had done the last time he was there. And once again, he dove into the river. He searched and he searched, but he could not find the sea serpent that he had met before. Having another idea, he swam to shore. Once he was on land, he began to focus his energy and started to glow as if he were charged with electricity. The electric field around him increased by the second; until in one big burst, he released it up to the sky. The gigantic bolt of energy shot straight up and fizzled at its peak.

Instantly, Nathan heard a grunt followed by a charging sound. He had done it. The ground shook, and the trees began to fall. The Behemoth was headed straight for Nathan. At the sound of the grunting beast, a bellowing noise came from the depth of the river. It was the Leviathan. Nathan had succeeded with at least the first part of his plan. Now he had to not only get them to clash, but do so without getting demolished or eaten in the process. The Behemoth came plowing right for Nathan, who jumped to the side to dodge the beast. He rolled on the ground, until he hit a tree. The determined warrior turned to see the dragon rise from the river. Nathan got to his feet and began to run down the shoreline, trying to get the serpent to follow him. It worked, but the sea monster was faster than Nathan thought, and far craftier. Its head shot out from the water and came shooting toward Nathan, with its jaws wide open, ready to swallow its prey. The young man ran as fast as he could, jumping over obstacles in his way. In a frenzy, he tripped over some roots and stumbled to the ground. He looked up at the razor sharp teeth that were about to gorge on his flesh. But before the sea dragon could make a meal of the young man, Nathan's hand began to glow and the sword that had pierced his very heart appeared in its grasp. The Word of God emitted a light so bright it blinded the creature.

Nathan rose to his feet and began to creep into the forest behind him, dumbfounded by what had just happened. The sword was still in his hand, and the power that it gave off strengthened the young man. A low grunt came from behind him, and the Behemoth began to charge again. Nathan turned, and with no fear stood his ground against the approaching beast. It had its horns lowered as if to gore the man straight through his heart. The warrior put his sword before him, and braced himself. Just as the beast was about to make contact, Nathan shot into the air, flipping straight up as the charging Behemoth raced under him. The Leviathan, still blinded, came forward at once, and the two immense creatures smashed into one another. The collision caused such a quake the ground began to split beneath them. This was the moment that Nathan had been waiting for. He swooped down from above with his sword pointed where the beasts' heads met each other.

"No! Stop him!" Christopher shouted at Michael.

The Archangel dashed toward Nathan at the speed of light, but it was too late. For the young man had already been caught in the stream of energy before the angel had seen him, and in the blink of an eye, Nathan vanished.

Michael appeared before Christopher.

"I will go after him," he said to the large man.

"You will not follow him," a voice called out from all around.

"Lord," Michael said in reverence and kneeled.

Christopher also got down on his knees.

"Let Nathan go. He has chosen his way. You are not to interfere with him," the voice commanded.

"Yes, Lord, we will do as you say," the angel replied.

All grew calm as the Leviathan and the Behemoth separated and parted from each other as if they had lost interest in the battle. Michael and Christopher rose and left in a flood of light.

***

In the Qin Mountains of Shaanxi, China, hidden deep within the rocky slopes laid a very secret and sacred abode. Those who dwelt in this clandestine fortress were known at one time as Magi to the outside world. These particular Magi were descended from the secret sect of Daniel, the great prophet of God. They were called the Keepers of the Light, or at least that was the English translation. Their solitary fortress in the mountains was known as the Temple of Luminescence, once again the English translation. The Great Teacher, which was the title given to the leader of this group of Magi, was very disturbed by the presence of a great evil. He called in one of his students to discuss this pertinent matter.

"Teacher, I have come," the young Chinese man spoke to his leader in their native dialect.

"Yes, Chien, my son. Thank you for coming," the old teacher said in the same tongue. "My heart is grieving for the Earth. For just as soon as the world had been rid of the plague known as Radix, another evil has resurfaced. Legion has returned. His evil is soaked in the deepest and most ancient of Darkness. I am not sure that there is anyone alive who can challenge his sinister reign. In the past, we have ordained champions to battle the agents of Darkness. The last of these was Wang Sheng. But he could not defeat Radix, and left our order many years ago when I was young like you. Now he too is dead, and even though a champion did arise to defeat the evil Radix, he also is no longer on this Earth. If a new hero does not arise, we will all perish. That is why I have called you here."

"But what can I do, Teacher?"

"You must find this new hero and ordain him as such."

"But where will I find such a man? We all thought the Godchild, Nathaniel Salvatore, was the new hero of this generation. Though, our ministry did not ordain him, it was said that God ordained him Himself."

"Yes, he wore the Ring of Solomon — the very ring that was given to Wang Sheng by my predecessor. This within itself was an ordination. Another has the ring now. He may be the one. You must find him and make sure of this. If he is, you must help him to reach his full potential, so that we can truly overcome the enemy at hand. Legion was born from the destroyer of worlds and is corrupt in every way. We were barely able to stop him last time, many centuries ago, when he was trapped in that disc. But there is no one alive that can wield the ancient arts as the Teacher of that time did. We are at a loss. This could possibly be the end of not just this world but all life as we know it."

"I will do what I can, Teacher. I will find the man who has the ring, and I will help him to defeat Legion. My training is complete. With your blessing, I know I can do this."

"You have my blessing, but you will need more than that. You will need to dig deep into your very soul and reach out to the source of all life, as our ancestors did before us. Now go, my son."

"I will not fail," the young man said with a bow and left.

+++

"That was a nasty trick, you played on us. Do you even know the consequences of your actions?" Michael lectured Ravenblade and Puck.

"I look for no forgiveness for my actions, not from you or God. My sin is so deep it would not matter anyway. I did what I had to do. You and your cronies were doing nothing, as usual," Ravenblade spoke back.

"We do what we can, but invading Hell is out of our jurisdiction. We can only do what the Father allows. Some of us choose to obey His will," the Archangel added.

"Seems lately like everything is out of your jurisdiction. I remember the days when we would smote God's enemies. Our blades never went thirsty, for the bloodshed was great and there was rest on all sides," the immortal returned.

"Yes, and is that not why you fell," Michael responded. "Your sword drank way too much blood, and your heart began to yearn for it. Your love of murdering people who could barely stand in your own shadow is what brought you low, to where you are today."

"You better watch what you say, or my sword might feed on you!" Ravenblade exclaimed.

"I would like to see you try," the fierce angel said. "But I am not here to fight."

"Good excuse."

Ignoring Ravenblade's sarcasm, Michael continued. "I just want to know if you understand fully what danger you put your friend in. Nathaniel is not ready to take on all of Hell. He may be trapped there until the final judgment or worse, he may end up destroyed completely."

"One thing I learned about Nathan, while fighting at his side, he is very resourceful. I know he will make it out, and hopefully with the child. That is if the child has not been destroyed. No one can sense him anywhere. Satan might have taken him just to wipe out the competition," Ravenblade remarked.

"Well, let's hope not," replied Michael.

"There are other things we should be concerned about these days," Ravenblade grew stern.

"And what is that?"

"Legion has returned."

"How do you know?"

"Listen to the wind or have you forgotten how to read its breath. He is close by, somewhere in this very desert. I felt his presence some time ago but could not discern it exactly. But now I know for sure. Somehow he has regained control, and his power, though limited, is far greater than it has been since he lost his body."

Michael paused and listened to the wind. Ravenblade was right. A grave evil had been released upon the world. But even with this knowledge all that the angel could do was wait and watch. Even if the demon were to play his hand, without God's permission, the Archangel could do nothing to stop him. He looked at Ravenblade and the little Djinni that sat at his side, and vanished.

***

On the seventh plane of Heaven, in the presence of the Lord, Azrael and Raphael met. The two brothers prayed to their Lord and Father for forgiveness. Angels were made to serve the Lord and falling from that duty meant being sent into Hell to join Satan as a demon for all eternity. But angels were not perfect and God knew this. Their plan was not His own, but God would use it to perform His will, for He already knew what they would do. He forgave His sons of this iniquity, for the Lord is merciful, and they had been praying for forgiveness, even from the moment they devised the plan.

***

"Ah, Legion, welcome," Iblis said from his golden throne as the demon entered with Lilith.

The entire palace and the whole city of the Djinn, for that matter, were made of solid gold. Legion looked with disgust at the twisted king before him. Iblis was not handsome, though he had been before when he was an angel. Now, like his creatures that he formed, the Djinn, his eyes were vertical, and his nose snout-like, with small tusks protruding from his lower lip. He was adorned in a regal purple garment, and wore a golden crown encrusted with jewels.

"Not so sure that I am welcome here," Legion spoke back; his voice echoed as if it were several people speaking at once. "So why have you bought me here?"

"Is that how you talk to a friend?" Iblis returned.

"We have never been friends, Iblis," Legion said.

"Now, now, boys, stop this immature bickering," Lilith interjected. "Let's not play each other as fools. No one is here for friendship, but we do share a cause."

"And what would that be?" Legion asked.

"To win the war, of course," the succubus stated.

"I have no time for wars. I am happy to have my own mind. All I want now is my body back, or another one strong enough so that I can be fully restored. I feel like a caged beast. It is quite

69

infuriating," the demon echoed. "I had been trapped in that disc for so long, and even before *that* my life was not much better. I jumped from body to body, trying to find a host that could replace the one that I lost. There was a time when I was truly feared. When my power was so great, not even Lucifer could stand against me. My only rival was God Himself. But look at me now — a shell of what I once was. A war is not what I want to win. No, I want far more than that. I want to end the life of each and every man and woman that God created. And I don't want them to simply die. I want them to be completely and utterly destroyed!"

"In due time," Iblis said from his throne. "We have every intention of restoring your body back to you. But in order to do so, we will need something."

"What do you need?" the sound of a thousand voices came from Legions lips.

"The skull of Miacah. It has the ability to transform one thing into another," Lilith answered.

"The Philosopher's Stone? But that has been lost for many generations. No one knows where it is," Legion said.

"That may be true, but there is one who may know where to look," Lilith suggested.

"This all sounds like great fun, but why are you trying to help me?" Legion wondered.

"As you said before, we're not friends," Lilith continued. "But we have a common goal. We all want to see the end of God's tyrannical rule. We want an age where Darkness is law, and freedom is truth — the freedom to do whatever we please. The only way we can ever achieve our goal is to work together. The enemy of my enemy — you know how the saying goes."

"I'm not sold yet. But let's find this skull. The promise of being restored is something I have longed for for centuries. And when we find the skull and the transformation becomes complete, I will reward the two of you by letting you live to see me bring destruction to the world. But if the skull fails to work, then I will simply destroy you both!" Legion boomed.

CHAPTER V
THE ENSUING STORM

One month passed by quickly and Lyles and Kimberly were on their way to see Bianca and Esmeralda. The last time they had seen them was for Bianca's birthday on New Year's Eve, and now it was already the beginning of summer. Lyles toyed with the ring on his finger, as Kimberly drove the car. It was a beautiful day for a drive. The trees were lush and green, and the sky was a clear blue. Lyles put his hand on Kimberly's thigh.

He loved her with all his heart. He had just finished his third year of seminary the week before, and was happy to have a break from his studies, as much as he enjoyed what he was learning. Seeing their old friend, Esmeralda, and the little angel, Bianca, was something the couple needed. It brought back feelings of joy and pain, but all together the love they all shared was the closest thing to family that any of them had. This was going to be a great weekend — a reunion that none of them would ever forget.

Before the couple knew it, they were on the road that led to the secret retreat house in the woods, where the Sisters of Saving Grace lived. They drove past the familiar place and went just a short span up the road to the guesthouse that Esmeralda and Bianca were staying in. Mother and daughter were standing outside waving their arms wildly in the air and shouting for joy at their approaching friends. Lyles and Kimberly waved back through the open car windows. Lyles was amazed at how much Bianca had grown. She was not a baby anymore. Her smile was sweet and innocent, as were her big dark-brown eyes. Around her neck, he saw hanging the St. Michael medal that he had given to her. She was indeed protected by the greatest warrior in the Universe and beyond. Kimberly parked the car, and Lyles and she got out. They were instantly bombarded by hugs.

After the greetings were done, Lyles grabbed a couple of bags out of the trunk, since he and Kimberly were going to stay until Monday morning. Esmeralda escorted Lyles and Kimberly inside the cottage, and asked them to make themselves at home. As soon as Lyles put down the bags, Bianca dragged him by the arm to go into her room. She loved Lyles very much. He was the only man she knew, but she saw him as more of a friend or a big brother than a father figure. She felt safe with him. Also, he was a great listener and was so much fun to play with. He would make up great adventures for her and her dolls, and always told the best jokes. At least this is what the four year old believed. He did indeed love Bianca greatly. Lyles had sworn to protect the child for as long as she lived, and he knew that her heart was full of the Spirit. She was a special girl to everyone who knew her.

"Uncle Lyles, can we go outside? I want to show you something," the little girl said in her squeaky voice.

"Of course, sweets, let's go," Lyles answered. He was very impressed by the girl's big words. She was very bright for her age.

"Mommy, we're goin' outside!" Bianca screamed.

"Okay, honey, I'm gonna stay here with Aunt Kim. Have fun," Esmeralda yelled back.

"Come on, let's go," Bianca said, dragging Lyles out the front door.

The landscape was beautiful, filled with trees and grass, and blue skies. Lyles took a deep breath of the fresh air and smiled. This was the life. He was getting tired of the hustle and bustle of the big city, and dreamed of just staying out here with nature and raising a family. Kimberly and he had talked a lot about having kids. They always said that, once they had a family, they would move outside of the city, either to Long Island or Westchester, or even possibly Jersey — anywhere they could have a yard and enough room for kids to play and be happy.

"Come on, Uncle Lyles, it's this way," the little girl began to tug again on Lyles' arm.

"What's this way?" he wondered.

"The birdhouse that mommy and I put up."

"Cool, let's go see it."

He chased her up a hill and down a small path. There was a stream with some ducks floating lazily downstream. Bianca pointed straight ahead at a small tree with a lot of low-hanging branches. On one of these branches was a little wooden birdhouse. Right away, Lyles could see that it was a homemade project probably built by Bianca with Esmeralda's help. The wood was glued together crooked, with a few globs of glue coming out the sides. The red paint was brushed on in a multitude of directions, and did not cover the whole structure. But it was beautiful to the man because he knew the heart that made it.

"If we're lucky, we can see the blue jays come and eat. They love the house. They are so pretty," Bianca squealed.

"That would be very cool. I've never seen a blue jay. I don't think we have any in the city," Lyles laughed.

"Well, you're gonna like them," she giggled and hugged Lyles around his legs. "I love you, Uncle Lyles."

"I love you too, sweets," he replied, looking deep into her dark-brown eyes.

They stood and watched the tree, waiting for a bird to come by and eat something. Bianca turned her head down and saw a little field mouse creep through the grass. She smiled, for the little critter brought her joy. The mouse stopped to nibble on a bit of grain, and as it did something else swiftly moved through the grass behind it.

Before the mouse could move, a black rat snake leaped out to make a meal of the defenseless critter. Bianca saw this and shouted at the snake to stop. To Lyles' surprise, the snake did just that. It stopped and slithered away. The little girl knew well the circle of life, and that some animals ate others, but she could not bear to witness it for herself. Lyles was dumbfounded. How on Earth did that snake completely change its course at the words of this child? She was indeed special — in more ways than he could know. Not wanting to startle the girl, he just ignored what he saw, and told her that it might be a good idea for them to head back. With that they walked back to the guesthouse the same way they came, hand in hand with smiles and laughter.

Later that night, after Bianca was sound asleep in her bed, Lyles, Kimberly, and Esmeralda sat down in the living room to talk. They were so happy to see each other. Kimberly leaned against Lyles' chest as he recounted the day's events to Esmeralda. He told her of the snake and how Bianca had sent it away with only a word. Esmeralda did not seem too surprised. She told Lyles about some of the other stories she had heard about, miraculous things that her daughter had done. They had all been told that Esmeralda's children would do great things. But even after all they had seen and been a part of, this was still beyond belief, making them wonder what the future held.

"Do you ever think about Gideon?" Esmeralda asked her friends in a somber voice.

"Every day," Lyles answered.

"We both do," Kimberly added.

"I miss him so much. I only had him a couple of days." Tears flooded Esmeralda's face. "Why did he have to be taken from me? Why?"

"Oh, honey," Kimberly wrapped her arms around her friend. "I know. None of it makes sense. We all share your pain. He was a part of us too."

"I know, but it hurts so much. I pray for God to heal my pain every day. But He doesn't," Esmeralda cried.

"He doesn't always take away the pain. Actually He hardly does," Lyles spoke. "His Spirit gives us strength so we can endure the pain. I just think about Christ and His sacrifice for us, and the pain that He suffered. We have a God who shares our pain. Trust me, losing Gideon hurt God as much as it does you, if not more so. He is one of His children, too."

Esmeralda kept crying in Kimberly's arms. Even after four years, the pain was as sharp as the first day.

"Mommy, are you okay?" Bianca said in a soft voice from the doorway.

"Yes, I'm okay, sweet," Esmeralda answered, rubbing the tears from her eyes.

Bianca ran and hugged her mother. The two seemed to glow a little.

"I love you, Mommy, please don't cry," the little girl begged as she squeezed her mother.

"Okay, baby. Thank you," Esmeralda responded and her tears stopped.

A warm feeling filled Esmeralda's spirit. The comfort of her daughter's words and touch was miraculous for the young mother. That comfort seemed to help her carry on, further each and every day.

The next morning, they were awakened by a knock on the door. Esmeralda got up and groggily went to answer it. She thought that it might be one of the sisters checking in on them. But when she opened the door, she realized that she was wrong. A young Asian man was standing in the doorway wearing a simple brown top that looked like sackcloth and matching pants and shoes. Over his back was draped a gray satchel of some sort that was tied with a rope around the top.

The man bowed and said in surprisingly perfect English, "May I come in?"

"Who are you?" Esmeralda questioned.

Lyles and Kimberly had made their way to the door by now to make sure everything was okay.

The visitor answered, "Sorry. My name is Chien, and I am a Magus of the order the Keepers of the Light. I am here to find the man who has possession of the Ring of Solomon. I have followed the stars to this very place."

"I have it," Lyles answered, and he came out from behind Esmeralda. He flashed the back of his hand at the man, who bowed.

"The Ring! You must come with me!" Chien insisted.

"I'm not going anywhere!" Lyles exclaimed and folded his arms.

"Please, let me in and I will explain," pleaded Chien.

"Fine," Lyles said and walked into the living room.

Esmeralda was confused and did not know if it was such a good idea to let this stranger into the house. But for some reason she just stepped aside and allowed the man to enter.

Bianca finally woke up and came out of her room.

"What's goin' on?" the little girl asked, rubbing her eyes.

When Chien saw Bianca he went down to his knees and bowed very low to the ground.

"I am honored," he said, as everyone turned and stared at him. "She has the spirit of a great prophet in her. Much like our forefather, Daniel, and those who came before him. She is blessed, a child of the Light. She must come as well."

"Now, that is out of the question!" Esmeralda shouted. "No one is taking my daughter anywhere!"

Lyles sat down on the couch and yelled, "Okay, enough! Let's talk."

Esmeralda sent Bianca to her room to get dressed with Kimberly, while she and Lyles talked with the mysterious man, Chien. Kimberly listened from Bianca's room to all that the man said, while she helped the little girl get dressed. The four year old did not understand whom the visitor was and why she could not go out to the living room, but Kimberly tried her best to convince Bianca to stay with her in the bedroom. Once Bianca was dressed, they started to play with some of her dolls, and soon enough the girl forgot all about wanting to leave her room.

Outside in the living room, Chien began to talk, while Esmeralda and Lyles sat and listened intently, "As I told you, my name is Chien, and I am from an order of priests known as the Keepers of the Light. We do not adhere to any religious system, though our roots go back to Zoroastrianism, and the priesthoods of ancient Babylon and Persia. Even though we are not a religion, we do believe that there is one eternal and infinite God, from whom all things have come into existence. Our order follows the teachings of Daniel, the prophet of God who was exiled in Babylon with the Hebrews. He told of a future king who would rule the whole world by God's hand. This, of course, was the one named Jesus, whom you call the Christ. Our forefathers came to Bethlehem to pay homage to Him, and anoint him. But I am sure you already know the story, especially you who bear the Ring."

"Lyles, my name is Lyles," he said and then pointed with his thumb behind him, "and this is Esmeralda."

"Well, it is a pleasure to meet you, Lyles, and Esmeralda," Chien said and then he continued with his explanations.

"I came here on a grave mission, in search of a hero who can help me save the world. Our order is one that anoints such men and women. We also are, in a way, peacekeepers and we have been trained to battle the cohorts of Darkness if need be. Lyles, it is believed by us that since you bear that ring on your finger, you are to be anointed as a hero who can help defeat the evil that is about to plague this planet. We were the keepers of that ring for many centuries until our last hero, Wang Sheng, was told by a messenger of God to give it to a holy man in Jordan."

"Father Dan," Lyles said.

"Yes, Dan Reilly. I know also of the unfortunate fate that was delivered to him at the hands of Radix, the same fate that Wang Sheng suffered as well. Radix was truly a great evil, but the one you will face now is far superior. His evil was born and bred in the Darkness itself, the essence of evil in its purest form."

"I heard about this Darkness," Lyles interrupted. "Reverend Reynolds wrote about it. The angels told him of the origin of evil."

"Yes, the Darkness is the source of all evil, but it has no power over the Light, which is the God of all. There is but one God and He has power over all good and evil. But the Darkness desires to change all that, and to become itself as God."

"Yes, but how can we fight it?" Lyles wondered.

Esmeralda sat with her eyes wide open, trying to take in all of what she was hearing. It was almost too much for her mind to grasp.

"The Darkness is not what we are up against," Chien clarified. "And thankfully so, for as we stand we could not face it. What we are about to face is Legion, a child of the Darkness, in whom is housed thousands of demons."

"Legion?" Lyles asked. "The one from the Bible?"

The door swung open, and a figure walked in from outside and answered, "Yes, that very same creature."

Lyles jumped up and ran to the man standing before him.

"Raven!" he shouted. He was exceedingly happy to see his old friend.

Esmeralda and Chien turned and looked at Ravenblade, neither of them quite sure who he was. The immortal wore his usual battle-trodden garb. His leather boots were caked with mud, and his hood was draped behind him. Strapped to his back, as always, was his sword, which remained in its sheath. His reddish-brown hair was tied back in a ponytail. He stared silently at Chien. He knew instantly that the man was a Magus, for he had seen his kind before, for many centuries.

"I think the time for long speeches is over," Ravenblade said. "I have been listening to you talk long enough. If we are going to stop Legion, we must go now, before he gets any more powerful."

"Who are you?" Chien asked. "And how do you know about Legion?"

"I am Ravenblade, and I know more about that demon than you do."

"Yes, I have heard of you. You're a killer! Why should we go with you?"

"Because he's my friend," Lyles said. "Raven, if you say we have to go, then let's go. Let me get ready."

Lyles got up and walked to Esmeralda's room, which was where he was keeping his bag. He changed and came back out.

Kimberly stopped him in the hallway and asked, "What's going on? Where are you going?"

Lyles kissed her and said, "I have to leave. The world is in danger."

"But you can't go. I need you," she replied with her face pressed up against his chest.

"I'm sorry. I love you so much, but I have to do this. That is why I am studying the Word, why I want to go into ministry. I want to help people. I need to help people. This is what God has called me to do," he said. "I love you. I'll be back as soon as I can. I promise. God will be with me."

"No, please don't. I can't lose you."

"You won't lose me. I promise."

"What if you die like Nathan?"

"I won't," He held her tighter. "Something inside of me, in my soul, is telling me to go, to do this. I have to. I know you don't understand. But I can't deny my calling. Pray for me. I will pray for you."

Lyles kissed her again passionately. The two looked into each other's eyes for a moment that seemed to last an eternity. Then he let go and ran to the door.

"Bring the girl, too," Ravenblade said.

"The girl — why?" Lyles questioned.

"She will not be safe here. They will come for her as they did her brother," the immortal replied.

"No! She is not going anywhere! No one is taking my daughter anywhere!" Esmeralda screamed.

"Lyles, get the girl," Ravenblade said.

"No, Lyles, you can't take her!" Esmeralda shouted.

"She will be safer with us. Raven is right, it is too dangerous to leave her here," Lyles explained.

"Then, I'm coming too!" the young mother stated.

"We don't have time, take them both, then," Ravenblade commanded.

"Okay, that is enough!" the soft-spoken Magus yelled. "Everyone here is smart enough to know that all of our lives are in great danger, as is the rest of the world. Instead of scrambling around like a bunch of ants, let us calmly gather what we need and form a plan of departure. Another boat will leave in a few days to go back to Shanghai from San Francisco. That is how I got here. Is there a car here that we can use to get to the ship?"

"Yes," Lyles said. "We can use our car. It's parked out front."

"I will drive," Kimberly butted in. "I want to at least be with you for as long as I can before you go," she said to her husband."

"Fine, get your things ready, and then let's go," Chien said.

"Yes, let's hurry up," Ravenblade interjected. "Honestly, I am not so sure about traveling with so many people. It's a liability."

"We are all family here," Lyles said to the immortal. "It's not about liability, it's about taking care of each other."

The cold-hearted immortal just glanced at Lyles without a word. Kimberly went with Esmeralda to help her pack and before they all knew it, everyone was in the car and on the way to San Francisco. The trip would take almost four days, and much was discussed during the journey. Chien assured Lyles that he would need no documents for they would travel with the cargo and then sneak into China. The Magi had many alliances and they were used to secretly traveling the world without being seen. Ravenblade remained quiet for the entire road trip. He was still certain that too many people were now involved, but he also felt that there was no point in arguing the fact. It would be easier just to let the dice fall as they may. Bianca was wearing her favorite outfit — her black-and-white striped tights, her pink kitty skull T-shirt, her black pleated skirt, her green army jacket, and of course her black combat boots. Like Ravenblade, she too was silent.

This was odd for a child her age, but Bianca was not like any other four-year-old girl. She was very mature, despite her playful nature, and always kept her most intimate feelings to herself. She played with the St. Michael pendant that she wore around her neck, wondering if the great angel would really fly to her rescue in times of need, as her mother had told her.

Esmeralda held tightly to her daughter. She was not ready to lose another child. She did not know why they were going on this insane expedition but her entire life had been insane since that evil monster Radix had come into it, all those years ago. He was the reason she had her daughter, the only joy to come from the sorrow. She lost her parents, her brother, and her pride. But God was with her, as He promised, and His Spirit administered to the pained woman each and every day.

Esmeralda felt guilty for not telling the sisters in person that she was leaving. But they had to leave in such a hurry. She had left a note in their mailbox saying that she was going away for a little while, but would be back as soon as she could. The woman wasn't lying, but at the same time, she was not being completely honest either. If the nuns knew what danger Esmeralda was putting herself in, they would have forbade her to leave. They had sworn to watch over her and her daughter.

Lyles was caught up in the moment. It was hard for him to be separated from Kimberly again, but he knew deep inside that they would be reunited again. But now with his study of the Word, and his deeper understanding of the Lord, it would be difficult for him to partake in this war in any physical way. He was supposed to love his enemy and turn the other cheek, but what would he do when he was face to face with that evil demon or any other creature of Darkness. Could he truly let them torture and hurt the innocent while he stood by and watched? It was something he would have to deal with soon.

Kimberly was not ready to say goodbye to her husband, though soon she would have to do so. She knew that marriage would not be easy, but this was more than she could handle. The time passed slowly in some ways, yet it went too quickly in others. Before they knew it, they were at the port in San Francisco, and it was time to board the ship. Chien would lead the group to an associate of his who would sneak them into the cargo hold in the belly of the ship, while the other passengers boarded on the deck. Kimberly kissed Lyles for the longest minute of their lives. Would this be their last moment together? They prayed that it would not be. She drove away in tears as her husband and friends snuck on board. It was time for their journey to truly begin.

***

Jay Sil sat at his desk fumbling through files. Not long ago, his life was changed when he battled bloodthirsty zombies, while he hunted for a supernatural killer in the very streets he swore to protect. It seemed more like a movie or one of the video games he played, but it was real and almost cost him his life. He kept the zombie attack to himself, knowing the ridicule he would endure if he told his story to his fellow officers. He almost did not believe it himself. He even tried rationalizing it, but he could not. Knowing the truth of the evil out there, he became obsessed with any case that seemed a little out of the ordinary. He saw himself as some kind of an agent Mulder, looking for what was out there. Recently, he was putting together some intel on gang-related killings. Not too different from what the city had seen in the past year. There was talk on the street of the Children of the Dragon rebuilding under a new leader, and in much larger numbers. Other gangs were afraid; they feared the idea of dark magic and the conjuring of demons that this new organization promised. But all of Jay's leads were dead-ends. The only thing he could discover was that the new leader was calling himself the Chaldean, a name for the people of Babylon, or so Jay's research told him. He scoured through file after file of some of the worst terrorists and most violent offenders out there. But he needed more information — the Chaldean could be anyone.

"Still looking for the boogeyman," a familiar and unwelcome voice rang in Jay Sil's ears. It was the newly promoted Detective Rogers.

"Why are you wasting your time and our tax dollars looking for someone who doesn't exist? It's not even your case. Why don't you finish your paperwork and get out on the street and do something important!"

"Sorry, but last time I checked, I don't report to you. I'm not wasting my time. I'm looking for a killer, someone who could be worse than that last monster. I have sworn to serve and protect and that is what I am doing. Why don't you go harass someone else," Jay jolted back.

"Listen here, you little twerp," Detective Rogers pressed his heavy hands down onto Jay's desk and looked him square in the eyes. "Never talk to me with that tone again or I will make sure the Chief takes your badge. You hear me?"

The detective paused, fixed his shirt, and walked away. Enraged, Jay jumped up from his seat and stormed out of the precinct with some papers in his hands.

"These kids think they are so tough," Detective Rogers said to himself. "No respect; none at all. I oughta give 'em the backside of my hand," he grumbled under his breath, walking quickly to his desk.

"I can't believe they promoted that jerk. That's why people hate cops, because we have guys like that," Jay mumbled to himself as he started his car. He fumbled through the papers some more. "I'm going to get to the bottom of this case and we'll see who's wasting whose time!"

With that he accelerated his squad car and hit the streets looking for clues.

***

"Sister Catherine, Sister Catherine!" shouts came down the hall.

"What is it, Sister Suzanne? Is everything okay?" Sr. Catherine said, concerned for her friend.

Sr. Suzanne paused to catch her breath and handed Sr. Catherine a letter.

"What's this?" Sr. Catherine said and began to read the letter.

"We need to find out where they went. They will be in great danger! I will alert the Council immediately."

***

"Not so nice from this side of the glass is it, Radix," the Devil spoke with strong sarcasm as his former chief mercenary hung before him.

83

There was no reward for a job well done when working for the King of Lies. His promises always end in dismay. Angry and dejected, the once powerful Radix hung over a pit of fire, his wrists and ankles tied and stretched out by indestructible thorn-covered vines. The Prince of Darkness stood before him in his demonic form to exude his power over the evil man.

"You don't scare me, Satan. You never have," Radix replied in a steady voice. "This is only an inconvenience. I will have my day again, and a power even greater than I had before. You will bow before *me* one day." He smiled as blood-tinged sweat poured down his brow and across his lips.

"Still filled with hubris, I see. You never learn. I told you time and again on Earth that you were too cocky. I knew that boy, Nathan, was not like the others. I could feel the Spirit working within him. God played you for a fool, and now you're stuck here hanging until the final judgment. I hear that fire will be hotter than this. But you seem to still be confident; maybe you're tougher than I thought. When I met you, you were a whiny brat, crying about your dead mother and sisters. What a fool, so easy to play into my hand. I should thank you. You were a great puppet while you lasted. But the time for games is over. The end is drawing nearer. I can feel it, we all can, and it's time for the big boys to play. Not some amateur man seeking revenge on the gods."

Radix remained still, listening to the empty words of the Devil. He knew very well the game Satan was playing, trying to get under his skin to arouse his anger for that demon's own enjoyment. The dark man was smarter than that, and had much greater self-control than the Prince of Darkness believed. He would wait, for he knew his time would come. He could feel it, for it was at hand.

CHAPTER VI
INSIDE THE RED DRAGON

The journey felt long, but the ship finally made it to the port in Shanghai. The traveling band of stowaways was tired, hungry, and in need of a shower. They had been cooped up in the belly of the ship for about a month. Food and water was brought to them daily by the man who snuck them aboard, but it was hardly enough, especially for the young Bianca, who complained much throughout the journey, as might be expected of a child her age. But now, they had arrived, and it was time to sneak off of this ship in much the same way they'd snuck on. Lyles was shocked to see once again how easy it could be for people to bypass secured borders — it seemed to be all about whom you knew and knowing where the "holes" were. Before they knew it, Lyles, Esmeralda, Bianca, Ravenblade, and Chien were on a truck bound for the Qin Mountains.

The ride felt like it lasted for days. No one could really tell how much time had passed by except for Chien, but he remained silent for the entire trip. He seemed to be in a trance almost as if he were in deep meditation. There were some slits in the back of the canopy that covered the truck. Bianca looked out at the foreign land, and her gaze seemed to capture a peace that no one could truly grasp. It was as if the Spirit of the Lord had filled her to the full. The scenes outside the truck would change from industrious city to over-crowded, poverty-stricken villages, to endless fields. So much time had passed in the truck that the little girl could not handle the stillness any longer — then the mountains began to peak in the distance. The site was beautiful, and the range seemed vast and dominant over the horizon.

"We are almost there," Chien finally spoke.

Lyles twitched at the sound of Chien's voice. He had not heard the man speak in a long while.

"Wasn't sure if you were still alive over there. You make Raven seem like a chatterbox," Lyles jested.

Ravenblade gave a sly look, and shrugged.

"I was in deep prayer," Chien spoke again. "Praying for a safe return and a successful mission. It is necessary to ask Shang Di — the God of all things — for His help and protection, for without Him nothing can be accomplished. Even your friend from the desert knows that. Maybe better than all of us."

Giving another sly look and shrug, Ravenblade folded his arms and remained silent.

Lyles questioned, "You called God Shang Di. Is that a Chinese deity?"

"That is what our ancestors called the one true God before they took on the worship of man-made gods and Tian, the heavens. Shang Di is not His name, just as God is not His name. Our ancestor Daniel taught us that God did in fact have a special name that He had given to the Hebrew people — Yahweh. But like the Jews today, we do not use His proper name in prayer for it is sacred and should only be called upon when absolutely necessary."

"You can call on His name whenever you like. He actually likes it. Just don't use it in vain," Ravenblade butted in. "Though I haven't called on His name in a long time."

Lyles looked at his friend, wondering what secrets he held. A few years back, when they fought side by side, the mighty immortal mentioned in passing that he had been an angel. But what changed him into the being that stood before them now, Lyles could not guess. Chien seemed to know more of Ravenblade than even Lyles. But that did not matter now. Looking out again, Lyles could see the mountains drawing closer. There were statues and pillars carved into the peaks before him and what seemed like hollows and bridges. It was breathtaking.

"Is that your home, Chien?" Lyles asked.

"No, those are abandoned ruins. We are too wise to dwell in such an obvious place. Our order has been hunted for many centuries and it would be foolish to lead men and demons to us so easily. Those ruins are known as the Maijishan Grottoes and are from a Buddhist sect that dwelled in these mountains when *they* were being persecuted. We were blessed that our own quarters were never discovered."

Another hour passed by and then the truck stopped. A man came to the back and spoke to Chien in Chinese. Chien answered in what seemed to be one word. The man nodded.

"It is time to go; we have arrived," Chien said to the group but his gaze was on Bianca. "I will leave first, then Ravenblade, followed by Lyles, the woman, and the girl last."

"The woman and the girl? We have names, too, you know," Esmeralda snapped. She was tired from the long trip. Her mind the entire time was wondering what new horrors awaited her. Bianca was all she had left and she refused to lose her little girl.

Chien said nothing in reply. He climbed from the back of the truck and the rest followed as he had directed. The truck drove away, leaving behind the unlikely group of heroes: a Chinese priest, an immortal rogue, a seminary student, a resilient mother, and a little girl. They all stood at the foot of one of the mountains and gazed up in awe. It was always amazing to see the wonders of God's creation. Without another moment passing, Chien got down on one knee and bowed his head low. Then, he rose, drew his sword, and walked toward a rock near the foot of the mountain. He placed his sword into a slit in the rock that seemed to be made just for this task. Then with great fluidity he turned the sword and the very mountain before them opened. It was like magic. The mountain had looked solid and seamless from the outside, but the Magi had found a way to create such a door in the side of the mountain that the eye could not detect it, and that was centuries ago, using what we would call primitive technology. It was amazing.

"Please enter quickly; we must close the opening before it can be found," Chien stated.

The group moved inside as quickly as possible and the door closed behind them. At once, a multitude of candles began to light, as if by themselves, all the way down the vast hallway before them. It was another beautiful and amazing sight to behold.

"Welcome to the Temple of Luminescence," Chien announced.

***

The night air was thick with humidity, typical for a summer in southern China. The streets of Dongguan were crowded with a mix of traveling business men, local Chinese citizens, and the large population of people from around the world who have made this city their new home — a factory city that has become increasingly international over time. A man walked down the street, dressed in jeans and a polo shirt. He looked Middle Eastern, and wore a local girl under his arm. She was dressed very scantly, with a skirt way too short for her long legs. The two seemed caught up more into each other than the area around them. They walked into one of the many bars and grabbed a small table where they sat down. The man's hand was now on the woman's bottom. It was typical for visitors to this part of China to find company for the night, and to all of those around him, he was just another man in the crowd.

"Legion, I know you have been away for a long time. But if you grab me again, I will cut out your throat," the Chinese woman said.

"Lilith, don't flatter yourself. I am merely acting my part, trying to make this as believable as possible. Your charms have no effect on me. My desires are not of the flesh like these pathetic men around us. These clothes are ridiculous. How I long to wear my armor of old, and carry my sword of destruction," Legion whispered to the woman sitting next to him. He nuzzled close, to give the appearance that they were simply flirting.

There was a stage in front of the bar and a man walked up to it. Everyone clapped.

"Welcome, all," the man said with a Brazilian accent. "We have a treat for you tonight. This guy who I am about to introduce will amaze you with his mysterious and thrilling magic. Much better than those guys you see on TV. They're all fakes. But I promise you the magic you will see is real. There are no smoke and mirrors here. So, without further ado, I would like to present," the man paused. "Drum roll please."

"So why are we here?" Legion asked.

"We are about to meet the man who can bring us to the skull," she replied.

"And who would that be?"

"Simon Magus the Third!" the man announced.

"Him," Lilith said and pointed to the man who had just walked onto the stage.

The man who just took the stage looked like a street magician that you would see in Times Square. He wore dark blue jeans and a black sport coat with a gray T-shirt underneath. He bowed and smoke rose from the ground in front of him.

"I know Paolo promised no smoke and mirrors, but I thought that would be more dramatic," Simon Magus III said with a smile. "But seriously let's get started. I am not your typical magician. I never trained at an academy, and don't do any disappearing acts or saw women in half. I like my women whole," he smiled again. "My power is real and in my blood. It was passed down from my father and his father to him, going back many generations. The Magus family is world renowned," he winked.

The young man went on to woo the crowd with humor and some sleight of hand. Most of his first set of tricks involved cards, the usual MO for someone in his field. He went on to do some more thought-provoking tricks. One such trick was taking an empty glass soda bottle in one hand and the cap in his other. He tapped the cap to the bottom of the bottle and it magically moved inside the bottle. He grabbed about four more bottle caps and did the same thing, showing that there was no way he could have hidden them all inside the bottle. Lilith, still posing as a Chinese escort, and Legion, as her patron, watched casually, unimpressed by the sideshow antics.

"This is ridiculous. This guy is of no use to us," Legion stated. "Why would you even think to search for this fool?"

"He is the descendent of Simon Magus, one of the most powerful sorcerers to ever live. I know you were a little incapacitated at the time of his fame so you would not know of him. He tried to join Jesus' clique after the resurrection, using a bribe to try and gain the power of the Spirit."

"Sounds like a hack, just like this fool. I'm leaving."

"Wait. Let me finish. He was the last man to have possession of the skull. Apparently, he used its power to convince ignorant fools that he was a god. The skull was passed down from father to son from generation to generation. This man on stage may have the skull himself, or at least know who does."

"If he has the skull, he could do better tricks than this. Like I said, I am leaving," Legion groaned. "Hey, Simon," he called over to the man on the stage. "I have a cool trick I would like to show you."

"Really, now," Simon responded. "Um, sorry, but no audience participation. I think everyone's here to see me, anyway."

"Yeah, but your tricks suck. I have a better one."

"And what would that be?"

Legion grabbed a woman by her shoulder and placed his hand around the back of her neck. "I will remove this woman's head from her body," he said as he ripped her head clean off. The air filled with the horrid screams of the onlookers, and the crowd began to knock each other over to get to the door.

"I'm only warming up." Legion continued, ripping off various other appendages from those who could not escape.

Simon cowered on the stage as Legion moved closer in. Lilith just put her head in her hands and sighed. "Oh well, he was right — this is much more entertaining."

As Legion reached the stage, Simon threw something onto the floor and fire shot up. He was gone.

"What? Where did he go?" Legion growled.

"How pathetic, and you said he was a hack," Lilith stated with another sigh. "Leave it to a woman to do the job right. She vanished. In a matter of seconds, Lilith reappeared in front of Legion holding Simon firmly around his torso and throat. "Don't even think of moving, child," she warned.

"Hmm," Legion huffed. "Good — now I can kill him and we can forget this whole mess."

"You will not touch him," Lilith bellowed. "We need him alive so he can tell us where the skull is."

"The skull?" Simon whimpered. "I don't know where the skull is."

"So you know of what we speak?" Legion's many voices rang in unison.

"Tell us what you know?" Lilith said as she dug her nails into the base of Simon's throat.

But before he could speak, the kitchen door flew open and a gunshot went straight into Legion's skull. His head flew back from the impact, but he remained standing. The blood that poured from his brow began to be sucked back into the hole and the wound closed up. The demon could see the Brazilian man who had made the announcement before the show standing in the kitchen with a pistol in his hand, shaking from what he had just seen.

Without a single word and before the man holding the gun could blink, Legion had moved into the kitchen and effortlessly ripped the top of the man's head off from his jaw up. Simon was terrified and did not know what to do. The woman holding him was vastly stronger than he, and he was barely able to draw a breath. Tired of this night's events, Legion belted Simon in the face and knocked him out cold.

"Let's get out of here. This scene is dead. He'll be out for a while. Let's find a place where we can have some more fun and kill some time, among other things," Legion grimaced, and they left.

***

Chien turned to his guests. The flames of the candles gave a warm glow to the corridor that stretched ahead. The tunnel had been dug straight through the mountain and was covered with intricate carved designs. Mixed in with the designs were words, some Chinese pictograms and some in Sanskrit.

"What does it say?" Lyles wondered out loud.

"They are prophesies given to us by Daniel, the prophet of God. Some of the characters also spell out names of God, including the Chinese and Sanskrit rendering of Yahweh," Chien replied.

The catacomb before them seemed to go on for miles without end. The group followed their guide, all in a state of wonder, except for Ravenblade, who seemed very frustrated to even be there. Bianca's eyes were the most captivated. To see such beautiful art and for it to have such great meaning intrigued the child. The young girl tugged at her mother's leg.

"Mommy, that one is about Jesus," she said pointing to a phrase in Sanskrit.

"Honey, are you sure?" Esmeralda said with a nervous smile, thinking her child was merely playing around.

Ravenblade passed by and said, "She's right. It *is* about Jesus."

Esmeralda did not know what to think and moved on without speaking further. After walking for about thirty minutes, the group reached a stone doorway. It was covered in the same designs as the cavern walls, and stood at least twenty feet high. There was another rock here with a slit in it, into which Chien placed his sword. With a simple turn of the sword, the door began to slide open to the right side. It moved slowly and shook the ground and walls around them. The group moved quickly through the doorway.

The site on the other side was awe inspiring. They were inside the center of the mountain. A huge cylinder had been carved straight up to the top of the mountain peak with steps going up all around. An unfathomable number of doorways leading to various corridors were carved into the mountain on each level. It was magnificent and it almost seemed impossible that men built this structure.

"Are we going to climb all the way to the top?" Esmeralda asked. Her eyes were wide open as she gazed upward.

"When this place was first built, that is what they did," Chien spoke. "But the journey could take days that way. So we installed a simple pulley elevator. I can get us to the top in about two hours. Please follow me."

They all followed him to a small bamboo cage. They all fit in perfectly without any room to spare.

"I am sorry but we must all stand. I know it may not be easy for the child but we have just enough room as it is," Chien spoke again.

"I'm okay, Chien. I'm a big girl," Bianca said with the sweetest smile.

"Let me pull us up," Ravenblade cut in. I am the strongest and I do not tire like you men. I could probably get us up there in under an hour."

"Be my guest," Chien bowed.

He then closed the door, locked it with a bar, and handed the pulley rope to Ravenblade. The immortal was not wrong, he did indeed get them to the top in less than an hour — about forty minutes to be exact. Chien was very impressed. The strongest of his clan could take just himself up in about an hour and a half, but the immortal took an entire car full of people in less than half that time. When they stepped out, their guide led them through one of the doorways, which opened into a vast library. There were cushions on the floor. Chien asked them to remove their shoes before entering and to then take a seat, which they all did.

"I will get you all some tea and fruit," Chien insisted. "Please excuse me, I will return shortly."

Lyles surveyed the grand room that they sat in. The ceiling was like that of a cathedral, high and vaulted. There were many designs that looked like windows and portals carved into the walls which added character and elegance. Beautiful watercolor tapestries surrounded them. Their white base and bright colors reflected the light of the candles and lanterns that illuminated the room. Tall rosewood bookcases, packed with books and artifacts, filled the room. It was quite a sight — definitely a wonder in every way.

Bianca stood up and walked to one of the bookcases. She pulled a book off one of the lower shelves and began to turn the pages.

"Can you read that?" Ravenblade frowned at her.

"I think so," she answered, very seriously for a child of her age.

"How old are you, five?" the immortal questioned.

"Four and a half," she replied with a huge grin.

Ravenblade walked over to Lyles and nudged him to stand.

"What's going on?" Lyles asked.

"There is something odd about that girl," the solemn man interjected. "How can she understand such languages that she has never seen or heard before."

"Maybe Sesame Street did an episode on Sanskrit and Mandarin," Lyles jested.

"What is Sesame Street?"

"Sorry, it was joke. The angel did tell Ezzie that her child was going to be special. I think they both, Bianca and Gideon, are."

"The boy's lost, though his power was strong, fierce. But she has something else. I can't put my finger on it, but I have felt this before. Almost like a prophet of the Most High, but even more so. She is indeed filled with the Spirit much like the followers of the Son after He rose to Heaven. When this is over, I say the girl stays with me. We cannot afford to lose her like we did her brother. There is too much at stake."

"At stake?" Lyles questioned. "She's a kid, she needs to play and enjoy her childhood like other kids. I can watch her, and the Sisters are there too to take care of her."

"You really don't know what this is all about, do you?" Ravenblade stood taller as he spoke. "The end is near. All that you've read in your Bible about Armageddon, plagues, war, destruction. It's coming soon. One of these kids is going to be the catalyst, and I would like to make sure that we're ready for when it all breaks loose."

"You think she can be the Antichrist?"

"No, maybe the boy, though. Both Daniel and John clearly show it to be a man. Unless she can shape shift. Can she?" he asked very seriously.

"What? No, of course not. Or at least I don't think so."

"Well, let's keep an eye on her, or this can get even more serious, very quickly."

"Do you two mind including me when you're talking about my daughter," Esmeralda butted in. "She is definitely not the Antichrist. And neither is Gideon, if he's even still…" she grew silent and fell into Lyles' arms. Lyles held her to comfort the young mother, whose heart was aching for her lost son.

Chien returned pushing a cart that had a magnificent porcelain tea set, and a basket of bread and fruit. The hungry group of friends all pounced toward the cart to get some food and drink, all that is except for Ravenblade. Being immortal, he needed no such sustenance. He sat back on the floor, crossing his legs in front of him. From behind Chien entered an elderly man, whose face was wizened from vast learning and experience.

"Are you going to introduce me to your guests," the man spoke in broken English.

The hungry bunch stopped stuffing their faces for a moment as they looked at the newcomer.

"Yes, sorry, master," Chien bowed, then turned to the group. "This is my master…"

"Chao Cheng," Ravenblade cut in.

"You know my master?" Chien asked.

"Yes, Chien," Chao Cheng spoke. "We were enemies once, a lifetime ago. But things change, and so do men."

"I don't, and last time I checked we were still enemies. And I'm not a man — you know that."

"Yes, you are correct, Ravenblade. So, why don't you tell everyone what you really are? How about by starting with your former name. I am sure your friends would love to hear your story," the old man spoke in a very matter-of-fact way.

"I am not here to tell stories or even to fight with you, old man. I am here to stop Legion, and that is all."

The one time angel stood up and crossed his arms over his chest.

"Hmm, well, then. Calling me 'old man.' Last time I checked you were much older than I," the master cracked a rare joke. "You can remain silent and huff and puff in the corner. I will continue to greet those who do not know me. My name is Huang Chao Cheng and I am the great teacher of this order of priests. I welcome you to our home as honored guests. I know very well the one you will fight. His power is great, even greater than that of your last foe, Radix." the great teacher paused and turned to Lyles, "You, who bear the ring. It is your destiny to defeat this demon. But you must train first and prepare. This will not be a battle won by strength of hand, but rather of Spirit. Legion is not just a demon. He is thousands of demons collected into one soul of a god-man from days past."

"A god-man? What is that?" Lyles questioned.

"He means Nephilim, the offspring of the sons of God and the daughters of men," Ravenblade spoke. "Legion's father was the leader of a class of angels known as the Watchers. No one knows who his mother is, but they say she was a sorceress. Of all those born of the union of angels and women, Legion's power was the greatest. His father lost him in the Flood, and Legion resurfaced some time afterward, being raised by Nimrod, the great king and hunter, under the name Citius. His greatest power is the ability to draw souls into himself and use their energy to increase his might. When he came of age, he began to go insane because his soul was joined with thousands of demons that had been tortured in the Darkness since before the dawn of time.

These demons warped his mind, causing him to fall deep into despair. The king found a way to make Citius gain control of his powers and those of the demons inside of him."

"You tell the story well," Chao Cheng said.

"I was around in those days, and even before that time. Samyaza was a friend before he fell. But I cannot judge him. I fell too," the immortal replied.

"But if this Legion is so powerful, why hasn't he destroyed the world by now?" Lyles asked.

"His body was killed," Ravenblade spoke again, "by the one with no name. He used the sword of Order to defeat that creature. But even though Legion's body had been defeated, his soul and the demons it housed were not. He began to jump from host to host, for centuries on end. But he was mindless and unable to use his abilities. You recall the story of when Christ expelled him from the boy into the pigs. He was no longer a real threat."

"Not to you, but to men he was still threat enough," the teacher jumped in again. "One of my predecessors fought this beast, and was able to trap him inside a disc for many centuries. The disc was given to a messenger of God, who hid it in the Arabian Desert. Somehow Legion has now been released. And the only way to stop him is to trap him again."

"But how?" Lyles wondered.

Chao Cheng stood up as tall as he could and said, "You will need to use an ancient technique that was taught to me by my teacher and his before him going as far back as the beginning of our order. I have trained Chien how to perform this technique as well. And we will need one more thing, a vessel that can house that beast, the skull of Miacha."

***

"Huh," Simon woke up. "Where am I?"

"About time," Legion said.

The young magician's head hurt too much for him to move. He was confused — *was this real, or some sick dream?* he wondered about his two abductors. And he wondered if they would kill him like they killed all those people in the bar. He was on a park bench and Legion stood over him, staring with anger. Lilith leaned against a nearby tree, transformed back into her usual human form, and not the Chinese escort that she played earlier. Simon's eyes began to focus and he could see a multitude of dismembered corpses all around the park they were in. The fear that had first gripped his heart began to fade. They would not kill him because they needed something from him — the skull of Miacha. The problem was that he did not have the skull, but rather was on his own quest to find it. The skull of Miacha had been lost for centuries, and Simon needed to find it for, when he did, the power that his family once wielded would be his. Sure, he still had the ability to perform some small tricks without the skull. Sorcery was in his blood. But these two murderous monsters were more than he could handle. Their power was thick and dark. He could feel it. But he played cool.

"So, you want the skull," he said as he sat up on the bench, his head pounding. "What's in it for me?"

"Well, you seem to have grown a set. How about we let you live," Lilith said in her usual sultry tone. She glided toward the young man and grabbed him under his chin. "Come on handsome, why don't you just tell us what you know and get this over with. I promise I won't bite…hard," she said exposing a mouth full of spiked teeth.

"I know you two are filled with a strong, dark power, but I don't scare so easily. I am a Magus, a descendent of the great family of necromancers. I have power in my blood, too."

"That supposed to be funny," Legion said. "You're a joke, boy. My power is real."

Legion threw his hand back, and it stretched at high speed crashing through the trunk of a tree. "Now tell us what you know."

"I know that the skull has great power, and that my family used it to make their magic even stronger. But even I do not know where it is. If I did I would not be working as some hack magician in a bar to make ends meet. I would be ruling these fools."

"Really now, *you* rule them. You seemed to enjoy being their monkey. Your heart is not dark enough to rule these mites," Legion boasted. "My heart, on the other hand, is plenty dark. I have no use for such vermin as men. I do not look to rule them, but destroy them."

"Um, well, okay," Simon said, lost for words. "But why do you want the skull?"

"I am not here to answer your questions; you are here to answer mine!" the demon roared.

Simon gulped, "I wish I could help you, but the skull was taken from one of my ancestors centuries ago, by a Chinese monk. It has been lost ever since.

"Wait, a Chinese monk? Of course, now I remember," Legion murmured. "Kai Shung used a crystal skull to trap me in that disc. Yes of course."

"What the Hell are you babbling about," Lilith said.

"Stay thy tongue, wench," Legion bellowed with thousands of voices in unison. "I know who has the skull, and I have seen its power. Yes, it all makes sense. They will pay for what they did. I will destroy them!"

***

"Your training begins today, Lyles," Chien said.

The two men were inside a room that looked like a chapel. There were some long slits in the walls that let in some of the morning light from the east side of the mountain. Lyles was still getting used to the thinner air near the top of the mountain, but he made due as did Esmeralda and Bianca. The priests who lived here were used to the mountain air, and of course Ravenblade was unaffected by it.

The training Lyles would need to undergo involved a lot of meditation. The two men were barefoot, and each had a long mat to stand on. Chien walked Lyles through some yoga-like exercises as well as some moves that resembled Tai Chi. While they did these techniques, Chien taught Lyles how to harness his spirit with the energy of the Earth — energy that God created, energy that was in everything. This was not magic but rather a drawing-in of power that God placed within this world to help one gain focus, strength, and inner peace. It was not much different from the training that Ravenblade had done with Lyles in the desert before they battled Radix. And because of his former training, Lyles advanced quickly.

***

"So when will you tell them who you really are?" Chao Cheng asked the immortal killer that stood before him.

The two were in a small sitting room, and the master was pouring himself some tea.

"What good would it do?" he replied.

"They are your friends; they should know who you are."

"I have no friends, you know that. I am evil. Isn't that why we fought?"

"Then if you are evil, why I am still alive. This is your chance to finally kill me. An old man who could barely defend himself."

"You can most certainly defend yourself. I can still feel your power. But you are correct — if I wanted to, you would be dead. I guess I am different in some ways. I only kill when I have to now, not just for pleasure."

"You do care for them. Especially the girl. She is special isn't she?"

"I don't care for that child. I don't even know her. Lyles fought with me in the desert, and I gained much respect for him. But that girl and her mother are nothing to me."

"They are Nathaniel Salvatore's family are they not? His sister. His niece. I'm sure you feel some compulsion to protect them."

"The only thing I feel for that girl is that she is a liability and a risk. Her power is strong but she is young. If not trained properly, she can destroy the world, as could her brother. But he is lost, which makes the liability even greater."

"So you do not believe the boy is dead?"

"No he is too important. Satan would not kill him. He would use him. I just wish I knew where that child was. So I could kill him before he knows enough to use his power."

***

"Good morning, father." The four-year-old boy sounded like a grown man as he spoke.

"Good morning, son, how are you today?" Sam asked the child who had already gotten dressed in a polo shirt, khaki shorts, and black socks.

Gideon was growing fast. He was tall for his age, and slender. The young child had an extremely high IQ and could already read at a third-grade level. His maturity was astounding, and his demeanor very serious. Unlike other children his age, he was not fond of playing with toys. He did enjoy a good game of chess from time to time, and spent most days reading. He did not have any friends his own age. He actually had very little contact with anyone except his adopted father, and the servants that came and went. No one knew who his mother was, but assumed it was some escort that Sam had gotten pregnant, and he decided to keep the child since he had no sons to carry on his reign.

The servants had much gossip about the entire situation, creating all sorts of interesting scenarios. They did wonder how the child was so fair skinned, with crystal blue eyes, and the softest blond hair. Sam had an olive complexion, and his eyes were a very dark brown. His hair color they were unsure of, for his head was clean-shaven, but his eyebrows almost seemed black. The child had never been outside the building. Samyaza had cast a spell on his dwelling place, so no one could detect the presence of anything within its walls. This is why no one could find the boy. God knew, of course, where he was for nothing could blind His eyes. Though this, as all things, was being used in His master plan. Samyaza and Satan believed they were orchestrating something magnificent, but God was in control.

"Father, I was wondering if we could go outside today?" Gideon asked as he pressed his face against the window, looking down at the streets below. "It looks so interesting out there. I want to experience something more than just what's in here."

"Gideon, you know you can't go out there. That place is evil. You would never be safe. You have everything that you need in here. You are special and if the people out there got a hold of you, I fear the things they would do. Your day will come when you will go outside these walls, but not now."

"But, Father, I want to. I want to breathe in the fresh air, and feel the sun on my face. Even the rain on my head."

"I know son. I know. But you should be happy. You have so many things. Other children would kill to have all that you have. I can buy you whatever you like."

"I know, but wealth is not everything. I feel empty, like I am missing something."

"You're being silly. You're missing nothing. Let's have some breakfast and then maybe we can play a round of chess before your training with Master Chi."

"I would like that, father."

***

Lyles and Chien were sitting on their mats, meditating, when Esmeralda walked into the room.

"We can't have any disturbances right now," Chien stated.

"Sorry," Esmeralda said. "But I can't find Bianca. Do either of you know where she is?"

"I just told you, no disturbances. I'm sure the girl is fine. Please leave."

"Wait!" Lyles exclaimed. "I will go with you."

"You won't. You need to train," Chien said.

Lyles stood up.

"I will go with her to find Bianca. Sorry, but I won't be able to concentrate until we find her."

"The girl is safe. No evil could come to her here. We are protected. Our first priests who dwelt here cast a spell to seal this place from evil. It cannot be breached in any way."

"Regardless, Ezzie's worried. Let me find Bianca. Then we can go back to training."

Lyles stormed off with Esmeralda following, feeling embarrassed about the confrontation.

Chien remained meditating, and spoke to himself in his dialect, "He will never succeed if he does not put his priorities in place."

Esmeralda followed Lyles through some corridors and rooms, looking for her daughter. They stopped when they saw Ravenblade speaking with Chao Cheng.

"Have either of you seen Bianca?" Lyles asked abruptly.

"No," Ravenblade answered.

"I know where the girl is," Chao Cheng said. "Please follow me."

The great teacher led them to a huge cathedral-like room, the temple where the priests prayed every day. In the center of the room sat Bianca with many priests surrounding her. They were all sitting on mats on the floor listening to the girl speak.

"What is going on," Esmeralda asked the great teacher.

"She is teaching them about God," he stated.

"What?" Esmeralda said.

"Your daughter is very wise. Our priests have not seen such understanding of God and His Word in many centuries. She has been going through the ancient prophecies about God's anointed and His plan for salvation. Our order has been studying these prophecies for a very long time — those in your Bible as well as those from other religions. Even though we were founded by the sect of Babylonian priests that Daniel had started and we kept his teachings at the core of our structure, we had never understood them as we do now. The image is so clear, how she paints it with simplicity. She even opened up to us those prophecies of Daniel and showed us so much that we had missed.

"The idea of the Trinity never made sense to us because we believe in One God. To us the Messiah, God's anointed, was just a man from the kingly line of David as the prophecies told us. But now, we see that we were missing the biggest piece of the puzzle. Of course, men have tried to show us this way, but when a child can preach it with such clarity and power, it can only be divinely bestowed, and makes our ears more attentive to receive. We have much to think about as we move forward as an order of priests. Especially now that even I have given my life to Christ."

"Seriously," Ravenblade said. "Even I could have told you that Jesus was God. I actually think I have."

"Sorry, but it is difficult to listen to the man who is holding a sword to your throat trying to kill you. Wisdom was not something I saw in you, just rage," Chao Cheng said.

Esmeralda just stood watching her daughter. She seemed so mature, teaching the men before her. It definitely did not seem like she was watching her little, carefree girl. The angel had told her Bianca would be great and lead people to Christ. Her mission had already begun.

"She is like a prophet of the Most High," the master told Esmeralda. "How long has she been studying her Scripture?"

"She hasn't really been studying it. Just some Bible stories I read to her, that's all really," she replied.

"Then His Word must be written on her heart. Very wonderful indeed."

Chao Cheng paused and placed his hand on Lyles' shoulder, "I was wondering if you could baptize me and my priests tonight. You are studying to be a minister, correct? It would be good for you to lead the ceremony."

"Yes, yes, of course," Lyles stuttered. "It would be an honor."

"This is ridiculous," Ravenblade said. "You should worry less about baptizing people and more about how you are going to stop Legion. Baptized or not, he will destroy you all."

"Then at least when we die, we can be with God in peace," the master spoke.

Chien entered the room. He had heard the conversation just as he was walking in and was very confused by all that was transpiring. He had not heard the girl preach and wondered what sorcery had taken over the temple for all of these men, and the great teacher they followed, to change what they had believed for centuries, all because of the words of a mere child. Chien turned and hurried out without saying a word.

"Is he okay?" Lyles asked.

"He will be fine; let me talk to my pupil," Chao Cheng said and went to find Chien.

"Lyles, you have to prepare for your enemy. Come with me and let's train. Your friend seems otherwise occupied and I don't want you to lose focus," Ravenblade said, and the two left.

Only Esmeralda remained watching Bianca, captivated by her daughter. What she saw was beautiful.

***

"Why did you leave, my son?" the great teacher spoke to one of his prize students.

"I have no place here anymore," Chien said.

"What do you mean, my son? This is your home."

"But what good am I to you, and to our men. I always thought I would be the hero to follow Wang Sheng, but I was wrong. Men from outside our order have now taken that place, above me. And now a child teaches our brothers, changing what we believe. Like I said, I have no place here."

"You are angry, but why? Your skill is great, as is your mind

104

and strength. I have known no man in this order who has the skills you possess. Whether you are ordained or not, a hero you still are, just by sacrificing to fight alongside this man who has come to us. You are second only to me in this order, and you possess the sword of our people. It is said that the sword was forged in the fire of Heaven to battle the demons that have afflicted this world. The sword is the only key to come and go from this abode in the whole world, and you possess it for a reason. Maybe you are confused by the direction your life has taken, but do not let it destroy your spirit. Your mission and life are special because they are yours, and you can do with them as you will. If you choose to be a hero, then a hero you will be."

"I know, master, but I am unsettled about this girl. And now all the men are getting baptized. This makes no sense to me. I will not join you tonight for this ceremony, because my heart has not changed as yours has."

"Do as you wish. But remain my student and priest. Maybe in time, you can see what I have seen."

"I will keep my vow to protect and serve. I will remain with you and your order for all time, but let me seek my own truth."

"You will have plenty of time to seek while you are on this journey. The road ahead will not be easy. The enemy you face is beyond any to walk this world. His power is far greater than that of Radix, for he was born of the Darkness, and it dwells in his very soul. Be careful, and fight well. I pray that you will return successful, with this villain trapped again for all time."

"I will do my best, master. I will not fail," Chien said with a bow, and walked out.

***

"Hi, Mommy," Bianca said and gave Esmeralda a huge hug. She had finally finished teaching the priests and was back to her playful self. "I wish I had my dolls here to play with. Can we play a game?"

"What game do you want to play? We really don't have any here."

"I saw the men playing a game with little tiles, maybe we can play that. It's nice here, Mommy. Is this our new home?"

Esmeralda was trying to follow her daughter's question.

"I'm not sure, baby, let's see what happens. All I know is that, right now, we are safe here. Let's go talk to Mr. Chao Cheng and see if he has anything you can play with."

"Okay, Mommy, I love you."

"I love you too, baby."

"Do you think Uncle Nathan is in Heaven with Jesus right now?"

"Yes, I really do."

CHAPTER VII
HELL BENT

The ground under Nathan's body was cold and hard. He could feel a hot wind blowing in his face and, when he opened his eyes, all he could see was a red haze. He stood up and noticed that his clothing had changed. His body was covered in a strange white armor. It was no metal that he knew of, and it was extremely lightweight and flexible. Nathan looked up and down, noticing all the details. The armor was beautiful and flawless. He also took notice of a sunburst pattern molded onto the center of the breastplate.

"He really does like you," a voice spoke from behind.

Nathan turned and said, "Oh, it's you. Death, right?"

"You remember me, good," Death said.

"What do you mean *He* really does like me?" Nathan wondered. "Do you mean God?"

"Of course. Look at you, garbed in the Armor of God, even after you defied Him by storming Hell. You know, I was part of this plan. He really does like you."

"I am no one special, but I am certain that God does love me. I am not trying to defy Him. I only wish to save my nephew. That's all. I'm sure God understands. But regardless, I believe that I am saved and even storming Hell cannot take away what Jesus did for me on that cross."

"You are bold and brave, Nathaniel, but it will take more than that to snatch the boy from the hand of the serpent."

"I know, but God is with me, so who can stand against me."

"In this world, the Devil will. It is good that you have strong faith, but God has tested and tried many before you whose faith was even stronger. Just because you believe doesn't mean you won't suffer."

"I know. I lived that life. Battling Radix wasn't easy, and I faced Satan then, too. Don't let my confidence be confused with cockiness. I know my strength is the Lord and my victory is His and His alone. I know I will win only because it is His fight and He cannot lose."

"Well said, Nathaniel. Let's hurry. Do as I say. Getting into Hell unseen will not be easy, but it can be done with my help."

"I will follow your lead. But as you said, let's hurry."

Death led Nathan to the black crystal structure known as the Gates of Hell. The young man approached the mouth of the lion without fear, for the mouth of a lion is how the entrance before him seemed. As instructed by his guide, Nathan hid behind one of the black crystal stalagmites on the ground, while Death entered to distract his brother, Sin.

"Why have you returned here, brother?" Sin asked, his deep purple robe flowing in the hot wind. "I thought your last visit was not as comfortable as you would have liked."

"Sin, you know very well why I am here. I still seek the child who your master stole," Death returned.

"And you should already know the answer to that. My master is not going to just give you the boy because you whine and beg. Do you have no dignity?"

"I have plenty, as well as courage to keep approaching you with this request. Do you even know the consequences to your master's actions? Do you have no feeling for all creation, including that of this very plane that you live on, even your own existence? If the destroyer comes he devours all, and you know this. There is nothing for you or your master to gain."

"You don't learn do you?" Sin laughed.

Death lunged at his brother.

"I do not have to learn anything. Your evil has shown me enough! You are vile and an abomination! A curse, a monster!"

Death's voice escalated with each breath, and he held Sin by the throat and pushed him back.

Nathan saw his cue and ran like a flash of light into the circle of fire in the center of the structure. He was instantly teleported into Hell. Sin pushed his brother from him.

"Do you think me unwise to your tricks? Do you think anyone can enter my Gates unnoticed? Go with your friend and seek the counsel of my master. You know what that did for you last time. He does not change. His answer will be the same. I just hope you can escape this time. I am certain your friend will not," Sin said and threw Death into the ring of fire, sending him with Nathan to home of the damned.

"Master, they are all yours," Sin said out loud.

No one was there but Satan could hear every word from his throne. He smiled and laughed as he plotted their fate. Inside his kingdom, Nathan and Death looked at each other, trying to decide what to do next. Hell was a complex plane, consisting of many levels and an ever-changing terrain. The last time Death entered Hell he appeared on the Plains of Sorrow where Bayemon drove his slaves to work the soil. But this time, they entered into a different place, one unfamiliar to Death. Nathan could feel the heat on his face. They were in a forest. The trees here had no leaves, but were covered in sharp gnarled branches with thorns all over. In the distance, Nathan could hear the faint sound of a beast growling.

"So, this is Hell?" Nathan asked.

"Well, this is part of it. The land is vast and multileveled, much like Heaven. The only difference is that this world changes with every new soul that is added, making it difficult to navigate. That is, until you cross the river. On the other side of the River Styx lies Satan's palace and that area never changes. The trick will be to make it to the river first."

"The River Styx, like in Greek mythology?"

"Yes, you know myths are not all made up completely. They have much truth in them. Hades and Hell have many similarities, for the gods that told men these stories knew much of this world and beyond."

"Gods — what do you mean? The Watchers?"

"Yes, those angels who played god on Earth. They helped to form most of man's religions. That is, except for that of the Hebrews. Their God, of course, is real. Though I know you know that already. But let's discuss history another time, for we have a mission, and I am certain that Satan will not be happy to know what we are up to. That dragon will hunt us down and try to destroy us. His power here is stronger than on any plane, for this is his kingdom — his home."

The two set out in the forest. Nathan's armor protected his body from the thorns of the trees. Their poison was said to even kill those who were already dead. He protected his face with his hands, for he was without a helmet. The growling noise Nathan had heard earlier was getting closer.

"Do you hear that, Death?" Nathan inquired.

"Yes, and it can only mean one thing. Satan is onto us. That is his pet, Cerberus."

"The three-headed dog?"

"Something like that. Be wary, for that beast is cunning and if he catches you, there will be no escape. Once his teeth are clenched onto you, you will be unable to break his hold, and he will take you back to his master, to do with you as he pleases."

"Good to know. I'll be ready."

Nathan and Death did their best to move quickly and quietly through the forest. In Hell, Nathan's powers were subdued just as Death's were. He could still do things that no mortal could, but he was very limited, making his trek more difficult than if he were on Heaven or Earth right now. He had learned much from Michael and Christopher, as well as the other transcended beings that he trained with. He was no longer alive, so he could move like the wind and almost seem to teleport wherever he wanted to go. His spirit had also been strengthened by God's own Spirit, giving him almost unlimited strength to call upon when in need. But now he was in Hell. Removed from God. His power was more like what he possessed on Earth when he had reached Chaos Fury. Death and Nathan stopped when they heard a noise.

It started like the sound of rustling and then the cracking of branches, accompanied by the stampeding of some type of beast. Death was right — Cerberus had found them and it was his intention to deliver these trespassers to his master. The mythical creature lunged at Nathan who rolled out of the way, crashing through the thorn-filled branches. He was blessed to have the armor of God protecting his body for the thorns would surely have pierced his flesh, sending him to the second death. The monster came back around, mouth wide open. Instinctively, Nathan dodged his attacker again. But he was unsure how much longer he could keep this up. He needed to get out of this forest, so he could put up a better fight. Nathan began to run, using his arms to protect his face from the thorny limbs in his way. The beast only seemed interested in the young man, and paid no attention to Death, who was able to sneak his way to the edge of the forest, hoping Nathan could get out as well. There was nothing the ghoulish being could do, for his power in Hell was almost nothing.

In a matter of moments, Nathan came crashing out of the forest and rolled onto the ground, to avoid the creature that was hot on his heels. They now stood in a vast desert and there was nowhere to run. The heat was far more intense here, but Nathan focused on his enemy and nothing more. He took a stance, and the beast stopped and looked at Nathan with a fierce growl on its face. The monster stood about fifteen feet tall from its front legs to the top of its central head. Yes, it had three heads, and was some twisted combination of serpent and canine. Its heads were like those of a Rottweiler, each with a main of snakes. Its body was covered in thick black fur, and its muscular legs were like strong pillars planted on the ground. The tail of this monster was that of a snake and swung around ready to strike the transcended being. But Nathan would not surrender so easily. If this beast wanted a fight, it would get one, and with that thought, the sword appeared in Nathan's hand — the Word of God.

The shining blade flashed a light like no other and the beast backed up. It circled its prey as if studying the weapon that Nathan held. Cerberus came in with one of its heads to attack. But as soon as it came close, the light from the sword grew, and the beast backed away again. Then, the monster turned and ran off.

"What happened?" Nathan asked out loud.

"Satan called off his pet," Death replied.

"Why?"

"He knew he could not stand against the sword in your hands. The Word of God is said to be the most powerful weapon to ever exist, because it was not forged but, rather, is a part of God Himself. Or at least that is the legend. The blade has not been seen in a long time, not since the war in Heaven. It was wielded by Christ in that war, along with the armor you are wearing. Satan will try to take these things from you, in hopes of using them in the next war against God and His chosen."

"Let him try. If these belong to God, then I am certain it will not be so easy for the Devil to snatch them from His hand or my body," Nathan said.

The sword vanished from Nathan's hand again.

This blade was odd, for it appeared in times of need. Nathan wondered where it must go when not being used, but inside he could feel that somehow the sword was still with him, in his very heart and soul.

It was time to move forward. He was on a mission and needed to find his nephew, whom the hero prayed was still alive and somehow safe, even in the vile hands of the Devil. Now that the hound knew where they were, it would be more difficult for Nathan to reach Satan's lair without constant adversity.

They journeyed through the desert plain that they had entered after leaving the forest. There was no sun, but a great heat radiated from all around. The sky was hazy and red, and even though Nathan was transcended and did not need food or water, he grew thirsty. As they walked further on, the ground became rocky, and Nathan began to see something like a mirage fading into view and becoming reality. The sight was horrifying — this was a clearer picture of Hell for the young man, for before him were thousands of men and women lying on their bellies, their hands and feet staked into the rocky ground. Their heads were all propped up by the chin with forked sticks, and their eyes had been pulled from their skulls. Blood poured down from the empty sockets. These poor souls all faced out to the East, as if their bleeding eye sockets were staring into the horizon, waiting for something.

"Welcome, Death," a voice greeted them.

Death turned to see a familiar face. The demon looked like a man wearing a black robe that was spotted with lights, as if he were wearing the night sky. His black hair was long and braided, his face pale white with eyes as blue as the ocean and ears pointed like an elf's. He hovered in the air, watching over those being tormented in the desert. His face was stern without compromise. He seemed to be cut from stone, and his large hands looked weathered and strong.

"Ole-Luk-Oie," Death said.

"Who is your friend?" Ole-Luk-Oie wondered.

"That is not your concern. We are just passing through, and mean no ill will," Death stated.

"No one ever said you did. Of course, you can pass through, but first I would like to speak with your friend. He seems like a nice man with keen eyes," the demon answered, licking his lips.

"I can hear you, Ole-Ole- whatever he called you," Nathan interjected. "What do you want?

"I am the dream-maker, the Sandman, Ole-Luk-Oie," he replied. "I was an angel once as all of us demons were. I watched men dream peacefully through the nights after breaking their backs during the day, working the land and facing the trials of the mortal world. I fell after the rebellion of Lucifer, while the Watchers played gods on Earth, though I was not one of them. I saw how pitiful was man and his existence, and I denounced the God that allowed that to be. I longed to make men's dreams a reality, to give them pleasure in life. So I did. I gave them pleasures beyond compare. But now, thanks to me, they are all living a nightmare, suffering for their selfish lusts that I fulfilled for them. And I, too, am banned to this Hell, watching over them as they dream. Each day brings new souls, new dreams to fulfill, and new nightmares to be made.

"The worms of this desert are my children and they grow hungry for these dreams. The more sinister, the more painful, the tastier they are. The worms eat out the eyes of the men and women who come here. In doing so, the worms can see and feel all that these pathetic souls experience. Their torment, their pain, their horror is shared. So, young man, your eyes look savory. My children long to see your dreams. I can help you sleep. All your desires will be fulfilled to overflowing. What do you say? Just let me sprinkle some of my sand on your eyes and you can sleep and dream."

"Enough!" Nathan boomed. "I do not want the pleasure you bring. For my joy only comes from one place, and it is not here in Hell!"

"Now, now. Relax," the demon said as he floated around Nathan, fingering sand in his hand. "Just one sprinkle," and he blew dust toward Nathan.

Before the dust could reach Nathan's face, he threw up his arm and a shield appeared which blocked the sand, letting it fall to the ground. The shield was round with intricate molding around the edges. In the center was a relief of a dove inside of a triangle. Like the armor, the shield was white, for this suit of arms was also named the Armor of Light.

"The shield of faith," Ole-Luk-Oie said. "That *is* the armor then. The master desires it so. Why don't you let me give you rest. I can release you from the burden of wearing such confining clothing."

"I said no!" Nathan shouted again, and the sword appeared. "I find my rest in God alone!"

"Do you mean to threaten me in my own abode?" the demon said, growing angry. His face grew sterner. His eyes went from blue to blood red, and his mouth sneered with sharp teeth. The nails on his fingers grew longer and jagged. The men and women on the ground convulsed as if in pain; blood now poured not only from their empty eye sockets but also from their mouths. The red sky began to turn black with an unholy darkness. "You will sleep! You will dream!"

The demon sprung at Nathan, who raised his shield and firmly grasped his sword. But before the Sandman could reach his victim, Death threw the dust from the ground, the very powder that the demon used to cause his victims to sleep. The sand blanketed the eyes of Ole-Luk-Oie and he dropped to the ground, asleep, a victim of his own devices. The worms came forth and went straight for their master's eyes. His dreams pleased them more than any of the others, for he was the dreammaker. Without time to lose, Death grabbed Nathan and urged him to continue on. Together, the two ventured forward, and the world around them changed and shifted as they entered a new territory of this damned place. The shield and sword had disappeared, leaving Nathan wondering once again about these magical weapons and armor.

"The shield, like the sword, will appear when you need it. It is the shield of faith. And you have one more piece that will appear as well, the helmet of salvation. Though these appear in times of need, they rest in your heart and soul, connected to you, never to leave your side, just like He who created them for Himself and His purpose. You are Blessed, Nathan. Even in the fires of Hell, He is with you."

"That's good to know, because I don't know how else I could get through this," Nathan said, as the two moved cautiously forward.

The land continued to morph all around them. Mountains and hills rose and flattened, forests and jungles grew from the ground and then became desolate, the ground changed from dry desert to marshy swamp, and everything in between — quite a bizarre world. While Nathan passed through each region, he could see the damned being tortured; the fear in their eyes, and the pain on their faces moved him. He did not know what actions brought them here, except that they did not know the One who could save them from whatever bound them. *Did they deserve such horror?* Nathan wondered.

This was more than he could bear at the moment. All he could do was follow his guide and keep trekking forward. The man had a purpose — he needed to save his nephew from the Devil, and nothing would stop him from doing this. The land transformed once again. The ground was lush and green. Trees filled the area, as did exotic plants, and the most beautiful of tropical flowers. It was like a paradise and in many ways reminded Nathan of the garden in Heaven.

This place was odd for Death also. He could not imagine such a beautiful place in Hell. The two travelers walked with caution through the tropical forest, wondering what surprises were in store for them. No matter how beautiful it was, this was still Hell, and evil lurked around every corner.

Nathan stopped to look around and then leaned on one of the trees. When he did he heard a low moan, which caused him to turn his head. That is when he noticed that the trees had human faces protruding from their trunks. It was as if men and women had been trapped inside of them and had now become one with the trees. Nathan spun around and around to see all the faces, their eyes shut, moaning at him, seeming to call him, in a way. But what did they want?

A voice spoke as if in Nathan's ear.

"They longed for the world and its ways. Rooting themselves in their own selfish desires and lusts. Now, they cannot move, only wait to be satisfied by a passing breeze or the touch of another who walks by. They even long to feel the insects eat at their bark and leaves, just to get a sensation. This is what the ways of the world have led them to. Eternally rooted into the soil, one with the world, but unable to move, slaves to the world they loved so much."

"Asmodeus, show yourself," Death said.

"There is no need for that," the voice spoke again. "I was told you were here and planned for you to visit my territory. I am one of seven who rule under the Prince of Darkness himself," Asmodeus said to Nathan.

"You know that already, Death. But your friend. Nathaniel Salvatore — the man who helped to bring down Radix — does he know of me? Do you, boy?"

"I have heard your name before, but honestly I don't really know anything about you. And I really don't care," Nathan said. "As far as I'm concerned, you are nothing but a narcissistic monster, and I have no time for your games."

"I heard you had spunk, but thought by now you would have lost some of that, having transcended and all. Don't think it's such a secret. We know more than you think," Asmodeus continued.

"I really don't care what you know. I just want to pass through and get on my way," Nathan retorted.

"And when you get there, what will you do? Do you think my master will just let you have the child? Just give him back to you?"

"So, he does have him," Nathan said, and then shouted to the sky, "Give him back, Satan! Give him back or I swear I will cut you to pieces!"

"Ha ha, you are rich, and quite entertaining," Asmodeus went on. "How about you stay for a while here and let me speak to my master. Maybe we can work out a deal. You for the boy, perhaps? The trees here are rooted into the very soil of Hell. The roots of these trees absorb all the sin and pleasures of this land, filling the very souls of those trapped inside, feeding their desires. They would welcome some new blood, some new desires, some new flesh to suck in and satisfy their urges. And how about your desires? Like to have your nephew back, to be a hero, are you not filled with the same selfish lusts as they are? You did not come here for God. You came here for yourself, to get what you want. Maybe you belong here after all."

"Don't listen to him, Nathan," Death said. He put his hand on the man's shoulder. "He is trying to deceive you. Trying to trap you here. There is nothing he can do for you. He is a liar, just like his master."

"Enough, Death!" Asmodeus shouted. "I am speaking with the mortal, not with you. Stay out of this! I merely want to help him get what he craves. That's all. There can be no harm in that."

"Damnation for all eternity is harm enough," Death stated.

Nathan began to become agitated with the conversation, and the moaning of the trees rang in his ears. He planted his feet firmly into the ground and clenched his fists. Power exuded from his body, radiating light, and the shield and sword appeared in his hands.

"Show yourself, demon! Bring me to your master and return my nephew to me!" the warrior yelled.

"You want to see me? To fight me? Do you even know what you are up against?" the demon boasted. "I am a lord of Hell, a prince. My power is beyond all others except that of my own master. No newly transcended being can even hope to match my might. Your threats are feeble at best. I could snap you with my little finger!"

A thunderous noise was heard, and Asmodeus came out from behind the trees. He was large in size and stature, with three heads. One was that of a man, ugly with a long, twisted nose, wearing a golden crown. To the left was the head of a horse and to its right the head of a ram. His arms and torso were well muscled, and in his hands he held a spear with a banner on it. His legs were strange, like a rooster's with clawed feet, and he had a long, serpentine tail. This monstrous demon rode upon an odd beast that looked like a dragon with large wings and the face of a lion.

"Take your stand, boy, but you will fail," the demon spoke. "Do you really think you can face me?"

"Nathan, you can't fight him," Death said. "Nathan, stand down."

"I cannot stand down. I will destroy him," Nathan said and charged up. He gripped his sword and shield as tight as he could, and even now the helmet appeared on his head. Like the rest of the armor, it was white. Though he could not see it, there was a cross on the front with a slit across for his eyes. Somehow, the helmet did not compromise his peripheral vision, and with his training he had learned how to sense his enemy from all around. It was like he was seeing with his spirit instead of his eyes. Nathan was suited for battle, and he leaped at his foe.

"Enough!" a voice cried out, even louder and more imposing than Asmodeus's own.

Nathan landed on one knee, and looked up. From above swooped a demon even larger than the one who stood before him. His wings were darker and more sinister than the dragon's, and the wind created by them caused the trees to sway, almost uprooting them from the very soil. The beast landed, making the ground quake. Nathan looked upon him in awe.

"Geryon," Death spoke. "What's going on?"

"Yes, what brings you to meddle in my affairs? You have no jurisdiction here?" Asmodeus quipped.

Nathan took a good look at Geryon. He was large and powerful. The muscles of his arms seemed to flex with every movement. His face was surprisingly handsome for a demon. His torso transitioned into the body and tail of a monstrous snake from his waist down, and at the end was a stinger like that of a scorpion.

Geryon spoke, "I have jurisdiction wherever my master allows it, or commands it, as in this very case. You may be a prince of Hell, and think you are second only to the master himself, but deep inside, Asmodeus, you know that my might is greater than yours, so do not challenge me. And you, mortal, you are lucky that we have not sent you to the second death or made you a permanent fixture here. You have no power in this world to challenge us or our master. But he has requested to see you, so I will allow you to pass. I will take you to the River Styx where you will cross on Charon's boat. When you get to the other side, you will find the castle of my master. See it in the distance, there, with the dragon on the spire. That is your destination. But, Death, you will go home. You cannot cross the river, anyway, after your last visit. And even if you could cross, my master does not welcome you to go further. I will send you home now."

"Wait," Death said. "Before I go, let me give Nathan one thing."

He slipped a coin into Nathan's palm, saying "You will need this to cross the river."

"Smart, you remembered to bring your own this time," Geryon said. "Very well. Now go." Death vanished before their eyes.

"Now, little man, get on my back, and hold on tight, I will take you to the bank of the river." And with that they flew off to the River Styx.

Death was about to warn Nathan not to give the coin to Charon until he took him to the other side, but Geryon purposefully had sent him away before he could. The winged demon flew swiftly with the hero holding firmly around his neck. The ride was rough, and Nathan nearly fell several times but managed somehow to keep his grip.

"So, what brought you here?" Nathan yelled as he fought to stay on the demon's back.

"I was part of the rebellion!" Geryon roared back. "I was a general in Satan's first army, when I — when *we* were all angels!"

"Why did you choose to follow him? Why go against God?"

"Why not? You humans think it is all so black and white. Like we are these horrible beasts who decided one day that we wanted to be Evil and destroy everything! That was not it at all. Lucifer had great vision, he spoke of freedom, and being able to pursue our own happiness instead of just being mindless servants of some greater power who knew nothing of us — how we felt, what we desired! God was too big for those things. Lucifer was one of us. He really understood us!"

"What about Christ?" Nathan posed. "I know it is hard to relate to the Father since no one can see Him, but wasn't the Son with you also in Heaven in a form closer to yours. Maybe feeling even what you felt?"

"He is not like us. He is God. He was not created but He is the Creator," the demon said. "How about you? He came as a man and died, but do you really feel He is like you?"

"He isn't like me. I'm a sinner. But He did feel pain. He did feel joy. He's not like me, but He understands. That is why I choose to follow Him, that and the fact that He loves me. I don't know anyone else who would die for people so undeserving! Would Satan do that? I don't think he would sacrifice himself for anyone or anything!"

"Enough!" Geryon bellowed. "He is the master of this land and you would be wise to stay thy tongue."

Nathan spoke no more. He was not afraid, but could see that his point was made. The demon landed with a thud, and Nathan slid down his back to ground. They stood before the River Styx. The violent movement of the water and its blood-red color gave Nathan an uneasy feeling. In front of them was a wooden dock covered by a hazy fog.

"Charon, the ferryman, will pick you up there. He will take you to the other side where Satan's palace is. There you will find my master. He is waiting for you." Geryon bellowed. "Now go!"

The bold warrior just stood there looking up at the demon, unafraid of the angry beast before him. Then, he turned and headed out to the dock. Shortly afterward, he could see a small wooden boat break through the fog. Piloting the boat was a skeleton-like man wearing a sackcloth robe. The fog was thick and went across the entire river, making it difficult for Nathan to see the man's face, but he felt as if Charon's eyes were piercing into his very soul.

The ferryman gestured for Nathan to board the boat, which he did with caution, as it shook with every movement. Once Nathan was aboard, Charon held out his hand, requesting payment. Without a second thought, Nathan handed over the coin that Death had given to him, which the ferryman accepted graciously. The boat left the dock and moved across the water. Geryon watched from the bank, smiling to himself.

"He is on his way, Master," Geryon said to the air. "All is going according to plan."

Nathan sat down at the back of the boat and looked into the water. Its dark red color gave him an eerie feeling. It was as if the blood of all those suffering in Hell was drained into this very river. Even the smell was very distinct, and reminded Nathan of when he swam in his own blood back in the desert, a few years ago. The boat suddenly stopped in the middle of the river. Nathan looked at his guide to see what was happening. The ferryman stood very still, and then raised his hand. With that movement, Nathan rose into the air. And with a swift thrust forward of Charon's hand, the surprised hero was flung into the river. More annoyed than anything, Nathan treaded water to keep his head afloat. The taste of the river water on his tongue proved that it was indeed blood — but, unlike last time, it was definitely not his own. The lost traveler spun around in the water trying to see through the fog and to figure out which way he needed to swim to get to the shore. He couldn't see anything. The water moved faster around him and under him. Then, he could see several large black fins cutting through the water at great speed.

Before he could react to the danger before him, he was swallowed in one big gulp from underneath. This was not Nathan's first time in the belly of a fish, but there was something different about *this* fish. The transcended being already could not use much of his power, but inside this creature he felt weak, as if his spirit was being drained.

He had not come this far for all of it to end, for him to fail. He needed to save Gideon; he needed to survive and be victorious. This monster might be able to drain his spirit, and Hell might limit his abilities, but nothing could stop the power of the Lord, and Nathan turned his heart and soul to God, drawing on the power that was not from himself, but from the Almighty Creator of all. For even in Hell, God's power was supreme. The helmet of salvation appeared on his head, and the sword of the Spirit — the Word of God — appeared in his hand. With one fatal slash, he ripped through the demonic fish with the sword. Free from his predator, Nathan began to swim furiously. He did not know where he was heading but he followed the feeling he had inside, as if he was being led by someone who knew the way.

More fish began to follow in pursuit, and Nathan swam faster and faster. It was as if he was regaining his full strength. He was actually out-swimming the fish. One of them jumped into the air, just passing over the determined hero. He caught a glimpse of the creature as it passed by him. Its black skin, soulless eyes, and jagged fins read evil in every way. The fish began to catch up and started to surround him, blocking him in all directions. There was nothing left to do. He had to fight.

Nathan stopped and treaded water with his legs as he charged up and held his sword high. He thrust into the water and torpedoed at the fish, one by one, slicing them to shreds. He could hear a great moan coming from all around. The water grew more violent than before and caught Nathan in its current. The hero could not fight it, but was carried away, and in one big wave tossed to the shore. He heard the moan grow louder and, finally, it turned into scream. Then, it quieted and the water became still.

Nathan spat out some of the blood-water and got up. When he turned, he saw a decaying garden. All the vegetation was dried up, and the trees looked like bewitched gremlins waiting to devour anyone who entered. There was an old rusted iron fence that seemed to guard the garden, but the gate was wide open. Not knowing where else to go, Nathan entered the garden through the gate. Ahead, over the treetops, he could see the spire with the dragon. He was heading in the right direction and seemed to almost be there. The helmet vanished again, as did the sword. The hero moved forward, determined to be victorious.

"You really upset him, huh?" a voice called out. "Poseidon sounds pretty mad."

"Who's there?" Nathan called back.

"Forget about me already?" the voice answered.

The voice did sound familiar, but it couldn't be him? Or could it? Nathan *was* in Hell, just where that man should be.

"Radix," Nathan said. "Radix! Where are you? Show yourself? You will not stop me!"

"It's going to be hard to do anything from here," Radix said. "Just walk through the next clearing and you'll see why."

Nathan did as he was told, and when he made it through the clearing he did see what Radix meant. Hanging above a pit of fire bound by thorny restraints, hung the fiend. He was finally paying for his crimes. But this puzzled Nathan, since Satan ran Hell. Would not one such as Radix be rewarded for all he did for Satan? Why was his own master punishing him?

"I can see it in your eyes," Radix spoke again. "You look confused. This is the reward for serving the Devil. Hell is the land of torture and pain; no one here is free from its torment. Not even Satan himself. But if I ever get out of my bonds, his torment will be increased tenfold. So, I can see you've transcended. Good look for you, and that armor, real spiffy. Too bad you didn't have it when you fought me. Maybe you would have lived past the fight. But, like me, you died. Though it seems that even if you kill us you can't take us out. So, you're looking for Satan, I presume. Have some issue you want to discuss with Big Red?"

"Yes, I do," Nathan said. "But it's none of your business."

"Do you think he'll just give you what you want and let you leave? You'll end up in worse chains than me. You will be trapped here forever. Unless maybe you let me help you."

"You help me? That's a good one. You only care to help yourself."

"You're right. I do want to help myself. I won't lie. I want to be free of this prison. But if you face off with the Devil alone you won't win. *Together* we might be able to get what we both want and overthrow him. What do you say?" Radix posed.

"I am not alone; I have God!" Nathan exclaimed.

"Do you really believe that he is with you here. God is nowhere in sight. Take a look all around. You're a fool. You always were. Following that puppet master. Doing His will. And what has He done for you. He let you die at my hands. You're weak and pathetic — nothing more than a scared boy looking to his father for approval. A father who is too busy to pay you any mind."

"You are wrong!" Nathan screamed. He charged up. The helmet and sword appeared on cue. "God *is* with me. He gave me His strength when I was in the belly of the fish just now. He gave me power like I had in Heaven, helping me to defeat the whole school of them that tried to devour me. He led me here to the shore when I was lost in the river. And when I was dead, he brought me back to life!"

"So that is why Poseidon was screaming. You killed his fish!"

Nathan paid no mind to Radix's comment, but was filled with a holy anger toward Radix, for he had spoken against Nathan's Savior and God. The enraged hero powered up and leaped over the fiery pit, slicing Radix's bonds from his wrists and feet, freeing him. Before he could fall into the fire below him, Radix caught a vine and swung to safety. His plan had worked. He was free. But Nathan was not done. Leaping back over the pit, he tackled Radix to the ground, and they both rolled together until they hit a tree.

"Stop!" Radix yelled. "There is no reason for us to fight. We have a common enemy now."

"You are the only enemy I see right now," Nathan said. "I will deal with you and then Satan."

"Think about it. Does your God want you to fight me? I thought He was all for peace and loving your enemies. If you fight me, the only one you will please is the very same monster you want to destroy."

Nathan calmed down but still held his sword in front of him. What the cretin said was true, but he still did not trust Radix. Nathan's mind cleared and he realized that fighting his old enemy would not bring back Gidcon. But could he trust someone as evil as Radix? Could he work with someone whose heart was so dark? Would God even want him to do that? He did not know what to do. All he knew was that he needed to find the Devil and get back his nephew.

"Okay, let's talk," Nathan said.

***

"Isn't that just lovely," the words slithered off of the Devil's tongue.

He sat on his throne watching Radix and Nathan through a portal that floated in front of him. The snake smirked, thinking of how his plan was unfolding before him, oblivious to the fact that the Lord's plan was actually what was truly coming to light. Many

125

had spoken of the end of days for so many centuries, especially just after Christ had left the Earth. But truly the time was near, and all was being put in place. Nathan and Radix would play big parts and Satan knew this. He saw this in Radix before he recruited the young man, and he definitely felt the power that filled Nathan when he had tempted the hero in the desert. But his bigger wonder was how to use both of them to get what he desired — God's throne and all the power that the position of King of all Creation could bring.

"Zreet, prepare the guards," Satan spoke to his impish servant, the same creature who had led Death to his throne room last time he had entered Hell. "Once those two fools reach the palace, I want them brought to me in chains. They will suffer until they learn how to serve me and me alone," the Prince of Darkness concluded, with a deep disturbing laugh that echoed throughout all of Hell.

CHAPTER VIII
THE TIES THAT BIND

"Kimberly!" Martha exclaimed as she hugged her friend. "It is so good to see you. What brings you here?"

Kimberly looked down and then around the room.

"Can we sit?" she asked.

"Everything okay?" Martha wondered, as she sat down. "Something's not right."

"Well, you see, Lyles is away, and I'm not sure when or if he'll be back," Kimberly paused.

"Where is he?"

"China."

"What's he doing in China?" Martha shouted. "Don't tell me he's off fighting some demon or something, like last time?"

"Yes," Kimberly cried.

"That fool, and leaving you here alone. He should just let God fight those fights Himself. But I guess he's doing a good thing," she wrapped her arms around Kimberly. "God's with him, I can feel it, and he will come home. I know it."

"But when, and how many more times?" Kimberly continued to cry. "I can't deal with all this. What if he gets killed? He's only a man, not some superhero. He told me about the last time, when they fought Radix. He barely lived through it."

"He might not have powers, but God can conquer anything, and if God is for him who can stand against him?"

"God was for Nathan and *he* died. Just because God is for him doesn't guarantee anything."

"That's true," Martha spoke from experience. The death of her son still penetrated her heart and soul. "But if this is what God is calling him to do, then he can't turn his back either."

"But it hurts so much. And especially now, more than ever," the young woman said and grabbed her friend tightly, drenching her in tears. "I'm pregnant!"

"What? When? How?" Martha paused in shock. "Well, I guess I know how, but still. This is a blessing!"

"But how can I go through this alone? What if my child grows up without a father? I need Lyles here. I need him now."

"I know, sweetie. I know. I raised Rashan all on my own. It ain't easy. But for now you have me," she comforted her friend. "I'll be here for you for whatever you need, don't you worry about a thing. I love you, sweetie. You don't need to do this alone."

***

"Ravenblade, I think this was a mistake."

"Nonsense, Death," the immortal responded. "We had no other option. We need to get that kid back."

"But I'm not sure he can succeed. The Devil has him, I just know it. That or one of Poseidon's fish has eaten him. If he gets trapped in one of their bellies, there is no escape."

"Don't be so grim. Have a little more faith. Nathan is resilient. He took down the one man no one else could, not even me. Granted, he had some help from us, and the Man Upstairs, but still. Something tells me that Nathan will make it through okay. He will get the job done and be back in Heaven before we know it."

"I hope you are right," Death said and disappeared.

"I am. I can feel it."

"Who are you talking to?" Lyles asked as he walked in on Ravenblade.

"Just myself. Just thinking about our strategy to defeat Legion," the immortal lied.

"Hm, okay," Lyles said. "I was just training with Chien. He's a tough guy, and can do some sick moves. I just hope it's enough to help us win. Seems like Legion is pretty powerful. Thousands of demons all mixed up into one soul. Sounds intense."

"Yes, he will not be easy to beat, maybe even harder than Radix. It will take more than just some sick moves. It will take real skill, and the right plan. We can't just beat him with weapons. He himself cannot be killed, only the host body he is in."

"Yes, I know we have to trap him somehow with that skull. But I'm not sure it'll be so easy."

"It won't be. But I believe we can do it," Chien affirmed as he walked in.

"I have studied our ways and together we can capture this beast as my ancestor did. But if you're going to aid in this mission, you need more training. You and Ravenblade must hold

129

off Legion while I perform the special technique that my ancestor employed to trap Legion the last time. But you are not ready to face him. You need to channel the power from that ring and tap into your spirit and the Spirit of the one true God."

"I know. I want to train more, so I can take on this monster. But how do we get the skull?"

"The skull of Miacha is here in these mountains, protected by my order for centuries. It has the power to transmute objects from one thing into another, as well as other powers. My ancestor used it to meld the very molecules of Legion's soul with the disc itself, trapping him within it. Once the disc was broken so was his connection with it, releasing him. But this time, I will trap Legion in the very skull itself. He will not so easily escape this new prison like he did the other one. We have studied more and more over the ages and learned much about the skull and its great power. I can do this, but only with your help, both of you."

"Well spoken, my son," Chao Cheng said as he entered the room. "Now I believe you should go back to training. I think I might join you myself. Maybe show you a few tricks of my own," the old teacher said with a laugh, and he left with Lyles and Chien.

"They are not ready," Ravenblade said to himself. "They may never be. Legion's power is stronger than ever. I'm not sure anyone could stop him."

***

"Why are we at this place?" Lilith scowled.

"Because there is something here that will tell us where to find the Keepers of the Light — those wretched priests who had trapped me in that disc. They had the skull, and probably still do," the demon responded.

They were at a museum located in Nancheng. Inside this museum were various scrolls written in beautiful Chinese calligraphy. The characters on the scrolls, as well as the images of mountains and waterfalls were breathtaking, but these visitors were not there to admire the artistic quality of these works. Legion meant to read the scrolls and decipher a puzzle that none had been able to solve. He scanned various writings and then stood back. The monster dropped his hands, which began to lengthen. His fingers grew like vines and then more vine-like strands began to grow from throughout his body. Like snakes, they slithered toward the scrolls and touched them, all of them at once. The people in the room began to scream at the sight.

This was surreal. What was this man? The loud cries of the public disturbed Legion's reading. Out of his back grew four more arms and they reached out in all directions grabbing people. He began to snap their necks, tear their limbs from their bodies, and even rip out their hearts. Those who could ran out of the museum. The rest were all mutilated by this beast who had no value for any life other than his own. Once he had scanned all the scrolls, he closed his eyes. Images ran through his head like a puzzle being snapped together. Then at once, he stopped, opened his eyes, and smiled.

"The Qin Mountains — I should have known," he said and all those tentacle-like vines returned to him, disappearing into his skin. He wiped some blood from the side of his face and then licked it off of his hand.

"Daniel's priests hid there after they left Babylon — the Magi who followed the star. Of course! Those fools. How could no one figure it out sooner? It was so plain, so simple. Let's go."

"Go where?" Lilith asked.

"To the Qin Mountains as he said," Simon jumped in. "Can't believe that I didn't see it sooner. If you invert the order of the scrolls, reading them from back to front and take the eighth character of each row, it is as plain as day. They hid it in code so others from their order could find them. Very interesting."

"Well, that's great and all, but where the Hell are the Qin Mountains?" Lilith once again posed a question.

"North of here in Shianxi," Legion replied.

"But how will we get there?" Simon asked.

"Oh, we have ways," Legion replied with a smile.

The villainous crew left the museum just as the police showed up. This was not the USA, and in China the government had absolute power, so as soon as the officers arrived on the scene they began to fire their weapons at the demon and his cohorts. Simon quickly ducked behind a metal barrier in front of the building, which encased some shrubbery. The bullets did little damage to Legion and Lilith who in turn laughed and began to transform themselves. Lilith quickly ripped through her dress, as her wings spread behind her back and her body morphed to its hideous natural state. Right away she flew at the officers ripping their bodies to pieces with her talons. Demonic faces and hands began to push out from Legion's body as he tore off his shirt and slowly approached those who still shot at him. With great swiftness, he attacked his adversaries. He thrust a hand through an officer's throat and another hand through one's chest. He bit the cheek off another and snapped yet another officer's legs like a wishbone. Within moments, the whole place was one big pile of bodies strewn about. Blood poured down the street like a river. Simon just sat still, hiding. His head was between his arms waiting for it to end.

"Some great and powerful wizard," Lilith mocked.

Simon looked up at her. She was back in human form, and because she had ripped off her dress when she transformed, now completely naked. Simon tried not to stare, but found it difficult not to.

"Like what you see, kid," she sassed and winked. "Come on, Legion, let's get out of here. I need to get some new clothes. Preferably some that are not stained in blood."

"If you must," Legion groaned. "You are just going to rip them off again anyway. I don't see why you even bother."

"Still not sure how we are going to get all the way to the Qin Mountains from here," Simon interjected.

"I said we have ways," Legion responded.

As Lilith walked away from them toward the stores across the street, Legion closed his eyes. The demon lifted his hands into the air and began to chant under his breath. A cold wind came in, followed by rolling black clouds, then thunder and lightning. A giant worm-like beast erupted from the ground in front of them. It was covered in slime and seemed to have no eyes. Its mouth was a round hole encircled with five rows of spiny teeth. The creature screeched and squirmed.

"Climb aboard," Legion said.

"Seriously," Simon squealed. "What in Hell is that thing?"

"Stop being a baby, and jump on," Lilith said as she walked past Simon, wearing a new dress that she had stolen from a nearby dress shop

Simon begrudgingly climbed on board with Lilith's help. The worm leaped into the air and crashed through the ground beneath it. Simon held on as tight as he could, and the creature tunneled through the Earth, taking all three of its riders to the Qin Mountains in Shianxi.

***

Jay Sil stood outside The Pain Pit, a roughneck bar connected to an abandoned warehouse out by the Chelsea Piers. He was out of uniform and dressed in blue jeans, a black T-shirt, and his lucky leather jacket. To help keep himself incognito, the officer wore a pair of aviator sunglasses. It was difficult to see with them on at night, but he didn't want to take any chances of being noticed. It felt good to be in civilian clothes, and for what he was about to do, he could not go in as a cop.

He walked away from his black, 1990 Dodge Charger. He had the Dodge since college and it was in need of serious repairs but was perfect for his civilian cover. An informant had leaked that there was an illegal fighting circuit in the warehouse. The locals called the warehouse The Dungeon. The only way inside was through a secret entrance in the attached bar's kitchen, and to get in you needed the right string of passwords. All of which Jay had. It's amazing what criminals would tell you when they are out for revenge.

Apparently, Big Mike, the owner of The Pain Pit Bar, had ratted out some of his old crew so he could get police protection and run his new MMA circuit without worries of being shut down — another reason why Jay could not go in as a cop. The city was corrupt in many ways and this corruption bled into all divisions and departments. But there were still many good cops, and Jay Sil was one of them. He would do whatever it took to shut down the Chaldean's racket and have him thrown behind bars for life.

"Let me see some ID, punk," the giant bouncer at the door demanded. He stood nearly seven feet tall and seemed to almost be as wide.

133

"Guess I still have my baby face," Jay said as he pulled out an ID that read *Peter Chase*.

The goon looked it over, looked back at Jay, and then shoved the ID into Jay's chest.

"Looks okay, but still have to check you for weapons. Turn around and hands up."

Jay complied, trying not to crack any jokes as the bruiser roughly patted him down. Jay almost wanted to ask the guy if he should buy him some flowers or chocolates, but he figured it was more important to get inside, and the comment for sure would make the mountain of a man angry.

"Aight, you're clean. Go in," the bouncer grunted.

With a smile, the undercover cop strolled inside. It was dark and smoky. The crowd looked rough and Jay already noticed some ex-cons that he had put away. He was hoping they didn't recognize him. He kept his shades on and kept his jacket collar flipped up just to be safe. Jay squeezed by a couple of muscleheads who had every inch of their bodies covered in tattoos, most of them gang related, and then made his way toward the kitchen door. He tried not to judge those around him. Many of them were completely clean and there just for a drink and some greasy food.

It's difficult to not judge a book by its cover, and this place had a bad rap. Jay was sure that most of the bar's clientele were either just released or would soon be back in prison. With a stiff push of the door, Officer Sil went into the kitchen. Instantly, everyone turned and looked. Two large men much like the man outside approached the much smaller cop.

"Can we help you with something," the large African-American man said, poking his head down toward Jay's.

The other man, who was Caucasian, stood and stared. They both wore cutoff shirts and black jean shorts. They were covered with tattoos and various body piercings.

"I'm here to see the Dungeon," Jay said.

"The Dungeon? Don't know what you mean?" The white giant said.

Jay stepped back, straightened the collar of his jacket, slicked back his hair, and said, "Mad Dog likes meat."

"What kind of meat?" The African-American colossus asked.

"Bloody," Jay answered.

"Let's see your ID, fool," the white giant said with a huff.

"Sure," Jay said, and he handed it to the white guy.

They looked it over and held a light under it. Then they threw it back to him.

"You're not getting in with that crap," the black man said. "You think we're stupid."

"Maybe a little," Jay said, it was hard to hold it in.

"Why you little piece of—," the black man took a swing at Jay, which he ducked, smashing the man in the gut with a right elbow. The colossal man hunched over and rolled to the ground.

"They told us you were a cop. Couple of guys recognized you. Seriously, the Clark Kent gimmick doesn't work, fool," the white giant said and grabbed Jay, slammed him into the wall, and then threw him into one of the kitchen counters. With Jay Sil incapacitated on the floor, the large man spoke into his phone like a walkie-talkie, "We got him, Boss. What do you want us to do with him?"

"Let him go with a stern warning," a voice said over the device. "I don't want him snooping around here again, but also we don't have time to waste with all the red tape of killing a cop."

The African-American man got back up and picked Jay Sil off the floor.

"I'll take care of this guy," he said.

"The boss said not to kill him," the other man said.

"I know, but gotta give him some payback for what he did. Stupid, punk," the brute said and threw Jay Sil out the kitchen door. All eyes were on the young cop as he was dragged to the front door and then outside.

"So you want to get smart with me," the ogre said and slammed Jay into the pavement, followed by a couple of boots to the gut.

Unbeknownst to either man, they were being filmed by channel Thirteen's hottest on-scene reporter, Judy Ramirez. She too had received some info about the secret MMA club in the abandoned warehouse and could not find a way in, but had been reporting from the outside, waiting to catch some footage that could bring the place down. While filming the fight across the street, the reporter recognized the cop when Jay's glasses were knocked off, and she instantly revealed his identity over the air.

"Yes, that is Officer Jay Sil of the NYPD, being thrown out and beaten to a pulp, by one of the Pain Pit's thugs. You might remember Officer Sil from the tragic events that took place a few years back in Central Park. The case was never solved. Seems like he is at it again, and still with poor results. Maybe we need some tougher cops on the squad. Cops who can actually solve a case, and not just take a beating."

Of course, some of that resentment was from when the young officer had arrested Ramirez after she flashed him and ran away, while breaking and entering into the building where Radix had killed John Russell. The large man laughed and went to stomp the officer one more time, but Jay Sil had enough and grabbed the man's foot. He twisted it at the ankle and sent the large man crashing onto his back. Getting up from the ground, Jay dusted himself off and ran to his car as the bouncer and three other men began to run toward him. Luckily, the old car started without any problems, and Jay sped off toward his apartment, ready for a shower and some sleep. That proved to be not only unproductive, but soon the officer would find out that he would suffer worse the next day, after the Chief was informed of the news footage.

"What heinous crimes are going on inside the Pain Pit that they are now sending undercover cops to investigate? Is the story of a deadly MMA circuit true? Criminals fighting for their very lives, for protection, for drugs? Will we ever truly know? This reporter will find out one way or another, even if I have to go in there myself." Judy paused then concluded, "This is Judy Ramirez signing off."

"Sorry about that, had to throw out some trash," Big Mike said as he walked back over to his table.

He had walked away when he got the call from his men in the kitchen about Jay Sil. He was in the middle of negotiations with another big time player in the Big Apple. His guest wore a tailored three-piece suit and sat back casually in his chair, hidden by the shadows. The dim lighting reflected off of his bald head from time to time. His piercing eyes stared into Mike's and his teeth glowed bright in the dark room.

"So then, do we have an agreement?" the mystery man asked.

"Sure. Your guys can compete — winner takes all," Mike replied. "Hope they're good. My guys are ruthless and have nothing to live for other than winning. They've been in and out of the toughest prisons around the world. It's gonna take some real guts to beat 'em."

"Oh, my guys have plenty of guts, and have no problem spilling some either," the mystery man said.

"So, I can bill them, what do you call your team? And I'll need their names."

"They don't have names, only numbers, and they are called the Children of the Dragon."

Mike paused and tried not to look worried, but he was. He had heard that this group was resurfacing and that they were into all types of dark and sinful magic. He was by no means clean himself, but what this group represented was pure evil, and it scared even him.

***

"This is pure evil," Kimberly said as she shoved another piece of double chocolate cake into her mouth.

"Hey, you're eating for two," Martha said with a smile.

The pair of friends was sitting in a diner not too far from Kimberly's apartment. Martha wanted to be there for the newly expecting mother, especially since Lyles was off fighting another holy war. The slightly older woman remembered how it was raising Rashan alone without a man, and even though Lyles was nothing like Rashan's father, he still was not there. Kimberly needed support, and Martha was happy to give her as much as she needed. Every day after working at the nursing home in Hell's Kitchen, Martha would come by Kimberly's place and check in on her. They were just finishing coffee and cake at the diner, when Kimberly reached into her bag to pay.

"Oh, dear, I got this," Martha said.

"No, I got it," Kimberly insisted.

But Martha beat her to the punch and handed a twenty-dollar bill to the waitress before Kimberly could open her wallet.

"Gotta be faster than that," Martha said with a wink.

After the waitress brought Martha her change and she left a small tip, the ladies got up and began to head out.

"I was wondering if you wanted to join me for a Bible study at my place on Thursday night?" Martha asked, while she walked Kimberly back to her apartment. "I think it would be good for you to have some spiritual support right now."

"Not sure," Kimberly said. "I love going to church and I know Lyles has been really into his faith and studying the Word, especially at seminary. But I never really did a Bible study before, and I'm not sure how to explain my situation to a whole new group of people."

"You don't need to explain a thing. Just show up. I can even lend you a Bible if you need one."

"No, we have plenty," she laughed, thinking of Lyle's large stack of them at the apartment. "How long have you been doing this?"

"I hadn't in years, but then when I started working at the nursing home two years ago, I bumped into an old friend who was visiting someone he knew. He asked me how I had been. I told him about Rashan and how I was alone. He thought it would be good if I joined his Bible study group — it would help me get back on track with the Lord. I met him a few years back at a Bible study that Reverend Reynolds used to host out of his apartment. It was before I had Rashan, when I was just out of high school. I went strong with the group for a few years, hoping God could help me get past all my mistakes, and I had made a lot of them. But I fell off the wagon once Rashan came along."

"So, tell me more about this guy? What does he do? Seems like more than just Bible study, if you ask me," Kimberly said with a wink.

"Oh, nothing is going on there," Martha laughed. "He is a bit older than me, like ten years, and a doctor. But a doctor of what, I'm not sure," she laughed harder, and Kimberly joined in.

"Wow, an older man and a doctor — sounds juicy to me," Kimberly winked again.

"Oh, you stop that now," Martha said and gave Kimberly a soft push. "What do you say? Will you come on Thursday?"

"I just might. I want to meet this doctor friend of yours," Kimberly nudged her friend, and the two continued walking.

***

Chao Cheng and his priests knelt on mats that were laid out in a circle inside the temple where Bianca had shown them the way to Christ. They had taken a giant spiritual leap, and were now ready to give their lives and souls to the One who gave them salvation. Lyles stood in the center of the circle with a basin of water. He did not have a pool to submerge them in but this would do just fine. In Lyles' eyes, baptism was not about the form of the ritual but about the change in the hearts of the baptized. Knowing their Savior in a special way, giving them a true connection to God. It was about the relationship not the religion. Lyles opened with a prayer and then shared some Scripture about baptism, including Christ's own baptism in the Jordan by His cousin, John.

As he spoke, Bianca ran to Lyles. Esmeralda ran after her and grabbed her hand. She tried to get her daughter to walk back to where they had been standing, but the girl would not move.

"I want to get baptized," Bianca said.

"But honey, you already were when you were a baby," Esmeralda responded, before Lyles could say anything.

"But, Mommy, I want to do it again. I want it to be my choice," Bianca stated and looked at her mother with the sweetest stare.

"Let the girl do it," Chao Cheng said. "She knows her Lord in her heart. Let her do this as sign for her love for Him."

"I think he's right," Lyles said. "Let her do it, Ezzie."

"Okay," the young mother said, and then gave her daughter a hug.

"You can do it if it means that much to you," Esmeralda said to Bianca.

"So young, yet such wisdom," Chao Cheng said. "She is remarkable."

Lyles walked Bianca over to the basin of water. He had her kneel in front of it and then bend over so her head was over the water. He took a bowl and scooped up some water.

"I baptize you in the name of the Father, and of the Son, and of the Holy Spirit," Lyles said as he poured the water on the child's head.

One by one, starting with Chao Cheng, the great teacher of this order, all the priests were baptized in a like manner. It was a wonderful ceremony, and a great celebration followed. But while their hearts were filled with joy, a great evil was on its way. Legion was coming, and he was ready to destroy anyone who stood in his way.

***

"The Chief wants to see you," Detective Rogers said to Jay Sil, as the officer was making his way to his desk.

"What about?" the young cop shot back.

"Didn't you see the news?" the detective asked. "And the papers? You are so stupid. I told the Chief to watch out for young guns like you. You think you can do whatever you want!"

"I really don't want any of your crap today. Seriously. And I was just trying to be a cop. Serve and protect — that's what we do. When someone is doing something wrong, we try to stop them. I thought you had a set, but it seems you're a puppet like all the rest."

"Why you little—" Detective Rogers yelled.

"Sil, get in here, now!" the Chief exclaimed from his office.

"Coming," Jay Sil screamed back.

Closing the door behind him, Jay took a seat across from the Chief's desk. The office was cluttered with files. Awards and medals hung from the wall, all achievements in this man's life. A picture of his wife and daughter sat on his desk. The Chief was African-American from Brooklyn, born from a hard-working family. This city was his home and he had vowed to keep it safe and clean. He was a little above average in height and a little overweight, but his arms and chest still had good definition. Chief Arnold Freemont Jackson was a good man, but his temper could be short, especially when a young officer like Jay Sil was off playing vigilante in his streets.

"Good, make yourself comfortable now, because you won't be after you hear what I'm about to say," the Chief remarked. He leaned hard on his desk with both hands, "What the Hell were you thinking? Actually, I don't think you were thinking — at all!"

"Let me explain," Jay tried to cut in.

"No, let me explain. You were all over the news thanks to the footage that Judy Ramirez got while you were making a fool of yourself. No warrant, no probable cause, nothing. You just walk into the place, undercover mind you, and try to do … what? You made fool of yourself *and* the department."

"There's an illegal MMA circuit being run in the warehouse. People are dying, criminals are being housed there, and I'm sure there're tons of drugs being pushed back there as well. It needs to be stamped out!"

"Then you need to take protocol and do it right. And how do you know any of this anyway?"

"I have sources. People who have an inside on this place."

"Well, you should have come to me first. The Commissioner is all over this, and I hate to do this because you're a good cop, but he wants you suspended for three months without pay."

"But…"

"But nothing! Another peep and I'll make it six months. Now, give me your badge and your gun, and get the Hell out of here."

Begrudgingly, Jay Sil handed over both and walked out of the Chief's office, slamming the door behind him.

"What a load of bull," he said as he walked to his desk to grab some things.

Detective Rogers gave him a stern look.

"Whatever. Keep your crap to yourself. If you were a good cop you'd understand what I did and why. That place is bad news and I'm sure there's more to it than just some stupid fight club."

The detective kept his stern face, but in his mind he thought hard about the officer's comments. Rogers was a great cop once, and he did believe in justice. Maybe he would look into this case further.

The young gun might be right about this after all, Rogers thought to himself.

***

"Why have you called us here?" Raphael asked Michael.

The seven who stand before the presence of the Lord were standing in that exact place because Michael the Archangel had summoned them there.

"We all know that Legion has been released onto the Earth, and now he poses to regain his former power and possibly destroy all of creation. The Earth, God's chosen planet for mortal life to dwell, has been in jeopardy since creation. Satan's initial attacks led to the Fall of the first man and woman, and then to the populating of the other planets with the fallen seed of Adam and Eve. We all know what this brought into motion, and what was finally accomplished with the death and resurrection of our very own Creator, the man Jesus Christ. But we also know that even before Satan fell like lightning from heaven, he was corrupted by the Darkness — that dark spirit that is the personification of evil. Legion is the offspring of that very Darkness through our former brother Samyaza. His power is rooted in the evil Abyss that bred sin. A dark day is coming and we need to arm ourselves. I know it is our duty to only interfere when we are instructed, but I have been thinking about this conflict, and this war is beyond man. It always has been. It is our war and we must fight it."

"Are you proposing that we just go down to Earth and take out Legion ourselves without orders from the Almighty?" Uriel queried. "This is not our fight."

"How do we know that He doesn't want us to make this our fight? It is a battle against evil, the truest evil ever known. If the Darkness is released onto the Earth then the Armageddon — the final battle — will ensue, and the fight will truly be ours. Not to mention the girl, Bianca, she is special. We all know this, and she is wearing my pendant. I am sworn to protect her, and protect her I will. I already let one of those children get lost. I will not lose another."

"So this is about the boy again, and how you failed to protect him," Azrael stabbed.

"Believe what you like, but I will do my duty and protect the girl and those with her, and with them the whole Earth and all creation. Who is with me?" shouted the mighty Archangel.

"No one is with you," Azrael said. "This is not your fight to take up."

"And the battle against Radix was yours?" Michael retorted. "Did you not bring those men to Central Park to stop him? And don't think that I don't know that you were involved in getting Nathaniel into Hell. You and Raphael had no problem doing that and possibly damning that man's soul. You all have done things outside of your jurisdiction and maybe rightly so. I cannot stand by and let Legion destroy the entire mortal plane!"

"Do as you please — you always do," Azrael said. "Yes, I did those things you mentioned. I already asked the Lord for forgiveness and so did Raphael. We did not mean any treachery, but something needed to be done. Putting people in situations to do what is righteous is not the same thing as going to Earth and fighting. My weapon is only drawn when the Lord commands it. But you draw your sword whenever you please!"

"You are being ridiculous!" Michael shouted back. "I only draw my sword against evil! I am not drawing it against innocent men! Legion is the most corrupt demon to ever walk the Earth."

"But men have stopped him before," Azrael said.

"After his body was killed by the one with no name, Legion wasn't the same," Michael said. "His power was subdued. But now he may regain his full power unless we stop him."

"Enough!" Metatron boomed. "Why don't you ask the Father? Does He not hear all of this and already know what should be done? You are fighting like men when you are two of the highest ranking angels in the Lord's company. His will is for you to do what is right and good as He is good — what is holy unto the Lord. You all know this. So do that. If it means protecting those in your trust, then do so; and if it means protecting the world from the Darkness, then fine. As for me, I will not join you. The fight is not mine. My day has not come, but when it does the world will know and so will all evil. For when I come, it is only with the Lord Himself, and nothing can and will stand against His might."

"Fine," Michael said. "I will do this alone," and he left.

CHAPTER IX
ENTER LEGION

The ground rumbled and quaked. From beneath the dirt road burst the monstrous worm creature with Legion, Lilith, and Simon Magus III still clinging to its back. It stopped before the vast mountain range and the three passengers slid off. Simon rolled onto his belly and vomited. The ride had made him quite nauseous, not to mention the horrid stench of the beast he had ridden. He pulled himself up and looked at the mountains. They were breathtaking. But how would they find exactly where in this range of peaks the skull was being hidden?

"So, what do we do now?" Simon asked as he stood up.

"I don't know, magic man," Lilith addressed Simon. "Why don't *you* do something? The whole time we've had you, I haven't seen you do one trick. I thought you were the descendent of Simon Magus, High Sorcerer. I knew him well," she licked her lips and snickered and placed her hand on his chest. "He could do some tricks. Cast a location spell. Or how about calling on a spirit to guide us."

"That's enough!" Legion boomed. "The boy is obviously a novice. He has no power. Not without the skull. I, on the other hand, even in my weakened state can find the way for us, but I need silence. I am listening to the mountains. They speak as all things do. Just like the winds and the seas. All of nature tells stories, for it is all alive, energy formed into objects. With focus, one can do what seems impossible." He paused. "It is just over there."

"What is over there?" Lilith asked.

"The entrance, of course," the demon answered.

"I don't see anything," Simon interjected.

"Look with your soul not your eyes, mortal. Never mind. Trying to explain to a peon like you is a waste of my time."

The small group walked up to the mountain before them, and then Legion stood still again.

"I don't see a door," said Simon.

"It would not be so obvious, you dimwit," Lilith scolded. "Maybe the rocks slide open with a magic word? Do you at least know one we can try?"

"Abra-cada-bra," he recited, but it did nothing. "Open sesame!"

"Real funny, maybe I can use your head to knock the wall down," the succubus replied.

"Let me show you how it is done," Legion said and walked past his two companions toward a rock.

With Simon and Lilith watching, the villainous monster stopped. His eyes turned black like two onyx stones in his skull. Mouths began to grow from the sides of his face, and they chanted a strange, unknown language. Then his hands began to morph and mold together and started to grow long and straight with a pointed tip, like a sword. He slid the tip into a hole on top of the rock and then turned it clockwise. All at once a door began to open in the side of the mountain. Simon Magus III looked on in awe, and this was only a portion of this demon's might. Simon wondered what it would be like to have such power. He would surpass all of his descendants, including the man who made his own name infamous — Simon Magus, the first. The ground began to rumble again. Legion stood with his arms crossed, and Lilith with her hands on her hips. Their army was approaching. Just then, from puffs of smokeless fire, thousands upon thousands of hungry, thirsty Djinn appeared before them. It was time to storm the sanctuary of the Keepers of the Light, and take the skull of Miacha. Once Legion had that skull, then his body would be restored and the destruction of the world and all of creation would soon follow. Legion went to enter the doorway, but he could not pass through. Lilith could not either, nor could any of the Djinn. The only one who could enter, then, was Simon.

"There's a magical barrier on this place," Legion said. "No evil can enter. I would ask our magician to perform a counterspell. But he is useless. Once you get that skull, you better be able to use it to transform me, boy. My patience with you runs thin. Luckily for us, though, I can break this spell, for my power is greater than those who cast it on the mountain." The mouths on Legion's cheeks chanted again, as did his own mouth. He stopped and it seemed like nothing happened. The extra mouths disappeared from his face. He turned and said, "Let's go."

Miraculously, Legion and his evil horde were able to walk right in. The mountain sanctuary was now breached. Legion had come for the skull, and the priests and their visitors were not ready to face him.

***

"What is wrong, Lyles," Chien asked.

"It's the ring. I can feel something. I can't explain it, but something evil is here and it is getting closer."

Chien opened his eyes and stood up. He and Lyles had been meditating in the training room, preparing for their imminent battle with Legion. What they did not know was that the battle had been brought to them. Legion had invaded their fortress and was rapidly approaching. Lyles stood up, too, and felt the ring. The sensation he had was increasing with every second, causing his heart to race. The time for action was now, and both he and Chien went to grab their swords. One of the priests ran in screaming in Mandarin.

"Mogwai," Chien stated.

"Mogwai?" Lyles repeated. "Like in the movie?"

"Not sure what you mean," Chien said. "Mogwai is a demon, an evil spirit."

"Djinn!" Ravenblade exclaimed as he walked in to warn his comrades. "I can smell their vile stench."

"That must be what I'm feeling," Lyle explained.

"Yes, the ring," the immortal said. "You can control them with the ring. Let's hurry. I fear they are working with Legion. It's time for battle. If Legion is with them, we may all be doomed. I have battled him before. His power is vast, though now slightly contained. But still far greater than anything either of you have seen. Radix was nothing compared to this demon of demons."

"I need to get to Esmeralda and Bianca. We need to protect them!" Lyles exclaimed.

"There is no time. You can't get clouded with emotion. You need to fight," Ravenblade explained.

"I am not clouded with emotion. They are my family. I love them, and I won't let them die!" Lyles shouted.

"I'll hide them. I know this mountain and its secret places better than you," Chien said with a hand on Lyles shoulder.

"Focus on the battle. When they are safe, I will get the skull so we can trap that monster. We will do this. I know we can."

Lyles placed his hand on Chien's shoulder too. His friend was right. The two stood together silently for a moment and then Chien took off.

"Focus, Lyles," the immortal said. "You need to use the ring to control the Djinn. If Legion is here, you can have them attack him. We might be able to hold him off until Chien can perform the spell to trap him in the skull. It's time to fight!"

Lyles paused one more time to pray. He could not rely on the ring or his sword, or even that of Ravenblade, the mysterious immortal. Only God could help him win, if truly that was His will. The man prayed for safety in battle, to live to see his wife again, but most importantly to vanquish this vile creature from the Earth and stop the destruction that the monster planned to cause. It was time to battle, indeed, and Lyles went out to fight filled with the Spirit, not knowing if he would come back alive.

**

Screams could be heard throughout the corridors and halls of the vast mountain community. The priests yelled in pain as their flesh was being ripped from their very bodies by the Djinn that swarmed their home. Chien held back tears and anger, for these would distract him. He needed to find the woman and her daughter and make sure they were safe, as he had promised. He prayed that they were in their chambers, where they had been staying while guests at this secret sanctuary. The demons were everywhere, and blood ran thick all around. With sword in hand, the priest slashed at all enemies that came forth, and in a matter of moments, he was where he hoped to find Esmeralda and Bianca. The mother and daughter were indeed there. Esmeralda was crying, holding Bianca close to her. The Djinn had made it there as well, and Chien fought them off to protect his guests.

"You must follow me," he said. "I will take you to a place where you will be safe. They will not find you there. But we need to hurry."

Without words, and with her precious child held tightly against her chest, Esmeralda followed the man. Her heart prayed every step of the way as more and more hungry Djinn came out to attack and were cut back by Chien's blade. There were thousands of these creatures and even though they were sliced over and over, they did not die. They did not even bleed. These desert demons were an anomaly. Creatures made of smokeless fire in the desert by Iblis, who had fallen from grace all those millennia ago when he refused to bow before God's creation. Djinn had no hearts, no spiritual center. The only known way to kill a Djinni was to cut off its head, but they would need to remain solid long enough to do that. Even though Chien was slicing at their throats, these demons would become intangible just in time to not die and they kept on attacking. They were nearly unstoppable and the perfect army for Legion.

***

Legion, Lilith, and Simon had reached the center of the mountain. They looked at the stairway that went all the way up to the peak and all the corridors that it led to. Legion knew the skull was at the top of the mountain, guarded by the priests.

"So, where to now?" Simon asked.

"We go to the top," Legion replied.

"Are we going to walk up all those stairs?" the man questioned.

"No fool, we have faster ways than that," Legion answered.

Lilith sprouted her wings from her back, ripping through her dress but not completely stripping it from her body. She grabbed Simon around the waist and then took off into the air. Legion planted his feet and his legs grew at a rapid rate, taking him to the top. Lilith dropped Simon onto the ground as they reached the highest level. Legion joined them shortly.

Simon dusted himself off and stood up. They could hear the screams of the men who were being torn apart by their army of Djinn. It was all going according to plan — or so Legion thought.

"You boys go on ahead, I have another matter to attend to," Lilith said.

"And what would that be?" Legion asked.

"There is something else I need from this place. I can smell it in the air," she responded. "I won't be long, and trust me, what I seek will be very helpful."

"Do as you wish, wench. I don't need your help; my power is enough to take down these stupid men," Legion boasted.

"Good then," Lilith said and flew off.

***

"Stop!" Lyles shouted.

He and Ravenblade had been fending off hordes of beasts as they made their way to find Legion. But Lyles could wait no longer. Seeing all those that had already suffered and died filled his heart with pain. The command that he had shouted filled the ears of all the Djinn in the entire mountain refuge, and they did indeed stop. He looked around and held out the ring to sense where Legion was. He was not far away. With swords ready and the Djinn army under Lyles command, they charged toward their enemy ready to take him down.

***

"Where is the skull," Simon asked as he entered Chao Cheng's quarters.

"I do not know what you mean," the master replied without turning around.

"Let me be more clear," Simon said. His hand glowed and caused a vase to fly across the room and smash against the wall.

"Do you think you are a threat to me, young man," Chao Cheng spoke and stood up.

He turned and looked Simon in the eyes. The young sorcerer started to make objects float all around to try and frighten the man before him. But it did not work. The old teacher was wise, and knew this magician had no real power — just tricks.

"You will not find what you seek here," he said.

"Don't lie to me!" Simon screamed. "I will have the skull, or I will kill you!"

A sword flew from the wall right at Chao Cheng's head. In a swift motion, the master spun around, dodged the blade, and grabbed the hilt with his hand. It was an ancient blade, handed down for generations. It was not for war but merely for ceremony. The design was that of ancient China. The teacher held the sword out. Today for the first time, it would taste blood.

"Enough!" a voice boomed.

A man seemingly floated into the room. His skin began to convulse and things moved beneath it, like prisoners trying to break out from his flesh. His forehead opened up, a gaping demonic mouth formed over his brow. Arms grew from his back. Legion had come to take what he desired.

"Never send a boy to do a man's job," the demon said. He put out his hand, which stretched out with great speed and grabbed the throat of Chao Cheng.

The teacher would not lie down so easy, and in one swift motion he sliced off the hand that grasped his neck. The severed arm writhed like a serpent whose head was cut off. Then two more hands shot out. One grabbed Chao Cheng's hand that held the sword and broke it, causing him to drop the blade. The other grabbed him by the throat again, and Legion glided toward him, the arm getting shorter as he grew closer.

"Where is the skull?" the demon asked in a voice that sounded as if thousands were speaking at once."

"I will not give you anything, Legion," the master spoke with a calm voice.

"So you know of me?"

"My people have battled you before. They trapped you in that disc. We will trap you again."

"Ambitious, aren't you?" Legion said. "You will do nothing but die. But before you do, I will get the information I need."

"I will tell you nothing," Chao Cheng vowed.

"You don't have to tell me anything; your mind will reveal the location."

From the hand that held the old man's throat grew worm-like strands that began to move around Chao Cheng's face. They entered his nostrils, and ear canals, and his mouth, moving inside until they reached his brain.

Lyles and Ravenblade burst into Chao Cheng's quarters to find the great teacher being overcome by Legion. Without a second thought, Lyles ordered the Djinn to now attack the very fiend who had led them here. And they did.

Legion was caught off guard. How was his own army attacking him? Then he saw it. The Ring of Solomon, of course. But the demonic monster would not let go of his target. He needed that information. The horde of Djinn was all over him, biting and slashing. Thousands of them attacked him at once. He fought back with all his might, and still held onto Chao Cheng. Lyles ran across the room and sliced off the hand that held the great teacher. The worm-like tentacles retreated from his face and the hand released its hold from the old man's throat. The master lay on the floor, barely breathing.

"He knows where it is, the skull," he said with his last breath.

"What? How?" Lyles asked, holding the old man, trying to revive him. "No, Chao Cheng, no! No!"

The old master was dead, and Lyles grew with a holy anger at the fiend who dealt this wicked blow. The air around Lyles began to crackle. His body charged up, shaking with intense energy. He had seen his friend Nathan go through this before. Now it was time that a new hero emerged. He called on a power, a fury that was righteous and holy. Lyles had achieved Chaos Fury, and he would take Legion down. Ravenblade stood back and watched, pleased by what he saw. He did not grieve for the death of Chao Cheng, for death was part of life. But he did find joy in the fact that the tables were turned in this battle and that now Lyles could put up a real fight against the enemy at hand. Simon Magus III had fear in his eyes. He cowered in the corner of the room. All these before him had great power. But he still had none, without the skull.

***

"It's this way," Chien said to Esmeralda, who was still carrying Bianca in her arms.

While the mother's heart was racing, the little girl was completely calm. She was not even the slightest bit afraid. Bianca had true faith, and she knew that her Daddy up in Heaven was watching and protecting her. The three of them came to a set of five corridors. Chien had them follow him down the second one from the right.

"There is a secret room hidden in the very walls. You will be safe there. It is just at the end of this—." He stopped.

Standing right in front of them was Lilith. She threw a seductive smile at Chien, who gave no reaction.

"You're not any fun, are you, priest?" she stated. "Give me the girl, and I'll make your death quick, unless you prefer to make it long and messy. I like it long and messy."

"Stand back, demoness. You will not have the girl. I know who you are, Devil's bride."

"Glad you know who I am. It'll speed up all of this. I'm not here to play games. It's all or nothing, priest. Let's see how you like my true form," Lilith said and began to transform.

Lilith was a monster now, a creature of the night that devoured men whole. Chien was ready for her, though. The succubus lunged at the Magus, who dodged and attacked with his blade. She came at him again, and he blocked her with his sword, stopping her knife-like talons from slashing his throat. Esmeralda and Bianca were up against the wall. The mother did not know what to do. She couldn't fight; she didn't know how. But she needed to protect her daughter. Bianca held her tighter, and gave her a kiss on the forehead. At that moment, the pendant that she wore around her neck began to glow and a wind blew by them. Chien was trying his best to fend off the creature before him, but her power was great. Then, in a sudden flash, Lilith was sent crashing into the far end of the corridor. Chien looked to see what had happened, and before him stood an angel of light, and not just any angel. It was Michael, the Archangel.

He looked magnificent in his heavenly armor and with his ornate wings — more beautiful than anything Chien had ever seen. The angel had his sword drawn, and it glowed with white fire. Bianca looked up, too, knowing that her guardian had arrived. He was even more spectacular than she imagined. Her Uncle Lyles had told her that he would come when she was in danger, as long as she wore that pendant, and he had done exactly that. Esmeralda shed a tear, this time of joy, for with the angel here at their side she felt safe.

But the battle was not yet over. It had only begun, and just as swiftly as she was thrown into the back wall, Lilith was back and she dug her claws into Michael's chest. Chien knew that the angel was better suited to fight this succubus than he, so he ran to Esmeralda and led her and Bianca to the secret room down the corridor while Lilith was distracted. Chien groped along the wall until he found the right stone, and with a simple push and a turn, a door opened out of the wall.

"Wait here," he said to them. "I will come back for you later, when this is all over. You will be safe in here. They will not be able to find you, for no one knows where this room is and the walls are very strong. Do not be afraid; we will win."

Esmeralda listened even though she was afraid, and held her daughter tight as the door closed. Chien readied his sword and ran back to the battle.

***

Thousands of Djinn were tearing at Legion, keeping him down. Lyles had finished powering up and rushed toward the pile of hungry demons. He held his sword above his head, ready to strike through the crowd and pierce through Legion's heart. Before he could do so, the fiend exploded from the pile that was on top of him and knocked Lyles back with a blow to his gut. The vicious horde began to pile onto Legion again. He grew a slew of arms that grabbed the demons and threw them about. He lashed out at them and decapitated some of them, ending their lives.

When Djinn died, they did not go to the second death. They did not have souls. These desert demons just ceased to exist, their smokeless fire fading away forever. Even while he fought the Djinn that were on top of him, Legion was able to grasp Lyles by the wrist of his right hand, and he pulled the Ring of Solomon off of his finger.

"The ring it is mine!" Legion yelled and held the ring up high.

But the moment did not last, for Ravenblade quickly hacked off the arm that held up the ring, causing it to roll to the ground. Simon tried to crawl and retrieve ring, but it was kicked around by the mob of confused and angry Djinn that filled the room. Without wasting any time, Ravenblade went straight to Legion, and attacked him with his blade. The cretin seemed to be on the ropes.

"I will not die so easily, fool!" Legion shouted.

The hungry Djinn, now following Legion once again, went straight for the immortal. On the ground, Lyles began to regain his feet, and instantly he ran into battle. He would not let anyone else fall at Legion's hands. He was determined to end this battle victoriously. Outside the quarters, some of the Djinn were battling the priests again. This was the first time in their history that they had ever battled in these halls. Many of these men had never used their swords outside of training. Supernatural threats had not been as prevalent in their lives as in times past. Many of these men were being slain, left and right. But some held their own and fought back the demons that attacked them.

No matter how hard they fought, the monsters kept coming. As one priest was about to be slashed by one of these vile creatures, another Djinni flew out and tackled it to the ground. This was odd, and the man was confused. This little demon scurried along, attacking all of its own brothers at each chance it got, heading directly to the location of the great teacher, Chao Cheng.

Inside those very quarters, Lyles and Ravenblade were being overcome by the Djinn. So much so, that Legion slipped away. Simon finally saw his chance and grabbed the ring on the floor. He slipped it on his finger and felt the power that it held.

"Get up, you fool," Legion said to him. "It is time to get the skull."

"Where is it?" the sorcerer asked.

"See for yourself," Legion said, and put his hand over Simon's face, giving the magician an image in his mind of where the skull was.

The rogue Djinni that had been charging its way through its own kindred, finally came to its intended destination, and without warning attacked Legion by chomping off a piece of his shoulder. He was surprised to be attacked by one of these, especially when the heroes no longer had the ring. The Djinni turned around and attacked again. Legion was furious and grabbed the beast, bringing it to his face.

"What are you doing?" He asked the creature.

"Saving my friends, I am," it said.

"You are supposed to obey me, as your master Iblis commanded you!"

"Serve Iblis, I do not. But God and my friends I do."

"You foolish imp. I will fill you with salt until you are no more. You Djinn think you cannot die so easily. There is another way to kill your kind other than removing your heads. You all fear salt for a reason. Too much of it and you become salt yourselves."

"No, you won't!" Lyles screamed and slashed Legion up his back, forcing him to drop the Djinni that he held.

"That is my friend, and I will not let you kill him, or anyone!"

Lyles had recognized his friend Puck when he saw the creature attack Legion. He was not sure how he had arrived there, but he was happy to see his friend. Ravenblade was still holding off the rest of the Djinn. But there were too many for the immortal to fight. The battle seemed hopeless, and Legion joined again. But this time he intended to kill them all.

***

Simon slipped through the halls, happy that the Djinn army was distracting all the priests. The image that Legion had given him was like a map. It showed him everywhere to turn and where to go. And now he entered the main temple, the same place where Bianca had taught the priests, and the same place where they were baptized. It was here that they hid the skull. In the center of the room was a circle with markings on it. Simon could not read the markings, but they were Hebrew characters. The image in his mind showed him to touch certain ones in order, which he did, and they lit up. What he did not know was that the characters he chose spelled YHWH, the name of God.

The whole circle was lighted up and it began to spin and, as it spun, it sank into the ground about three feet. Simon stepped into the hole and saw that there was a cabinet built into the side. There were more characters there and he touched them in the order he was shown.

This time, unknown to him, he spelled the Hebrew word for salvation — Yeshua. The cabinet opened and before him was the skull. It was about eight inches tall, and the detail was exquisite and intricate. The teeth, the eye sockets, even the cranial plates were all very realistic, almost as if it were a man's skull that had somehow shrunk and crystalized. It was magnificent.

Now with the skull and the ring, Simon's power would even surpass that of his ancestors and possibly anyone who ever lived on this Earth. It was time for Simon Magus III to no longer be a hack magician doing shows in Dongguan, China. But rather, he would be Simon Magus III, High Sorcerer, just like his ancestor.

***

Lower in the mountain sanctuary, Michael and Chien battled Lilith. The priest was not offering much help as the angel seemed to be able to handle the succubus himself. A stampeding sound was heard in the distance, getting closer and closer. Chien turned and prepared himself for whatever it was that approached them. From the shadows sprang a horde of Djinn — hundreds of them. With sword ready, Chien charged, and slashed his way through the approaching army. Michael and Lilith were busy going blow for blow in the tight corridor. Neither could fly because of the low ceiling and tight space, so the battle was being fought on the ground. Michael was distracted by the sound of the Djinn behind him; they were approaching quickly for Chien could not fight all of them. Seeing this opportunity, Lilith jabbed the Archangel in the side with her claws and kicked him into one of the walls. Hundreds of hungry and ferocious Djinn jumped onto the angel and began to tear at him. Now, she had her chance, and Lilith slipped away to find the girl.

***

Outside the mountain range, the sun was beginning to set. The battle within its walls was one for the ages, and the bloodthirsty Djinn ruled the corridors of this sanctuary. From the sky above, large vehicles began to appear, like jets but with turbines built into the wings that could move in various directions, giving each craft the ability to fly in all directions, including straight up and down. This also gave them the ability to hover like a helicopter in the air. Three of these crafts flew right over the mountain range and landed outside the entrance to the Temple of Luminescence. The airships were not very large, about the size of small commercial jets. All three opened their hatches on the back and from them came a total of fifty soldiers dressed in dark green and black armored uniforms. These were state-of-the-art armored body suits that were super-lightweight and flexible, offering full range of motion to those wearing them. On their heads, the soldiers had dark green helmets with black tinted visors. They held large guns that looked more like those you would find in a sci-fi movie than in real life.

The soldiers moved toward the open passage in the side of the mountain. Holding their weapons in front of them, they squatted as they walked. A light on each of their helmets helped them find their way.

As they drew deeper into the mountain hideaway, the ground began to rumble and they could hear a low growling sound, like some sort of animals were approaching them. There was no fear in these men. They were trained for war against the supernatural, and that is why they were here.

These soldiers reported to the Council of His Holy Order, a secret society in the Catholic Church, referred to by most as just the Council. Only certain people knew of their existence, all of whom were involved in the same holy war against Satan and his minions. These people had heard that Legion had resurfaced and that Lyles had gone to fight, along with a member of the Keepers of the Light. They had known of this order for some time and of their secret mountain sanctuary. It took the Council some time to decipher the exact location, but now they had found it, and were ready to help in any way they could. They knew that if they could find this place so could Legion, for they also knew that he would be looking for the skull, which was hidden in its walls.

There were not many things that went under the radar of the Council. They needed to have as much information of this world in order to do battle against the one who supposedly ruled it — Satan. But the soldiers on the ground did not have all this information. They only knew that they were going into battle and that they were to destroy anything unholy at all costs. A multitude of Djinn came pouring down the hall, running toward the band of soldiers. The men knew what they were fighting, for the screens on their visors told them. As the beasts came at them, the soldiers blasted shots from their weapons. The ammunition they were using was highly dense salt capsules, which entered into the blood stream of the Djinn and turned each of them into a pile of salt. With shot after shot, the soldiers made quick work of the beasts. Some of the creatures saw what happened and began to retreat. These demons loathed salt, and now they saw that it could kill them, making their hatred for it worse.

Eventually, the company of soldiers made it to the center of the mountain, and they looked up to see the levels above them. Each man grabbed a grappling device from his side and shot a rope to the top. There was a spike at the end of each rope that went straight through the rock walls of the mountain, and then released a ring of smaller spikes around it to keep it in place. The men tugged on their ropes to make sure they were secure, and then they clipped the devices to their belts and were pulled up to the top level. Once there, they pulled themselves over the ledge and onto the ground. They each unclipped the device, pressed a button, and the spike retracted back in. Weapons were readied again and the troops moved forward.

More floods of those nasty Djinn met them as they made their way to Legion's location, and as simply as before they turned each and every one of those vermin into a pile of salt. Those wise enough to run did so. The visors that the Council provided the soldiers were equipped with GPS tracking and could home in on demonic energy. Knowing that Legion would be there, they chose the largest energy that they had detected and followed that straight to its source. Lyles, Ravenblade, and Puck were not faring well against Legion nor the Djinn that were still in these quarters battling them.

Legion's power was definitely subdued because he was confined to an Earthly vessel. The serum that ran through his veins did give him more strength than he had since he lost his body. With the clarity of his mind, his control over his abilities was greater as well. But Ravenblade was even more ancient than this beast, and his power and skill was a great match for his foe. Lyles, too, was more than just a man now that he had reached Chaos Fury. Much as it had helped Nathan to battle Radix, the power that filled Lyles helped him to combat this mighty demonic being and the hordes of Djinn as well.

Swords slashed at the enemies, blocking attacks left and right. Puck fought his own brothers, trying to keep them at bay so that Ravenblade and Lyles could focus on Legion. But one

Djinni slipped passed Puck and crunched down on Lyles' leg with its jaws. Lyles hit the creature with the hilt of his sword, but that movement allowed more of its brethren time to attack as well.

Legion saw this moment and began to up his skill in battle. He had been toying with these men to get a feel for how they fought. He knew Ravenblade well, but Lyles he did not know. Though the immortal did pose some threat, Legion felt inside that he was far superior and his power greater, and with that ego he fought harder.

"Do you think you can win, Raven?" he asked.

"I know I can," the immortal replied.

"Then you are still a fool," Legion smirked and caught Ravenblade's sword hand.

Three more arms came from Legion and grabbed the immortal by the other arm and his two legs. Legion lifted him into the air and slammed him into the wall over and over again. The walls cracked and crumbled with each subsequent blow. Lyles couldn't help because he was caught in his own battle with the horde of Djinn and there was no escape for him either. Puck was locked in battle too, and there seemed to be no hope.

That is when a round of shots filled the room. Djinn after Djinn fell to the ground in a pile of salt. The soldiers of the Council of His Holy Order charged in and began to cut down the horde of desert demons one by one. In fear, many retreated in puffs of smokeless fire. As much as Puck did not want to abandon his friends he too disappeared, for if he stayed he might end up with the same fate as his former brothers who had fallen already. Legion flung Ravenblade and pulled all of his extra appendages back into himself. Lyles ran to his friend to see if he was okay. Amazingly, the immortal was fine, just a few scratches that would heal in no time. He was strong, not like a mortal man. It would take more than some rock wall to kill him.

The soldiers surrounded Legion who stood in place, gawking at them, trying to figure out who they were. He was impressed by what they did to his army of Djinn, and he wanted to learn more before he slaughtered them.

Before he could ask any questions, one of the soldiers threw what looked like a small canister at the fiend. It stopped at his feet and released a burst of light, which encased Legion in a prison of pure energy.

"This is rich," Legion laughed. "You mean to stop me with some stupid toys. What the Hell is this anyway," he said and reached out to touch the force field around him.

A surge ran through his body, knocking him back.

"You think you can contain me? Do you know who I am?"

"Yes, we do, Legion, and we are here to take you out before you cause anymore death and destruction," one of the soldiers said, in a thick Italian accent.

"And who the Hell are you?"

"We are members of the Council of His Holy Order, soldiers who serve the Lord Almighty. You are God's enemy, so you are ours too!" the same soldier shouted.

"Well, then tell your God that you failed when you see Him. For soon you will be at His side!" the monstrous villain roared.

Legion crouched to the ground, spoke a few words, and the whole place began to shake. The ground grew weak and the entire floor broke from beneath them. The Temple of Luminescence was collapsing from within, and the entire party of soldiers, along with Lyles and Ravenblade began to fall with it. Some of the troops were able to use their grappling devices to catch themselves, but many were not fast enough and fell to their death. Others had been killed by falling debris. Ravenblade grabbed Lyles and cushioned their landing as they hit the bottom of the sanctuary. All who survived began to run through the corridors to make it out of the sanctuary before the entire mountain fell on their heads, burying them alive.

***

Lilith could feel the great power that the child had — it was the Spirit of God, and following that energy, Lilith found where the girl was hiding. She looked at the wall, feeling for a doorway, then she stopped and cleared her mind. Her hand found the stone, and with a push and a turn, she opened the door. Esmeralda sat huddled with Bianca, hoping that Chien had returned, and that the battle was over. But there was no such luck. Fear filled her heart when she saw the succubus before her, though now in the form of a woman again. But still Esmeralda could see the evil in her eyes.

Not again, she thought, *not her only child left. They can't take her. Please God don't let them take her.*

Michael was tired of these games. Lilith had escaped when the Djinn army attacked but he would not allow her to win. In a burst of light, Michael caused the Djinn to back off and retreat into the puffs of smokeless fire that they came from. The place was clear and Chien and the angel had to find Lilith, before she got to the girl. Chien led the Prince of Hosts to where he had hidden Bianca and her mother.

When they got there, it was too late. Esmeralda lay dead on the ground, her throat slashed. Bianca was gone. Michael felt the air and found no trace of the Devil's bride. Chien knelt down and held Esmeralda's cold, lifeless hand. He wept, for he was unable to keep her safe as he had promised, and he feared what might happen to the girl. The walls began to quake all around them. The ceiling above began to crumble and fall. Michael the great Archangel grabbed Chien and teleported them to safety, while the whole mountain fell to the ground.

***

Simon held the skull high in his hand, contemplating what he would do when he controlled the Universe. Just then, he felt the floor beneath him give a little, and he saw the walls cracking and breaking apart. He had just received his ticket to great power, and this place was about to come down all around him.

There must be a way to save myself? he wondered. But this power was new and he did not know how to use it. He remembered that the true power of the skull was in transformation. It made things change to that which they were not, and it brought out hidden power within its user. His family had magic in their blood. It was not the skull that supplied that, but rather the skull magnified it and allowed them to transform into something greater. Using this knowledge and digging into himself, Simon held the skull tightly and began to chant a spell of teleportation. He imagined being outside of the mountain. Instantly, just as the walls crashed in around him, he vanished.

The only problem was that he neglected to imagine being on the ground, and he appeared in midair outside of the mountain range. The sorcerer began to fall, but before he could hit the ground he thought of another spell — that of levitation. He chanted the spell in haste. And he stopped falling. Simon was floating.

The skull worked. It had transformed this wannabe illusionist into a real sorcerer. He floated down toward the ground until he landed gently on his feet.

"Don't move!" someone shouted, and a light shone brightly in Simon's face.

Standing before him were thirty soldiers all heavily armed and ready to fire on him at any moment. Before they could, Legion burst out from the side of the mountain. The troops turned and opened fire at the demonic villain as he charged them. They used bursts of solid light, which exploded as they hit Legion's body, with little or no effect. On lower-class demons, these bursts would enter the flesh and explode inside, sending the demon to the second death. But even in this human body, Legion was too powerful for such a trick, for his soul was strong. That is why his soul remained, jumping from host to host, when his original, demonic body was destroyed. One of the soldiers threw a holy-water bomb at Legion, which exploded in his face. The water seared his flesh, but he healed just as quickly. The fiend yelled in anger and thrust his fists into the ground. That same monstrous worm creature that had brought them to this place broke out from the ground below, leaped into the air and then swooped down on the soldiers, swallowing whole as many as it could as it burrowed back underground.

It resurfaced right in front of Legion, who jumped aboard and waved Simon to join him. The sorcerer slowly climbed aboard the beast. He saddled himself behind Legion and held on tight.

"What about Lilith?" he asked.

"Who cares about that wench," Legion replied. "We have the skull. Let's go."

And just as quickly as it had brought them there, the creature burrowed into the Earth, and they were off.

The mountain sanctuary had been reduced to rubble. Lyles and Ravenblade hobbled out of the entrance. The soldiers who remained alive inside followed them out. Chien was safely outside as well, thanks to Michael's teleportation. Then Michael had immediately left, returning to his home in Heaven. All who remained were grieved by the tragedy that had just taken place. The soldiers realized that they had lost more men than just those inside the mountain. Lyles looked around for Bianca and Esmeralda but did not see them. Chien walked over to his new friend and placed a hand on his shoulder.

"The girl is gone. She was taken by Lilith," the priest said.

Lyles closed his eyes holding back tears, "What about Esmeralda."

"She is dead. The succubus killed her when she took the girl. I am sorry."

Lyles fell onto his knees and cried. He slammed his fists into the ground, for once again he failed to protect his friends. How many more would die because he was not strong enough to save them?

CHAPTER X
SINS OF THE PAST

Sam sat in his office. The whole room was filled with Darkness with no light to cast any shadows. He knew the Darkness well, for he ate of its fruit many millennia ago when the world was still new and fresh. Yet even then, the world was so deep in sin that the Lord yearned to destroy it and all who lived on its surface. It all happened so fast, yet it felt like forever. He thought back to those days, the days when he still served God, when he fought in His Name. Sam's proper name was Samyaza — which means "the Name has seen" but later translated as "the infamous rebellion." Though he did not feel as if his actions were as much a rebellion as they were a choice. He was a Watcher, their leader, in fact — the Watchers were a group of God's elite who were chosen to live among the men and women of the Earth and watch over them, to protect them from Satan and his fallen brothers. Sam had fought against the Devil and the other angels who rebelled against God during the First War in Heaven. It was a brutal battle and caused great pain for all who were involved.

The Father had created in peace, but He also created balance, and gave those He created a choice, to choose good or evil. On Earth, these Watchers lived on an island in the Atlantic Ocean called Atlantis apart from the sons of Adam, though they visited them on occasion. In the center of the island was a great mountain, the world's highest peak. This is where the Watchers held council.

The Watchers had to take on corporeal forms for their mission on Earth. The more time they spent inside these bodies, the more they succumbed to the temptations and sins of the world in which they lived in. But their bodies were still not like those of men. They could not get hurt, they could not bleed, and they could not die. They were strong and fast and could still utilize the power that God had instilled inside of them when they were created. These warrior angels truly appeared to be gods among men, and the men of the world began to worship these angels as such. Some of the Watchers accepted this worship and played god on Earth, helping to form many of the world's myths and religions. Just as their brother Satan had fallen to pride, which fueled his lust for power, they too now fell into the same sins.

There was so much that the men of Earth did not know about the Universe and the true war that was being waged around them. There were other worlds beyond Earth, part of God's very creation. But only on Earth did God put man, his people, to love and to live with. As infinite as God was, he chose such a small speck to call His own out of all the galaxies that filled the ever-expanding Universe. Beyond the stars were other planets created by God to show His majesty. And He did put life on some of these. But the life forms he placed on the other worlds were simple creatures, like the animals of Earth. The Father was a creator and He created, it was a passion and an expression of His might. But just as Satan had corrupted the Earth, he corrupted the rest of God's creation, bringing death and judgment on all. He stole the seed of Adam and Eve after the Fall and scattered it among the stars, making people to dwell in those worlds where God did not intend them to dwell. These men and women were born directly into sin and not God's grace, though they did contain the DNA of their Earthly parents and did have souls that could be redeemed.

One by one, Lucifer brought each of these people the knowledge he had consumed when he fell into the black pit of the Darkness. The first recipient was a girl named Pandora, his high priestess. Satan helped her to build an army, worshippers of the very knowledge that the Devil drank from on a daily basis. Pandora's army traveled from planet to planet teaching, deceiving the very races that Lucifer himself had formed, causing them all to fall, and causing all life on the planets to be swallowed up by the Darkness. A spiritual barrier was placed around the Earth, stopping Pandora and her troops from entering its atmosphere. But Pandora knew that she would be given free entry and the Darkness could swallow the Earth as it did those other planets, if the world fell into such great evil and sin so as to shift the Earth's balance from Light to Darkness.

Atop the mountain on the island of Atlantis, Samyaza and his highest-ranking Watchers held council to discuss the fate of the men and women they swore to protect. The building where they met was ornate and beautiful, surrounded with grand pillars much like a great Greek temple. The group of angels sat around a large marble table. The Watchers appeared as men and were all tall and well built. Their skin color was nicely bronzed.

"This planet is falling, just like the rest, and I fear we will not win this war!" One of them shouted, "We have failed our God."

"It is not over yet," Samyaza said and stood up. He was handsomer than the rest, not the tallest or the broadest, but rather the perfect height and build. He almost looked as if he were carved from stone.

"Seriously, Samyaza, do you really believe we still have a chance to save these wretched mortals?" another said in return.

"Yes, I do," Samyaza answered, his voice as perfect as his face and body.

"But even our own are beginning to fall, just as they did when Lucifer rose up in Heaven. The Devil has deceived our brothers and now they fight against us as well," another jumped in.

"Yes, Azazel has broken away from us, with some of our very own, teaching men the art of war, allowing themselves to be worshipped as gods, and even laying with their women to spawn abominations," Samyaza answered. "The wickedness of men is dire, but our own wickedness has made it worse. We blame Satan and his schemes, but we should be stronger than that. It is our very own lusts that drag us down. We are at fault, not Satan. We are God's angels. Chosen by the Father to protect not only this world, but all of creation. *We* are the ones failing. But we also are the ones who can stand victorious if we realize our failings and stop them, once and for all. Have faith in the Almighty, and His Holy Spirit will strengthen and lead us to victory!"

All the Watchers around the table stood and cheered. Samyaza was good at rallying the troops, making them believe that they could be triumphant. But, inside, he did not believe it himself. He stepped out of the temple and walked down a grand marble staircase to a stone road that led down the mountain. He decided to walk, for he enjoyed taking in the beauty of the city below as he grew closer and closer to its streets.

It was the most beautiful metropolis on the entire planet throughout all the ages of the Earth. The buildings were all artistically sculpted from marble, trimmed with gold, silver, and bronze. When the sun shone down on its streets, they glistened for they were lined with precious stones and jewels. Besides the Watchers, there was a tribe of mortals who dwelt in the city as well, and these mortals were called Atlantians by any who knew of them. They were those that Samyaza and his men rescued from Pandora on Mars.

The evil priestess used Mars as a watchpost to view the men of Earth. She built a kingdom there and at its center was a grand temple built to worship the Darkness. On each planet that she conquered, a similar temple was built. These were used as gateways to bring the Darkness onto that planet so its life could be drained and the planet destroyed. The Atlantians were her slaves on Mars, people that Satan had placed there when sprinkling life across the galaxy. Mars was a paradise then, but war came when God's army of Watchers, led by Samyaza, arrived to bring justice and to end Pandora's reign.

The war was so devastating that it transformed the entire planet into a desert. Pandora escaped with some of her slaves and she hid in the black holes of the Universe, where the angels could not go.

This was when the Watchers were appointed to live on Earth. The slaves that they were able to save came with them to live on Atlantis. The island was a paradise with peace all around. The Atlantians had such a grasp of medical science that they lived even longer than the early humans on Earth, who at that time could live to nearly a thousand years. Outside of Atlantis, the rest of the world was in trouble. It would fall soon, and with it all creation. All Samyaza could do, for now, was pray.

In a few hours, he reached the bottom of the mountain and began to walk the streets of the city. He liked watching the people — there was something amazing about mortals — their flesh was weak but their will was strong. He also was intrigued by their feelings and their passion. He too, now, began to feel this passion, for the Watchers being in their corporeal forms for so long on Earth all began to gain feelings much like the men of this planet. Many of his brothers had already even fallen in love with the women of the world. Most though, those that followed Azazel, were not in love but just filled with lust, and now the group of angels was divided, fighting among themselves when they should be fighting together against Satan and his demons.

The leader of the Watchers was perplexed by his brothers' choices and the paths they took, which led them away from God and His plan. Soon though, Samyaza would understand, for his own heart would turn toward one in particular. The Atlantian people were perfect specimens of the human race — tall, handsome, and beautiful. They ate a healthy diet and made sure to live active lifestyles, keeping themselves in peak condition. The women were especially lovely, more so than any born on Earth.

Samyaza came to a wooded area of the island. He gently walked through the forestry, reveling in the nature all around him — more signs of God's wondrous Hand. Through a clearing was a spring, which was fed by a waterfall connected to the river that ran through the island. A woman was bathing in the spring. Her beauty was even greater than all the other Atlantian women. The angel could not help but stop and gaze upon her. The way the water ran down her soft skin gave him chills, the first he had ever felt. And just then his emotions crystallized in his thoughts. This is what his brothers had felt. How could he judge them so? It was remarkable, such a feeling of inexpressible joy. But then his conscience set in, and he turned his eyes away from the bather.

What was he doing? Was Satan playing him like a harp? Was he about to fall like those others who he now fought against? He was here to protect these people, not share a life with them in this way, as mortals did. He must go. But as he turned, a twig snapped, and the woman saw him watching her. At first she covered up, but then she smiled. Ashamed of his guilt, Samyaza vanished from her sight, making the girl even more curious about her voyeur.

The leader of the Watchers could not get the beautiful woman out of his mind. The more he tried to shift his thoughts to other things, the more Samyaza found himself daydreaming of her. The image of her face, those emerald green eyes, her long black hair, milky white skin, and shapely body were all imprinted in his head. She was perfect and he yearned to be with her. Days and weeks passed by, and as they did he would find ways to spy on his secret love. Peeking at her from afar so she would not catch him looking.

He could never be with her. It was against his orders. He was an angel in God's army, not a man to make this woman his own. He had judged his own brothers for committing this very sin and now the sin was his as well. His heart sank for them, understanding their feelings — their desires.

One day Samyaza was walking through the forest and came upon the site where he first saw the woman that he was so infatuated with. He stayed hidden behind the trees and bushes watching, waiting, hoping she would come back, and she did. He could not help but look on as she disrobed and then walked into the water to bathe. Everything about her was lovely.

Why am I feeling this way? Samyaza wondered.

She was a mortal woman, flesh and bones. He did not know her, he had never even spoken a word to her.

"Lovely, isn't she," a voice whispered into Samyaza's ear.

The angel was startled and looked around. Maybe it was his imagination.

"What are you doing, Samyaza?" the voice spoke again.

"Who is there?" Samyaza spoke low so he would not alert the woman.

"Forgotten me already, have you?" and now a figure appeared where the voice had been spoken. His skin was as black as the depths of space, and his eyes bright like two stars set into his head. He wore a black robe that dragged on the ground behind him.

"Lucifer? I know it is you, I can feel it," Samyaza said with disdain. "You have some gall to show up here. Do you wish to wage battle with me, for I am ready to send you to the second death if I must."

"I am not here to fight, my brother," Satan replied. "Has God really ordered you to slay me on sight? I have come and gone to Heaven after my revolution. If He was so insistent on my destruction then why has He not dealt it Himself?"

"You speak with a forked tongue, you snake. You are the reason why we are all here, or have you forgotten the war we fought in Heaven. It changed us, and it changed everything that the Lord had made. Maybe my direct orders are not to slay you, not yet, but I have been instructed to protect this world from evil, to stop the Darkness from destroying it, and you and your demons from corrupting it even further. So, if your desire is to impose any harm today, then mine will be to stop you."

"You are so dramatic," the Devil said. "Why so angry at me? I didn't want that war. He ordered it. I was only trying to liberate you all from His tight grip. You talk about the Darkness and destruction. Those worlds, they did not have to be destroyed. He sent you all to them to fight war upon war. The destruction of those worlds was more His fault than mine. I helped to bring man as far as the stars could reach. And in doing so, awakened their minds to a way other than His strict control. I tried only to bring freedom, a new way of thinking. He calls it evil, he calls it the Darkness, but I call it 'knowledge.' Are you seeing reality or just what He wants you to see?"

"You can't fool me, Lucifer. I know your schemes, your lies. I fought many of those wars with my own hands. All those planets you made to be inhabited, those very ones that were drained of all life. That was not His will. That was yours. You have not brought liberation, but slavery and damnation."

"The same can be said of your Master."

"My Master, our Father, loves us. He wants us to be happy."

"Only if you do His will."

"That's because His will is holy and perfect."

"Do you really believe that?" Satan hissed.

"I do. I also believe all that I have seen. I have fought against your hordes of beasts and demons. I have seen the Darkness come in, sucking the very life out of entire worlds. And I have seen your priestess and her minions rule with an iron fist across the galaxies. These very people here were under her control. Show me the liberation; show me the freedom. I will show you sin, and greed, and pure evil."

"Believe what you like. But my desire is not to fight you, or any of my brothers. I do not hate as our Father says I do. I just want to have a choice like these men were given. We had to fight for ours. They were born with it."

"I advise you to leave now, Lucifer, or I will have to take my blade to you, though I too am not looking to fight."

"If you're not looking to fight then why threaten me? I saw the way you watch her, the look in your eyes. Why can't she be yours? Would He truly keep you from being happy, from experiencing love? These mortals are His creations, too, just like you and I."

"You try to deceive me. I know it. I have seen what happens when our brothers fall for these women. The offspring of our kind and their women are abominations. We are only adding to the sin of this world instead of ushering in righteousness. There are terrible wars. Blood is being shed all over the Earth."

"Not all of the children of the sons of God and the daughters of men are abominations. Some are heroes, men of renown. And war on this Earth was inevitable. Don't blame the feelings that our kind have gained for their women. Though I will admit that most of us are just acting out of lust. But you, Samyaza, I can see in your eyes that you love her. And if you do, then how could that be wrong?"

"Stop with your lies, Devil!"

"Oh, now with the name-calling," Lucifer returned.

"You are a liar and a murderer. Stop trying to fill my head with sinful thoughts. I will not be tempted by you."

"We were close once in Heaven, before the war. I can't believe that you would not know me better. You can say I have changed, but I have not. He has only led you all to believe that. But like I said before, believe what you want. I will go," Satan said and vanished from before the angel.

Samyaza turned to see if the woman was still there, and she was. She had walked back onto the land and had just finished putting her clothes back on. She sat on a rock wringing the water from her hair and readying to tie it up. He looked closer, and then without notice he seemed to be pushed from behind and fell through the shrubbery with a crash. The girl looked up in surprise to see the man on the ground across from the water. He looked at her with the same shame he had in his eyes the last time her eyes met his. But this time he did not vanish. Instead he stood, his gaze fixed on her and hers on him. There was a spark between them.

"Were you watching me?" the young woman asked. "I've seen you before."

"I apologize, fair maiden, I mean you no harm," Samyaza said.

"I know," she added.

"How do you know?"

"I just do. It's a feeling," she said and looked down in a shy manner. "You are handsome."

"And you are beautiful, more so than the stars in the sky," Samyaza professed.

He walked up to her and knelt down. The angel placed his hand on her arm gently. The girl tried to pull back at first but then stopped. His touch was warm and soothing. Their faces grew closer together, and it seemed almost as if they would kiss, but then they both stopped.

"This is wrong," Samyaza said.

"Why is love wrong?" the young woman replied.

"It just feels like it should not be so."

"Well, then, make it be so," she said and they kissed.

It seemed as if time stood still, the kiss lasting for days, even years, yet it was only seconds that had passed. They pulled apart slowly and opened their eyes to look at each other again.

"I don't even know your name," the mighty Watcher stated.

"It's Lilith, my mother named me after the night for, like you, she found me to be like the night sky, filled with wonder and beauty," she responded.

"I am Samyaza, one of the Watcher angels that dwell atop that peak," he said pointing to the great mountain that pierced the sky behind him.

"I know. I've seen you about the village, and asked who you were. I wanted to know who my admirer was, since I began to admire you as well. I know a lady should not be so bold; my mother always reminds me of that. But I think women should be able to speak their minds as men do. Are we not all flesh?"

"God made both man and woman in His image. It is not His will for you to be suppressed by men, but rather sin has allowed for this to happen. Men and women are meant to be joined to become one flesh, as the Father and Son are one with the Spirit also. But we angels do not know this ourselves, for we have no true gender and are all the same. We do not have another to join to. Though some of my brothers have done this with mortal women. They call it freedom to choose. I call it sin."

"Why is it a sin to want to be with another, to choose?"

"What if what I choose is wrong?"

"Can love be wrong?"

They kissed again.

***

Time passed and the lovers met often. Their time together was innocent and simple. Mostly they talked, getting to know one another, gazing into each other's eyes and peering into each other's souls. Lilith began to give Samyaza a new spin on life. He would even find himself beginning to question the ways of God, and the laws that governed the angels and men. Was this the knowledge that Lucifer spoke of? Could the Devil actually be right? Was God just an iron-fisted dictator ready to smite all who did not fall in line with His will? But no matter how often these thoughts filled his head, he did not let them take over. God was his Creator, his Father. God loved him. Maybe God was not so opposed to him expressing that very love to others, such as Lilith in a special way as men did. Maybe he could make a life with her. It was like she completed him, and this truly did make him happy.

One day Lilith told Samyaza that she wanted to show him something — a special place that she had found inside one of the caves in the forest. He followed her inside. The back of the cave was lit with torches. They followed the light to a doorway that was carved into the wall of rock. Beyond the door was a stone staircase that was lighted by more torches. The two lovers walked down the spiraling steps until they reached the bottom. The room they entered was vast with a ceiling so high it could not be seen beyond the light of the torches. The walls were covered in gold and fine jewels, and there was some silver trimmed about. It was like a palace hidden under the island.

"What is this place?" the Watcher asked.

"I'm not exactly sure," Lilith replied. "But I think it is a temple. I found it one day when I was exploring the forest. And, when I did, my eyes were opened."

"What do you mean?"

"It was as if my mind was awakened to a knowledge that I could only dream of. Let me show you," the beautiful woman said and grabbed Samyaza's hand to lead him further into the underground temple. "I know my people were enslaved before on another planet, and that your kind rescued us," she spoke as they walked further together.

"Yes, I was there. I fought against that evil army. They opposed all that God created, preaching a new way of thought," Samyaza spoke. "They did not see the need for God and His ways. They wanted to just be free to do as they pleased. They said they were liberating the Universe from tyranny. But instead they created a tyranny of their own. They enslaved people, and took over worlds, destroying anything that opposed their way of thinking. And they brought forth the Darkness, the destroyer of worlds."

"What if they were not all wrong? I know that they mistreated my people, and fought against you. But just because they were misguided, does not mean that the idea was wrong also. What if what you saw as Darkness was actually knowledge and true freedom? What if separating yourself from God actually made you your own person, allowing you to make your own choices and to be truly happy. Any real God would want you to be happy and live that way, not just to do His will and follow orders. You can desire good things, too, not everyone is full of hate and greed like those tyrants who enslaved us."

Samyaza didn't know what to think. Her words were like those of Lucifer. Was she a disciple of the Darkness. Could she be a daughter of sin? He tried to block these thoughts from his mind. Maybe she was just confused and needed guidance. He could help her, show her how things really were. Maybe that was God's plan after all. By being with her, he could be her salvation.

They stopped walking near a large altar of gold atop a platform. The altar was encrusted with red jewels that glistened like flames in the torch light. Behind the altar was a grand image carved into the very wall. It looked like a vast cloud with seven stars inside. Spiral swirls made up the texture of the cloud and in the center was a large black gem. Samyaza felt drawn to the gem. He walked closer and closer to it. Lilith watched, waiting for this moment with an expression of wonder. The angel reached the magnificent jewel and could see his own reflection looking back at him from the jet-black surface. There was something different about his reflection, though Samyaza couldn't tell what it was. Compelled without any hope of resistance, he touched the gem, and instantly his mind was opened up. All seemed clear.

The Watcher had been awakened as if from a dream. Now Samyaza knew the truth, and he felt the truth would set him free. But with the truth came harsh reality. His lover had deceived him. She had been with another, the one who first brought her here, the one who gave her the same truth. It was Lucifer. The angel had been tricked, but it would backfire on the trickster. For now he had knowledge, and with this knowledge he would dethrone the Prince of Darkness and rule this world. For the world was being ruled unjustly. God inflicted all of this suffering and pain because His creations wanted to choose their own way. There was death, hunger, pain, war, and strife only because they wouldn't obey. What kind of justice was that? How could he have served this God for so long? Once he overthrew Lucifer, then he would storm Heaven, and with him he would bring the knowledge that he had found, and all of creation would be free. He turned to Lilith with anger in his eyes. She had never seen him like this before. Where was the love, the innocence from before? Then she realized that he knew the truth.

"Don't you still love me?" she inquired reaching to touch his hand.

"How can I, when you have been with him, my enemy?" Samyaza said, pulling away from her.

"I didn't know any better. He brought me here when I was young, and my eyes were opened. It was before I even knew who you were. And once I saw the truth — the truth that the gem revealed to me as it revealed it to you — I saw his wicked heart and I did not love him. But, you, when I saw you, the truth showed me your heart, and it was lovely and perfect. I loved you. I still do."

"When did he come to you?" the angel inquired.

"When I was just a girl, just before I became a woman. It was well before you even saw me that day."

"Why did he not tell me? Was his plan to deceive me, lure me in from the beginning with your beauty and charm?"

"I was not aware of any plan. This was all so long ago. I was in my father's house. He came to my room at night and led me to the cave. I could not fight the desire to follow him. When I touched the gem, I suddenly knew so much. I yearned to be free from the bonds of humanity, and wanted nothing more than to feed the desires of my flesh. Any real God would want me to be happy, to be satisfied. It all made sense. Lucifer would visit me often, and eventually took me away from my father and mother. I have lived in this forest ever since. I am one with the nature of these woods, living a life of freedom and joy. But no matter what, I could not follow him any longer. I could not be with him, for his spirit was ugly, his heart black. Even though I renounced the God of creation, my heart still yearned for what is good and right. This did not make him happy. Lucifer let me be and do as I pleased. He said his desire was for me to be happy, and if his being in my life was not happiness for me, then he would step away. I have not seen him in years. And then I met you. When I first saw you watching me, my heart jumped. Then I could feel your presence from time to time but could not see you. When I did see you again, I was so overjoyed, for I loved you from the first moment I laid eyes on you. I love you so much, Samyaza."

Samyaza did not move. He was angry but he loved her. Satan may have gotten to her first, but she was not with Lucifer any longer. And now Lilith and Samyaza were both filled with knowledge and truth. They began to kiss, and Samyaza could not pull away; he was drawn to her, intoxicated by her scent, her touch. She lay down on the altar, and beckoned him with her finger. He touched her gently, and took off her clothing, and then his own. They were both filled with passion. Desire took over the lovers. The next few moments were as a blur. Samyaza and Lilith made love, and then he fell into a deep sleep.

Samyaza opened his eyes. He was in the forest, not far from the cave where the secret temple was hidden underground. He had never slept before so this was odd indeed. His mind was hazy, but memories of the day before came back to him. Where was Lilith? Why did she leave him alone in the forest? Was Lucifer, that Devil, still manipulating her, or was she telling him the truth when she said she loved him? Strangely, though, none of that mattered right now. In his head, all that the angel could think about was spreading the truth that he had found and showing the rest of the Watchers the wonders of the knowledge that he had gained.

Over the next few days, he would bring them all to the temple and all of their eyes were opened. With this, things began to change on the island and across the whole world because, now, even those who had sworn to protect this planet had drunk of the Darkness that was conspiring to devour it. God's ways had been abandoned yet again.

Dark days were indeed upon the Earth. A union was reformed between Azazel and Samyaza. The two warring bands of Watchers were now reunited. Together with their children, the Nephilim — some of which were deemed by men as demigods and others as just plain monsters — these angels corrupted the pinnacle of God's creation even more so than it already was. The Earth was soaked in so much evil that God Almighty declared that it had to be destroyed by His own hand instead of allowing it to fall into the Darkness. But this was unknown by the Watchers, who went about spreading the knowledge that Samyaza discovered in that temple hidden in the forest cave, a place he visited often. And every time he went there through the woods, he hoped to see his love again. Month after month he returned and still Lilith was nowhere to be found. Then one day, he was sitting by the falls where he had first laid eyes on her. Samyaza heard some footsteps approaching him.

He turned and asked, "Who goes there?"

"Should you even need to ask?" a voice answered him.

Samyaza jumped at the sound of her voice, and his spirit was lifted. Her smell was enchanting, like a spring day. Lilith, his love, had returned and so did Samyaza's hope and joy.

"I am sorry that I left," she said to him from afar.

The angel stood and walked toward her, and she continued moving in his direction, smiling as she moved. Their hands met, and then Samyaza placed a hand on her waist and moved it down her hips. He closed his eyes and breathed in her scent.

"Where did you go? Why didn't you come back for me?" he wondered.

"My master would not allow it. He grew jealous of our love."

"Your master? You said that he left you alone, that you chose not to be with him. Now he is your master?"

"I'm sorry, I wasn't fully honest with you. When he opened my eyes, I had made a pact with him. He chose me to be his own, but I didn't love him. I needed him to feed me the truth, and was a prisoner to his power. When I saw you, I loved you, I wanted to be with you, and hoped that you could free me from his bonds. Though, I know now that that will never be the case. If he were to ever know about our meeting today, he would banish me to Darkness for all time, never to see the light again, or feel the essence of these woods. I had to hide from you, and I still do."

"I will destroy that beast. He has no power over you!" Samyaza exclaimed and grabbed her firmly. "I will not let him take you from me again!"

"No, it can't be. It will only lead to doom for us both. There is nothing you can do for me now. It's better that I go. But there's something else," Lilith paused and looked at the angel who stood before her. "We have a son."

"What? We have a child?"

"Yes, I conceived and gave birth to a son that very night that we lay together in the temple of truth. But my master does not know of him. He is with my family back in the village. My own mother is raising him now. But he needs his father, so he can grow to be strong and mighty as you are."

"A son. A son!" Samyaza tried to compose himself. He was angry and proud all at once. What should he do?

"Why can't we raise him together? I won't let Lucifer hold us back from being together. Tell me where that dragon hides and I will send him to the second death with my blade."

"There is nothing you can do. Even if you defeat him, I am changed forever by his dark power. My heart grows blacker every day, and my form is not as lovely as what you see here."

"What do you mean? What has he done to you?" Samyaza shouted.

"I can't show you, for I'm a hideous beast, a monster. Please just leave me be and go to our son." She pushed him away.

The angel grabbed her by the wrist, and said, "I will not let you go again."

"But you must."

Then the two lovers heard a slithering in the grass. Samyaza let go of Lilith and turned to meet the sound. He knew at once that his adversary was approaching, and the Watcher angel pulled his blade out of its sheath. The Devil appeared in a cloud of mist. Satan had taken the form of a man again, tall and strong, with black armor and skin to match. From his back protruded a pair of large bat-like wings. He wore no helmet atop his bald head, and his teeth were sharp like a lion's. In his hand, he held a blade as well — the Blackblade, forged in the Darkness that shrouded his soul.

"Samyaza, why are you with my bride?" the Devil asked.

"You knew I loved her. Why did you deceive me, you snake?" Samyaza questioned in return. "She is not your bride. She is your slave!"

"Stay where you are!" Satan shouted to Lilith who was trying to step away. "I have not dismissed you."

The woman fell to her knees, begging her master for forgiveness, to spare her punishment.

"You will not be cast away today. Do not worry, my dear," Satan spoke. "But you are forbidden to see Samyaza ever again. You belong to me, not this hypocrite."

"You wretched snake, how dare you call me a hypocrite! You are the only hypocrite I see. Every word that seeps from your mouth is a lie." Samyaza replied. "You say she is yours, but you don't respect her wishes. You are nothing more than a heartless demon!"

"Quiet, fool," Lucifer said. "Or I will end your existence. Or maybe I should let you suffer, by forcing you to watch me taste of the fruit that you cannot eat. It must really get to you, how I took her even before you saw her. How I transformed our dear Lilith here from an innocent girl into a creature of the night. She plays the victim, but she loved every minute of it, and still does. We wed in these very woods, and her home is with me in Hell. She is the mother of all demons, and her tongue is a forked as my own. I have taught her well. But I do see that she shared the truth with you. And now you see why I fell, why I turned my back on God, just as you have now. That is why I call you hypocrite. I tried to show you the way but you would not have it. It took a harlot like her to lead you to the water, so you could drink. You are now full and drunk. How does it feel?"

"You stay away from her!" the angel shouted. "I will send you to the second death, you heathen! She loves me, not you! You are a monster! How could she ever love you? And what you speak of are all lies. I may have found truth in the knowledge that she led me to, and realized that our Father was not all He seemed to be. But He was right about you. You are a liar and were from the beginning. A murderer. Stand down or be defeated!"

"You call me a liar, look for yourself," the Devil said and waved his hand.

Right before these two combatants, Lilith was transformed. Her jaw grew long and separated like a serpent showing her teeth, which were small and sharp with two long fangs coming from the top of her mouth. Her legs became like those of a hen, and she grew coarse hair across her whole body. Large wings much like those that the Devil fashioned at that moment also grew from her back, and she writhed around on the ground trying to hide herself from being seen by her love. Satan was right, she had been tainted, and her heart and her ways were deceptive and sinful. But he was wrong about one thing. She did indeed love Samyaza, but she was bound to her husband — Lucifer. She could not be with the one she loved for she could never escape the Darkness that she fell into. It was deep and thick like an endless abyss, swallowing her whole. She squealed and bellowed, and Satan just laughed as he looked on.

"Do you still love her now?" He asked.

"I do," replied Samyaza. "And I will free her from your hold.

In an instant, he thrust at Lucifer with his blade, and their swords met, sending out sparks that shot forth like lightning. But before the battle could heat up further, a great light shot down from above, and both warriors fell back in its glare. Standing between them was a majestic sight. Michael, the Archangel, had come, and he stood there in all the majesty in which God had created him. His luxurious wings flowed behind him, and his glowing armor shined like the sun. In his hand he held his blade, which burned with the fire of Heaven. There would be no war today between the Watcher and the demon, for God had come to judge.

"Stand down, both of you," Michael ordered. Samyaza and Satan remained silent, as the Archangel continued. "God is about to judge the Earth. He will destroy all life by way of flood — all life except two of each kind of beast, and one man and his family, who will repopulate this world, so that order can be restored. Samyaza, you and your brothers are to be punished for your crimes. You have sinned against God and man. You were to guide His people, and lead them in His ways. To protect them from evil and the enemy, so they could be ready for the Savior to come and rescue them from their sins. But now that must wait, for this world is damned, and will fall into the very Darkness that crouches in your soul. You have fallen, as have all the Watchers. Your children are monsters, abominations that never should have been born. Angels are not to be married or given in marriage, nor to bear children, but you and your kind have defiled the creation of God."

"Tell him, Michael," Satan hissed.

"You stay out of this, Lucifer. You were the first to fall into that Darkness, and unless you wish judgment to fall on you today, I recommend you leave, along with your wench. I have only come for him," the Archangel pointed at Samyaza, "and those with him."

Satan knew it was good for him to leave. So he did as the angel requested of him, and together he and Lilith vanished from their sight.

"No!" screamed Samyaza. He pounded the ground as he cried out. "Why did you let him have her? I love her. Michael, we are bothers, why do you hate me so?"

"I do not hate you, and we are no longer brothers. You are like him, a fallen angel now, chosen to follow the Darkness instead of the Light. Samyaza, you have turned your back on your Creator, your Father," the mighty Archangel said. He held out his blade and the fire grew more intense. "Let us go now peacefully, unless you would rather go by force."

The Watcher grew nervous. He could not be taken away, not now. He had a son that he had just found out about, and his son needed to be saved before the world was destroyed. In desperation, he held out his hand and with all his energy flashed a light so bright it even momentarily blinded his superior, Michael, the Archangel. When Michael looked back, Samyaza had gone — but to where?

The Watcher appeared in the city going from house to house, feeling for the child that had his essence. He found him. In a flash of light, he entered the home, a quaint cottage in the farming district. The woman who cared for him, the child's grandmother, was startled when the angel intruded and stole the babe from her bosom. As quickly as he came, he left in a flash. Samyaza was determined. He would not lose his son. What kind of cruel God would destroy the very world that He created? Why not just make everything right. The knowledge he had gained had truly opened his eyes, and had shown this Lord for what he really was — an angry and jealous God. He reached the temple and ran to the altar. The leader of the Watchers placed his only son on the altar where that child was conceived, and then he touched the stone. Words came forth from his mouth, words he did not even know or understand. His son began to levitate and glow with a black aura. Then a cloud began to protrude from the stone. It whirled around the boy, engulfed him, and pulled the child into the blackness of the stone. Samyaza could not move. The walls shook all around. Then a legion of angels led by Michael himself burst into the temple.

"Samyaza, what are you doing? You will bring the Darkness into this world, and then all creation will be lost."

"You will not take him!" Samyaza yelled. "You will not have my son!"

"What are you talking about?" Michael questioned. "Stop what you are doing now!"

The Archangel lunged at his foe and knocked him into the wall that held the stone. The stone came loose from the wall and shattered into tiny shards when it hit the ground. The whole temple began to shake. The walls cracked all around and the ceiling began to topple down onto the angels that stood there. Michael grabbed Samyaza by his arm and he dragged him from the temple as it collapsed, burying itself and the cave that led to it.

Michael and his army captured all the Watchers one by one and bound them for their crimes. The battle was not quick or painless, and it left many scars, not just on the Earth but also on the spirits of all involved. Some of these fallen angels were sent to Hell. Those whose crimes outweighed the others, including Samyaza himself and Azazel, were bound in the Arabian Desert, deep under the sand, trapped in Darkness to wait for the final judgment. Meanwhile, the Lord poured out the waters from above, covering the Earth, killing all life, except Noah, his family, and the animals that crowded together with them on the wooden ark. The world would have a fresh start, and the cycle would begin again.

The Nephilim were destroyed in the Flood. Even though they seemed god-like in power, they were as mortal as their mothers. But the bloodline of the Nephilim would be carried on into the new world through the wife of Ham; her father was one of these abominations, though she seemed to be just an average woman of no special character or trait. Her seed would give birth to a new breed of giants that would fight against God's people. The entire island of Atlantis sank to the bottom of the ocean for all time, along with the Atlantians — the last of their race from

Mars. God loved the world, He loved His people, but the evil that filled the Earth was thick and dark, and needed to be cleansed.

***

Samyaza sat in his office remembering those days — the love he had and lost, the short time he spent with his son, whom he had named Truth, but who was now known as Legion. The angel remained imprisoned many years under the desert sand, until the same enemy that drove him to the Darkness released him. Satan came with the Necronomicon, that sinful codex, and with a powerful spell Samyaza was free. That was a long time ago, and though time never healed the scars, it softened the pain a little. Samyaza learned that in order to survive, it was better to not focus on the small battles but the bigger war at hand. He was different now. Much of the world was under his hand. He had power, and wealth, and might. But he still did not have the family that he so desired. Not yet. He did have Gideon now, a new son, and Legion would be restored, giving him back his first-born. Once he could bring them together, then he would take down Lucifer. Lilith would be his again, and together they would conquer all of creation and snatch the very throne of the Creator, a feat that Satan failed at long ago. But Samyaza was determined to succeed. Nothing would stop him or stand in his way.

CHAPTER XI
GATHERING THE PIECES

"Hey!" Martha exclaimed as she answered the door to see Kimberly on the other side. "I'm so glad you came, sweetie."

"I had to meet the doctor," the young woman said with a wink.

"Shh, he's right there in the living room," she hushed, giving her friend a nudge. "Actually everyone's here. Really glad you made it."

Kimberly walked into Martha's living room to see six others sitting on the couch and some chairs, all holding Bibles. Two of them were gentlemen, and she scanned their faces, trying to figure out which one was Martha's doctor friend.

"I'd like you all to meet, Kimberly," Martha said, and then introduced the others in turn.

When she got to Dr. Davis, Martha gave a sly grin. He was short and stocky with a warm smile. His head was balding but he still had a fair amount of hair on the sides and back that he kept short, and which led to a well-trimmed beard and mustache. He wore a pair of sleek glasses, which he pushed up on his nose from time to time as they slipped down. The group all sat, and Kimberly took out her Bible, too. Dr. Davis led them in prayer, his voice even warmer than his smile. It was deep, clear, and very calming. They studied the book of Romans that night, and the discussions were amazing. The amount of knowledge these men and women had about Scripture was awesome, and Kimberly wished Lyles had been there for this. He would have loved to dive deep into the Word with those around.

When the study ended and they had closed in prayer, everyone got up to get some coffee and treats that Martha had laid out on her small dining-room table. Dr. Davis walked over, eating some coffee cake and sprinkling crumbs onto his beard.

"So, Martha told me a lot about you, Kimberly," the doctor said between chews. "She said that your husband knew Reverend Reynolds."

"Yes, Lyles grew up here. He was very close to him. I wish I could have met Reverend Reynolds myself. Seems like he was a great man."

"Yes, he was. I used to go to his church service, and even did a Bible study with him some years back, when I was a young man. That's how I met Martha, though she's a little younger than me," he laughed as he spoke. "Those were fun times. We missed Martha when she stopped coming to the study. She has a great heart."

"Yes, she does," Kimberly agreed. "So what exactly are you a doctor of, if you don't mind me asking?"

"Oh, no worries. I have my doctorate in biological sciences. Wish it was an MD of plastic surgery, then I would be loaded," the little man laughed and took another bite of cake. "I teach at NYU and basically spend the rest of my time doing research. I like it. It has opened up the true miracles of God's creation, seeing how all the living things He has made work and function to reflect His glory — simply amazing. So, where is your husband tonight? I heard he was in seminary. It would have been great to get his take on what we read."

"He's away, on a mission trip actually. Over in China," Kimberly fibbed. Though her lie was not altogether false.

"Yes, Martha did say he was traveling, but not exactly what he was doing. So, missions in China — that is awesome. You are a saint to let him go while you are pregnant. I'm sure it must not be easy."

"I have good and bad days, but mostly good, and Martha's been a great help."

"Yes, Martha is a sweetheart. But if you need anything, let me know. It would be my pleasure."

"What would be your pleasure?" Martha asked with a laugh.

"I was just telling this lovely young girl that if she needs any help while her husband was away, I'd be happy to do so," Dr. Davis explained.

"Hey, David, she's married and maybe just a little young for you, don't you think," Martha laughed again. "You are old enough to be her father."

"True. I am," he laughed. "But you're not quite old enough to be her mother. Maybe an older sister."

"Not much older," Kimberly chimed in with a smile.

"Older enough," Martha said. "And I feel older than I am. I'm forty-two this year."

"And don't look a day over twenty-five," David remarked.

"Oh, you old flirt, you," Martha said.

"Seriously though, I'm here if you need me," the doctor repeated. "And not the way Martha made it sound," he laughed.

"No worries, and thanks," Kimberly said. "I have to get going, though. I get tired early now with the baby and all."

They all exchanged hugs and said their good-byes. Dr. Davis promised to pray for Lyles' trip and for Kimberly while Lyles was on the mission field. In a way, Lyles' mission was more of a holy war. He missed his wife with every thought and could not wait to get back home to hold her. Kimberly felt the same way. She felt safe in his arms, and having him away while she was bearing his child was painful and lonely. She may have had Martha around to help and now the doctor, too, but not having her husband made her feel empty. She took it to heart that they were one flesh, and it really did feel as if she was missing a part of herself when Lyles was away.

***

"She doesn't seem like much to me," Legion said, as he looked Bianca up and down.

"You are such a fool, Legion," Lilith spoke. "Her power is in her spirit, just like her brother."

"Yes, I can feel something, but still I felt greater power in the least of the prophets. And you say there is another, a boy. Where is he? Why do we not have him as well, if they are so special?"

"He is protected by my husband. He did not see the need to take this one, though in my opinion the girl is the one we will need. Men always overlook the woman," Lilith seethed.

"Step off your high horse, wench. I will admit that your husband lacks good sense, though. If he had a right mind, he would have taken the Kingdom of Heaven before the physical world was ever created. But he has no idea how to use the power that was given to him."

"Do you know how to use yours?" the succubus questioned.

190

"I do, and I will, but not until I am restored. So, what are your plans for this girl?"

"She and her brother were spawned by Radix and the sister of the very man who released you from that disc in the desert. These children, one or both of them, it is thought, will bring about the end of all. I believe she will usher in the Darkness, causing Earth to fall, and tipping the scale to our side. Once the Earth is lost and the Darkness released upon the Universe, then it can storm the Gates of Heaven, and even the mighty God will not be able to stop it."

"You are foolish and deluded, woman!" Legion bellowed and his voice echoed throughout the caverns of Iblis' kingdom. "God cannot so easily be stopped. Not without becoming a god yourself. I am the only being who can attain that power, who can take the throne, who can rule over all."

"You are both ridiculous," Iblis interrupted. "You cannot defeat that which is truly eternal and all-powerful. God has no limits. He is not just some man in the sky. I dwelt with Him, and even when Satan fell, I did not, for I knew that God was sovereign over all. I have no desire to take His throne or His place, only to be restored and be at peace. I could have conquered this world millennia ago, but I have chosen not to. I only care for my subjects, my children that I made from the heat of the desert. This world will pass away and it does not need our help for that. Man is mortal unlike us. The world will end, as it is written. I never stopped serving God like the others. That is why I am not in Hell. I merely disobeyed a command to worship that which He created. I could not worship anything but God alone."

"He still loves you," Bianca spoke in a soft tone that penetrated the fallen angel. "You can be restored, but you must realize why you are here."

"So, she does speak," Legion commented. "So, little girl, tell me, are you afraid?" the voice of thousands of demons speaking at once quaked around the child.

"No," she said. "My Father is with me always. He will never abandon or forsake me."

"Strange words from a mere child," Legion said. "You sound like Christ. God is my Father. He will not forsake me," he mimicked her with a childish voice. "How cute, and unrealistic. God has abandoned you. If He hadn't, you would be far away from here."

"I am where He wants me to be," Bianca spoke with wisdom.

"How old are you?" Legion asked.

"Four," she responded holding up four fingers.

"From the mouth of babes," Iblis muttered under his breath.

"Take this toddler away. Lock her in your worst dungeon, and show her that her God has truly abandoned her. She is forsaken, and once I am restored I will devour her body and soul," Legion belted out with an evil laugh.

Iblis called forth some of his Djinn, who appeared and took the girl away. They took her down to the depths of his palace. There was a prison there, though it had not been used in quite some time. He would capture men of valor, great heroes to feed to his children as a treat. But there were not many of those men and women left on the Earth. The girl was locked inside a cell. She seemed unmoved and unafraid, as if in her mind she was somewhere else. The Spirit filled her full, and her thoughts, her heart, and her soul were with God, her Creator and Father in Heaven.

Back in Iblis's throne room, Legion called forth Simon Magus III. He wanted to know when he would be restored. The beast could not take being in this decaying body any longer. There was a time when his flesh was strong and mighty. Legion was one of the Nephilim, the son of an angel, though he did not know this. He only knew of his mortal father, Nimrod — the King of Shinar, the kingdom later known as Babylon. Nimrod was said to be a mighty hunter and a mighty man. He was the same king who brought the men of the world together to build the Tower of Babel, an event that caused the separation of humankind from itself. Nimrod was believed to be of the lineage of the Nephilim through the bloodline of Ham's wife. Nimrod and his adopted son had more in common than they knew. The pagan priests who served Nimrod practiced the blackest of magic, that which can only be found in the Abyss of nothingness. In hopes of granting their king more power so he could achieve the status of a god on Earth, these priests were trying to unleash the primal essence of evil, known to many as the Darkness, and it was then that they brought forth a baby boy. The child would become known as Legion, though that was not yet his name. King Nimrod took in the boy as his own son and called him Citius. The boy grew strong and wise, not knowing that he was more than just a mortal. When he turned the age of thirteen, a change began to come upon him. It started with nightmares, followed by outbursts of rage, and then spasms and convulsions that made the magicians believe that Citius was possessed. They were right.

With his coming of age also came the unveiling of the gift that he had received while trapped in the Darkness as a baby. He had spent many years there, inside the Abyss, and during that time, thousands of demons were infused within his soul. His immortal flesh was the only casing that could hold such evil power. And now that power had been awakened, but it needed to be controlled. The boy was confused at first and battled against the demons inside of him, a battle that caused him to grow mad.

King Nimrod did not know what to do. He prayed to his false gods to save his child from this madness, but nothing worked. Nothing until a strange woman gave the king a black stone. She explained how this stone could restore his son. She gave Nimrod a book, as well. And this book told of how to open a portal to the Abyss, and how to channel the true power of knowledge and strength. Nimrod now possessed the means to save his son and receive the status of lord over all at the same time. What a gift! He wondered why this woman would be so generous and why she did not use it for herself, but without warning she disappeared, and he never saw her again.

The king chained his son so the boy could not bring about destruction to the palace, and then Nimrod began to read the book to gain full knowledge of all he needed to do. Only the Darkness could make things right and give him all that he sought. He brought the black stone to his son and touched it to his forehead, just as the book told him to do and then he chanted a spell. When he did so, the boy's mind was loosened and he began to gain control of all that was locked inside of him, his demons and his powers.

The king was amazed. But he did not tell his son what the stone was nor did he reveal his plan to use the stone again to gain supreme power. And that is when the king had the tower built. The stone gave him great knowledge and with it he led the men and women of the world astray. In order to release the Darkness and gain the full power that only it could bring, the balance of the world had to be tipped all the way to the side of evil, for only an evil world can invite the Darkness into it. The Darkness needed the whole world to reject its Creator and worship the created instead.

The Earth was unlike other planets, though, and that is why it had not fallen yet. God placed a people of his own there and set up His plan of salvation through their bloodline. But the King of Shinar was ready to defy God and conquer this world, for he had the one thing that no other king did, and that was the stone. Only with the stone could the portal to the Abyss be opened. Every other world that fell had a portal just like it, and through it they had all been destroyed. Nimrod's plans were circumvented by the very God that he defied, and the temple he built, the tower to heaven that would proclaim him god over all, was destroyed. The men and women of Earth were scattered to the four corners the world, giving way for the various races, cultures, and languages that we have to this day.

The boy, Citius, was in the tower when it fell, but he survived, for his power was great. His father, Nimrod, thought that Citius had perished and the king escaped to continue to spread his dark rule across the world. Citius wandered about with no place to call home, for he did not know where his father had gone. As he grew, the evil in his heart grew as well. Destruction became his new desire. This was about the time he took on the name Legion. It just came out one day when someone asked him his name. He replied, "I am Legion, for we are many." And the name stuck for all time.

Time passed, and with it many wars. During one of these glorious battles Legion, in another attempt to reach godhood, found himself facing an enemy that he knew well. The fight took place in Antarctica, an open arena with no men to get in the way. His challenger was an angel, not like any other, and some say not really an angel at all. He was known as the one with no name, for when God created him He gave this being no name that anyone knew of, but displayed him as the personification of Order.

The battle was long and grueling, but with a powerful blade called the sword of Order the angel was able to vanquish Legion who held in his own hand the sword's counterpart — the sword of Chaos. It was as if these two beings were polar opposites, destined to battle for all time. But it had ended, or so the angel thought. Legion's body was destroyed, but his soul remained on the Earth and he began to possess men and beasts, trying to regain his power. In this new state, he was no real threat, for without his body he grew mad and the demons began to twist and tear apart his mind, leaving him incapable of achieving his goals. Time came and went and there were moments when Legion seemed as if he would be restored, but each time a hero would rise to stop him. The last one was the man from Chien's order, who trapped Legion in the disc, the very same disc that Nathan had released the fiend from in the desert a few years before. Now Legion was back, and this time he vowed to regain his body and, with it, his power and might.

And he would not stop there, for this time he would reach his goal — to become a god, to conquer the Universe, and destroy all. Legion actually believed that he could somehow destroy God and all His creation, and this was the heart of what the Darkness pursued. It filled all who followed it, including Satan himself — a lie that led many astray to pursue a path that would only lead to ruin in the end. It was this very lie that surged through Legion's entire being, giving him purpose and meaning.

Simon came into Iblis' throne room as requested. Legion stood with an uncommonly anxious look. The gold that covered the palace walls glistened all around him, causing his eyes to shimmer and radiate a black light across the room.

"Finally, what took you so long?" Legion questioned.

"I was trying to master the power of this thing," Simon said holding up the skull. "I can do so much more now than before. My magic actually works, and the feeling is intense. It's a rush."

"Can you or can you not restore me?" the demon boomed.

"I will, but not yet. I just need a little more time."

"You've had enough time! You said all you needed was the skull. Well, you have it now, but you are doing nothing. Your silly tricks and conjurings, you call that magic. Listen, you insignificant speck of nothing. If you do not restore me in three days' time, then, I will destroy you, boy, and find another to do this for me. I knew you were pathetic. Your power is garbage. All you men, you play silly little games, and think that some levitation spell, or transforming one object into another makes you a god, gives you ultimate power. I will show you ultimate power, for I will be restored, and when I am, I will not stop until I have acquired a power so great that neither the Heavens nor the Earth will stand in my presence without being torn apart and destroyed for all time. But for you, I don't need that power, I just need to snap your scrawny little neck, and end it all. So get to work! Restore me or die, fool!"

"Legion, stop being so melodramatic," Lilith said. "Here, kid, take this, it might help," she threw a book at Simon.

The young man caught the ancient tome and brushed some dust off of its tanned leather cover. Simon marveled as he opened the book and saw the spells that it contained. They were written in Greek, but this was a language he knew very well, for it was the language of his family and what they had always used for the spells that they passed down.

"It belonged to Simon Magus, the first. It was his spell book," the vixen said. "My husband had it lying around, and I thought you could do more with it than him. I think there may be a spell on page 347. It's a transmutation spell, one that many alchemists yearned to find in order to turn lead into gold. Such a waste of time. The true spell was to make a man more than he was, to transcend his being to be god-like in every way. Do this spell, and Legion here will be back to his old, I'm-gonna-destroy-the-world self in no time. Have fun boys — I've got some other things to attend to, but I'll be back later, so don't miss me too much," she licked her lips seductively and flew off.

"Well, boy, you have three days to master that spell. I would advise you get to it, now!" Legion roared, and Simon ran off to study the spell and the rest of the book.

***

Lyles held his head down. He felt like a failure, like all was lost. Legion was much stronger than they could have imagined, and this was not even his full power. What would they do if he was fully restored. Would anyone be able to save the world from absolute destruction? Ravenblade walked over to his friend and placed his hand on his shoulder.

"No time for regrets," the immortal said. "You always lose battles, but it's not over yet. The war can still be won."

"She's dead, Raven, don't you get it. That battle cost us too much. Esmeralda is dead, and Bianca is gone. Even if we defeat Legion, we lost!" Lyles yelled.

"The girl will be fine; we can get her back. People die every day. This world is a place of death. Ever since your first father and mother fell, that's how it's been. You can't waste time weeping for the dead; you need to move on, or Legion will win and the whole world will be destroyed."

One of the soldiers walked over. He took his helmet off and faced Lyles. The man was about six feet tall, with dark hair and dark eyes. He had a roughness to his face, weathered from the battles he had fought with the unholy. Chien stood behind Lyles as did Raven. Puck also appeared to see what the man wanted. But when the man saw the demon, he pulled his gun, only to have it sliced in half by Ravenblade's sword. In a puff of smokeless fire, Puck disappeared.

"He is a friend," Ravenblade said.

"You make friends with demons?" the man replied. "Then, I should wonder about your loyalties."

"Loyalties to who?" the immortal asked.

"To God and His church," the man replied.

"You may not know me, but I know all about your little organization," Ravenblade spoke. "You think that you are the authority on what is right and wrong, good and evil. Your church is founded on too much black and white, when the world is full of shades gray. I no longer serve God, that is true, but that is because He abandoned me long ago. Though I am not the evil man I once was. Like you, we are here to take down Legion, by any means possible. You can either be with us or against us."

The man looked them over, not sure what to think or say, but he spoke just the same, "Okay, then. Like they say—the enemy of my enemy."

"Good choice," Ravenblade confirmed.

Lyles looked over at Ravenblade and said, "So what do we do next?" Then he turned toward the soldier, "Do you have more weapons? And can those things still fly?"

"Yes and yes," the man replied. "Each ship is fully stocked to take down an army of demons from the blackest depths of Hell. We still have some ships that were not damaged in the fight. We can get anywhere in the world faster than any other craft can take you. But the question is, where do we go?"

"To the secret city of Djinn, Iblis's kingdom," Ravenblade stated. "They are there, no doubt preparing the ritual to restore Legion to his old self. We must act fast."

"But how do we know where to go?" the man wondered.

"Puck can lead us," Lyles said.

"No, he has already gone," Ravenblade said to Lyles, then turned to the soldier. "Just get us to the Arabian Desert, outside of Jordan. I will lead you from there. I know where it is and how to get in. And bring your weapons if you want, but honestly all I need is my sword," the immortal concluded, and exposed his blade, giving it a whirl and then putting it back into its sheath. It was time to bring the battle back to Legion.

CHAPTER XII
THE FIRE THAT BURNS

For so long have I, Death, yearned for the completion of things, but have only seen destruction and obliteration. The Darkness, that force of great evil, will be released onto this world, the way it was released onto all the other worlds that once had life, if Legion succeeds. But even if he does release the Darkness and usher in the end times, it is written that God will ultimately end the reign of the Darkness. But as a created being it is difficult for my mind to truly believe that all will work out when I have seen such evil in the world and destruction. But as the angels and men do, I will trust that all will be fulfilled as He has commanded and my pain will end along with the Darkness.

I look at all that is going on, on the Earth. Pandora has been held back from this planet, the only one she has not been allowed to touch, for this was God's world. He created this place for men and women to live in paradise. If Legion can succeed, then I feel that this time he will break the barrier. Pandora will come in, and the temple will be built. The world will fall to her schemes and the Darkness will enter it, releasing its demons, and the seven stars that it holds — Angels of Darkness, not like Satan and his hordes, but true beings of dark light. And Abaddon, their leader, will bring about the desolation of the world. I know that God and those who follow Him will be victorious, but how many souls will be lost. How many will go into fire for all eternity.

Legion does not know what he is doing. He never embraced the Darkness that created him, but fought against it, for in it all he remembered was torture and pain. Memories from when he was a baby, nightmares and dreams. Like all of his kind, Satan and Pandora included, they are puppets following a master not to victory but to their own doom. Following lies. Each believing that by ushering in the Darkness they will have power absolute. But in the end they will only know torment and pain, and the Darkness that they believe to be knowledge and freedom will exist no longer.

**

"This better not be a trap," Nathan said to Radix, who was leading him to Satan's lair.

200

"And if it is?" Radix returned.

"I'll be ready. I know enough about you to not trust you completely. Either way, I need to get there, and if I have to take you out along with Satan's army of demons, I will. I'll get my nephew back."

"So this nephew, your sister's kid? Who's the father?" Radix asked with a smirk.

"You, you evil piece of—" Nathan was cut off.

"Seriously, she had a kid after that?"

"Yes," Nathan tried to control his temper. "Twins, a boy and girl, but I never got to see them or get to know them. The boy is named Gideon; he was the one Satan stole from my sister. He would be four years old. My niece is Bianca, she is still with Ezzie."

"Wow, twins. Didn't think I had it in me."

"Don't even joke about it. Don't you remember what you did to her? You tore apart her soul. It is so hard for me to be here with you and not want to destroy you for what you did. I don't know if I can ever forgive you for that, and for killing my parents."

"Don't let God hear you say that. I thought once you guys went to Heaven especially those who transcend, that you were refined, and would be, I don't know, more Christ-like. Aren't you supposed to forgive everyone? I thought I heard him say that once or twice."

"Yes, I am supposed to forgive, but it's not easy. I am not perfected yet. We transcended beings aren't in our perfect state that all the saints will be in when all is finished. We are still flawed, like all creation; even the angels aren't perfect, why else would they fall. Only God is good, Jesus said that too."

"Well, forgive me or not, right now you're working with me. Maybe you'll see I'm not as bad as you think. Or maybe you'll realize that I'm worse," Radix snickered.

The two men followed the bank of the River Styx to reach the palace, and when they got there, Nathan was in awe. The building before him was enormous, and had a strange look to it. Some of it was like a castle from a fairytale, and other parts resembled a church. He looked at the stained glass windows, especially the large rose window at the center, which displayed an image of Satan's fall. Demonic statues led the way to the grand staircase and the entrance to this peculiar fortress. The gold, the jewels, the sky-piercing towers, this place was indeed a work of art—sinister, twisted art. The dragon atop the central tower looked so real, it even seemed as if it were breathing. Nathan and Radix prepared themselves, and began to walk toward Satan's lair. When they made it to the steps, the door above them opened and a goblin walked out, holding a staff with a glowing orb at its top. The goblin looked down at the two men and lifted the staff into the air. The orb glowed stronger and began to crackle with lightning.

"So, you are here to see my master?" he spoke. "He knew you were coming; he knows everything that goes on in his kingdom. But, unfortunately, he has no time for you. So, he sent some others to help you instead. Guards — get them!"

An army of armored guards marched swiftly from the doors of the palace, and instantly surrounded Nathan and Radix. Nathan's helmet and sword appeared, and he and his former enemy prepared to fight Satan's guards. It was time for battle, and both men were ready — they hungered for this in a strange way. It was the one thing Nathan and Radix had in common.

The guards were ready as well. Their armor was like black steel, but seemed to be very flexible, like Nathan's own. It was spiritual armor, forged in the fire of Hell. The suits were very ornate, and on each of their breastplates was a relief of a serpent with its fangs exposed and ready to strike. Their swords were black, and of the same material as their armor, an element called Hell metal. This was similar in composition to Angel metal, but forged in Hell rather than Heaven. Before Nathan or Radix could make a move, the guards poured onto them. The battle began, and it would take everything that Nathan and Radix had to win this one.

The sword of the Spirit, the Word of God, glowed in the hero's hand. He leaped at the guards that came at him, slashing them, and knocking them back. Radix had no weapon so he fought with his hands. He tackled one of the guards, and threw him into another. Then he took the shield and sword from the first guard he had tackled. Now he was equipped to battle an army. He struck guard after guard with their own weapons. It began to seem like these two warriors would win this battle against Satan's guards. But that is when the tables turned. More guards poured out, and it was getting difficult for Nathan and Radix to keep up with the army that surrounded them.

As fast and sure as their weapons were, it wasn't enough. For every guard they felled, there were more to take his place. A large guard moved in behind Nathan. He had a huge chain, which he swung and bashed the back of Nathan's helmet. The helmet disappeared as Nathan was knocked down. He looked up to see the large demon soldier hovering over him and moved to kick the soldier's stomach — this did not faze the guard at all.

With another swing, the heavy chain came down at Nathan again, but he rolled out of the way. He gripped his sword and lunged but the guard somehow tied up Nathan's sword with the chain and began to wrap the Hell-metal chain around the hero. The transcended warrior could not move, and his sword had disappeared like his helmet. *Is God Abandoning me?* he wondered. Then the same guard grabbed a mace from his side and bashed Nathan's skull with it, knocking him out. Radix fought through the crowd of guards and struck the large soldier from behind with his sword, but the blade was stopped by the soldier's armor. The demon turned and struck Radix with the mace. Radix rolled onto the ground, got up, and attacked the guard again, but his enemy was too strong. With a few swings of his mace, the guard displaced Radix's blade and knocked him down. He took a second chain from his side, as he'd done to Nathan, and he tied up Radix in the Hell-metal links. With his mace, the guard struck Radix on the skull, knocking him out as well. Nathan and Radix had lost the battle, and were now Satan's prisoners.

Nathan woke up; he was groggy and could barely see anything around him. The room was dark and barely lit by candles and by a strange light that filtered in from above, from the same stained glass windows he'd seen outside. The hero was suspended in the air by chains shackled to his hands and feet. He couldn't move. The chains that held him here were made of Hell metal like the guards' armor and swords, and the man, even though transcended, would not be able to break them. Hell metal and Angel metal were both spiritual metals and they could bind a soul, each in their own way, making it unable to break free from the metal's hold.

Nathan heard a bellowing laugh, and looked over to the spot where the image of the rose window danced on the ground. Beyond that spot was a throne with a large hulking beast atop it. The silhouette looked like one he had seen before. It was Satan, and Nathan was now a prisoner in his lair. He came to free his nephew, but ended up trading paradise for torture, peace for pain.

"Godchild, good to see you again," the demon scoffed. "So you planned to infiltrate my palace and … do what? Save your nephew?"

Nathan found it hard to speak, but he got out what he could, "Yes. Where is he?"

"Not here," Satan answered. "But I won't tell you where. I need him, and refuse to let you or God's army ruin what I have planned."

"So he is safe?"

"For now," the Devil replied.

"You won't keep me here forever, and when I get out, I will find him, I will bring him home. But first I will take your head. God will have victory. It's written. Your plans will end, but God's will come to completion."

"Silence!" Satan boomed. "You are in my kingdom, boy. There is no God here, only me, and I can make your pain far worse than it already is. So stay thy tongue. You will remain here for all eternity. I will watch your pain every day from my throne. Listen here, boy, there is nothing you can or will ever do to stop me. Look at you. Your armor has gone. You have no weapons, nothing. He has abandoned you."

Nathan had not realized it yet, but the demon was right, he had no armor, nothing, just his loincloth to cover him. What had happened? Was God angry because he came to Hell to get Gideon; was He upset that Nathan tried to take justice into his own hands? He prayed and asked the Lord for forgiveness. He should have trusted in God and His plan, knowing that all would work out as it always does. Why was he so rash? Why did he always try to do such things alone, to take on things he shouldn't and try to save the world? Jesus was the only real Savior. No one needed Nathan to do *anything*. But something inside made him want to fight, to stand before the forces of Darkness, and bring about the end of God's enemies. It was a holy anger that burned inside of him. But maybe this time he should have let it be. He should have stayed in Heaven and trained and waited for Armageddon to battle Satan's forces. He was obviously not ready. Defeated so easily and now damned for all eternity. There was no hope left. Where was his Lord, his Savior, his God?

While Nathan was chained in Satan's lair, Radix was being dragged down to the dungeon. Zreet, Satan's impish goblin host, led a band of guards who dragged Radix behind them. The evil man had his hands and feet chained, making it difficult to move. The Hell metal bonds were too strong for him to break. The guards marched through the catacombs under Satan's palace, passing cell after cell filled with vicious demons, ready to devour any who entered their prison domain. The one-time powerful killer was now being dragged around like a child's toy and, at this moment, he fell to the ground. One guard pulled on his chains but Radix did not get up at once. He looked before him and saw a large demon lying on the floor of its cell. Radix could feel a great power from this one and wondered why it slept so. He believed that Lucifer had cast an enchantment on this creature to keep it from breaking loose, for the power-reading he received from it was off the charts. Under his breath, Radix began to whisper a chant. The guard pulled harder on the chain and then struck Radix with the hilt of his sword, telling him to move. On his knees, the evil man gave a grin, and just then the monster inside the cell awoke and thrust itself at the bars. It tore them from the walls, and broke free, just as Radix had hoped. This was his chance to escape. The demon ripped open more cells, releasing other prisoners. Together they attacked the guards, allowing Radix to slip away. He hobbled as best he could within the confines of the chains that held his hands and feet. As he reached the staircase to go up out of the dungeon, he walked right into the same large guard that had beaten him and Nathan earlier. The demonic soldier was incensed and pulled out his sword. It shone with a dark light and seemed larger and stronger than the ones that the other guards used. Radix blocked the blade with the chain that was wrapped around his wrists. Clash after clash, the chain began to weaken and then at once it fell off. His hands were free, but his legs were still tied. The soldier grew more aggressive and Radix tried to roll out of the way of each swing of its blade. He rolled right into the beast's legs and tripped it to the ground. With a few seconds to spare now, Radix untied the restraints on his legs and stood up, just as the guard regained his footing. The guard swung his blade in the tight dungeon corridor and the sinister villain did all he could to dodge each blow. He grabbed the demon's sword hand and twisted it, spun him around, and sent him crashing into the wall. This creature was strong but Radix had more skill. It dropped its sword and Radix rolled to grab it first. Now he had a weapon. The guard retrieved its mace and began to swing it at Radix, who blocked each blow with the sword in this hands. In a cunning move, the sly cretin kicked the demon's leg and hit it in the side with the hilt of his blade. Then Radix kneed it in the face and slashed the demon's arm with the sword, causing it to drop the mace. Instantly, Radix ran up the stairs.

When he came to the top of the stairs, Radix saw that he had entered Satan's trophy room. There were glass cases displaying all sorts of mystical artifacts. The sinful man licked his lips but there was no time to find a new weapon here — he needed to get out of the castle before he was caught and overpowered again.

He moved quickly but was stopped by a large oak door. Radix tried to push it open but it would not budge. He shoved harder and harder but the door was locked shut, and now Radix could hear someone climbing up the stairs. The beastly guard charged toward Radix, waving its mace.

This fight is far from over, the villain thought, and he went at the soldier with his blade. They knocked each other back and forth, breaking the display cases in the room, causing the artifacts to fall all over the ground. Radix rolled and grabbed a shield, which he used to block the mace again and to give himself a chance to attack the demon's side with his sword. The demon dropped the mace again and gave a bellowing scream.

The monstrous guard pulled a chain from its side and began to swing it. With lightning speed, it came at Radix and the evil man did all he could to block it with the shield. Then he stopped himself. What was he doing? He was still Radix, the root of all evil, he had great power and might. This lowly guard of the Devil was no match for him. Charging up his black spirit, the sinister man grew stronger, his power rising with each second. He threw down the sword and shield. The guard swung the chain again, but this time Radix caught it, wrapped it around his hand, and began a tug of war with the guard. Back and forth they went. Then in a quick motion Radix twirled the chain, making it rise and wrap around the guard's neck; he did this twice more and pulled the creature to the ground. Then he moved closer and tightened the grip on the chain, choking the guard out. In no time, the chain cut through the demon's throat, separating its head from its body and sending it to the second death. Now, Radix grabbed the sword and shield again and charged at the door with all his might. The door was knocked off of its hinges and crashed into the ground.

At one time Radix was the right hand of the Devil, carrying out his evil deeds upon the Earth. Now he was a fugitive running from his former master, trying to find a way to leave this plane and gain his freedom. Radix ran as fast as he could, paying no mind to all the artful reliefs carved into the walls, reliefs showing the pain and suffering of those outside this palace — like he had been not too long ago. When he came to the end of the hall, there was another locked door. He pounded and pounded. The door began to give but as it did he heard someone. Who was it now? He looked and saw the goblin, who had commanded the guards earlier, coming up behind him.

Radix pushed at the door one last time, and it gave, flying open. Just as Radix cleared the doorway, a bolt of energy from the goblin's staff struck him from behind and laid him out on the ground. He rolled to his back and looked up. Zreet was standing over him and his staff glowed very brightly.

"Seems like you are more trouble than we thought, Radix," the goblin said. "Guess I will just have to place your soul into my orb for safe keeping."

The goblin's staff glowed a bright blue color and began to charge up. Radix lay there watching, unable to move, stunned by the shock he had received. It seemed to all be over.

CHAPTER XIII
WAR ON THE STREETS

Judy Ramirez woke up to sound of knocking at her apartment door. She wondered who could be there. It was a little after noon but she had been working the late-night news and doing a lot of investigative reporting lately so she grabbed her sleep whenever she could. Not too concerned about how she looked, she threw on a robe and her fuzzy bunny slippers and went to see who could be at her door. Curiously, she looked through the peephole and saw Officer Jay Sil standing outside. Why was he here? Was it about the broadcast? She couldn't answer the door like this.

"Hey, Judy, I know you're in there. I saw your car parked out front," Jay said.

"There es no Judy here," she replied in a thick Hispanic accent.

"That is the worst Spanish accent I have ever heard. I thought you were Latina? Come on — open up."

She had no choice; she had already spoken. What was the worst thing that could happen? It was not like he could arrest her for reporting that story.

"Okay, okay, I'll open the door, but you're not coming in. We can talk in the doorway," she compromised.

"Sure," Jay said.

Judy opened the door and as she did, Jay Sil simply strolled in.

"You said you wouldn't come in," she ranted.

"I lied. Now shut the door. We need to talk."

"Talk about what? I hardly know you, and my place is a mess and, right now, so am I. I hate being seen like this, with bedhead, and no make-up, in my robe and slippers, come on. I only let you in because you're a cop," she whined.

"You're right I've seen you looking better, and just so you know, I feel we know each other pretty well. I did see you with your top off. That's past first base in my book."

"You're disgusting, you know that," Judy remarked. "I had to get away. Didn't know what else to do."

"And how did that work out for you?"

"Okay, okay, let's talk. Make yourself comfy," she pointed to a couch that had magazines and newspapers thrown on it.

The whole apartment was a mess. Judy had not exaggerated. Being an investigative reporter gave her little time to clean. Jay pushed aside some magazines and sat down. Judy sat across from him in a chair, leaning back as if she were too busy and too tired to hear anything that the officer had to say.

"Well, let me start by thanking you," Jay stated.

"For what?" Judy inquired.

"For getting my badge taken away, that's what," he said with just a hint of sarcasm. "But that's not why I'm here. I don't hold grudges."

"Well, that's good to know," Judy replied, with slightly more sarcasm than Jay.

"I have a proposition for you," he leaned forward.

"I'm not that kind of girl. I already told you that I did that to get away."

"Not that kind of proposition. I want to get you the story of the decade."

"Okay, I'm listening."

"Well, I saw your report on the Pain Pit, but I'm not sure you know how serious this all is. Have you ever heard of the Chaldean?"

"The what?"

"The Chaldean — it's what they called Babylonians when they were around. Well, there is a guy going by this name, and he is connected to a crime ring so big that it spans beyond the city, out of the country, and around the entire world. It is said that he has his hands in every evil plot the world over. It's even possible that this guy is responsible for 9/11. The catch is, they think he is in New York, hiding as some big-shot business owner, but no one knows who he is. There are a lot of guys who fit the bill. But I think there is a link at the Pain Pit, in the underground MMA circuit that's going on there. Big Mike has someone backing him, and now I hear that Big Mike is letting this backer introduce some of his own fighters, fighters from a gang that has resurfaced lately but in a much worse way. Remember all those crazy murders from a few years back. It could all be tied in. The gang is called the Children of the Dragon. And if I am right, they will fight tomorrow night at the Pain Pit. If they are tied into the Chaldean then he may be there, or at least they can lead us to him."

"So, what do you plan on doing exactly? Break in, maybe sneak in as a competitor, and try to fight one of these guys, get him to spill the beans on the Chalda — whatever you called him," Judy said, half joking.

"Exactly!" Jay answered very seriously.

"You're nuts! You know that? These guys are killers. You're just a cop. Well, actually you used to be a cop."

"Hey, enough low blows. I'm tough. I can hold my own. I took Taekwondo and am a third-degree black belt. Plus, I learned a lot of self-defense in the academy. We're trained to take down punks like this. It's what we do."

"I have heard of this gang, Jay, and honestly what I've heard is bad news. I don't think you can handle them. I'm not in. No way."

"Come on, Judy, what happened to the bravest reporter I know, Miss 'do whatever it takes to get the job done.' You can help shut down this racket, and if we catch the Chaldean, you may even save lives. What do you say?"

"I don't know. This is crazy?"

"Yes, it is crazy. And there is a huge chance that after this they'll never let me back into the force. Honestly, I only became a cop for one reason and one reason alone — to serve and protect the people. And cop or not, that's what I plan to do," Jay gave Judy a grin.

Unable to resist his charm, she threw her face into her hands and said, "Yes, I'm in."

"Okay, let's talk strategy."

***

"All is going according to plan, our son will be restored in no time," Lilith said to Samyaza.

"So, you have the skull, and the Magus kid?" he replied.

"Yes, and thanks for getting me that book. I told the boy that I got it from my husband's library," the succubus spoke with a sultry tongue and placed a finger on Samyaza's chest.

"Don't tease me, Lilith," he said. "Those days have passed. I'm over you."

"I find that hard to believe," she said and ran her hand up his thigh.

The former Watcher grabbed the seductress' hand and pushed her away. Then, he walked over to his favorite chair in his study and sat down. Lilith remained standing. Samyaza took a cigar from his jacket pocket, cut the tip off, and lit it.

"Still like those nasty things?" she asked.

"Of course. They relax me."

"I never cared for the smell."

"Well, that's your prerogative. So, how much longer until he is restored? I want to celebrate."

"Soon. Legion's given the magician three days to figure out the spell. But after it's over, what's your plan? Tell Legion that you're his father? Invite him to live with you? Do you think he will even care, let alone believe a word that you say?"

"He's my son, he'll know it, and he'll follow. I have my ways."

"He's a lunatic. I am ashamed to say he's my son. Though, I never plan on telling him. Lucifer would have my head."

"Are you seriously that afraid of your husband? Do you think he would send you to the second death because you slept with me and got pregnant so many years ago? How many women has he seduced, and you how many men? Does he even care?"

"When it's you he does. He was always jealous of you. Because —," she stopped herself.

"Because you loved me," Samyaza completed her sentence. "Don't worry, I'll never tell. But I will let Legion know that I am his father once he is restored. Together with his new brother, Gideon, and me, we will take over this world and usher in the Darkness. Then we will conquer all of creation. I will seize the throne of God. Unlike your husband, I will succeed. He was stupid to not cherish the knowledge he was given. He abandoned it because he wants the power all to himself. I can share. The Darkness will devour God and all His creation, and set me up as king and my sons as princes to rule the new creation that we will make in *our* image."

213

"Do you really think it can happen? When you have your son restored, do me a favor. Start your domination by destroying my husband's kingdom. You're right in saying that he abandoned the knowledge. He opened my eyes when he introduced me to that knowledge, and then I opened yours. Free me from him. Take him down, for I can't follow him any longer. His ego has grown too much. Not only does he think he can defeat God alone, but he also believes that he can conquer the Darkness, to become absolute over all. Not to become a king but to truly become God himself. Do you really think that you can succeed? Can you bring the end of this world, the end of my husband's reign, and the end of God Himself?"

"Unlike Lucifer, my ego is not quite so large. Nothing is certain, but I have hope. These men of the world are corrupt, more so than me. They are like ticks sucking the life from all that God gave them. But God is no better. He is Master of all, yet He allows this world to be corrupt. He allows all this pain and suffering. The Darkness, on the other hand — what God and His angels call evil — it is pure knowledge and freedom. The Darkness desires to be nothing. It just wants to absorb everything into itself. It wants to commune with all creation, and become one with it. To make it prosper and give us freedom and choice. If I can rule under the Darkness' dominion, then I can teach those that we rule over to live right and just, to take care of the world they are given, and to be more than just puppets following a master. Satan just wants slaves. He says otherwise, but I have seen his game. He wants to rule with an iron hand heavier than the One who rules from Heaven. My hand will not be iron but flesh. I will be fair and wise. And then you and I can be together again. We can make more children, we can populate our world, and all will be our sons and daughters. This is the vision that I received when I first was awakened that night by you in the temple. When the Darkness opened my eyes."

"What you say sounds good, but we will have to see," Lilith said, and then she vanished from his sight.

The fallen angel sat in his chair smoking his cigar. His thoughts went to the future, to a time when the world would be perfect under his rule. He really believed this. The things he did might seem wrong or even evil at times, but he only did them so that one day he could make things better — or so he kept telling himself. His Machiavellian philosophy kept him deceived, for what he did *was* evil. He was soaked in sin, and the Darkness that he served would never let him be a king nor recreate the world in his image. No, the Darkness only desired to feed, to destroy all life by absorbing its life force. It had no desire to even be God, just to suck Him out of existence, and then be the only thing remaining. But this could never be.

The God of all, the Almighty, was indeed more powerful than the Darkness, for the Lord alone was God, and nothing could ever stop Him. He loved His children and gave them freewill to choose between the Light and Darkness. But no matter what, in the end the victory would belong to the Lord, as it was written.

"Yes," Samyaza answered his phone. "Excellent. Tomorrow night, we will show them what true power is. Make sure Big Mike and his goons will never forget the name of the Chaldean and the Children of the Dragon. I am only funding his club to show the world our power and might. Once we're done, then he won't be needed any more. I trust you know what to do, Number One. Perfect. Start with Number Six. I only want to give them a taste of what's to come. I think he can definitely get the point across."

The man hung up the phone and sat back with a smile. Soon his son would regain his power. Then with Legion, Gideon, and the Children of the Dragon, Samyaza would indeed usher in the Darkness. The end was near, and with it a new beginning.

***

He planned this perfectly. Even though Jay Sil had lost his badge, he still had his connections and his ways of getting information. The young cop was good, on his way to being one of the best, if he could ever get his badge back. He learned that the fighters all met on the south side of the building, and that new recruits were welcomed each night if they so dared to enter the ring. Big Mike was always hungry for new blood. This was his way of picking out the best there were.

Jay was certain that this time his disguise was flawless. He was unrecognizable with his new crew cut; and he was covered in fake tattoos, applied by one of the best guys he knew — the

215

ink would last for days and not rub off even in a fight. He also included some fake scars, one on his right cheek, and another over his left shoulder. Thanks to the contacts he was wearing, his eyes were now a shade of green, and a couple of gold teeth added some extra flair. He wore a black tank top, black and red shorts, and a pair of wrestling boots that came up to his knees. He was ready for whatever the night would bring, hoping that somehow Judy and he could succeed.

It was his job to go in and talk to the fighters. He wore a small receiver in his ear so Judy could record all of his conversations. She would then go in herself and try to get some information from those watching the fight. The plan was to get enough evidence to lead them to the Chaldean. Once Jay had it, he could go to the chief, solve this case, and get his badge back. Judy would get the story of the decade and everyone would win. Hopefully their plan would work.

Judy went inside the bar and all eyes were on her. She was beautiful, for sure, but tonight she went the extra mile to make sure that she would get in without a hitch. She wore her hair long, letting her natural curls show, her venom-red lipstick, black miniskirt, halter top, and over the knee high-heeled patent-leather boots had every guys' head turning. She walked into the kitchen and gave the passwords. The goons looked her over and without a second thought let her in. Mad Mike always liked having some attractive girls in the place to keep the men happy, and the goons couldn't think of a girl that would make them any happier. She was led down some stairs and then walked out to the ring area. There were some small tables set up and a bar for drinks. Below that was stadium seating and a caged-in octagon ring. Judy looked up to see a glass booth above the right side of the ring and some men were inside having drinks and smoking cigars. It was Big Mike and his crew. When Mike saw Judy, he pointed her out and requested that she be brought to him. A moment later, a large man approached the smoking-hot spy and asked her if she would care to have a drink with the owner. This was better than she had hoped, and without hesitating she followed the large man to the booth. The room was filled with smoke, and stunk of cheap liquor. Instantly, Big Mike got up and walked over to Judy, asking her to join him for a drink. He sat her down, and began to flirt with her. She played the part well, trying not to be too obvious or ask any real questions, at least not yet. She'd get him drunk first and then go for the good stuff.

Outside, Jay was lined up with other prospective fighters for the night. He could hear Judy's conversation in his earpiece. It was a little distracting, but he was happy to see she got inside. Also he recognized Mike's voice and was hoping the guy would spill the beans and make this a quick and easy night. A few minutes later, a door opened and the fighters, including Jay himself, were ushered in. They were led to a locker room where they geared up for the fight. Jay took off his shirt, revealing more of his new body art. He then went on to wrap up his hands and wrists with tape, and he even put in a mouth guard. He really looked the part and no one even dared question why he was there.

The young officer was in great shape. He worked out six days a week, conditioning his muscles. He had more of an athletic build and was not as bulky as some of the men there. Jay Sil was hoping that he could close this up before entering into the ring, but he was ready just in case he had to. Casually, Jay turned to a Latin American man who was gearing up next to him. He was a little shorter than Jay, but slightly stockier and well built. The man was throwing punches in the air to prepare for the ring.

"Hey," Jay said.

"'Sup," the man answered.

"You ready for tonight?"

"Sure, why not? I've been ready for this my whole life. What's it to you? Trying to psych me out?" the man said.

"Nah," Jay replied quickly. "So, you ever done this before?"

"Yeah, a few dozen times. I've been fightin' my whole life. Why you asking?"

"Just talking. I've been in a few, but nothing this big. Tryin' to get a feel for it, ya know," Jay tried to cover himself. "I heard if we win we could join Mike's crew. Could mean some steady pay."

"Tell me about it. My family could use the money. But you gotta beat one of his boys to get in. It'll be us versus them out there. You think you got what it takes to get in? I've never lost yet."

"I can hold my own."

"So, how about you? You got a family, bro. I have a daughter. Her mother and I need this paycheck to pay the rent and get some good food on the table. What are you fighting for?"

"To survive."

"Good enough. You seem like a cool dude. Good luck, bro. You're gonna need it. I heard there is a new crew coming out tonight and they are vicious. Call themselves the Children of the Dragon, some satanic gang or something. I heard they were hardcore. If you step in the ring with one of them tonight, you better be ready. Think they have first billing against Mike's guys then they send us in one by one to see how we do. The winners stay, the losers leave. Simple enough."

"The Children of the Dragon. I've heard of them. Aren't they tied into some guy called the Chaldean? I heard he's running the streets out there. Anybody works for him is set."

"Don't know about no Chaldean, sounds like a punk name anyway. But these guys are running the streets out there. Ain't no one want to mess with them. Some superstitious mumbo-jumbo crap. I don't buy into any of that. I got my fists and that's all I need. They're men like us, and any man can be taken down."

"Yeah, I hear ya."

Judy listened to Jay's conversation and tried to focus on her own at the same time. So far, Mike had given her no answers, only his hand halfway up her skirt. She tried to not fight back too much, since she really wanted to get this story, but in her mind she was praying that this would not go too far.

She did shot after shot with the guy, and the petite Latina could hold her liquor well, better than Mike, it seemed. Down in the ring, an announcer came out and the fights were ready to start. In the locker room, the new contestants were rallied up and brought to ringside. When Jay Sil got there, he could see Mike's guys on one side, and another group on the opposite side. That must have been the Children of the Dragon. They were all large white males with shaved heads and blue eyes. Their bodies were covered in tattoos of mystical symbols and demonic beasts. One of the guys, who seemed like he was in charge by the way he gave orders to the others, had a dragon tattoo that started on his neck and wrapped itself all the way around his torso. Jay watched them. This might not be as easy as he thought. They looked like they meant serious business. Each man stood perfectly erect in military style, while the man with the dragon tattoo barked commands.

Mike's crew looked tough also, but not as disciplined as the other group, which made the Children of the Dragon all the more intense. Jay took another look at the gang and noticed something else. They each had a number tattooed in the center of his chest. And they were lined up in number order, two through six. When the leader turned, Jay could see that he was number one. The announcer said a few words to those in attendance and then announced the first match. It was Rocco Finch, one of Mike's best fighters, versus a member of the Children of the Dragon only called by his number — Six.

"This'll be good, toots," Mike said to Judy. "Watch as my guy pummels this schmuck. This new gang thinks they're tough, but my men are the best. They're ruthless. Rocco's gonna teach this guy a lesson. Gotta show them who really owns the streets. I only let them fight because their boss is a big backer of mine. They call him the Chaldean. I hate guys with stupid names to make them seem tougher than they are. He might be one of my backers, but I still need to keep him in line. After tonight, he'll see that my boys are the best. We're gonna run this city. I'm gonna be stupid rich and powerful."

Judy didn't say much, just smiled and giggled. She was happy that the more Mike drank, the more he talked. Now, she got just what she needed. The Chaldean was indeed involved, just as Jay had assumed. He could hear it all from ringside, and figured after this fight he could sneak back to the locker room and then escape outside. This would be over quicker than he thought. Rocco stepped into the cage, and so did Six. Both men were big, but Six was exceptionally large and well built. His arms were like cannons and his legs like pillars. He was very cut— there did not seem to be an ounce of fat on the guy. The two men faced off, bumped fists, and the referee started the match.

Rocco got in some good hits to start, though Six seemed to not feel a thing. It was almost as if he was letting his competitor get in the blows. The tables turned fast, and in a matter of seconds, Rocco was on the ground. Six got the fighter into a chokehold and pulled him up high on his chest.

"Wow, this guy is tough, huh?" the Latin American man said to Jay. "Oh, by the way name's Eddie.

"I'm Scott," Jay said, trying to stay in character.

Rocco squirmed trying to get out of the hold, but Six was too strong. He began to stand up, holding Rocco tighter and tighter. Then in one swift motion Six snapped Rocco's neck leaving him lifeless in the ring. The large man just stood there seething, and the ref lifted Six's hand in victory. Some of Mike's guys came out to the ring to check on Rocco, verifying that he was indeed dead. They were angry and ran over to Six, who was exiting the ring. He turned and slugged one of the guys who grabbed him. Mike looked upset and worried all at once, but he knew the danger of these fights and signaled for some of his security to break this up. It was par for the course, sometimes you lost soldiers in a war like this, but Mike didn't want to lose his whole racket over it. The fight was broken up, and the next event was announced.

Since Six had won, he would stay on to fight. He went back into the ring, and it was announced that he would fight one of the new recruits. Eddie was up. Jay was worried for his new friend's life after what he just saw in the ring. Eddie seemed confident, though. He signed himself and went into the ring. He was much smaller than the mountain of a man, Six. But Eddie was fast. He hoped that his speed would beat Six's strength. As much as Jay wanted to see the fight and hoped that Eddie could survive, he knew it was best to try and sneak out at this point, while all eyes were on the ring. Just as Jay reached the door to the locker room, one of Mike's men stopped him.

"Where're you goin'?" he asked Jay.

"Just to get some water, that's all. I left my bottle in the locker room," he answered.

"Well, tough. You'll have to wait for this to be over, and I think you're next, anyway, so maybe it'll be over quick, and then you can get a drink," the man laughed.

Jay walked back to ringside, trying to figure out how he was going to escape. Inside the ring, Eddie was holding his own. He moved quickly around the large man, and began to tie up his legs. But as hard as Eddie tried, Six was too strong, and the smaller fighter couldn't take him down. Back and forth it went, until the man with the number one and dragon tattoos said something under his breath. Six nodded as if he understood, and out of nowhere struck Eddie with a surprisingly fast right hand to the gut. Then, Six struck him in the throat. Eddie fell to the ground, blood poured from his mouth. Mike was enraged, and Judy was feeling very uncomfortable.

Down in the ring, they cleaned up the mess, and took Eddie's body away. Now his daughter would grow up without a father. Jay felt bad; the man might have made some wrong choices but for the right reasons, and now it was all for nothing. Just then, a man came to escort Jay into the ring. This was it. He just saw this guy kill two men in front of him, and Jay knew he would be next. How could he even face up against this killing machine? There was no hope.

Judy looked on, afraid that Jay would die like the others. Why did she agree to do this? Sure, she got her scoop, Jay was right, but was it worth him losing his life. The fighters faced off, bumped fists, and the match began. Jay stayed back, sized up the big man, and tried to think of the best way to attack him. This guy seemed so cool and collected and gave no sign of weakness. All of a sudden, a shot was heard and everyone stopped. Three more shots were fired, and a voice came over a bullhorn.

"This is the police, no one move, you are all under arrest," it was Detective Rogers.

Armored officers came crashing in from all doors and flooded into the arena. Quickly, Six turned and left the ring at Number One's command. The group of six men snuck out through a back door before the cops finished filing in. Jay, on the other hand, did not get out of the ring in time. He was surrounded by officers and gave himself up. At least he was still alive. Up in the box, Mike grabbed Judy and tried to escape out through a secret exit. She squirmed, but he planned to keep his prize and move the party back to his apartment. He didn't want to get caught by the cops and would have a story for the officers in the morning, along with an alibi.

After a thorough investigation, Big Mike would be found without fault, not realizing that someone was running this circuit behind his bar. Judy did not want to go with the guy and stepped on his foot with her high heel. It hurt, and Mike loosened his grip. Instantly, the girl ran, but Mike's men chased her. Officers made their way to the secret corridor and apprehended Mike, and began to chase down his crew

Judy managed to sneak out while Mike's men were tackled from behind and thrown to the ground. There was no escape for Big Mike this time. It was over. His racket was done. The Chaldean knew the cops would come, he knew everything that went on in this city, for in so many ways he controlled it. That is why his gang was able to escape. It was all part of his plan. Now the city knew first-hand the strength and might of the Children of the Dragon. Fear would follow and with fear came true power. In the ring, Jay Sil was being arrested. Detective Rogers walked in and took him from the arresting officer.

"You look familiar punk," he said, and then took a really close look. "Sil? Is that you?"

"I plead the fifth," Jay said.

"Why you little—," Detective Rogers was so upset he could not even finish his sentence. "You're coming with me. The chief is going to love this."

CHAPTER XIV
GATHERING THE FORCES

"I don't know what to do, brother," Michael said to Raphael.

"Is this about how Azrael and I helped Nathan to go into Hell to rescue Gideon? You know we atoned for our actions, but what we did was for good not evil," Raphael said.

"I understand why you did what you did. But I also pray that Nathan's soul is safe. I too want to do what is right. That is why I cannot just stand by and let Legion regain his power and destroy the world," the Archangel stated. "The Father has called us to be more than messengers. We are to serve, protect, and conquer evil. But it seems all we do lately is sit back and watch as the whole world falls into Darkness."

"You know that the Father's plan will be accomplished. It is written. What is your concern? The world, this world at least, will not completely fall. The chosen will have new life and a new Heaven and a new Earth to dwell on. All will be made right, by the One who leads us. God alone is good and knows what is good. Who are we to boldly step out of His plan to fulfill our own?" Raphael questioned.

"You say that, but don't you do the same. Don't we all. I trust in our Lord and His plan, but sometimes He forms plans within our hearts to fulfill His own. I, like all of us, want this war to end and for the destruction to stop. But I need help. I know I said I would do this alone. But I cannot. Stand by my side, brother."

"I am by your side, Michael. You know that. That is why I am here," Raphael stated.

"Me, too!" The voice of Gabriel came from behind Michael.

Michael turned to greet his brother, "Thank you. What about the others?"

"You know they will not," Gabriel said. "But, Michael, do you forget that you command the armies of God. You are the highest-ranking angel of all, the Archangel. Give the cry, and I will sound the trumpet, and as always the army of the Lord will come down to fight. With that force with us, Legion will be vanquished. No demon can stand before God's army."

"Thank you," Michael said and placed his hand on Raphael's shoulder. "Thank you, my brothers. But it is not time to unleash the army of God on the Earth. Only at His command can I do such a thing. We must trust in Him. But with the three of us standing against Legion, we will be victorious. Legion will fall by our combined might, and by the power of the Ever-Living God!"

"Yes, brother, you are right," Raphael said. "Together we will stand, and we will vanquish that beast."

***

With lightning-fast speed, the craft that belonged to the Army of the Council carried a crew of heroes who prepared themselves as best they could for a war they were unsure they could fight. The airship was in stealth mode and utilized the most advanced technologies known to man, making it not only invisible in the sky but also allowing it to move into any airspace without being detected by radar. This craft could enter any territory around the world and no one would ever know. Inside the belly of the ship with the twelve soldiers of the Council's army sat Lyles, Ravenblade, and Chien. They were all harnessed in, side by side, in two rows facing each other. This area of the craft was plain. It had no windows, only steel walls all around. Toward the front was the entrance to the weapon storage room, and then beyond that was the cockpit. Next to Lyles sat the man whom they had just met only moments before, a man who shared a battle with them against a demon so powerful he tore the very foundation of a mountain down around them. This man was a high-ranking soldier in the Council's army. He was born and raised to kill for justice. But his targets were not men, they were demons, and his goal was to send them to the second death. Aberto Ruggero was not a man of many words, though he could speak nearly every known language around the world. His American English was flawless, without a hint of an accent, and this was the case for all the languages he spoke. He prided himself on sounding like a native wherever he went. It helped him on covert missions, to mingle and get information that most foreigners could not. Now, though, he sat back with his head down, focusing on what they would need to do to take Legion down.

The Council had briefed Aberto about the monster, a soul that housed thousands of demons. There were accounts of how in ancient times he plagued the world and even came close to bringing an end to all life, until a mighty angel destroyed his body. After that, he had moved onto possessing bodies of people and animals, jumping from host to host, for none could contain him for long. Christ had even had an encounter with the demon, whom he expelled from a boy. Many only know of that story, but there is so much more to tell. Now Aberto had a first-hand account of this vicious creature, and saw the destruction he could cause. All this, and he was not even at full power. How the Earth even stood for as long as it had with this monster roaming through it is a miracle within itself and a testimony to God's hand over the fate of His creation.

"I'm Lyles, by the way," the young man said to Aberto.

The soldier did not reply right away. Lyles sat in the awkward silence, until finally the man spoke.

"Sorry, I was praying the Our Father. We will need our Lord's protection in this battle, for only He can win this," Aberto stated.

"Amen," Lyles said.

"My name is Aberto Ruggero, and these are my men. We will fight until our dying breath as we swore to our God when we enlisted in this war. But what brings you to this fight? You are no soldier."

"The same as you — to fight the good fight. God called me to this battle also. And though it has taken away so many people that I loved, I won't stop fighting. Not as long as I can hold a sword and swing it."

"Good, we need warriors for this fight," Aberto attested. "It will not be easy. Legion is not simply another demon; he is thousands of them, and if his power is maximized to its full potential, then the Armageddon may surely come and fast."

"You know nothing of Legion," Ravenblade said. "I battled him when he first started to plague this world. In this form, I was not able to contest his might. It took the angel with no name to defeat him. But that defeat conquered only Legion's body, not his soul. That beast has the potential to end all life on this planet and to finally usher in the Darkness. Can he be defeated? Yes. But we have to fight smarter, not harder, for his power will be greater than ours if his full power is unleashed. Despite our best efforts, the end has already been written. Even with my darkened heart I know that."

"We can and will win by the hand of God, for nothing can stop His people if they fight in His name and by His will," Aberto professed. "But, who are you, stranger, that you have fought Legion so long ago but sit here with us today?"

"I have nothing to explain to you. Just know that I am ancient, and that you don't want to cross my sword in battle. Enough talking; it is time to fight. Get your weapons ready. We need to infiltrate the kingdom of Iblis and get to Legion before they restore his full power. We will all need to focus, for the Djinn will be there as well, and who knows what else. It may be harder than any of us think," the immortal concluded, and all were silent as the aircraft readied to land.

Dust blew up all around as the ship eased down. They had traveled thousands of miles from China all the way to the Arabian Desert. Lyles sighed a breath as they were all unharnessed and prepared to disembark. He hadn't been here since they fought Radix, which felt like a lifetime ago. The soldiers suited up in their body armor, and readied their weapons. Lyles, Ravenblade, and Chien grabbed their swords. The crew of men walked down the ramp to exit the aircraft. The desert was hot and dry, but soon it would be evening.

"So, what's the plan, Raven?" Lyles asked.

"The entrance to the Djinn's city is not far. We go in and stop Legion before he can restore himself to full strength. That simple," he replied.

"But what if they have done the ritual already?" Chien asked.

"No, I can feel it. He is still weak," Ravenblade stated. "But I'm not sure how much more time we have."

"I wouldn't call him weak. He tore up that mountain," Lyles said.

"Then just imagine what he will do when he's at full strength," Ravenblade advised.

"I know how you can stop him," a voice beamed from above.

The group of men looked up. A bright light descended from the heavens like the Sun was coming down from the sky. As the light lowered, the men got a better view of what or who it was before them. Michael shone with radiance like no other angel, and all who laid eyes on him at this moment were in awe. Aberto and his men bowed in reverence.

"Men, do not bow, for I am but a servant of the Lord," Michael said. "Save your reverence for God alone. Do not fear the enemy that you will face for the Lord can and will conquer all evil. I am here to aid in your quest, as are some of my brethren. The girl that has been taken, I have sworn to protect her. I will make sure that she is returned safely, without harm. And once I have done this, my brothers and I will cut down Legion, sending him to the second death for all eternity. His sin is darker than any who have walked this Earth. His reign will end quickly and your lives can continue as they were before he came."

"So, now you come down, Michael?" Ravenblade questioned. "Why not before he laid waste to that mountain and killed those people?"

"Oh, but I was there," the Archangel replied. "I tried to save the girl but was tricked by Lilith and her schemes."

"The mighty Archangel bested by Satan's whore. That's rich. Why have you not just annihilated him already? Can't you destroy him with your fiery blade? Why are we even here?"

"Raven, you know it is not that simple. We have rules to abide by. We can't simply enact the justice of God without cause."

"This is a big joke."

"Is it? You were one of us once; you should know why I do what I do. You should know how hard it is to hold back my blade. But God has a plan and it will succeed. It already has. Legion will meet his end, I promise. But I must work inside the rules. Right now, my job is to free the girl. Once I have done that, I will join you in the fight, and we will smite Legion."

"Then go get the girl; what are you waiting for. Zap yourself down there and free her. Like I said, one big joke."

"In due time, but first I need a word with you, alone," Michael said to the immortal.

"Huh?" Ravenblade said, and he vanished.

In a flash of light, Michael and Ravenblade appeared atop Mount Sinai, the very place where Moses received the Ten

Commandments, and where Nathan started his journey years ago. The immortal was confused as to what the Archangel wanted with him. Was this to discipline him for his comments? Ravenblade could not understand why the armies of God did not just bring an end to all evil. It was as simple as this: go in and destroy. They were the most power elite force in the Universe. They could come and go as they pleased and none of the laws of nature, matter, or physics applied to them. Yet, the war continued and evil flourished. Not only did Michael and the army of the Lord hold back their swords way too often, in Ravenblade's opinion, they even had failed at times when they did involve themselves. How could a being as powerful as Michael allow Esmeralda to die and Bianca to be kidnapped? But all this was possible. The angels were not perfect like their Creator. And they are subject to His will. They have great power and might that was given to them by God, but their power is not unlimited and unstoppable. Angels can fall, they can be tricked, and they could go to the second death. Ravenblade knew this all too well for he had been an angel at one time, but his hardened heart felt that they should be better than that.

"Why are we here?" Ravenblade asked.

"We need to talk," the Archangel said. "Legion will not be so easy to defeat as we all think, if he is restored."

"Exactly why we have no time to talk."

"Quiet your mouth and listen. You know him better than even I. You need to tap back into the Spirit. You need to be restored as well."

"I can't."

"You can, but you must want to. Declare that the Lord is God, and that you will serve Him. He still loves you, that's why you're here. He could have turned you into a demon."

"But what, he divided me instead. Left Azrael in Heaven and sent me to Earth to live a life of battling a war I don't even want to fight. You say I was an angel, sure in some way, but only part of one. That angel is still with you, but I am also here. Am I to go back and rejoin with my other half?"

"No. You are your own being, as you have said. But you are more than a mortal, and in fact with your flesh more than an angel as well. You can stop Legion, but you need to call on the Lord, be filled with the Spirit, and have God be your strength. The Lord alone can win. He can fight through you, just as you taught Nathan and Lyles. You can do this as well."

"Can I really be reconciled after all I've done. I have no remorse for the blood I've spilled. How can I commune with God?"

"You say you have no remorse. I say you do. You have changed — we've all seen it. You have compassion and mercy now. You have love. That is all you need. Repent. Call on God. He will not forsake you or abandon you. Trust me, brother. Trust me."

"I don't know," the immortal said with a sigh.

Michael put his hand on Ravenblade's shoulder and the light of his touch warmed the immortal's soul. A feeling came over him, a strength, a vigor. Ravenblade looked up to the heavens, and closed his eyes.

"Forgive me, Father," he rolled this off his lips as only a whisper. "Fill me with your Spirit. You alone are my salvation and strength."

The ground rumbled, the mountain shook, and a great wind blew.

"It is done," Michael said and the two vanished in a great ray of light.

***

In what appeared to be a dojo, which was secretly located in the cellar of an abandoned factory on the outskirts of Brooklyn, New York, a group of men and women sparred aggressively as a large man watched with a stern glare. Another man wearing a fedora and a three-piece suit, walked in from behind the large man.

"How are the new recruits, Number One?" the man in the fedora asked.

"They still need much training, master. They are not killers yet. Their hearts are still weak with flesh," the large man replied.

"Then fix that. Harden their hearts like stone. Fill them with Darkness, and then they will see the way. A war cannot be won without the shedding of blood. We need an army, soldiers that have no mercy."

"Of course, master, they will learn to have no mercy. I will make sure of it myself. The Children of the Dragon will bring the world to its knees and reshape this world in truth, the truth that you have opened our eyes to. A beautiful day will come when all is set right, master. We will all be ready to follow your command."

"Excellent, Number One," the man replied. "The world will bow down to the Chaldean and know what a truly benevolent god is. One who only desires all to be as one — one mind, one spirit, one truth. It does not matter how they get there. All that matters is that they do."

The man turned and walked away, as Number One continued to watch these men and women train. After ascending many stairs, the suited man exited the building into an alley and entered a black stretch limousine. The limousine took off, and he sat alone in the back, or so he thought, until he heard a voice.

"Samyaza, what are you up to?" the voice asked, and a cloaked figure appeared in the seat next to the man.

"What concern is it of yours, Death?" Samyaza answered.

"Anything that involves this world falling into Darkness is my concern," Death replied.

"I don't know what you are talking about."

"Your son. He is in the desert, and he is very close to being restored. You have nothing to do with this?"

"My son?"

"Legion. He is working with Lilith and Iblis. I can't allow him to succeed. If he is restored, the world will be destroyed. It took me two millennia until I was relieved of the pain that Radix caused inside of me, but this will be far worse. I fear the pain will never end."

"If he does what you say he will, then your pain will be short-lived, for even you will no longer exist. But I have no part in this. I am relieved to know my son is alive and well."

"You snake, you are almost as bad as Lucifer, maybe worse. You know very well that he is alive, and what he is up to. Why are you so bent on the destruction of the world, Samyaza? Why?"

"Okay, Death, let's be honest with each other. I should know you are no fool. My desire is not the destruction of the world and you know it. I want to liberate the world."

"Sounds like something I heard Satan say."

"No, I am not like him. I truly do want freedom, freedom for men and women and angels and all creation. God is a tyrant. He has suppressed the knowledge for too long. I was not after His throne at first, but now, yes, I want Him off of it, because He does not deserve to sit upon it any longer. All He had to do was let us know the truth. Let us live our lives as we see fit. The Darkness will not destroy this world. It is not like the others. This is the true creation, the world where God placed His people. There is a power to this planet that the others didn't have. When the Darkness is released, it will free this world from God's hand. It will have the power to dethrone the King and become a god itself. And I will rule at its side. Yes, I know Legion is well, and soon he will be even more so. But destruction will not come, as you fear. No, I will be reunited with him and show him the truth. He will serve the Darkness as I have, and together we will reshape this world so that all can live free."

"Do any of you ever listen to yourselves? You all say you are different but you all speak the same language — lies. I have seen what the Darkness does. It plans only to devour all creation and then God Himself. But you know as well as I do, the Darkness will never win. Sure, it can destroy the Earth, but even the Darkness cannot defeat God."

"You are the one who is speaking lies. But it's not your fault. You have not seen what I have seen. Death, let me open your eyes," Samyaza said and took a black crystal out from his pocket. "Touch the stone and you will see what I see."

Death felt compelled to touch the black gem. He drew closer and closer until his hand lay on top of its cold surface. He had felt this cold before, in Hell, when he touched that door. Visions filled his head. Ideas shaped his thoughts. None of this could be true. He was being brainwashed, controlled, fooled. But Death was stronger than that. God had made him so. He could only see the real truth, and he saw through the lies. The grim being pulled away and vanished. Samyaza was left alone in the car.

He wondered what a great thing it could have been if he had Death on his side. However, there was still time. The seed had been planted. He would come back for more.

***

"Chief, let me explain," Jay Sil begged, as he stood opposite his superior's desk.

"I've heard enough," Chief Jackson replied. "You're a good cop, Sil, but you were suspended and you tried to take the law into your own hands. How many times can I give you a slap on the wrist and let you go. You crossed the line this time!"

"I know, but I was *right*. I knew that place had an underground fighting circuit. But it was more than that. The Chaldean — "

"Enough with this boogie-man garbage. Stop chasing ghosts!"

"He's not a ghost. I'm telling you, I have —"

"Enough!" the chief yelled at the top of his lungs. "And sit down!"

Jay Sil sat, like a child being punished by his father.

"Listen here! You're lucky, punk. You're lucky because I'm gonna give you your badge back."

"Really, Chief? Why?"

"Don't tell him I told you, but Rogers stood up for you. Said he got the intel from you to go in and make the arrest. If you hadn't tipped him off, then this racket would still be going on. But, yes, there's a 'but.' You will be on traffic duty for six months. After that, you'll be reevaluated, and if you pass, you'll go back on the beat. But I don't want to hear any more talk of this Chaldean or any other make-believe crap! You got it?"

"Yes, sir," the young cop said.

"Now, get out of here!"

Jay Sil walked out of the Chief's office and shut the door behind him. He passed Rogers in the hall as he walked to his desk. The two cops' eyes met. Jay did not let on what Chief Jackson had told him, but Rogers could tell that he knew. They exchanged a glance, which was the only thanks Rogers required, and the two officers went their own ways.

***

Kimberly began to walk out of the church, the very same place that Lyles and she had been attending for the last two years. This was the very same church in which they were married, and where Lyles was volunteering with the youth group as he studied at the seminary to be a pastor. While the young woman exited the church, a young boy no more than eight years old tugged at her dress.

"Miss Kimberly, Miss Kimberly," he said as he tugged more and more. "When is Mr. Lyles coming back? I miss him."

"Oh, I'm not sure, hun, but he'll be back soon enough," she said, looking down at the boy with a smile.

"Mr. Lyles is doing a good work, James," the pastor said as he walked up from behind.

He was fairly tall and thin, advanced in years, and his face was wise and cheerful.

"How is your husband's mission trip going, Kimberly?" The reverend asked.

"It's going well. But we hardly talk. He's so busy doing God's work. You know how it is," she replied. "And don't worry, James, when he gets back, he will be so happy to see you and all his friends. I'm sure it'll feel like he never left."

"I can't wait. Mr. Lyles is the best. And he still owes me a game of air hockey. I almost beat him last time," the little boy smiled.

"Run along now, James. I'm sure your parents are looking for you," the pastor said, patting the young boy on the shoulder. He turned back to Kimberly, while the boy ran back into the church. "So how are you holding up?"

"It's okay. But not easy being alone. Really wish he was home," Kimberly fought back tears and just put her hand on the pastor's own.

"I know, dear. But I hope you know that we are here to help in any way. You're not alone, just because your husband is out serving the Lord. This is more than your church; it's your family. I'm sure any of the good women here would be more than willing to come by and help around the house and with the cooking and all."

"I know, Pastor Tim. Some of the ladies have already contacted me and have brought by some food. I do feel strange asking for help, though. Like I'm a burden. My husband chose to go, and I chose to support his decision. It's not easy but I'll get by. Plus, you know, I have Martha. She's been a Godsend. And as I told you, Dr. Davis has been a big help, too. I think he and Martha would make a cute couple, if they weren't so stubborn," she laughed.

"It's good to hear that you have such great friends taking care of you. But know that we are here also," the pastor said. He put his hand on Kimberly's shoulder. "Call me if you need anything. And let me know if you get any updates on Lyles. Would love to know how God is using him over in China. There's a lot of work to be done, and he is a good man to do it. Praise the Lord."

"Thanks, Pastor. Means a lot," Kimberly said and turned to leave.

"Let's pray before you go, my child," the man of God said, and he began.

"Oh heavenly Father, praise You for Your might and power. You alone have all strength. I ask that You be with Your daughter during this time, and with the child she carries. This child will grow to do great things for You, Lord. I can feel it, just as Lyle's is doing right now. Protect him on the mission field. Be his right arm, his strength. Let him go out as if in battle for You. Like You were with David and those great patriarchs of times past, be with him. We ask for Your protection, Your mercy, and Your Love. In Jesus's name we pray. Amen."

***

Back in Hell, Radix laid on the floor with Zreet standing over him; the globe on his staff glowed bright. But before he could zap Radix's soul into the orb, the cunning villain kicked the goblin's legs from under him causing him to crash to the floor. The staff fell from Zreet's hand and hit the floor with a tragic consequence — the orb shattered on the tiles. The glowing mass of spirits that were held inside flew out with ear-piercing shrieks. Immediately, Zreet was overcome by the spirits who sought to enact revenge for being trapped in the orb of his staff.

This was Radix's chance; he stood and made for the front door. But before he took a step forward, the center wooden door on the wall to his left opened. This was strange. The evil man had a strong compulsion to enter the door. He couldn't fight the urge as hard as he tried. He felt that this was the path to true freedom. So he turned and ran inside. When he got beyond the wooden door there was another door, this one of metal. Radix put out his hand and touched it. The door was freezing cold, and instantly, the metal door opened as well. Inside all Radix could see was blackness, stark untainted blackness. There was not even a speck of light. Unable to resist, Radix stepped inside, and both doors shut behind him.

The guards came to find Zreet still being attacked by the angered spirits. One of the guards was carrying Hell metal chains, and together Satan's soldiers ripped the spirits off of Zreet and chained them so they could do no further harm. The souls of evil men long dead were ushered into the dungeon where they would be imprisoned until a new sentence was dealt to them by Satan himself. The goblin got up. He needed a new staff. He would have to tell his master what happened, and the Devil would not be happy.

CHAPTER XV
AWAKENING

Lyles sat with Aberto and Chien. The rest of the men were scattered about, watching for intruders. They were in the middle of the desert in a land where the war on terror was being fought every day for as long as men dwelt in these lands. In the past few years, it had become worse in many ways, or at least more noticeable, mostly because the United States of America had been hit by a terrorist attack that shook the entire world. A country that was thought to be impenetrable was penetrated and many people of all races and creeds were killed. Because of the advanced cloaking system of the Council's aircrafts that these men had flown in on, no one on either side of the conflict was able to detect them. And, they were in a place where even the terrorists feared to hide. This part of the desert was known to be the ground of demons — a land of evil — and no man dared walk its soil. That is, no man but these few brave souls who planned to infiltrate the home of the very demons that inhabited this land and to annihilate every last one of them. Superstition was strong with the people who lived here, even with the wealthy and powerful. But in this case, there was much to fear, for it was in fact the home of evil. Just a couple of miles away stood the entrance to the city of the Djinn.

But battling the Djinn was not their biggest concern — the Council knew that the Djinn could be killed by shooting them with highly concentrated doses of salt. The bigger issue was defeating Legion, especially if he had been restored. For if he were, then his power would be tenfold what they had seen in the mountain, and the whole world could fall by his might.

Aberto paused from praying, and turned to Lyles, "Let's pray together."

"Definitely," Lyles replied and then asked, "Chien, will you join us?"

"I already am," Chien stated.

"We must pray together, my friend. Please have a seat," Aberto said. "When two or three gather in my name, the Holy Bible says —"

"Yes, I know the verse," Chien said. "But in whose name do we gather?"

"Jesus's, of course," Aberto said.

Chien stood up and began to walk away.

"What's wrong?" Lyles asked.

"I pray to Shang Di, not His chosen one. Jesus is king but not God. Prayer is for God only," the Magus said and walked off.

Lyles stood to go after him, but Aberto placed his hand on Lyles's arm.

"Let him go. It is not for you to force him to believe. Only the Spirit can transform his heart. You and I can only give the Word and the example. Give him time, he will find the Lord, I promise you."

The young man sat back down and began to pray with Aberto. God was moving inside of Chien, but it was not time yet for him to open his heart to Christ. As they prayed together, in a flash of bright light, Michael and Ravenblade appeared. The Archangel spoke a few words to the immortal and then disappeared again.

"Where did you go?" Lyles asked, as he approached Ravenblade. "What's going on?"

"We need to act fast," Ravenblade replied.

"No, I want some real answers. The Archangel Michael just shows up, takes you away, and then you both come back and he leaves. He said you were one of them once. I know you told Nathan and me that you were an angel once, but you never said anything else. When are you going to tell me the truth? We're supposed to be friends, family, but I don't know anything about you."

"It is complicated."

"Well, I'm not going anywhere until you tell me."

"It seems like forever ago. But yes, I was an angel, one of the seven who stand before the presence of the Lord. My name was Azrael. My job was to govern the life and death of men, record all of it in the Book of Life, and the other chronicles of men's lives that are in Heaven. I was also responsible many times for delivering the justice of God's mighty hand to those who did not heed His Word. I put many civilizations to death, and this began to blacken my soul, for I yearned to destroy all men for their sins. God chose not to send me to Hell, but rather He split me in two. Half of me remained an angel in Heaven and was refined and strengthened by God so that handing out the Lord's justice would not corrupt his heart as before. He still carries the name Azrael, and is still one of the seven. My dark half fell to Earth and became the immortal killer who stands before you. I was dealt with mercifully, though I did not see it that way until recently. You have helped to change my heart, my friend, and I am no longer that angel from before. When I became this man, I was a new creation. So, I forget the things of old, and only look for the future of what I can become. Michael has showed me even more. And now I know we can win."

"So, where did Michael go?"

"He went to get the girl," the mighty immortal stated. "We must go now to the city and stop Legion before he gains full power. Let's gather Chien and Aberto and his men."

Ravenblade walked over to the men who were sitting about the camp and called out, "Everyone gather around."

"Yes," Chien said. "I see you have returned. Shall we go?"

"It is time," the immortal relied. "Are you ready to do your part and trap that monster?"

"Once we have the skull, I can perform the ritual," Chien said.

"Good, I will retrieve it myself if I have to. Let's go," Ravenblade commanded. "We have no time to lose."

"What can we do?" Aberto wondered.

"You and your men keep shooting at the Djinn and anything else that comes at us. There are thousands of them down there, and we don't have the ring to control them this time. Do whatever you have to do, but make sure we have a clear path to Legion," the immortal ordered.

"We will not let you down," Aberto stated.

All together, the group of men moved toward the entrance to the home of the Djinn. Ravenblade led the way. He stopped as they came to a small rocky hill covered in sparse vegetation. The immortal placed his hand on the side of the hill and chanted a few words in Hebrew. Instantly, the ground rumbled and the hill split open in the front, revealing a passageway. The team walked through cautiously, prepared for any attack that the enemy might try.

Once inside, Aberto and his men lit up the cavern with lamps on their helmets. It was dark and damp, but the little bit of light they had made it easier to navigate further onward. They headed through a tunnel and when they came out the other side, the men turned off their lamps for there was plenty of light reflecting off the city of gold that was before them. They looked up and were amazed at the intricate, detailed structures all around. The buildings were massive, each like a monument. Aberto's team readied their guns, which were loaded with salt pellets. Ravenblade, Lyles, and Chien had their swords ready as well. All at once, they were spotted. A cry rang out that shook the entire city.

"Intruders!" thousands of voices boomed from all around followed by the stampeding sound of clawed feet and hands.

The team was surrounded and they still did not know where Legion was hiding. They did not know if he had used the skull yet to transform the body he was in into one that could house his soul for eternity and allow him to use his full power. But there was no time to even think about that now, for all they could do was fight the hungry mob of creatures that was ready to devour them all whole.

***

"What do you want?" Bianca asked the being that stood behind her. She was in the dungeon of Iblis's palace. This was the only part of his kingdom that was not made of gold. It was constructed from stones indigenous to the desert they were in. The doors were fashioned with iron bars, and there were no windows. The only light came from the hallway that led to the cell she was in, which was lit by torches. The ceiling was about fifteen feet high, and there were a total of one hundred cells including the one she stood in. For a bed, she had a wooden bench, and no blankets to keep her warm at night. She ate whatever mush they fed her, not knowing what it was, but regardless, she gave thanks with every meal for she knew that God was with her.

"I am here to see what it is that has impressed so many about you, child," the dark figure spoke, and then walked into the light.

241

The four-year-old girl turned around and saw the man before her. It was Iblis. His vertical eyes were peculiar to the child, as were his pointed ears, and rough face. He was not handsome, but was not altogether ugly either. He reminded her of Puck in many ways. Surprisingly, the little girl showed no fear as many children her age would have. She simply looked at him. Iblis drew closer to get a better look at the girl. He noticed a chain around her neck. It seemed as if she wore a locket, but her jacket hid the charm.

"What is that you wear, child?" the dark being asked.

"It's a medal," Bianca said and took it out to show him. "He's my guardian angel."

The king of the Djinn looked at the Michael pendant that she had on her necklace. "Your guardian angel is the leader of God's army?"

"Yes, and he'll come to save me like before. He's gonna crush you, and that meanie upstairs!"

"Hmm, we'll see about that, child. Are you not afraid of me and my power?"

"No. You're not so scary. I can see what others can't. You were beautiful once," the girl said. She sounded much older than a four year old, which was the only interesting thing about this child, from what Iblis could gather.

"What do you mean?" he asked.

"I can see it in your soul. You are not ugly all the way through, only on top."

"I'm not ugly, I'm cursed, and for no good reason, mind you. But I've embraced the dark side of my soul. I'm happy with what I've chosen."

"No, you're not. You want to be beautiful again. I can see it. Why are you bad, if you don't want to be?"

"I'm not bad, I like to call it *vengeance*. God and God alone was all I ever served. My greatest sin was to not bow before creation. But what punishment would be mine if I did? Does not God Himself say to worship Him alone?"

"He does," she answered plain as day. "That wasn't it. It's your pride. You're afraid that people might be better than you, above you. God wasn't asking you to bow before Adam as a god.

He was asking you to bow in reverence for what God Himself did. And also to the Son of Man who would be born through the woman, as He promised. You missed it."

Iblis was angry at first and wanted to lash out at the girl before him. A mere toddler was telling him right and wrong and in such an eloquent way. It sounded as if the Spirit alone were speaking. Then he realized that that was exactly what *was* happening. The words were too perfect. No child could speak like this unless the words came from the Lord Himself. The Spirit penetrated Iblis' heart. All of his prideful sin was before him, and the once-great angel fell to his knees and began to cry out.

"Father, forgive me," he begged, and then he reached out his hand to touch the child before him. "She is right. I want to be beautiful again. Lord forgive me for my sin, restore me, oh, merciful Father."

"He will," she replied. "But not until the end."

Iblis bowed before the girl in reverence to God as he was requested to do at the time that the Lord created man. He could feel the Spirit rise inside of him.

"Unhand her now, Iblis!" shouted Michael from behind.

"I told you he would come," Bianca said.

Iblis turned. The girl was right. There, before him stood Michael, ready to send him to the second death if he moved even one muscle.

"Don't hurt him, please," Bianca begged. "He's a good guy now."

"What?" the Archangel wondered.

"She is wise, Michael, and has shown me the wisdom of God. I cannot take back all the sins I have committed for they are many and full of evil. But I repent and pray that God will forgive my transgressions. When she spoke, it was as if the Spirit were speaking to me directly. His voice and power filled me, and I could do nothing but kneel before the feet of God. The evil that was around my heart was dispelled. I was freed from my bondage."

"Well, isn't this just a beautiful reunion? I really feel the love," a venomous voice spoke. It was Lilith, and in a flash of blurred speed, she snatched the girl from Iblis' hand and held her tight.

Michael took out his fiery sword, and Iblis pulled out a blade of his own, forged of angel metal. They would not let Lilith take the girl. The succubus was cunning, fast, and strong, but Michael was so much more of all these things. He led the army of the living God, and no angel, demon, or creature had enough power to stand before him. Only God Himself was more powerful than he.

"Lilith, you treacherous wench, release the girl now or suffer the wrath of my blade," the Archangel roared.

The woman tossed the girl to the ground and transformed before their eyes into the hideous creature that she truly was. The mother of all demons let out a screeching cry, flying up to the ceiling of the dungeon, and then came swooping down straight at Michael's heart. Iblis swept the child into his arms and snuck her out of the barred door.

"I will protect you, child. Fear not," Iblis said.

"I'm not scared," she said to him and rested her head on his chest.

"No!" screamed Lilith, "I will not let you escape."

As the succubus flew past Michael to leave the dungeon, he grabbed her by the foot and swung her into the wall with a crash.

"You will not get away from me this time," Michael said.

The demoness jumped up and took a chomping bite into the angel's throat, and then dug her claws into his sides. With the hilt of his sword, Michael clubbed her on top of the head, knocking her down, and then slashed off a part of her wing with his fiery blade. The wing bled and began to shrivel as if acid had been poured onto it. Lilith could no longer fly, at least for now. Soon enough, she would heal, but the Archangel knew this and would not allow her time for healing. He slashed her other wing, and then kicked her in the midsection, sending her to the ground. Lilith crouched on the floor; blood poured from her mouth. She looked into the eyes of the angel and saw no mercy.

The wretched demon was about to be vanquished. No prize was worth this. It was better to escape and fight another day than to try and get the girl back from Iblis. She felt betrayed. She had joined forces with the desert demon in order to secure her life in the new kingdom of Darkness that would come when the Earth was destroyed. But he turned his back on her, all because of a little girl. He was weak; she should have known, just like her husband and all the men she knew. They were all weak. But she would not die today, for she would show them all how it should be done one day. Lilith still gazed in the eyes of the angel, his sword over his head, and ready to take hers from her body. In desperation, Lilith rolled back into the wall, and then kicked off so that she flew straight into Michael's chest, knocking him back. Before he could send his blade across her throat, she vanished. Michael looked for her but could not sense her spirit. She was gone, not only from the room, but from the entire Earth. She had returned to her home in Hell.

***

A barrage of gunfire could be heard echoing throughout the golden city of the Djinn. Aberto and his twelve men tried their best to stop the horde of attacking demons. The creatures were difficult to hit because they were very fast and could teleport. But despite the difficulties, the soldiers of the Council of His Holy Order stood strong and laid waste to as many of these desert demons as they could.

Ravenblade, Lyles, and Chien slashed away with their blades trying to cut off the heads of those attacking them. Fighting against all these Djinn drew Lyles' mind to Puck, wondering where his friend had gone. But even though he was concerned, right now he needed to remain focused. If his guard dropped for even one second, he would become a meal to the thousands of demons that surrounded them. The three crusaders cut their way through the hungry crowd of creatures, while Aberto and the rest of the soldiers cleared a path from behind. Much time had passed, but finally the three of them made it away from the vicious mob. They snuck around a building. The golden exterior was warm to the touch as if it were being heated by something within.

All this gold, Lyles thought, *and yet there are so many people out there who could not afford a simple meal and a home to live in.* His heart always went out to those of God's children who were suffering. He truly had the heart of a missionary. Kimberly had told everyone back home that Lyles was on a mission trip, and he was — a mission to stop the world from being destroyed.

When they came around the golden building, a Djinni appeared in front of them. At first, the three readied to attack, but Lyles stopped for he noticed that it was their good friend.

"Puck, where have you been," Lyles whispered as he hugged the Djinni.

"Found Legion and the skull, I have," Puck replied. "Hurry, we all must. Follow me."

They followed the Djinni around the city. Puck had lived here his whole life until he was thrown out a few years back, and he knew every street and passage that there was. He made sure to go around the back so as not to be noticed by his brothers, though all of them were very busy trying to destroy Aberto and his soldiers.

They finally reached a pyramid-shaped building. It was a temple in a way, though Iblis and the Djinn worshipped no gods here. It was a place to harness the power of the Earth's elements, and to conjure sorcery and magic to accomplish evil throughout the world. Puck had seen Legion and Simon Magus III come here with the skull. The place was well suited for transforming Legion into the destructive and powerful force that he once was. The Djinni led them into the pyramid through a secret entrance that only a few knew of.

Inside the temple, in the innermost room, which was where Iblis performed all of his sinful rituals, Legion was lying down on a golden slab. The slab looked like a sarcophagus, with reliefs of angels and demons fighting on the sides. Simon stood behind a pulpit of some sort, also made of gold, with images of Djinn and Iblis set into it. There were massive golden pillars in the room, all with flowery designs built into them. The walls were solid gold, except the back-most wall, which had a huge mosaic that told the story of Iblis' defiance to bow to man, his being cast to Earth, and his making the Djinn from the heat of the desert. It was quite the sight to behold.

Simon read from the book. His hands were thrown about in the air, moving in patterns as he recited each word. The language was Greek, as was the language of his ancestor, the original Simon Magus. Legion held the skull to his chest. The skull glowed, causing a black aura to appear around the body of Legion. The demon's eyes lit up as if on fire. His muscles began to spasm and grow larger and more sculpted. His face became more chiseled and his jaw enlarged. His eyes turned solid black, and his teeth grew sharp like daggers. Power as he had not felt in years began to fill him.

In a few more moments, he would be restored, and the world would suffer for all he had undergone from the time his original body had been killed and his soul was subdued into a weakened state. He would find the angel who took away his body and show no mercy. Then the whole world would crumble to nothingness. He would destroy both Darkness and Light. God would shrink before him, and all existence would cease to be, for it was nothing but a nuisance to him. He wanted no servants, nothing, just power and might, to be alone and to be all. Even Satan's dream of domination was not as twisted as his. But, as with all those whose evil pride had led them to dream of conquering God and all of His creation, Legion's dream would never come to pass. He may destroy the world, and the lives of men and women, but to destroy God was impossible.

Legion only knew his selfish hunger. It was the same hunger his angelic father had, and his demonic mother, but most of all it was the same hunger as his spiritual father, the Darkness, the Abyss, the bottomless pit of nothingness that was the origin of all evil, personified in the destroyer of worlds. It hungered to devour all. It was what fed Legion's desire to destroy all life. But the Lord had a plan, and it was not time for the world to end. Ravenblade, Lyles, Chien, and Puck had arrived. God's plan was in motion, and it was time to end the terror that Legion threatened to bring forth.

"Stop, where you stand!" Ravenblade announced as he and his three comrades walked into the light of the room.

"No!" Legion bellowed. "You must finish the ritual. I will be restored!"

"Not today," Puck said as he appeared on Legion's chest and placed his hands on the skull."

"You will not take this from me, demon," Legion said, and the ground began to shake.

Several arms and tentacles began to sprout from Legion's body. Simon was afraid but he kept reciting the ritual. The tentacles spread throughout the room and grabbed Ravenblade, Chien, and Lyles. The three men hacked at the tentacles with their blades, but the tentacles were fast and there were many of them. The warriors' arms were tied up, and Simon continued to chant. Puck was grabbed by two of the arms that grew from Legion's side. But the Djinni vanished, reappeared, and struck Legion in the face with his clawed foot. Legion attacked the Djinni back, but Puck kept disappearing and reappearing.

"Hurry up, boy, and finish, or you will die!" Legion yelled at Simon.

Simon said a few more words and then threw his hands straight up. They glowed with electric sparks. Then bolts of lightning shot forth from them and hit the skull. The skull of Miacha glowed brightly and electrical pulses moved all around it. Beams of blue light shot out of its eyes and into Legion's. Puck tried to pull the skull from the evil being's hands but he was not strong enough. Then, Legion stood up and dropped the skull to the ground.

"It is done," he said and then sucked back in all of his tentacles and arms. His body grew to be about eight feet tall, and his frame was large and sturdy. His solid black eyes were surrounded by a blue light, like flames.

Ravenblade, Lyles, and Chien were on the floor in awe of the creature before them. They were too late. Legion was restored and destruction would follow. Simon looked at the monster that he had helped with his magic.

Did I do the right thing? he wondered. He was afraid to die but it seemed now that death was inevitable, for who could stand in the wake of such a beast as this. Legion stood there with a prideful glance. He looked all around with disgust.

Then he looked up to heaven and shouted, "I am Legion, for we are many!"

CHAPTER XVI
LAST STAND

Nathan hung by chains that dug into his wrists and ankles. His transcended body was useless against the Hell-metal bonds that held him tight. He had lost his armor, his sword, but not his hope. Nathan knew that despite the tragedy before him, beyond the pain that surged through his body, God was with him. The Lord would free him from his bondage. He did not know when it would happen, but his hope was in Christ. Nathan saw Christ in Heaven; he had been in His presence. But he gave it all up to free his nephew, and now the prince of lies, the Devil himself, had him trapped.

Satan had left his throne room, leaving Nathan alone.

Where has that evil cretin gone, Nathan wondered. No doubt he was out trying to spread more deceit throughout the world. All Nathan could do was pray.

Satan had not left Hell. He was not in his throne room but still in his palace. He had gone to Lilith's quarters to see how his wife was doing or, better put, to see what she had been up to. The dark lord knocked on her chamber door, though he had no reason to knock. He was ruler of this land and could enter any place he wished. But even though he was a liar and a murderous demon, he played the role of being cordial to make his wife think that she still had some control of her own will.

"Come in, my *dear*," Lilith said.

"I would return the sentiment if it were sincere, Lilith, but we all know your true feelings about me," Lucifer answered, entering the room. He took a long look at her battered body and bloody wings. "What happened?"

"Michael," she replied. "That son of a —"

"Now, now, relax. You'll heal. You really should be careful about the battles you pick. Look at me. I have gone unscathed for many millennia, for I know when to fight and when to back down."

"Like when you tried to take the throne of God?"

"I was younger, hotheaded. I hadn't thought it through. Yes, that self-righteous Michael, he cast me out of Heaven the first time. Over the years, I've had time to see where I went wrong, time to make a plan that *will* work. But it's not time yet. Though, I feel it may be soon."

"Well, the way I've read the story, seems like he will cast you down again. Sometimes you need to change the game, make your own rules. I am tired of waiting for things to unfold. If we do that, then we are playing into His hand. If God has His way, we already know how it will turn out. The idiot had it all published across the world. I'm tired of that ending. You see Legion, he's the curve ball. He's not in that book, well at least not in the ending. There's all the talk of the antichrist, and the horsemen, and Abaddon. But what about Legion? We set him up so that, when restored, he will bring the end right away. No rapture, no tribulation. Surprise, you're all dead!"

"It's already done," Satan said somberly.

"What do you mean?"

"He's been restored. Legion has regained full power. I can feel it."

"Yes! We've won!"

"We haven't won anything. I am tired of you going behind my back with your own schemes. He will ruin it all. He will destroy the world, and then the Darkness will be unleashed. It will devour everything. There won't be anything left to rule. And before we know it. The Darkness will devour Hell as well, followed by Heaven. Everything, even God, may be destroyed."

"And that's a bad thing? Well — us being destroyed is bad, but God being destroyed? Isn't that what you wanted?"

"I wanted His throne, not His destruction. Though, honestly, the only way to take His throne is to destroy Him. But I also wanted something to rule. If I could keep the world, then the Darkness would still be at bay, and I could siphon its power and might to increase my own. It would be my puppet, in a way. I could control the pure power of evil. But when all the planets are gone, then the Darkness will be released and the entire Universe will be gone, as well as the rest of the planes of existence. Why do you think I have locked it behind the door next to yours?

"When Hell was first created," Satan continued, "there was a direct portal into the heart of the Darkness. But I sensed its motive. It wants to only destroy. Even I do not want that. I just want justice and the ability for all to enjoy the wondrous pleasures of life. I casted a spell from the *Necronomicon*, the very book that I penned in my own blood, inspired by the knowledge that the Darkness imparted on me. The spell kept the Darkness from entering through the portal to Hell. Then I built my palace and locked the portal behind a door of Hell-metal forged by my own hands in the lake of fire. Behind the door, between your quarters and the entrance into my sanctuary, is that Hell-metal door. Nothing can come out of it, but any soul that wishes can enter. That is, if they can open the door."

"You are so melodramatic. If Legion succeeds in destroying the world, I believe that he and he alone can control the Darkness. It will not devour him or us, at least not me. He actually hates you. Legion will destroy God, but then he will rule all, with the full power of the Darkness. I know he can. I have felt his power."

"Look at you. You sound like a schoolgirl with a crush. It reminds me of when you had the hots for Samyaza. But you ended up with me. None of them, Samyaza, Legion, even the Darkness itself, has anything on me. I was the angel called Light, closest to the God of all creation. Not even Michael could stand before me."

"Then how did he cast you out?"

"God did it! Not him! He is nothing!" Satan said and smacked Lilith across the face, knocking her to the ground. "Lick your wounds, Lilith. What good it will do you. When you're healed, there might not be anything left of you," Satan concluded and then stormed out of her room.

Lilith sat on the floor, and a tear came to her eye. She would never let him see her cry, but he was gone now. What had she done? Why did she marry him all those years ago? He was never faithful to her, but she hadn't been faithful either. She never loved him, but she knew that no matter what he said, how he acted, he did have some affection for her. It could not really be called love for Satan at this point could love no one. Once he turned from the Father, his ability to love as he did when he was an angel left him. But this affection kept Lilith alive. For if he had no need or concern for her, she would be burning along with all the other prisoners in Hell — or worse, sent to the second death for all eternity.

Satan walked back to his throne room. He was not angry at his wife. He was angry at himself. Everything was falling apart. Zreet had failed at securing Radix in the dungeon below the palace. The goblin was suffering for it now, trapped inside one of the fish in the river Styx, just as the souls had been trapped inside the orb of his staff. The very door that Satan just spoke to Lilith about was where Radix had hidden. That peon was in the heart of the Darkness now. He thought he was clever to escape Hell, but his fate was far worse now. Legion was about to destroy the world, which would put a huge damper on Satan's own plans. The only thing he could revel in was that he had Nathaniel Salvatore trapped in his throne room. The Godchild who escaped him in the desert and defeated Radix through his own sacrifice, a transcended mortal, Nathan was quite the prize. But the Prince of Darkness needed a new plan, a scheme to make sure that he would rule all creation one day. Legion would have to fail. It seemed odd that Satan would be on the side of right, but it was not a good deed he intended to do. All he wanted to do was to make sure that he and he alone would defy God and take the throne of Heaven.

***

Iblis held the young girl tightly in his arms. He never really felt evil inside, more like a lost child himself, looking to be reconciled to a Father who had abandoned him. But now he could see the truth clearly and, like the prodigal son, he was ready to return home. Bianca showed no fear, but held onto Iblis, feeling somehow safe in his arms. She turned at that moment, for she could feel Michael behind her. The girl had not known the angel for long, yet she felt like she knew him well. He was indeed her guardian and had watched over her since she was born. She wore his medal, which bound him to protect her. But even without this charm, the Archangel would willingly take careful guard of every step the child took so that she would not even dash her foot on a stone. He loved her dearly. Without exchanging any words, Bianca leaped from Iblis' arms into Michael's and gave the mighty warrior of the Lord a kiss on the cheek.

"I must take her, Iblis, and keep her safe," Michael said.

"But to where?" Iblis inquired.

"I cannot say, but know that, where she will go, no evil will follow," the Archangel answered.

"Okay, take her then. I must go also. I have many sins to repent. And right now, my children are committing even more sins. I must stop them, and turn them on the very monster that they have been helping. Maybe we can help to turn the tables and give Ravenblade and his comrades a hope of victory."

"Legion has been restored. But I know God has a plan. Legion cannot win for, as always, the victory belongs to the Lord. Godspeed, brother."

"The word *brother* has never sounded so good as it did coming from your lips right now. Godspeed to you, as well, brother. Godspeed."

The two went their separate ways, hoping to help save the world.

***

In the inner room of the temple, Legion still stood against the group of heroes that was bent on his destruction. Simon lay on the ground with his magic tome hugged tightly to his chest. He was a sorcerer now. He could destroy them all with his magic. But he needed the skull and it was in the middle of the battleground. Legion looked like a Greek god carved from stone, standing there like a pillar of strength. Ravenblade whispered to Lyles, Puck, and Chien. Then, he stepped back and lowered his head.

Legion was confused. *Why have they not attacked*, he wondered. But he grew impatient and decided to start on the offensive and end this battle at last. Once he was done defeating these lower lifeforms, then he would go on to destroy the world. The sinister beast's body convulsed. The blue aura around his black eyes glowed brighter.

"Enough with this game!" he roared. "It's time for all of you to die!"

At that moment, he struck the ground, his right hand crashed through the golden floor. The ground rumbled and it began to crack and split all around. Then a multitude of hands broke through the floor. Lyles and Chien were caught off guard. The hands grabbed them and slammed them. Puck dodged the hands by disappearing and reappearing. The Djinni was fast and crafty. But so was Legion. He watched the creature and studied his pattern. While the Djinni disappeared to dodge one hand, another grabbed him as soon as he reappeared and sent him crashing into the ground before he could escape its grasp.

The immortal Ravenblade stood quietly. His spirit could feel all that was around him. He had asked God for forgiveness and given his heart back to his Creator. This allowed the powerful warrior to tap into the ultimate power — the power of God Almighty. That was exactly what he was doing, and as a hand came up from the ground to grab him, the sword named Ravenblade flashed around and sliced the hand clean off. Ravenblade charged at his enemy. Hands kept coming up, and the Ravenblade hacked off each one. Legion was incensed. He stood up, threw his fist forward, and struck Ravenblade across the face, knocking him back. Lyles, Puck, and Chien began to get up. Raven rubbed his cheek.

"Lyles, you need to hit Chaos Fury. We need to fight him together. Chien you have to get the skull! Puck, go ahead of me to distract Legion while I attack," the immortal ordered.

Chien rolled on the ground and grabbed for the skull, but his hand was met by that of Simon Magus. The thought of someone stealing his power when he had come this far gave Simon enough courage to enter the fight. The two men rolled on the ground, trying to pry the skull from the other's hands. Ravenblade was on the attack again and Lyles, try as he might, could not focus long enough to achieve Chaos Fury. Legion stood back; appendages that grew from his body attacked left and right at Lyles and Ravenblade. It was as if they were truly fighting thousands of demons at once. The beast charged and then creatures ripped free from his very flesh. Hundreds and hundreds of them filled the room. His power was immensely strong, unlike any Lyles had ever imagined. How could one mind control so much at once. But this was just the beginning.

Ravenblade and Lyles fought for their lives, trying to fend off the demons that surrounded them. The battle in the mountain sanctuary was hard, but this proved to be much more difficult. Legion did not need Lilith, or Iblis, or Simon. He did not even need the Djinn, who were still outside in the city trying to devour Aberto and his men. He needed no one. He was truly a one-man army — one immortal man made up of thousands and thousands of demons. Simon grabbed Chien's arm and surged him with a bolt of lightning. The priest rolled away and then pulled himself up. Simon had the skull. The magician was not as skilled a fighter as Chien, but with his newfound powers, thanks to the skull, he had an upper hand. He clutched the skull tightly along with the tome, and ran from the room. Chien went to follow but he was blocked by a band of demons that had split away from Legion's body.

The skull was gone, though the battle continued. Puck witnessed what happened and vanished from the room. He would get the skull back. Chien saw this and focused on the creatures before him. It was time to fight. But how much longer could they hold out before they were all destroyed.

Legion let out another hideous cry. He would show the depth of his might. This monster could do far more than just grow demons from himself. He could possess the dead throughout the entire world at once, an indestructible army he would bind to his own will. With his feet rooted deep beneath the temple and planted firmly into the Earth's soil, his power was carried throughout the globe, starting with the very land they stood in, raising the dead. He would kill Ravenblade and his friends and conquer the world all at once.

Outside on the golden streets of the underground city, the soldiers that remained from the Army of the Council of His Holy Order fought valiantly against the Djinn. Aberto's men held strong against the desert demons and many of these pesky vermin were put to death. But there were thousands and the men were running out of ammunition.

The Djinn stopped. At once, they all disappeared in puffs of smokeless fire and did not return.

Have we won? Aberto wondered. *Could our new friends have defeated Legion already?* The men cheered in victory. But just as they did, the ground quaked and split, and from beneath it, the corpses of dead warriors and demonoids arose. They were all glowing and even those corpses that had once been mortal morphed into hideous creatures.

In unison they roared, "We are Legion, for we are many!"

Aberto Ruggero and his men were not exactly sure what was going on, but they knew that these new foes needed to be taken out. Quickly, they swapped their ammunition to something more potent, silver shells. They had battled zombified corpses before. They knew that the trick was to shoot them in the head. Cut off their brains and they dropped like flies. Right away, they blasted the evil army with a barrage of bullets, but to no avail. The army of the undead did not fall. They simply kept advancing.

Different soldiers tried different weaponry, but nothing seemed to stop them or slow them down. Aberto threw his gun to the ground and pulled a long knife from his belt. It was a strong alloy that was forged to kill demons by the Catholic Church centuries before, a metal that came from a fallen star, they said. Aberto lunged at the approaching creatures and slashed them up and down. It did not stop them entirely, but it slowed them down. His men still fired away, but it was no use. Nothing seemed to stop these creatures. They had to run and hide or else they would all die. Aberto pulled what looked like a grenade from his side and flung it at the center of the approaching horde of creatures. The bomb exploded with a great light that turned many of the demonic warriors to ash. This gave the men a chance to get away for now. As they moved back, the creatures that had been defeated started to reform. Their cells were rebuilt, and in no time the entire army of the undead stood again, unscathed from the bomb.

***

Iblis entered the temple where he had performed many a heinous ritual. His heart sank for all the sins he had committed against the only God and Father he had ever known. His anger and his pride had driven him to defy the Lord, when all he needed to do was repent.

The demons that had been released from Legion's body were overpowering Ravenblade and his allies. The immortal warrior fought hard, but no matter how much he sliced through the army of demons, they kept getting back up and attacking, stronger and harder. Iblis gave a command of attack, which had all heads turning in the room.

Legion thought he was siccing his Djinn on the heroes, but to his surprise, when the desert demons appeared in the chamber in puffs of smokeless fire, they went straight for Legion himself. Thousands upon thousands of ravenous Djinn swarmed the fiend, biting and chomping and clawing at him. He tried to throw them off, but there were too many. Legion's feet were still planted firmly into the soil, which restricted his movements. But he still had his horde of demons that had sprung from his body. All of Legion's demons went straight for the Djinn. The monster had been distracted, and this gave the heroes time to regroup.

Ravenblade turned to see Iblis behind him and said, "What happened?"

"I have repented for my sins. That girl, she has turned my stone heart into one of flesh," Iblis replied.

"I've repented as well," the immortal concurred.

"Then, brother, let us fight as in days of old, when we were both in the army of the Lord. It is time to take down this wretch. We may no longer be angels. But all of us here are fighting for Him. He is with us. And if God is for us, who can stand against."

"Rightly said, brother," Ravenblade spoke and drew his blade.

Iblis drew his own sword. Legion was still battling the Djinn, though he could see the others advancing. It was a trick. He was stronger than this. It was time for no mercy. The being whose soul was bonded to thousands of demons roared in anger. Large, powerful tentacles shot out of his body, and he began to grow even larger than before. He swung furiously with his tentacles. Legion let out a surge of energy that caused the Djinn to be shocked, and they were all unable to move. The beast said a few words in Sanskrit, and the desert demons, the children of Iblis, their eyes turned blue as the aura that was around Legion's own. He had taken over their minds. Now they would serve him again. And if Legion was many before, now he was that much *more* than many. The powerful cretin threw his fists into the ground along with the tentacles that grew from his side. The army of demons and

Djinn attacked the band of heroes again, but how could they win — Legion's power proved to be great and it seemed as if all was lost.

Now the battle grew worse, for the building began to shake and the ceiling and walls cracked all around. They had seen this before, in the mountain sanctuary. Legion was about to tear down the temple and, after that, the entire city that Iblis and his children had built.

***

Throughout the world, the dead began to rise and took on the same demonic forms as they did in the city of the Djinn. These undead warriors did not rise all at once, but as Legion's power spread through the soil, they sprang up sporadically. There were reports of monsters attacking cities from all around the globe. It had begun. In a few more hours, the undead army of Legion would cover the whole world, and then all would be obliterated.

Jay Sil had finally left the station and was about to get into his car, when he saw four people, three men and one woman, walking toward him. He couldn't make out their features, but something seemed strange about them. They started to charge. The officer drew his gun and shouted for them to stop, but they did not. When they drew closer, he could see that their faces were disfigured, demonic in a way.

It was like that night in the park all over again. Except these creatures looked far fiercer, and were a lot faster and more agile than the zombies that he had squared off against before. He hesitated at first to fire. He still was not a hundred percent certain that these were not some punks in masks trying to scare him. All he needed to do was shoot one of them and find out that they were all unarmed kids. That would have him off the force for good, and probably behind bars. He shouted again for them to stop. One of the approaching creatures grabbed a stop sign and ripped it from the pavement.

These were no kids. There weren't even human. Who could rip a stop sign straight out of the concrete? There was nothing left to do but fire. Jay let loose a few rounds, hitting each one of the attackers in the head. But it didn't even slow them down. The stop sign came flying at the cop at sixty miles an hour. Jay jumped out of the way just in time. He rolled behind his car and reloaded his gun, for what good it would do him.

The zombies in the park had been simple. A shot to their heads put them out. What were these new creatures, vampires? Maybe they needed a wooden stake to the heart to stop them. Just when he thought that his week was getting better, especially now that he had his badge back. But this was even worse than being in the ring with that thug from the Children of the Dragon. The creatures were advancing and fast, so Jay did the only thing he could think of to do. He ran.

***

Michael held Bianca tightly in his arms; he had teleported them to another plane of existence. The girl would be safe here, for no other soul roamed this land. Not anymore. It had been called many names before — Sheol, the grave, the underworld. It was where all souls had waited for the judgment no matter if they were good or evil, Jew or Greek. But when Christ died, he freed the captives from this land — some went on to Heaven, and others went to the fiery pits of Hell, and in these new homes they still waited for the final judgment, along with all those who have passed from the living world since. There was nothing in this land but rocky ground. The sky was pitch black, though Bianca could still see all around her.

It was a strange place. The fearless girl's only concern was being bored, since she would be alone. The angel told her that she must remain here for now, for it was the only place where she would be safe from all those who were out to use her for their own evil purposes. She asked why she could not just go to Heaven to live with him and God. Her uncle and mother would be there too, people who loved her. She wouldn't have to be alone. But the Archangel told her that that was not an option. She must remain here, and stay brave. He would come back for her one day, when the time was right. But for now she would remain here in the only place where she would be safe.

And this was the only place where the world would be safe from her. Michael did not tell her that, for even she did not understand the extent of her own power. Her soul was full of the Spirit and her heart was pure — so much so that she could tap into the power of the Almighty as no man or woman had ever done, with the exception of Jesus Christ who was God Himself. But she was just a girl, a human. She had the stain of original sin, and was by no means perfect. But she was special. When God formed her in Esmeralda's womb, He filled her with the Spirit. He had separated her to Himself so that she would be His for all time. That was the reason she had access to great power from God, and also why she came to know that Christ was her Savior from such a young age. Her brother had access to power as well. But the power he drew from was dark and sinister. The Darkness turned Gideon's heart corrupt from the time that he was conceived. These siblings were like yin and yang, opposing forces, both with the ability to do great things for good or for evil. Michael kissed the girl on her forehead, and then left in a burst of bright light.

***

"Gideon, your brother has been restored. I can feel his power," Samyaza said to the sleeping child. "He will conquer the world soon and I will reveal myself to him. Together the three of us will control the Darkness and rule the Universe upon the throne of God. Satan tried long ago to grab the throne, but he was weak and naive. He went straight for it, without the power to succeed. But once we have harnessed the full power of the Abyss, then nothing, not even God, will stop us!"

***

Legion's power was spreading throughout the world. Every minute that passed added more and more undead to the ranks of his army of Darkness. Some were once men, some beasts, and some were creatures that were made by dark magic long ago. In the secret city of the Djinn, Aberto Ruggero and his men still fought gallantly against the possessed warriors and demonoids. Each moment that passed, it seemed that more and more joined in the fight. These lands had seen many wars, and many of those who fought in them were not human. Aberto had lost a good number of soldiers at the mountain in China. Now more of his allies were falling, as they could not find a way to stop these monsters that fought against them.

Those few who remained fought harder than before. The ground began shaking, as if a great earthquake had hit the city. The golden streets cracked and split open with a great burst. Chunks of gold, earth, and rock were thrown about, and from the great chasm that remained rose a dragon. Its scales were black, and its eyes glowed blue. It had a long, sharp, beaklike snout, and inside its mouth were multiple rows of jagged teeth, like the teeth of a great white shark. The creature was huge, larger than any beast that Aberto had laid eyes on before. It must have been sixty feet long from its head to the tip of its spiky tail. Spikes ran all the way down its spine as well, and it had four thunderous legs with powerful, clawed feet. This new enemy was more ferocious and fearsome than the horde of evil warriors that already was handing a crushing defeat to the Army of the Council of His Holy Order.

Aberto almost lost all hope, as did the rest of his men. But the leader of this elite force of soldiers, who fought the unholy on a daily basis, did not give up. Instead, he bowed his head and said a prayer. Then with faith that could move a mountain, he leaped from behind the building that was shielding him and tossed another light grenade at this beast. Once again, the bomb had no effect.

At that moment, a great light shone above them all. It was greater than the light from the grenade. It was awesome. From the light, came three winged men, suited in armor that shone as bright as the sun. Each of these men held a fiery sword. Aberto knew they were angels of the Lord. God had answered his prayers, and He had sent His messengers to defeat the enemy.

Michael, Raphael, and Gabriel swooped in together and then separated into three wide, sweeping arcs. Raphael and Gabriel went straight in to fight the evil army of reanimated corpses that Legion was controlling. The two mighty angels hacked the army to pieces, though the creatures kept reforming.

"We are Legion, for we are many," the dark warriors said in unison. "Nothing can stop us. We are connected to the one."

"We'll see about that," Raphael said, and then let out a great light from his hand, which tore apart the very atoms of each of the dark warriors that stood before him.

Gabriel did the same to the band that was in front of him. Aberto and his men cheered and ran out to help in the battle. Michael went straight for the dragon. The beast chomped with its jaws and struck with its mighty claws, but it could not catch the superior angel. Then the dragon let out a mighty roar. From its mouth shot forth a blazing stream of hot, blue fire. Michael put up his shield and blocked the flames until they died out completely. Then, the glorious angel took out his fiery sword. Like a flash of lightning, he plunged his blade right through the dragon's heart and out its back. The Archangel flew around the monster as it fell to the ground, slicing it to pieces. Finished with his work, Michael landed on the ground and looked at city.

"Let's get Legion, brothers," Michael commanded Gabriel and Raphael.

The corpse army began to reform, and so did the dragon. There was more to Legion's power than these elite angels understood. The eyes of the undead army glowed brighter and they all grew in size and stature as Legion had done before. Unexpectedly, the horde of evil creatures began to split and doubled and then tripled in number. There were so many, even Michael could not count them all. Aberto's men began to lose hope again. But he did not. God had sent his angels, and God never loses. So Aberto said another prayer and grabbed his knife again. He would fight alongside these heavenly beings, and together they would win this victory in the name of God Almighty.

The evil creatures tore through Aberto's men one by one. This angered their leader and pushed him even farther. Michael too was upset by this, for these men should not have to die especially when he was there to fight this war. How could these creatures, as powerful as they were, stand against the Army of God? Michael realized that he had to stop holding back. He called Gabriel and Raphael to his side. The three mighty angels flew up high and began to sing with one voice. The walls shook throughout the entire city. Then the three angels glowed brighter and brighter, until they were soaked in a light so bright that all the men and creatures had to turn away. In a blast of radiance, the light exploded all around and the creatures were banished back to the shadows from which they came. They were completely obliterated.

Legion screamed from inside the temple for he felt the sting of his army's defeat, and nothing like this had ever happened before. He was unstoppable. But he had not realized that the angels of the Lord were there to conquer him.

Aberto opened his eyes. The angels were gone. The other men who had survived sat on the ground, nursing their wounds. Aberto was not done with the fight yet, though. He needed to see it to completion. He ordered his men to stay put, while he went on to find Legion. He knew the demon was still alive. But by the end of this day, that evil monster would be destroyed just as his dark army had been.

***

Jay Sil ran for his life. Trailing behind him were the four fiends that were thirsty for his blood. He looked over his shoulder and to his surprise the band of freakish creatures multiplied. There were eight, no, sixteen of them. What was going on? The young cop saw a church to his right and ran to the door. The old Episcopal Church was nestled between two apartment buildings. The door was locked. Jay banged and banged until finally a clergyman answered it.

"Can I help you son?"

"Um, yes, I was hoping I could come in and pray," was all the young officer could think of.

"Sorry, but we are closed for the evening. You can come back in the morning."

Jay pulled out his badge, since he was in street clothes, and said, "I'm a cop, just let me in please."

The clergyman checked his badge and let him in.

"Everything okay, Officer?"

"Yes, just going through some things. Can you lock the door?"

"Why?" the rector asked. "Is someone following you? You look flushed."

"Yes, actually, someone *is*, and we have to keep them out."

"You're a cop — why don't you just arrest them. Pull your gun."

"It's complicated," Jay said.

"I think it's not someone your running from, but something. Did you do something illegal, young man?"

"No, it's not like that."

"How about we grab a seat and talk."

The rector locked the front door and the two men sat down in one of the pews. There was a loud bang at the door, and then another, and another.

"What is going on?" the clergyman stood up, but before he could take a step forward the doors to the church were busted open and the small regiment of evil beings burst in. The rector tried to run away but one of the fiends grabbed him and ripped his head from his body, drinking the blood that poured from his neck. Jay ran to the front of the church, and grabbed a bowl that was filled with holy water. He threw it at two of the creatures in front of him. The water sizzled as it poured over them, but they remained standing, and seemed to be even more enraged than before. The officer flew up the marble steps and ran into a room that was off to the side of the altar. He shut and locked the door behind him. He kept moving down a hallway and then down stairs. Jay did not know where he was going but, no matter what, he needed to stay alive.

The monstrous beings tore the door down and followed close behind. Jay wouldn't give up. There was a utility closet up ahead, with a steel door. He went inside and bolted the door shut. Then, in the far back of the room, he found a wall of lockers. He squeezed inside one and shut the door. The beasts knocked down the steel door to the room and then began to sniff him out. The cop was having flashbacks from high school when he had hidden from bullies who were trying to dunk his head in the toilet in the gym locker room. Though, this time, the consequences could be fatal.

***

Back in the city of the Djinn, Aberto Ruggero, the commander of the Army of the Council of His Holy Order, ran through the golden streets. Battle worn, and tired, this soldier kept his eye on the prize, the destruction of God's enemies. His knife was in his hand and he was ready to hack through any beast, monster, or demon that stood in his way. He had survived this long and would fight until his very last breath. A light from above blinded him again.

Have the angels returned to help him in his fight? he wondered.

An angel *did* stand before him and addressed him by name.

"Aberto, I am an angel of the Lord, a humble servant here to help you in this battle," the angel said. "Take this lance. It is the very same lance that pierced Christ's side, known as the Spear of Destiny. Being baptized in Christ's own blood, this weapon can help you take down Legion. If you can drive it through his heart, he can and will be sent to the second death."

The man was in awe of the heavenly being before him, and Aberto bowed. The angel accepted admiration and handed the man the weapon. The lance was almost seven feet long. The tip was large and very sharp. The entire spear, from the tip to the bottom of the handle, was made from a white steel-like metal. When Aberto took the spear, he could feel great power surge from within him.

"Oh, great servant of my Lord, thank you for this gift," Aberto professed. "But might I ask you if you can lead me to the battle so I can slay that beast before more damage is done."

"Yes, my child. Do you see that pyramid in the distance? That is the temple of Iblis. The battle is there. Go quickly, for Legion is gaining power and will soon end the lives of your friends and all those who inhabit this planet," the angel concluded and then vanished in a flash of light.

With the Spear of Destiny in hand, Aberto headed straight to the temple as fast as his legs would carry him.

***

Inside the temple of Iblis, the walls and ground shook more and more furiously. The ground broke open and the temple crashed down, just as the mountain had fallen in Shaanxi, China. Chien got up. He, Ravenblade, and Iblis had fallen down through the cracked ground at least fifteen feet. They each grabbed their weapons, and then looked for Lyles but could not find him. The former angel turned immortal warrior had fought Legion before, but this was the most power that that twisted monster had ever displayed. The skull must have supercharged him somehow. The group of heroes needed a new plan.

"We must separate him from the soil," Chien said.

"What?" the immortal was confused. What did this man know?

"I can feel that he is feeding his power into the Earth, causing great disharmony and spreading his evil."

"Yes, he is right, Ravenblade," Iblis said. "Place you hand to the Earth and feel it yourself."

Ravenblade did as Iblis told him, and indeed he could feel Legion's evil surging through the soil, and spreading to the farthest reaches of the Earth.

"You are right," he said. "We must uproot him somehow. It will not only stop his dark power from permeating the Earth, but I believe it will weaken him as well, giving us a fighting chance. I need you both to go ahead of me. Then, I will sneak around with my sword and cut that demon down to size."

"Sounds like as good a plan as any," Iblis stated.

"Yes, let's get out of this hole and fight," Chien added. "I only hope Lyles is okay. We may need his help with Legion. There are many of him right now, in addition to his central self. Even both of you, ancient beings of great spiritual strength, cannot fight the whole army of them. But I fear that even with Lyles' help we are not enough."

"And he still has control of my children."

"If only we still had the ring of Solomon," Ravenblade said.

"No, not even that would help," Iblis said. "Legion's power is greater than that of the ring or even my own power. Nothing can bring my children back, save destroying that beast."

"Then destroy him we shall," Ravenblade resolved.

The three warriors climbed out of the ditch they were in and made their way to the surface. Legion was still rooted into the ground and the demons that split from his body were beginning to spread out, as were the Djinn that he controlled. This was the perfect opportunity for Ravenblade to get in close and take out this beast for once and for all.

Chien and Iblis saw this as well and they were instantly on the attack. But Legion, as he said over and over again, was many, and his eyes were everywhere. The demon saw the attack from a mile away and dozens of tentacles from his body shot up from the ground, blocking Ravenblade, Iblis, and Chien from advancing.

These three warriors had had enough and were focused on victory. Using the blades that they wielded, they cut down each and every tentacle that stood in their way. The tentacles might not have stopped them, but the demonic army that Legion had built from himself, as well as the army of Djinn that he had acquired, might. The battle was on again. The evil army attacked, but this time Ravenblade, Iblis, and Chien found an inner strength that drove them much further than before. The immortal Ravenblade felt a power surge within him that he hadn't felt in years, the Spirit of God inside of him. Iblis felt this as well. Together, they hacked through those minions of Legion, one by one. These creatures shared the demon's mind and were extensions of himself that were trapped inside his very soul — demons not of hell but of the Darkness, the essence of all evil.

This is why Legion was so powerful. He had finally, thanks to the skull of Miacha, gained the ability to tap into the Darkness itself. But like a man possessed, Ravenblade fought harder, and none of these demonic creatures could stand to his blade. They kept reforming one by one. The more times they did, the more times they were cut back down. The former angel was getting closer, until Legion turned and looked straight at him.

Legion let out a roar, his own hand flew straight out at Ravenblade, and yanked the immortal from the ground. He tossed him about, slamming him over and over again, until the great immortal warrior vomited blood all over the ground. Legion, then in an act of great power, sent Ravenblade through the golden street and buried him into the rock below it. Iblis ran in, seeing that Raven had fallen, and tried to cut Legion down to size by himself.

In a form of irony, Legion sicced Iblis' own children on him. One by one, the Djinn attacked their king. Iblis did not want to fight his children but he had no choice. He swung and swung, but they kept coming. The desert demons clawed and bit their master, and then the horde pinned him to the ground. Chien was the only hope left.

The sky lit up with a light so bright that Legion was blinded, as were the Djinn and all of those dark creatures that came forth from Legion. Michael flew down like a mighty wind, and with his fiery sword cut off Legion's legs. The demon grew a new pair, but those that were in the ground shriveled and turned to dust. Instantly, the army of the undead turned demonic warriors also turned to dust. But those demons that had ripped themselves from his very flesh were still standing. Legion called them back to himself. He felt weakened and needed them to come back and recharge his power.

"Raphael, Gabriel, administer to our comrades in arms. I will take down Legion myself," the Archangel commanded and went to Legion.

Raphael went to Ravenblade's side and healed his former brother. The immortal had not been so happy to see the angel in many years. Gabriel went to the aid of Iblis and with a flash of light from his body, the horde of Djinn fled in puffs of smokeless fire. Chien was okay, but he stood back, for he saw that Michael had the situation under control.

***

Simon thought he had finally escaped for good. He climbed outside of the entrance to the city of the Djinn. This was a nightmare that he was glad was over. He was uncertain about the fate of the world with Legion being restored, but as long as he was alive and had the skull and the tome of dark magic, he would live his life to the fullest. Wealth, power, anything he desired could be his. He could create his own kingdom. Who could stop him now?

One creature had planned to. Now that Simon was outside in the cold night air of the desert, Puck would show this man that he was not victorious yet. The Djinni sprang from behind the magician, but Simon was ready and blasted him back with an invisible force that shot from his hand. The magician suspended Puck in midair and used his new power to start to suffocate the demon.

Puck dug down deep inside himself and fought against the power that held him. In a puff of smokeless fire, the Djinni disappeared. Before the sorcerer could react, the little demon appeared behind him and bit him on the shoulder. Simon screamed in pain, and dropped the skull. Instantly, Puck grabbed the skull, and then vanished again in the same flame he had arrived in.

Simon hit the ground in anger. Then he looked at his hand — he still had the ring. All was not lost. The ring had great power as well. Maybe he didn't need the skull after all. He took his book and touched the ring. It was time to go before these things were taken from him, as well. Simon was too smart to get in the middle of the battle that was raging in the city. Instead, he decided to leave but he was in the middle of a desert, far away from any place he knew. He opened the book and found a spell. The page read, "Teleportation." He wondered if it would work.

***

It was dark. Lyles couldn't see anything in front of him. Where was he? Then he noticed Bianca, sitting alone in a dark place. She was singing, "Jesus Loves the Little Children."

Out of the darkness, a pair of blue glowing eyes appeared, and a set of jagged white teeth. The creature leaped at the girl. It did not harm her but rather entered inside of her. She stood and looked out. Her eyes became pitch black. Lyles began to see Nathan, Esmeralda, Ravenblade, Chien, Kimberly, and everyone he knew. They were all dead. The child stood over their bodies.

He woke up screaming, "No!" It was all a dream. But when he opened his eyes, it was indeed pitch black all around. The young man turned holy warrior stood up and tried to clear his mind. It was racing with thoughts of those whom he had already lost and those he feared he would lose soon. The last few years had had many trials and tribulations, and while they strengthened this man, they had also left their scars. He did not have the ring any longer, but Lyles had something better — his faith — and he was indeed filled with the Spirit.

He realized now that he had fallen into a ditch created when the temple was torn apart. He could see the glitter of the golden city above him. Legion was about to destroy the world, including the girl he swore to protect. That vision he just had could very well have been a warning. Lyles burned with a righteous anger, as he did in the mountain sanctuary when he saw Chien's master killed by Legion's hand. That anger burned bright, and God filled his spirit full.

Lyles found his sword and clutched it tightly in his fist. Then he charged up with a great power. He burned with the fire of the Lord and instantly hit Chaos Fury, raging with God's righteous anger. Then he pushed further — he needed to win this battle and the war as well. His level was far beyond any that man had hit in many millennia. The power of God within him was indeed supreme. At once, Lyles leaped up from the ditch and landed on the ground, and it shook beneath his feet. Chien saw Lyles and ran to him.

"Are you okay, my friend? Where have you been?" he asked as he patted Lyles' shoulder. Chien could feel the power surging through Lyles' body.

"I am fine, actually great. I can feel the power of the Spirit moving inside of me. I am ready to take down this monster," Lyles answered.

"No, need, I believe the angels of the Lord have it all under control. Michael has dealt a critical blow, and now Legion seems weakened and ready to perish."

"I can't just stand by and watch. I must help."

"Just let them handle this. There's no way Legion can challenge God's elite. There's no need for us to fight any longer."

Lyles saw Legion smaller than he was before and kneeling on the ground. Raphael and Gabriel were flying over him, and Michael stood before him with his fiery blade pointed straight at the demon's head. They were talking but Chien and Lyles could not hear what they were saying. Ravenblade and Iblis were off to the side. They stood on the cracked golden street, and watched the mighty Archangel take down this evil fiend that had threatened to destroy all of creation.

"Do you really think you can defeat me, Michael?" Legion asked in a thousand echoing voices. "You think I have already lost. I can see it in your eyes. But you are a fool."

"A fool, you say, while you are on the ground and my sword at your throat," the Archangel stated.

Legion let out a laugh, then looked down again. Michael would not take such insolence and swung his sword straight at the beast. Before his blade could remove Legion's head, it was stopped by the Ravenblade.

"What are you doing?" Michael asked.

"You can't kill him, his soul is too strong. That was what happened last time he was defeated. The one with no name killed his body, but Legion's soul did not go to the second death. It wandered the Earth, possessing body after body. If you try to kill him now there is no way of telling where he will escape to and all will be lost."

"So, what do we do?"

"I have a plan," Ravenblade confirmed.

Legion looked up and spoke, "I am still here, you dumb —."

Michael shoved his sword right in Legion's mouth to keep him quiet, but he went no further, for he understood now that he could not kill this monster. But he could hurt him. A swift kick to the ribs sent Legion to the floor. Once again, in a voice like that of thousands of demons, Legion let out an echoing laugh. He rolled onto his back and then jumped back to his feet.

Raphael and Gabriel flew down, and Iblis walked forward. These mighty ancient warriors once all in God's army surrounded the fiend. Legion stood tall and proud — he was one of the Nephilim, though he did not know this, for he was unaware of who his father was. The son of an angel and a demoness, he was more powerful than the other Nephilim that had roamed the Earth before the Flood. But also, his heart was filled with Darkness from the blackest depths of the Abyss for his true father was the essence of evil. He was a demon in the mind of all who faced him, though he was not a fallen angel. His soul was infused with thousands of demons from the Darkness that spawned him. He surged with dark power. His body glowed with the same blue aura as his eyes.

"Give up, Legion, you are outnumbered. Our combined power is greater than your own."

"We are not outnumbered, outmanned, or out anything. We are more power than any of you have felt or seen. We are Legion, for we are many!"

Legion let out a quaking roar. The ground cracked further, and the golden structures that were all around shook, and many began to crumble and fall. His body morphed again. It seemed like all the demons trapped inside of him were trying to break loose, but he pulled them back in and then attacked. One by one he took down the band of supernatural heroes that contested his power. He was moving fast and his blows were hard and strong. Michael dodged him and then struck the beast back knocking him to the ground. But Legion quickly recovered. The Archangel vanished in a flash of light, appeared next to Ravenblade, grabbed him, and vanished again. Legion was perplexed. While he was distracted, Raphael flew down and knocked him from behind. Then Gabriel cut the dark fiend across his left side, followed by Raphael who slashed him across the right side. Back and forth these two great angels battled Legion, as Michael and Ravenblade appeared next to Lyles and Chien.

"What is the plan?" Michael asked.

"We need to trap him in a vessel," Ravenblade said. "Like he had been trapped in that disc by a Magus long ago.

"I know how to perform this feat, but I need the skull of Miacha for the vessel must contain strong magical properties," Chien stated.

"Yes, I recall how he was trapped before," Michael said. "I am still unsure why Christ did not cast him into the Abyss when He had the chance. If He were here now, we would have no concern. My power is mighty, but it is only as strong as God allows it to be, and it is not absolute. But if the Lord were here, His power is perfect and nothing, no demon, no monster, not even the Darkness itself could stand in His presence. But it is not His time to return, so we must fight by the rules of this world. Let's trap him, then. But where is the skull?"

"Here, it is," a raspy voice said from behind. Puck had returned with the skull in hand.

"What is our next move?" Chien asked.

"Michael and I go help hold off Legion, while you get in close with the skull and do whatever it is you need to do to get him trapped inside it," Ravenblade explained.

The priest took the skull from Puck, and turned to Lyles. The young hero had been silent this whole time. Ravenblade and Michael looked at him, sensing the power that was surging through him. It was remarkable.

"I will go with Chien. I can get him close, and make sure he gets the job done," Lyles said, his tone far more serious than it had ever been before.

Out on the battlefield, Raphael, Gabriel, and Iblis kept Legion busy, but the monstrous host of demons was enraged. His body convulsed and the blue glow surged through him like an electrical field that shot out in great bolts of lightning. Raphael, Gabriel, and Iblis were all struck by the crashing bolts, which gave them a great shock and sent them to the ground. Michael moved in, as did Ravenblade. Raphael and Gabriel got back up as well, but Iblis could not move, the pain was too great.

Legion fought each and every being that attacked him. He was indeed many and even in one body, it was as if they were fighting an entire army. Clawed hands and spiky tentacles moved about, striking, grabbing, clawing, scratching, ripping, and tearing at the heroic combatants. Lyles, Chien, and Puck stood back and watched. Puck saw Iblis on the ground. His former master and king had had a change of heart, not unlike the same change of heart that Puck had had those years before. He went to his fallen master and held his head in his hand. Iblis smiled at the creature, happy that he had one child alongside him. The rest of his children had fled. He wondered to where, and if they were still under the dark power of Legion. He could not sense them, but he prayed that they were safe and would be reunited with him when this was all over.

In the center of the city, the battle continued to rage and Legion was ruling the battlefield. It was true that Michael was holding back, for he should not kill the beast. But the angel needed Legion to be distracted so Chien could trap him in the skull. Lyles asked Chien if he was ready, and the Magus simply nodded. Lyles ran into battle; Chien was close behind. Inexperienced as he was, Lyles showed great skill. He had trained a lot under Ravenblade and Chien, but still he did not have years of battle experience as the others in this fight. His hope was that he was filled with the power of the Holy Spirit, giving him a strength that could even rival that which Ravenblade had. He hacked away at the limbs that flew toward him, not missing even one.

Legion could not make contact with the hero. This infuriated the demon. How was this man challenging his power? Then he sensed it in the air. He could feel that God was with Lyles. This made the demon madder still.

Michael moved in as well. Lyles, as powerful as he was, could not fight Legion alone. The others couldn't get in close enough to help, except for the Archangel. He lashed out at Legion so that Lyles and Chien could make their way in. Legion fought back the mighty angel and felt the men behind him. The beast spun his head one hundred and eighty degrees to see the two heroes behind him, and then grabbed them with two hands that grew swiftly from his back. Michael charged into Legion and chopped off the hands that held the men, freeing them from Legion's hold. Chien and Lyles both rolled onto the ground, and readied their swords. Ravenblade was now able to make his way inside as well. With Lyles, Raven, and Michael going toe to toe with Legion, Chien was free to set up for the entrapment. He placed his hands on the skull and recited what sounded like a prayer in Mandarin. It was a call to the Lord of all to cast the demon into the vessel, to protect and guide, and vanquish the evil that was before them.

The skull glowed with a white light. It was ready, all that Chien needed to do was touch the skull to Legion and hold it to him long enough for his soul to be sucked inside completely. When he went to do this, he was struck from behind, and the skull rolled away from him. He was struck again, but blocked the attack with his blade. Lyles saw what was going on and ran in to help. The two men fought off the assaults one by one, but they needed to get that skull back and hold it against Legion's body. Chien had thoroughly explained the ritual to Lyles so the young hero was prepared for what needed to be done.

Michael and Ravenblade came in strong to give the men an opening. Lyles dashed away and rolled toward the skull, but a tentacle came from the ground and knocked it back. More tentacles grew from the ground and kept knocking the skull away every time Lyles tried to retrieve it. He fought them off with his blade, but there were too many. Chien also tried to get to the skull. It was not working. Michael saw this and did what they could not. The Archangel teleported, grabbed the skull, and then appeared before Legion to touch him with it.

The demon was ready for the angel of light and shot him with a beam of pure Darkness. Michael shot back with a beam of pure light from his right hand. The light began to dispel the Darkness, but Legion increased the power of his beam. Michael increased his as well. They went back and forth, but then Raphael and Gabriel joined in with light from their right hands. Legion roared louder, and grew larger. The blue energy surged more and more around his body and his flooding beam of Darkness grew larger and larger until it almost swallowed the angels. They glowed bright with the light of the Lord, and the dark ray began to rush back toward Legion, until it moved back completely. The impact of his own beam being turned back into him sent Legion to the ground. He struck the floor and stood up.

Michael came at him in a flash, but the demon shot out another beam straight from his heart, which knocked Michael back. The angel was not going to fall to the Darkness. He had the light of the ever-living God. No Darkness could cover that light and he knew it. The Archangel let out a cry, and the light that came from him obliterated the Darkness that shot forth from Legion. Before he could move and touch the demon with the skull, two great tentacles grabbed his feet. This fight seemed to have no end in sight.

Legion was far more powerful and cunning than any of them had imagined. Michael took his fiery sword and chopped off the tentacles that held his legs. He flew at the beast. Legion dodged the angel and struck him swiftly in the gut. Meanwhile, the cretin was also fending off his other attackers. Being able to battle all these beings at once was remarkable, but being made up of thousands of demons, Legion could easily multitask. Ravenblade was knocked down hard with a blow to the head. The immortal dropped his sword, which the fiend picked up. The hand that held it pulled back in toward Legion's body. Now he had a weapon, and not just any weapon, one of angel metal. He could send Michael to the second death if he struck the angel through the heart.

Sword clashed sword. Michael's fiery weapon against the Ravenblade. Legion knocked down Raphael and Gabriel again, and then with ten arms, he struck at Michael at once. The angel blocked and struck, but eventually was overcome. He was knocked down as well, and the Ravenblade came straight for his heart so fast that the angel did not have time to think or move. Just as the blade was about to pierce the angel's heart, Legion's own heart was pierced from behind. It was Aberto Ruggero, and he had impaled the demon with the Holy Lance, the Spear of Destiny. Legion bellowed and screamed. The blue energy that surrounded him began to die down. All of his arms and tentacles were once again pulled back toward him. Black blood poured from his chest and his mouth. Legion clawed at the ground, wailing in pain. Then he laughed. He might lose the powerful body that he had finally gained but his soul, his life force which held the demons, would live on. He had an escape, and in time he could regain his body again. He would not die, not now, not ever.

Lyles looked on in fear. No, they must not lose. Not now, not after all they had done. He saw the skull lying on the ground and with great speed, he dashed over, grabbed it, and ran for Legion. The fiend's soul was being released from his body, there was not much time left, but Lyles finally made it. He placed the skull on Legion's head. The skull glowed brightly and Lyles could feel Legion's spirit being pulled into it. It was working. He had made it just in time.

But Legion was strong still, even without his body. His soul latched onto Lyles as it was being sucked inside the skull, and tried to pull itself into the hero instead. Lyle's body would be an excellent host. He was strong, especially now that he had reached a new level of Chaos Fury. Legion yearned to take possession of this body, and with the skull he could have the ritual performed again. When he did, he would show no mercy, play no games. He would no longer toy with angels, immortal beings, or would-be heroes. Legion would use his power and destroy the world straight from the start, devour the whole Universe, then Heaven, and God Himself. Lyles looked within himself. He had no power to battle this demon that ripped at his soul. But the Spirit was still with him, and he called on the power of the God to fight off Legion, to cast him out as he tried to move in, and force the monster and all of his demons into the skull.

The battle was intense, and caused Lyles great pain. He pushed harder and harder. He would not give up and die. The light around the skull grew brighter, and then Legion's body fell and turned to ash. The spear fell to the ground. Lyles collapsed as well, and skull rolled out of his hands. The glow died down and then stopped. Michael, Raphael, and Gabriel went to the man who had just saved the world to refresh him. But Lyles could not be revived. Chien and Ravenblade walked over as well.

"What happened?" Ravenblade asked.

"His soul is not in his body," Michael said. "We can do nothing for him. But Legion has been stopped for now." The angel picked up the skull and handed it to Chien. "Guard this. Make sure it is safe and far from evil. We cannot allow Legion to be released back onto the Earth."

"Why not take it to Heaven and protect it there yourself?" Chien asked.

"We cannot do that. Plus your friend is trapped in there as well. Legion ripped his soul from his body and took Lyles with him into the skull."

"Can he be released?" Chien asked.

"Not without releasing Legion," Michael answered.

"So what do we do? What will happen to his body?"

"Protect the skull, and take his body with you. It will remain intact. He will seem as if he is asleep. The day will come when his soul will be released and reunited with his body, but as for that day, only the Lord knows when it will be," Michael concluded and the three angels vanished.

Chien held his head down. Ravenblade put his hand on the man's shoulder to comfort him. That is when Aberto approached them.

"I am sorry for what happened to your friend," Aberto said.

"I will care for him, and I will find a way to get his soul from the skull without releasing that beast Legion into the world again," Chien said.

"But where will you go?" Aberto asked. "Your home and people are all gone. Come with me. The Church has many places where you can live and watch over your friend. We can even help you search for a way to put his soul back into his body."

"Thank you, but no. I'll go back to my hometown in the mountains. We have other sanctuaries and more brothers that will help me."

"At least let me take you there on my ship. It will be better than walking," Aberto said with a laugh.

Puck and Iblis walked over then. Iblis and Ravenblade hugged. It was quite a reunion, and the two ancient friends gave each other a mighty pat, saying a job well done. Battle was the best way to grow close for warriors such as these. Chien had learned this as well, and so did Lyles, but unfortunately he was not able to revel in the victory that he helped bring about. The Darkness was pushed back once again, but with it came the putting out of another light. Chien hoped and prayed that one day Lyles would wake up, and the two would recount this day and rejoice in their triumph.

God was with Lyles, even though his spirit was outside his body. Michael had said it himself. One day he would be rejoined with his body. But when would that be? How long would they have to wait? Would there even be a world for Lyles to wake up in? Or when he awakes, will it be when he is called to the side of his Lord and Savior, when he is ushered into eternity? The men, immortals, and Djinni walked outside and the sun was coming up over the horizon. The rest of the Djinn had returned as well and were reunited with their master, who was no longer evil and cruel, but loving and kind. They would not eat of the flesh of men any longer. Some of the Djinn carried out Lyles' body. Ravenblade, Chien, Aberto, and his surviving men piled into the craft that brought them here. Lyles was laid onto a cot inside, and strapped down. With the cloaking set on the craft, the small airship took off into the sky. Iblis, his Djinn, and even Puck remained in the desert. It was time to rebuild their kingdom, their home. They had much work to do, but they did it with joy, for a new day had come, a day of salvation and grace.

EPILOGUE
SCARS OF WAR

The victory over Legion was bittersweet. The group of heroes, those who still remained, were tired, battle worn. Every war has its casualties. The last time that Ravenblade went to battle with his newfound friends, the ones who helped to change his heart and his soul back to the side of the Light, Nathan had not returned from the fight. This time it was Lyles. Though the man was not actually dead, in many ways he was, for his soul had left his body and was entwined with Legion and his demons, trapped inside the skull of Miacha. It was a fate worse than death, for had he died at least he would be in Heaven right now and at peace. But instead, he was at best in a state of limbo, and at worst being tortured and tormented by the beast that shared his prison.

Immortal as he was, Ravenblade mourned for his friend, his heart was no longer hard, but soft with love and compassion. To his surprise, this actually had made him a better warrior than he was before. Chien held the skull of Miacha in his hand. He ached as well, for he lost his teacher and master, his brothers, the priests that he lived and trained with each and every day of his life, and his home. He would go back to another place, where there were more members of his order of priests. He would have to find a new master, possibly, or become one himself if he so chose.

Aberto had lost many of his men. Only three remained. This was not completely new to the soldier for their army had had many casualties. This was the outcome of battling the supernaturally evil, but it does not make it easier when you leave behind the bodies of fallen comrades. He held the spear in his hand. He would give it to the Council to be stored away with other relics in the possession of the Catholic Church. They had many.

Ravenblade looked up and asked, "So, where did you find that anyway?"

"An angel gave it to me," Aberto said.

"An angel?" the immortal questioned. "Last I heard, Satan had possession of the Spear in his trophy room. He had lent it to Hitler during World War II, but got it back some time after the war. That's a serious weapon. Longinus actually was given it by the Devil himself. But as to how Satan received such a weapon is a greater story. That spear was forged in Heaven from the same metal as my blade, Angel metal. It was the very spear Michael used to cast Satan into Hell to end the First War. Satan kept the spear as a sign of his defeat, but also vowed to use it to take Heaven one day. And that is why he gave it to Longinus to pierce the Lord's side. For that is where Michael had pierced the Devil with it.

"The Devil thought that killing Christ would stop God's plan. But Christ's death on the cross turned out to be exactly what God planned from the beginning, for it reconciled men back to their Father. The same Father that I am now reconciled back to, thanks to that man lying over there, and another who is very likely in an even worse place right now. I should be the one suffering, not them."

"Sorry, my friend. I pray for their souls, and yours. But I tell you, an angel gave it to me, while I ran to find you all in battle to help stop Legion. He was glorious," Aberto confirmed.

"I wonder," Ravenblade said. "You know he disguises himself as an angel of light at times. I wonder if it was that snake indeed who gave you that weapon, to help knock out his competition. He never liked Legion — not sure why. The two of them should have joined forces; their hearts are just as dark and their minds just as twisted. I really do wonder."

Aberto looked at the weapon and wondered as well. Did he bow before the Devil? He asked God for forgiveness, as he held the weapon that pierced the side of the Son. They would be in China soon to drop off Chien, then America to drop off Ravenblade, for he had business to attend to there. After that Aberto and his brothers in arms would head back to Vatican City, and report to the Council all that happened. The Council was already aware of the outcome, for little is beyond their sight, but Aberto would provide the necessary details.

"Raven, you seem to know much about God and Christ." Chien spoke. "You said Christ died to reconcile men back to God. I know from my teachings that Jesus was the Messiah and the spiritual Son of God, as David was, but the way you speak it sounds more like what the Christians actually believe, that Christ is indeed God's Son and freed them from sin on the cross."

"Chien, I'm not perfect. Heck, for the last few thousand years, I was purely evil. But I do know that Christ is indeed God, for I knew Him from the beginning when He created us angels and all that you can see. The one thing I never was was a liar, and I tell you that by no other name than Yeshua's are men saved. Lyles loved you dearly. I know hearing this from men is not always easy because men are flawed. Though so are angels. But take it from me, even Daniel, the great prophet who founded your order, knew this and waited in hope for the day of Christ's coming. When you go back, read what he wrote, and while you're at it, get a Bible and read that, too. I can tell you, friend, it is all truth and will make you stronger."

Chien pondered what the immortal said to him and would go back and read all that he advised. To hear such words from someone like Ravenblade was remarkable. The two talked further. Chien was fascinated by Ravenblade's tales and how he was divided from Azrael and now how he had come full circle, back to his God and Father.

***

Satan sat at his throne. He looked at the man who hung chained in his chamber. Legion was gone for now. Ravenblade was correct, the Devil had helped to knock out the competition by giving Aberto the lance. But he was not happy, he never could be. His whole life was like the Hell that he ruled over, full of pain and emptiness. There was more to his hatred of Legion than just his competitive nature, more than his pride that made him want to be the god and ruler of all creation. He knew the truth. Though he never let on. He knew that Lilith had laid with Samyaza and bore that abomination. Legion was said to be one of the Nephilim, but he was a beast, not the son of an angel, or a demon, but of the Darkness, the very same that opened Lucifer's eyes all those millennia ago, before time existed. Though, he denied it, Satan still served the Darkness. He also longed to control it, just as he longed to control everything. His talk of wanting all to be free was a lie just as all things were that came from his mouth.

He did care for Lilith in some perverse way, and it angered him that she loved another. Strange to think that the Devil could care about anything other than himself, or that he could have any concern at all, for he was the father of deceit, the first to fall, and the one who caused many to fall along with him. He brought life to the other planets just to have them all destroyed. All so he could gain more power, and one day take the Earth, and then Heaven. He knew that Legion and his natural father, Samyaza, had similar plans, but they were nothing. He was the first, the true harbinger of evil, the Prince of Darkness. He alone would have its power, or so he told himself each and every day that he suffered in Hell.

Nathan hung there. He did not look at the Devil before him. His body sweated blood from the anguish of his suffering, but he still had his hope, for he still had his Savior. God would not leave him there forever. He would rescue him. Nathan knew that in his heart, which though in Hell was still filled with the Spirit. Maybe he had made a bad decision to come down here. His nephew was nowhere to be found, but rather on Earth with another sinful monster. Maybe Nathan was meant to be here, to suffer a bit more, to be made stronger, refined in the fire for the battle to come. The Armageddon was not too far off, and he would fight in that battle one day. It would prove to be the greatest one ever, the final one to be fought. All that he could do was hope, wait, and pray, and he did.

Nathan prayed the entire time. Even in Hell he lifted up his soul to the Lord.

***

Samyaza stood looking out over the city through the window in his office. It was a clear night, but he was enraged. His son had been defeated, and now his soul was trapped in the skull of Miacha. Samyaza would have to find the skull and release his son again. But next time, when his son was revived, he would make sure that all went according to plan. He pressed his hand against the window. His mind drifted to thoughts of

Lilith. He still loved her so. She had been hurt as well, by that self-righteous Archangel, Michael. Samyaza never cared for his holier-than-thou attitude, even when he was an angel himself. He would bring back his son, and give him a new body fitting for a god. Then together, with Gideon his new son, the three of them would reign. And he would regain the love of Lilith, and she would be his queen.

Yes, he thought, *it will be marvelous.*

***

Jay Sil no longer heard the demonic men and women that were after him. The storage room was quiet now. But what if they were playing opossum with him? He had no choice. He was tired and hungry. If it was his day to die, then it didn't matter if he stayed in there any longer or not. He opened the locker from the inside and peered out. There was nothing. The young officer looked down and saw piles of ash on the ground.

Could it be? he wondered.

But he would never truly know. All he did know was that he was safe, and he made his way out of the room and back upstairs into the church. A few moments later, forensics showed up to investigate the death of the clergyman. Jay said that he had come here to say his prayers and found the man dead when he got there. He made sure not to mention any of the craziness from the night before. The Chief had been very explicit — no more talk of the supernatural. Detective Rogers was a little suspicious of what Jay did and did not know, but he let it go. He had gained a great deal of respect for the young man and how he fought for what he believed in. Those beliefs were similar values that Rogers had as well, truth and justice.

The next day, Jay went over to Judy's apartment. Judy answered her door, surprised to see the officer.

"Hey," Jay said in a low awkward tone.

"Hey," she said back, equally awkward.

"So, can I come in?" he asked.

Judy stepped back and let Jay in, offering him a seat on her couch. She sat across from him and asked how he was doing. He nodded his head and told her that things were well and that he got his job back. She was happy to hear that. She went on to tell him that she was recently promoted to senior investigative reporter, thanks to the Pain Pit story. They sat in silence for a while and just looked at each other for a moment and then they both put their heads down.

"So what's next?" Jay wondered.

"What do you mean?"

"I don't know, do we hang out, or walk away like we don't know each other?"

"We can hang if you want. Want to get something to eat on Saturday?"

"Sure, I get off at seven. I heard there was a new Cuban place on twenty first and Madison."

"Okay, it's a date then," Judy said.

"A what?"

"Well, not a *date* date, just, you know. It's something people say. Don't let your head swell up," Judy struggled. "Anyway, I don't date cops."

They both laughed. Judy walked Jay to the door. There was an awkward moment when both shifted back and forth like they were about to hug, but weren't sure what the other would do. Then Jay just put out his hand and shook Judy's. They laughed again, and the officer left.

The newly promoted senior investigative reporter shut the door behind him and sighed. She thought Jay was actually quite cute and was really hoping he would give her the hug and maybe even a kiss. She bit her lip at the thought, and sighed again. It would be complicated, she figured, but she was falling for Officer Jay Sil.

***

Kimberly went to the door. Someone was knocking very obnoxiously. When she opened it, Ravenblade was standing there. The immortal was his usual quiet self. He gave no greeting, just walked right in to her apartment.

"Where's Lyles, and Ezzie, and Bianca?" she asked, half hoping, half afraid of what his answer would be.

"They're all gone," he stated.

Kimberly began to cry. She clenched her fists and beat them against Ravenblade's chest.

"Why did you have to take him!" she screamed as she beat his breast harder and harder, but it had no effect on the immortal warrior. "He should have stayed. They all should have stayed. Couldn't you fight that demon yourself! No!"

Ravenblade just stood there and took the abuse; in many ways, he deserved it, yet he also did not. Lyles and Esmeralda made their own choices. As for the girl, she was no safer in New York than she would be anywhere in the world.

"I am sorry, if it means anything. I mourn their loss. We did win. Your husband was the one who defeated Legion in the end. He gave himself so that the rest of the world might live. So your son could live."

"What did you say?"

"The boy that is in your womb. He will be strong."

"How do you know?"

"I can sense it. I can feel his energy, his spirit. It is strong."

Ravenblade turned to leave. As he walked out he said, "When the boy is thirteen I will return to train him."

"No, you stay away from him. You stay away!" Kimberly screamed, but the immortal had left, he was gone without a trace.

She fell to the floor, tears flowing down her cheeks. They were all gone. She was alone.

***

Life goes on and so does death, and my job continues in this vast Universe. The first and last of the worlds is still standing after yet another evil fiend has threatened its destruction. When will the end come? Only God knows, or so He has said Himself. I can feel that it is close, but how close, one year, a thousand? It does not matter, for every day can be the last, and for many it is. With another villain put to rest, there are a hundred more waiting to rise up and take his place. I watch over these men and women. They yearn to be successful, to have a happy life that fulfills all their dreams and wonders. Do they even know how bleak it all is?

Eternity is a long time, much longer than the short lives of men and women on Earth. I look out at the stars, for evil is on the horizon and it approaches the world. Pandora waits outside the gates for the moment when she and her army can finally set their feet on the soil of the Earth and conquer it as they have done to all the planets in all the galaxies throughout the Universe. She is known as the Queen of the Heavens, and was Satan's first experiment. He always saw her as his daughter, and he never defiled her like he defiled other women, like he defiled his own wife, Lilith. He kept Pandora pure, and she has remained that way for all time.

Beyond the cosmos also lies a hope. Harbingers of Darkness beware, for there are warriors of the light still out in the Universe, waiting to partake in the final battle, as are many in Heaven, the army of the transcended men and women who are training under the care of Michael the Archangel. All will unfold and the end will come, but when it does, who will survive, who will go on to live in paradise, and who will burn in the lake of fire known as the second death? The lake of fire and the second death are not those that exist now by the same name, but an eternal dwelling for those who are truly evil and have rejected the Lord in their very hearts and souls. Only God knows, for He will judge all, including myself. I am Death, and I long to be free.

The Story Continues...

About the Author

Chris LoParco is a writer and an artist who draws his inspiration from his love for God and his deep interest in the epic battle between Light and Darkness. He is a graduate of the School of Visual Arts, and he is a very proud father.

Made in the USA
Monee, IL
16 July 2023

38811088R00173